Riordan
The Anak of
Dagon

Will McDonald

Brookside

Press

www.brooksidepress.us

Maybe this wasn't such a good idea . . .

Rising from the wreck of his tanniyn the Anak once again held aloft his jeweled scepter. Air molecules condensed above the glowing orb until they formed a dark catapult projectile that flew at Riordan striking him straight in the chest. His ribs and sternum cracked. The blow launched him backwards several feet and dropped him unceremoniously into a heap. Body and spirit broken, the air forced from his lungs once again, he watched helplessly as the sorcerer stooped over and picked up the Riail dlí out of the dust.

"Any number of attacks I could have used to destroy you boy . . all were dismissed as being too quick—much too painless. Ah, but it strikes me that slow dismemberment by your own blade, now *that* would have such delicious irony . . . even a soul long dead such as mine can still enjoy a good laugh.

My name is Anbhás. I intend to kill you slowly, painfully–violently. Perhaps your screams will prove useful to lure more vermin out of their holes so they may be exterminated."

Riordan's family and friends always said his impulsiveness would get him into serious trouble one day . .

Riordan The Anak of Dagon ©2014 by Will
McDonald. All rights reserved. Printed in the United
States of America. Published by Brookside Press
   ISBN-13: ISBN-13:
   978-0615966090 (Brookside Press)
   ISBN-10: 0615966098

To my Mom
love for her children
required such extravagant
sacrifice.

And to Grandpa
The father of my heart.

Special acknowledgments to my son Corin
for all of his editorial input
(What *were* you doing during 5th grade
Grammar dad?).

And to Annette
For ripping the proof copy to shreds
and helping me put everything
Back together again.
Also for helping me come to know Yeshua
& C.S. Lewis.
I'm forever in your debt.

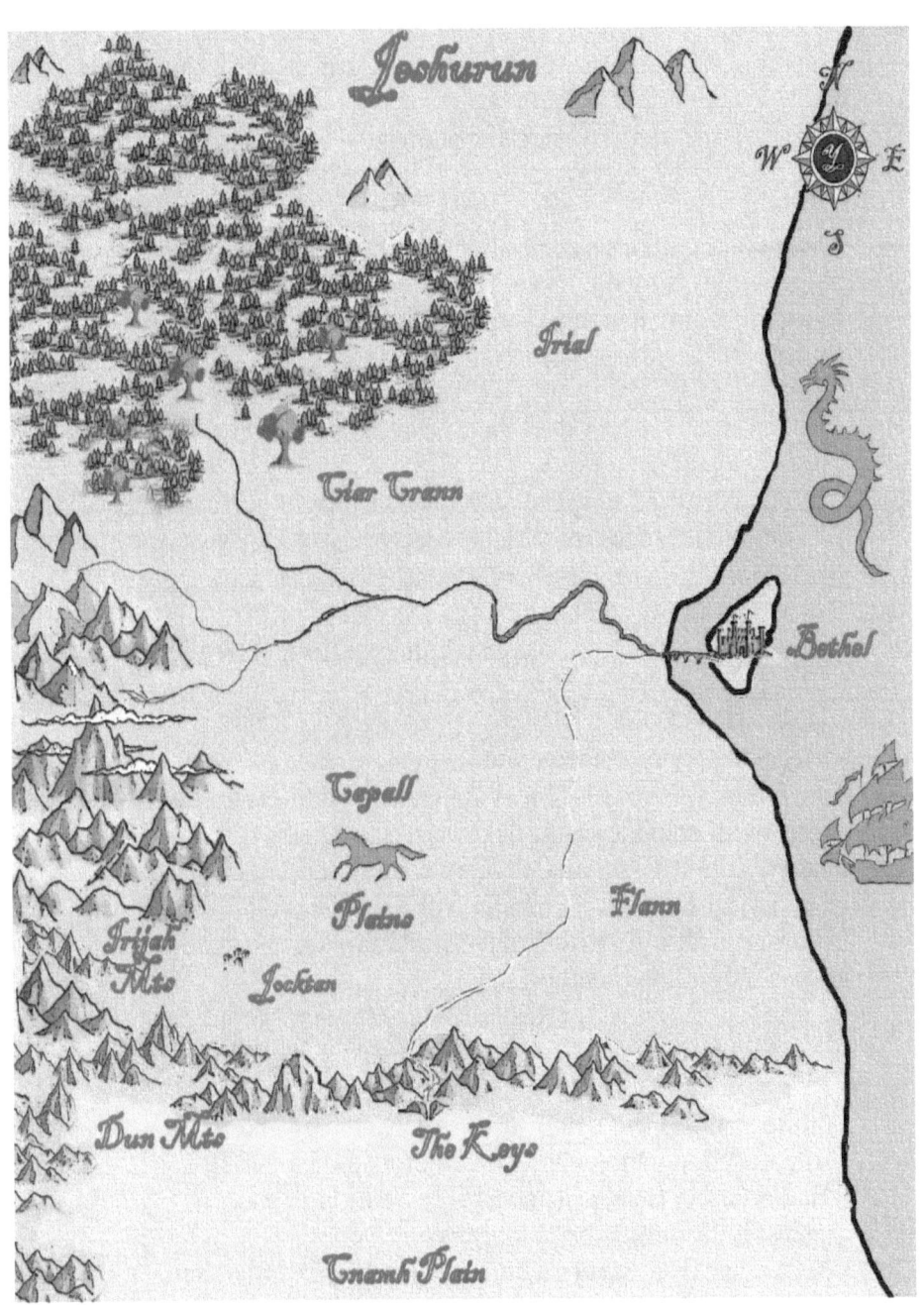

Jeshurun

Trial

Ciar Crann

Bethel

Capall
Plains

Irijah
Mts   Jocktan   Flann

Dun Mts   The Keys

Cnamh Plain

Riordan: The Anak of Dagon

Reader's Reviews

"I loved it. If attending the epic film version (hope there is one) movie patrons would be yelling, 'Hey you, down in front, because I'm standing and cheering for Riordan!"

> – John Prescott Athens GA

"Offensively stereotypical, Mr. McDonald doesn't seem to understand that most evil sorcerer's that plot for world dominion, do so from a heart that only seeks the highest common good."

> – Suariman the No Longer White

What category or Genre would a person place Riordan? The author weaves historical archeology, and biblical poetry with ancient myth; throws in some personal history, stirs it all up and ends up writing a book in a category all by itself. You can call it Christian historical Celtic American devotional fantasy. I'll call it good, a good book, a good read.

> –Michael O'Conner New York

"While at times the author uses inflammatory and derogatory language when describing sheep, over all I found Riordan to be a wonderful recreation of the greatest under-dog story of all time."

> – Mary (who had a lamb once) Shepherd

"So good my tail came unfurled!"   – Mr. Tummynuss

"I found his lack of faith disturbing."   – Durth Vader

"My Billy has been telling good stories all his life. Like
the time he took the car for a spin when he was only
four. Or how about the one explaining setting the
neighbor's garage on fire, ha ha, those were all good.
Wait-a-minute . . . is he telling stories again? Alright,
what'd he do this time??

                                        – Billy's Mom

AUTHOR'S NOTES:

Inspired by historical events, Riordan is a work of fiction. While attempting to remain true to the spirit of the original text and events, I have expanded on an already incredible story and retold it in a fantasy genre and context. Some similarities to characters living or dead are usually intentional, but not always factual. Tebel, is a parallel world to our own, distinct, but sharing many common elements, similar histories, and a common Creator.

Also please note: as in many of our own ancient source documents, several names are used for one God. Modern translators as a rule translate several different names to generic forms. In Riordan, in most instances, the names of God are left untranslated and used in ways appropriate to the context.

Glossary of Names

Aella - Whirlwind. Korah's horse.

Anak - Shaman magic user of the Anakim.

Anakim - Offspring of the unholy union between the Watchers and the peoples of Tebel.

Anbhás - Anakim shaman, or sorcerer.

Capall - People of the horse. Youngest of the seven children of Elohim.

Cnámh - bone. Battle plain south of Jeshurun.

Drochshaol - The bad times. Global destruction ending the first age.

Dun - Son of stone, Third Born of Elohim's children.

El - Great might or power. The common name for Jeshurun's God.

Elohim - Compound name for Jeshurun's God, combines mighty power with sworn oath or covenant.

Eoin - First born son of Captain Korah, of the Capall.

Rapha` - Race of giants. Fourth Born of Elohim.

Irijah - The race of Centaurs. Fifth Born of Elohim's seven children.

Irial - First Born children of Elohim.

Jephthah - Yahweh sets free. Jeshurun's liberator and law-giver.

Jireh - He sees. The last Shophetim of Jeshurun.

Joktan - Small. Village birthplace of Riordan.

Korah - Cavalry captain of the Capall.

Lithos - From litho, or stone. Dun Chieftain.

Mamzer - Illegitimate.

Mara - Bitter. Riordan's Step-Mother.

Mereah - From rea, means friend. King Ruarc's son and Crown Prince.

Meribah - Quarrel/contention/strife

Jeshurun - Marked. Riordan's nation and people.

Nomos - Laws that governs workings of universe.

Ruarc - Storm, Jeshurun's Rapha` king.

Quillan - Irial lieutenant.
Ra`ah - Shepherd.
Ragnhildr - Captain of the Irial.
Riail dlí - Rule of Law. Mythical blade forged by Yahweh Elohim from the nomos.
Riordan - King's poet or song.
Ro'eh - Prophet or seer.
Ruwach - Spirit, wind of heaven.
Skandalon - Offense, Bait of Satan. One of the Watchers
Shophetim - Judge/prophets of Jeshurun before the age of Kings.
Sióga - the faerie people, Second Born of Elohim.
Tanniyn - Dragon, monster, serpent.
Tebel - The world.
Torin - Chief. Eldest son of Brannan and Riordan's brother.
Watchers - Fallen messengers that acted as evil guides to the fallen races during the first age.
Yahweh - Noun form of verb "to be". Name for Jeshurun's God revealing His nature to be love, truth, law and judgment.
Zaquen Esh - Aged flame.
Zilliah - The Red Shade, an amulet and talisman of power created by the Watchers. It may have been used as a portal and communication device.

Riordan
The anak of Dagon

Prelude

"Cast your eyes on the ocean
Cast your soul to the sea
When the dark night seems endless
Please remember me"
~ Dante's Prayer
Loreena McKennitt

The stars were bright and a first moon shown as a harvester's sickle above the plains of Capall. A woman moved through waist high grass toward a hill outside the village of Joktan. In her arms she cradled a bundle with a small face wrapped in blankets. Not a newborn, but a boy of three summers and quite a burden for the arms that bore him. Even in the dim moonlight, fatigue displayed itself clearly on the woman's face, betraying the distance and the struggle her exertions required for her to carry the child. Despite the woman's hurried, jostling movements, her son slept, seemingly undisturbed, a strong hint of the child's own weariness.

She reached the summit and collapsed completely out of breath. She selected this particular knoll as a landmark that could easily be found in the dark–plus it commanded a view in all directions. Now she only needed to watch, and wait.

Looking out over the landscape, she didn't see any evidence of movement. The new moon yielded so little light a rider could easily move across the grass plains without her knowing. In her mind she feared that no one could be seen, because no one *would* be seen. If he didn't come, what would she do? Still, her heart felt a sense of relief in the thought; after all, if he didn't show then perhaps she wouldn't have to go through with this nights business after all.

Her vigil yielded views of an endless expanse of stars, and pale blue moonlight reflecting off snow capped mountains some forty miles East. The grasslands of Capall appeared endless, but she knew they were only one part of Jeshurun's territories. The nation itself seemed to the women's limited understanding vast and beyond her ken. If a person has never journeyed more than twenty miles from their birthplace, the world can either be a very small place, or as big as the universe. It all depends on the boundaries of their imagination.

Satisfied for the moment that nothing moved on the grasslands below, she relaxed and let down her guard just a bit. She returned her focus to the child on her lap, and pulled back the blanket to reveal more of his face. Never having a looking glass, she didn't really understand that the young boy's face mirrored her own. Any observer would quickly note mother and son shared the same petite nose, high cheek bones and gray blue eyes. Her sun gold hair, a trademark of the Capall tribe, seemed to be the one trait her son failed to inherit. Not familiar with her own face, only the father's facial features seemed apparent. And yet the light-blue eyes were a characteristic they both shared. The boy's dark hair however, a rare trait among the Capall, and a cleft in the chin came from a man she knew for a night and never saw again. Not until just recently.

She kissed the child's cheek and pulled him close so that his head rested on her shoulder. Her own head came to rest on the boy's soft, black hair making it damp from tears that gathered and fell.

"Ah El, how can I do this?" She murmured "Give me strength." Despite her appeal to the ancient God of her fathers, she felt little comfort, and no strength for the task at hand. She clung to her little boy so tight as too almost squeeze the air from his lungs as she considered the consequences of what she sought to do. She knew it to be the right thing; she could no longer feed and care for the child herself. Nor could she bear it any longer to see the boy go hungry, as she herself went hungry. But to give him up? How could she do this? The child she knew would never remember her; never again cry to her, call her his Mamma.

"El, I know I am not worthy of making any requests of you, but I beg you to watch over him. I make this vow, though I perish from hunger, I will never sell myself again; if you will only watch over this boy. I don't know if you will even accept this gift but I offer him to you. I will never see him grow beyond this; he will never know how proud I am . . . of him, I could never be proud of myself. Take him please, be a father to him . . . and mother."

The woman's fervent prayer became interrupted by thundering hoof beats. She rose to meet a man driving his charger hard up the hill. Her sudden rising out of the grass took even the horse by surprise causing the large black to skid to a rearing stop. The rider kept his saddle superbly and his body swayed in perfect balance as though the man were an extension of the horse. One of the sons of Capall, the rider like all of his people did not need a bit or reigns to control his mount.

The rider looked down gruffly at the woman and child before him, offering no greeting. In a very stiff voice he let her know he intended the whole affair to be an emotionless business transaction.

"That's the whelp there? Not much to look at, are you sure it's mine?"

The woman's tears abruptly ceased and her voice hardened to match his. "Selling myself is not a profession, I did what I needed to survive. It was several months before you that I sold myself, and you were the last. He is yours, a simple search of his face, hair, and eyes will reveal all you need to know." Pulling the blankets back from the boy's head and face she revealed a mop of sable hair and gray blue eyes to match the riders. The man bent down from his horse to get a closer look and simply grunted. After a moment of consideration he finally made his response.

"Woman, this child would only bring shame to my house. For this reason he can not bear my name, nor know the honor of being my son. He will be raised as an orphan, the son of a relative killed in the wars with the Dagon. You must never contact the boy or see him again–*ever*. That he will be fed and cared for is all I can promise, he will receive little else. Are you content?"

"Content? How can I be content? What I do, I do to save the boy's life! If there were any other choices left to me, I would take them. How can I be content when I must choose between the child's abandonment or his death?" The man's stunned silence added crushing weight to the depths of the pain caused by the consequences of her limited, discontented choices.

"NO, I am *not* content!" she screamed, her anger echoing across the hills. Then in a quieter voice, "But I am decided. Take the boy and raise him as a son of Capall. However hear this, though a prophetess I

14

cannot claim to be; the day will come when you will wish you could call him your son."

With a final tender kiss, the woman handed the boy to the rider, who placed him to rest on his lap at the front of his saddle. With a snort of contempt as the stallion veered sharply away he muttered, "Woman, I doubt it."

The sudden swift movement of the horse's leap into flight woke the child. A quick assessment of the situation confirmed the separation of the child from his mother. Howling in protest, as only a toddler can, the boy cried into the night for his Mamma. Every piercing scream stabbed the woman's soul with searing anguish. In agony she collapsed back into the tall grass, weeping. The nights only mercy came from the speed by which the large black charger bore her only son's anguished cries out of the range of her hearing.

After several hours, exhaustion at last put her to sleep, but with no relief for the agony in her soul. Deep into the night, in tormented dreams she watched the boy being torn away from her, his shrieks fading into the distance. Over and over the images of his horrified face replayed in her mind. Time and time again she replayed the memories of her son's frantic accusations of betrayal and abandonment. Time and time again the sound of her toddler's high-pitched voice screaming Mamma, Mamma over and over were haunting echoes of indictment.

Nightly, an internal prosecutor would introduce her young son's cries into evidence. Nightly the accuser verified the validity of the moral and criminal charges against her.

Unfaithful.

Loveless.

Cruel Abandoner.

The names all became synonymous with mamma in her heart. Silent whispers gleefully repeated her new identities, taunting her. Haunting her. Throughout the night, the next day and to the end of her life.

One

"Joy flickers on the razor-edge of the present
and is gone."

~C.S. Lewis

amzer watched with eyes of envy as his cousins made preparations to go on an excursion to the mountains in search for wild horses. Pretty much all of the male household would be going except for him. Growing up in his uncle's house, even after fifteen years, he knew that while he shared a blood connection, he wasn't family.

Even a casual glance would confirm the young man's relationship to Brannan his uncle as being at the very least that of a close, blood relative.

Unlike most of the blonde horsemen of Capall, his uncle possessed raven black hair, and blue eyes, a perfect match to Mamzer's, and to three of his four cousins.

Despite his being the son of a younger brother, a close relative, his uncle always seemed angry at him. Mamzer, or Ra`ah as they often called him, never knew what sin he committed to cause so much animosity, but their scornful treatment convinced him it must've been something real bad.

The best treatment he could expect from his "family" was to be ignored. He'd learned long ago nothing good ever happened whenever he did something to attract anyone's attention. Meanwhile, his cousins were almost without mercy in their picking on him, and they too seemed to have an unstated cause to hate him. And of course how could he forget dear Aunt Mara? She seemed to despise him most of all. With all that animus lurking just beneath the surface, Mamzer spent most of his life feeling like an unwelcome intrusion.

He normally felt relieved when his Uncle Brannan and the cousins went away. Life on the remote farm always proved to be so much more peaceful when they were gone. This trip however, would be going to the Mountains of Irijah, some forty miles East. He could see the snow caps in the far distance from a few of the farm's hilltops and something about those distant hills called to him. Perhaps the longing he felt emanated from the mountains seeming so forbidden, so out of reach. Even on foot he could get there in two, maybe three hard days. However, since he would never be permitted to make the trip, those far blue hills might as well have been a million miles away.

Knowing in his heart if he asked to go the answer would be no, he didn't even dare mention it. He would be told no, simply because it was the Mamzer who asked. "What if . ." he reasoned, "What if I seemed excited about *not going?*"

Then his sense of reality kicked in, "Naw, it'd never work." After a lifetime of disappointment, the Ra'ah's experiences taught him to no longer place much hope in hope.

Brannan and his four sons were making the trip searching for feral horses. Believed inferior to the horses of the Capall, they were still considered valuable as pack animals, or for general farm work. The sale of the wild horses would bring much needed income to the family. The market was certainly there, work animals were needed for the simple reason that no son of Capall would ever consider hitching his charger to a plow!

Torin, the oldest of Brannan's sons called out rather bluntly, "Hey Mamzer, take these water skins, fill them, and be quick, we don't have time to wait while you dwaddle or daydream."

Cavan, the next oldest, chimed in, "Yeah Mamzer, and when you're done water the pack animals. After that, you can go back to watching the sheep." The rest of the brothers, who really weren't much older than Mamzer just started to Baaaa and laugh.

The Capall were horse people. Although they owned herds of cattle and sheep, the tending of these animals was deemed beneath their warrior sons. They gave Mamzer his nick name of Ra'ah or shepherd years ago, as much for the purpose of humiliation as identification.

Taking up the skins and walking to the well, he began drawing water, the sounds of his cousin's laughter still ringing in his ears. The Ra'ah didn't mind watching sheep really. The sum total of his life experiences convinced him the critters were

19

far better company than people most of the time—plus he enjoyed the solitude.

As a shepherd he found himself at the bottom rung in terms of prestige and importance. Servants and slaves ranked higher, and certain privileges were denied to him; among them, the right to ride and own a horse. His personhood might just as well have been rejected. More than status, being a rider meant freedom; freedom to see the world beyond Brannan's farm; freedom to see those distant mountains that beckoned to him for as far back as the journey of his memories.

As the ra`ah filled the water skins, Brannan's father, and Mamzer's Grandfather Brónach, rode up to join the expedition. Riding an aged blood red roan, the horse and rider seemed a near-perfect match; both were old warriors with lingering evidence of great power and strength.

Close to forty years older than Brannan his first-born; a stranger would never guess Brónach's true age, at least not by appearance. He always rode straight and tall in his saddle, while displaying a quiet confidence, a bright eye, and a sharp mind. Only the white assimilating his blonde hair and beard betrayed the years spent under Tebel's sun.

On a lead rope Brónach led a pair of mules, one with packs loaded for travel, and another saddled for a rider. Mamzer watched his grandfather ride up to Brannan, lean over and speak quietly to him. Even a lip reading novice could see that whatever the request entailed, it inspired an immediate, emphatic *no* as a response. This gave him a sliver of reason to hope. Whenever his uncle opposed anything so strongly, it usually involved something he really wanted.

With a sudden thrill, Mamzer realized that his grandfather went through the trouble of preparing the second mule for another rider–and none of the men in the family would ever ride a mule, except–for maybe him.

20

Hope started to creep into Mamzer's heart–quickly he pushed it back down into the black hole where all his other dreams were kept. He suffered from an almost terminal case of disappointment, and so no longer dared allow his dreams to escape.

The debate raged for about five minutes, but in the end Brannan gave in to his father's suggestion. Loudly voicing his displeasure, Mamzer's uncle simply threw up his hands in disgust and walked away. Brónach then walked his horse over to the Ra`ah and dismounted.

"Finish filling the water bags, and water the animals as you were told lad, then go gather some of your things, and roll them up in a blanket. You'll be traveling with us today."

The boys heart skipped a few beats and his eyes widened from shock as he stammered, "But, what about . . . the sheep?"

"They will be tended, Mara and some of the servants will see to it. I convinced your uncle that someone will be needed to watch over the horses we capture while riders search for more." Brónach changed the tone of his voice slightly when he called Brannan "*your uncle*" but Mamzer felt way too excited to wonder about this.

"I'm not sure I have really done you a favor lad, this is going to be hard work. Also, your presence will only be cause for further resentment. However, I've also seen you gaze at those hills and I believe you need to see a bit more of the world than this farm."

Mamzer thanked his grandfather profusely and rushed to the barn where he often slept to gather his things, completely forgetting the task at hand. Brónach merely rolled his eyes, smiled, and gathered the lead ropes of the pack animals to bring them to the well.

A few hours later Mamzer and Brónach were bringing up the rear of the expedition. Riding a mule felt rather humiliating. But if it meant the chance to see the mountains, the Ra`ah figured he could endure it. He even ignored Cavan when his cousin looked back

21

from his own horse and shouted, "Well Mamzer, looks like a suitable mount has been found for you at last. Although having you saddle a sheep might have been even better!"

Ignoring the laughter, Brónach quietly asked Mamzer a question, "Lad, do you know what it means to be meek?"

After a few moments thought the boy answered, "Isn't it sort of being like a mouse, weak . . afraid, always ready to run?"

"Well it's interesting you would say that, and I believe many would think so. But ages ago, when Jeshurun first became a nation, our people were led to freedom by Jephthah the lawgiver. Did you know ancient scrolls describe our nation's liberator as being meek or gentle?"

"But," Mamzer responded, "How can that be, he's the greatest warrior our people have ever known!"

"Well, you're right, and I don't rightly understand it myself. I've given it some thought though, and I have watched many men through the years; I believe the man with the greatest weakness must try to hide behind a lot of bluster. Those truly confident in their strength have no need for demonstrations, or for cruelty to prove themselves to anyone. Also, he knows when to use force. Rarely is it needed for example, to respond to the taunts of another, who is merely being a buffoon."

Mamzer smiled as he got the point, and together they rode on in silence. After several hours on the back of a mule, the mid-morning sun felt terribly hot. A slow pace combined with the heat, made the young inexperienced rider feel like they were never going to get there. He never actually opened his mouth, but several times he almost asked, "Are we there yet?"

Brannan's farm sat at the edge of the mountain foothills, so shortly after starting out they gradually started gaining elevation. With every hill the ascent proved longer and higher than the last. Long uphill

22

climbs were followed by much shorter descents, so that they gained almost four thousand feet in the first ten miles.

Mamzer started to notice changes in the vegetation. The grasses grew shorter, and the hills rockier; yet despite the sun climbing ever higher in the sky, the real mountains never appeared to get any closer. It really seemed this part of the trip would take forever. In part, perhaps because for fifteen years he'd never traveled anywhere. Worse yet, for fifteen years he also never rode, well . . . anything! Discomfort adds as much to the length of a trip as a slow pace, and the clock in his saddle started to sound an alarm!

To pass time after a long ride in silence, Mamzer asked, "Grandpa, will we see any of the Irijah when we get to the mountains?" The Irijah were the great centaurs who made the mountains their home and gave them their name.

"As interesting as that may be, I am hoping we do not. The Irijah don't like anyone taking anything from their homeland, including its creatures. They see themselves as stewards and guardians of the mountains and its animals. Now they are wise enough to know that no son of Capall would be abusive to any horse, unbonded or no. Still, if a centaur got testy about our presence, and our rounding up wild horses from their mountain valley's, . . . well, let's just say no one in their right mind wants a quarrel with one of the sons of Irijah–certainly not a group of 'em."

"But I thought the Irijah were friends with our people?"

"And they are, and allies in war. But each of the people groups of the Jeshurun have their own territory. The different tribes really are a loose confederacy of sorts. Being united under one king is a very recent development, and each tribe remains sovereign in their own domain. And make no mistake, these mountains belong to the Irijah. We're not exactly trespassing, but we must be careful not to do anything that would provoke their anger."

The party stopped at mid-day to take a simple meal of breads, dried meats, and some cheese. They selected a place beside a rushing stream so they could also rest and water the horses. Mamzer took his meal on a rock next to the clear water. At home a creek flowed through the sheep pasture, but the water always seemed dark, quiet and slow moving. Here the current hurried, rushed and hurdled over legions of rocks, roots, and other obstructions giving the spring a musical quality. Something about the water's voice called to some unknown place in his heart and spirit. While he found it soothing, and felt refreshed by the song, it also struck a chord of melancholy. The young ra`ah noticed this, but didn't understand why he suddenly felt that way.

Mamzer winced as he climbed back into the saddle, and out of the corner of his eye he noticed his grandfather trying to hide a grin, "The pain will pass in a day or so lad, and I'm sorry to have to be the one to tell ya, but the only way to get used to being in a saddle is to stay in one."

Despite feeling the ride would take forever, by mid-afternoon they topped a rise and could see over a broad valley where the first real mountains rose dramatically above the foothills. Brónach guessed where they stood to be about 5000 feet, but the mountains across the valley were almost twice that. Gazing beyond the next ridge, the elevations rose to nine, ten, even twelve thousand feet. Seeing the granite rock faces, and the snow caps rising so dramatically before him for the first time, the sight became seared into Mamzer's memory.

"Quite a sight isn't it boy?" Brónach came up from behind Mamzer almost unnoticed. "Mountains are among the world's most beautiful places. There's music in the waters, and being on a high rise with the whole world before your eyes, . . well it stirs something inside a man. I insisted Brannan allow you to come along because I wanted you to see this. Lord knows you haven't been given much chance to see the world in your fifteen years. But as beautiful as they are, the mountains are dangerous, and you'll need to keep a sharp eye. There are bears up here–an amazing sight to see–when they stand they're near as tall as a giant, incredibly strong, with great claws. They also can kill a horse, or man with a single swat of their paw. If you see one, look for the closest climbable tree, then pray 'es got too heavy to climb."

The ra`ah got a puzzled look on his face, "If I'm riding shouldn't I just urge the horse into a hard gallop?"

"Well you could," Brónach replied, "except big as they are these bears can out run even a fast horse for quite a pace. Running only makes sense if you've got a pretty good head start. And remember bears are not the only danger. Wolves generally avoid man all-together. But they're cunning, and a wolf pack if they can catch one separated or alone, won't hesitate to take down a horse, or mule. There's cats up here as well, some of 'em weighing two, three hundred pounds. They're able to leap forty, fifty feet from a hiding place catching their prey completely by surprise. If you're alone and one decides to take you, a man could be dead before ever knowing what hit him. As if that's not enough, there are rock, mud and snow slides, all kinds of dangers from the mountains themselves."

They started down the slope and into the valley, riding in silence for a while. Finally Brónach broke the silence as if finishing his thought. "In a lot of ways, when I leave this world and go see Elohim face to face, I think he'll be much like these mountains. Lots of folks think our El is some kind of benevolent nurse maid. I look at the works He's created, and see something quite different. When I stand before Elohim face to face–and I expect I shall in the not too distant future–but when I'm before Him, I reckon it will be the most beautiful

25

experience I have ever known. A beauty much like these mountains, wild . . . untamed, . . a beauty that better be respected."

They rode on for most of the day, climbing steadily before finally making camp late in the afternoon on a saddle between two low mountains. Mamzer dismounted and walked around a bit trying to work some feeling into his backside. Brónach lightly dropped to his feet from his horse's back and got his attention. "While everyone unpacks and cares for the horses lad, why don't ya go gather some wood for a fire, while there's still light. I'll come help in a bit."

He searched for dry, dead and down wood, not needing to be told about the futility of burning, or trying to burn what's still green. After carrying and dragging in a couple loads, Brónach walked out to join him. "That's plenty for tonight lad, but we'll need some kindling and fire starter as well. Start with this big fir tree. Go ahead and lift the branches, then go inside underneath. All the small twigs and brown needles burn easily, and they're always dry, even in the middle of a heavy rain. In a pinch you can weave the limbs together and make a pretty fair shelter. I know I told you about the perils of bears and mountain cats, but being wet and cold is the greatest danger. Knowing where to find shelter, dry wood and some kind of fire starter could very well save your life."

Trusting the horses to alert them to danger, the party slept that night with no watch. Mamzer lay awake watching the stars and snow capped peaks in the distance, glowing pale blue from reflecting starlight. He couldn't remember ever being so content, but despite his best efforts to stay awake and take everything in, he drifted off to sleep quickly.

The party left before dawn the next morning. Mamzer could barely walk with his backside so sore from yesterday's ride. Looking up at a mounted Brónach the ra`ah volunteered, "I think the mule is still tired from yesterdays hard ride . . I'll walk the rest of the way."

Chuckling, Brónach tossed a squishy pouch to the boy, "Take a minute and go off into the bushes. Drop the britches and put some of this salve on yer backside, especially any sores. Your gunna need it . . we'll all be in the saddle most of the day today. Way to much to do, and I don't think you want your uncle or cousins thinking you can't keep up."

About mid-morning they rode between two granite walls, coming to a narrow gap with a crude pole fence and gate, badly in need of some repair.

"I first discovered this place and the feral horses long before you were born." Brónach spoke as if answering Mamzer's unasked question. "Mostly I like to leave the horses to run free, but sometimes there is a need to take a few to make ends meet"

Working efficiently, with everyone having assigned tasks the family took care of the horses, and then went to work repairing the enclosure. By mid-afternoon the rails were mostly replaced or repaired after a lot of hard work and sweat. Just as Mamzer began to take in the magnificent surroundings, Brónach called out, "Mount up boys, then spread out a bit and ride through the canyon. It's a bad idea to fill the valley with horseflesh just to have em get eaten. Be sharp now, we're looking for predators, and . . " here the boys grandfather flashed an impish grin, "It'd be a terrible thing for one of you to end up as some critters afternoon snack."

A collective groan greeted Brónach's instructions. Mamzer's backside told him in no uncertain terms he didn't want to sit on a horse or mule, again–*ever*. Taking some comfort from his cousins groans and complaints he realized he wasn't the only one feeling that way. Listening to all the protests and moaning,

Brannan flashed an angry scowl their way, sending the clear message he wouldn't stand for complaints or argument.

Brónach observing their long faces smiled to himself and offered a word of encouragement to ease the sting just a bit, "Lads, we would have needed to move on regardless. We can't make camp here at the gate for one thing, we want the feral horses to go through, right? We just need to be sure there's no danger waiting further up in the canyon and we'll make camp there. I know you're hot and tired. I promise, you won't regret riding on just a bit more."

Spreading out, the whole family moved on in silence and without incident. Riding through extensive groves of massive fir and pine, the towering granite canyon walls came into view only occasionally. Alone, while ever mindful of his seat, Mamzer also felt overwhelmed by the majesty of his surroundings. In thirty minutes the ra`ah heard the reward that his grandfather promised. Guided by the roar, the riders finally broke through the trees, entering into a high meadow. Mamzer jumped off the back of the mule and walked to a sand and pebble beach, on the south shore of a small mountain lake. A couple acres in size, and fed by a cascade that flowed over a twenty-foot gray granite wall, the fall's turbulent hydraulic worked to carve out a perfect swimming hole on the canyon floor.

Like a starving man standing in a king's banquet hall, Mamzer didn't know where to let his eyes feast first. Beyond the lake and fall there appeared to be a narrow cut that ended at a much higher cliff and a second waterfall. Everyone stood stunned. Their grandfather seemed to be enjoying everyone's reaction immensely. Finally he laughed, "Well now, who could have guessed *this* would be here? This appears to be a likely spot, how about we make camp? Go on, tend to the animals, and then if you wanted to jump from those rocks into the pool there, I'd surely appreciate it. Yer all getting a little ripe."

In minutes they were climbing the rock wall and running along the flat ledge over which the water cascaded into the small lake. Stripping their outer garments, the young men all looked over the edge as they got ready to take the plunge.

Shouting down at his Grandfather, Torin who didn't even bother to stick his toe in, asked "How cold's the water?"

Brónach grinned and shouted back "Jump on in. These mountain streams have a natural heat source, practically warm as a bath back home."

Mamzer learned from this to distrust anyone's advice about "Jumping in" when they happen to be standing dry on shore. But Torin, needing no further assurances, ran and jumped with a loud whoop that turned slightly high pitched when he actually hit the surface with a loud smack. After a few seconds he popped out like a cork and shrieked, "Ow that's cold!! Grandpa, you said the water was warm!"

"No, I said it has a natural heat source, which it does–the sun! Why, did you know the sun does such a good job heating things that just a few hundred feet up the mountain and a only a few moments ago, that water was solid ice?"

The brothers laughed and despite the cold plunge waiting for them, like lemmings one after the other they took their turns jumping in.

When it came to Mamzer's turn, he hesitated and looked once again over the ledge. His first impression– it sure looked a long way down! Then, gazing past the foam of the fall, he saw the deepest, most intense blue he'd ever seen. Earlier Brónach said he believed the face of El would be a reflection of these mountains. Mamzer thought if that were true, then right now he just might be staring straight into His eyes. The thought startled him so much he started to shut out everything else going on around him, until the voices of his cousins pulled him back.

"C'mon Mamzer, quit being a chicken and jump!" Torin yelled from below.

"He's not being a chicken," taunted Cavan, "He's a sheep! He's afraid the water will wash away the smell and the little lambs won't know their mama!"

Mamzer responded to the laughter and the taunting by stepping back a few paces; he then ran across the top of the smooth rock, and leapt in the direction of his cousin while rolling into a cannon ball. The worst thing about jumping from this height? The few seconds a person has to reconsider their actions before hitting the water. Just enough time to realize . . . this is a really dumb idea! Cavan of course found plenty of time to scramble and get out of the way; but the rotation on his descent caused Mamzer to hit the water with a smack– flat on his back! It stung like all get out and took his wind away. More than cold, the crystal water's intensity almost burned his skin, his head hurt from an instant brain freeze. After a small eternity of fighting to reach the surface and warm sunlight, the ra`ah surfaced too stunned to even whimper in protest.

Brónach kept right on laughing at the startled looks on the swimmer's faces. The brothers were already headed ashore seeking to share the experience with their grandfather. The old man proved much to quick, and discerning. Sensing their hostile intentions he retreated well away from the water's edge before the brothers could drag him into the frigid water.

"Sorry boys, but you'll have to admit, if I actually told you how cold the water was, you'd never have taken a much needed bath."

Torin protested, "What about you grandfather? Don't you want to take a Bath?"

"Not on your life. A man would have to be crazy to jump in any of these mountain lakes . . and my mama didn't raise no fool."

They rose before light the next day. Going without a fire, they packed a cold breakfast of dried meat, cheese, and dark bread that could be eaten while riding. Brannan explained the simple plan as they rode out across the valley, "We'll ride around on that ridge boys and form a wide line making a net of sorts before sweeping down through the valley. Once we reform our line, we just need to ride back towards the canyon. Ride slow, and make sure the gaps between riders gets smaller and smaller as we draw closer to the gate. With any luck, the horses will be wary, but not frightened–sure ya don't panic em now–simply keep em moving ahead of the line."

Brónach cautioned everyone about what to expect once the horses reached sight of the fences. "They'll be on to us sometime before they get to the open gate lads. At least some of them will try and make their break, you'll have to be ready. By that time it should already be too late, and we just have to close the net. Whoever is on the outside of the line will have to be alert; it's likely, the ones that try to escape will attempt to get around our flanks. Make sure ya leave em no other option than going through the gate."

Mamzer would ride with Brónach in the center, since the mule and his big red roan were not as fleet of foot as the other's horses. At this Brónach grumbled, "You might be surprised what the mule could do, and at one time folks considered ol' Esh the swiftest war horse in all of Capall. He might not be a spring chicken anymore but he's still got a lot left."

Brónach's argument however, was brief and primarily to stand up for the old stallion's honor. So after kicking up a little fuss and dust, he and Mamzer took their places in the middle of the line.

Still a little stiff in his blanket saddle, Mamzer watched as the morning light first struck the peaks turning them a pale gold. The valley while getting lighter, would still be in shadow for a few more hours, while the sun climbed above the ridges and peaks.

Using hand signals, Brannan got everyone's attention and pointed down below. In the center of the vale a small herd of horses were enjoying an early morning breakfast of clover and grass. A veritable equine feast, the clover stood hock high and glistened from being dipped in early morning dew.

Mamzer heard the low whistle that repeated on down the line signaling everyone to start moving forward. When drawing within fifty paces of the herd, the lead stallion, a large black with a small white star on his forehead, spotted them and snorted a warning. Most of the animals in the herd reacted pretty casually, with maybe just a nervous nicker. Riordan guessed they lacked a reason to be afraid. Why should they be? Never having seen a man before, certainly not on the back of a horse, likely they didn't find the sight particularly frightening, just strange. Sort of like a centaur but with the human parts in the wrong place.

As they drew closer, the herd just nervously trotted off a few hundred paces and settled back down to graze until the line moved in close again. This was repeated for an hour or so, until the lead stallion decided he'd seen enough and took off. The herd followed and as expected tried to do an end around on the line. Brannan and Torin were ready for the attempt, and they cut off their escape. The lead stallion and a few of the mares might have made it, but for some of the young foals and colts in the herd. These would not be abandoned. In the end, they chose the path of least resistance trotting through the gate and into the canyon without too much protest.

Brónach on Esh pulled along side of Mamzer on his mule. "I think that stallion has a noble heart lad. Without the weight of a rider, not one of us could have matched his speed. He could have gotten away easily I think–chose not to."

Puzzled, the ra`ah asked, "Why would he do that?"

"Love, loyalty, faithfulness. To get away required abandoning the mares, and foals. Loving something is dangerous lad because you become vulnerable; Vulnerable to enemies–even more vulnerable to pain from the ones you love."

Mamzer sat on his mule and thought about what Brónach just said and after a moment asked, "Is it better not to love then?"

Brónach looked at him solemnly, "No, not better. Perhaps safer. Love is not for the weak or faint of heart, I'll tell ya that." That said, Brónach urged Esh into a gentle trot through the gate and on into the canyon, leaving his grandson with his thoughts.

While Mamzer found the chase exhilarating, he soon realized that driving the horses into the canyon, had been the easy part. Now each horse must be individually caught, given a lead rope and hobbled. To do this a person must tie a short rope to the front legs just above the hooves. This allows the horse to walk freely while making it impossible to run.

For the riding and roping Brannan didn't allow Mamzer to participate. Once the horses were captured however, the brothers at least seemed more than happy to allow him to attach the hobbling ropes, the trickiest and most hazardous job. A far cry from tame ponies, trying to hobble wild horses required dealing with their best and most dangerous means of defense–their hooves. The lead stallion proved to be particularly cantankerous, stomping Mamzer's hand and nearly taking off his head with a kick.

It ended up being a pretty profitable days work, with about twenty horses captured. The proceeds would equal about half a year's harvest of seed crops. Brannan however, planned to go out again for the next couple days and leave with a total of forty to sixty animals.

In the morning Brónach pulled Mamzer aside to give him the bad news. "You did fine yesterday lad, I want you to know that, but today someone needs to stay here and watch after the horses we've taken. As might be expected, that someone is you."

"But Grandpa, I . ." The old man immediately raised his hand to silence the protest.

"Your performance of this duty is how I convinced Brannan to allow you to make the trip. We can't change that now. But lad, there's no shame in this. You might think–and have been told often enough I expect–that watching over a herd, be it sheep or horses, is not warrior's or even man's work. But let me tell ya, those ponies out there because of the hobbling, are nearly defenseless. You're their protector Lad. A true warrior does not fight for treasure, riches, gain or glory. He fights only when he has too, and then in protection of the innocent or helpless. I've told you of some of the dangers in these mountains. If a bear, spotted cat, or pack of wolves came along finding horses unable to run or defend themselves, what do you think would happen? Any predator coming into this canyon would think he'd found a carnivore's banquet hall. Also, there are even more dangerous creatures that make their way into these hills. In truth, you will have the hardest and most dangerous job of all today. So much so, I am of a good mind to stay and help. But if I did, I'm afraid your cousins would say I stayed to be your nursemaid, and I wouldn't want to give further occasion for your shame."

Turning, he centered his light leather saddle on Esh. Capall saddles lacked a cinch, or stirrups so the saddle could not be grasped by the rider to help with mounting. Brónach however, leaped up and swung his leg over Esh's back with an ease that defied his age. Looking down from the saddle, he gazed at Mamzer again with a wrinkled brow, "Lad, I know most of your life people have called ya names, and said you're no good. I've known lots of people who were treated like that, and it became a fulfilled prophecy of sorts. Everyone said they were worthless, and they just fell into believing what folks said. I want you to know, despite all that's been said and done, you still have a choice. One choice is to be the very best man ya can, and prove em all wrong. I expect you're going to become the sort of man who can do just that."

Brónach looked the boy in the eye, and the corner of his mouth lifted into a slight grin, "Now don't ya disappoint me."

Mamzer spent a good part of the morning moving among the hobbled horses. The black would not let him get close. The best bribes of apple or even a lump of brown sugar got him nothing except close to getting killed. From a safe distance however, he stopped to admire the stallion. The power and muscles in just his neck were so incredible, Mamzer decided he could ride on the horses head while sitting between its ears. This was of course only, if the big black would actually let him.

"Fat chance," he thought. The stallion seemed like such a proud animal, he doubted it would ever submit to any man's yoke. Far too spirited to tote packs or pull a plow, Mamzer couldn't imagine anyone ever thinking he would, or should.

Taking some dried meat, bread and cheese with him, Mamzer climbed the lower wall to the top of the first waterfall. After looking over the edge again, and realizing how far down it looked, he chastised himself for the stupid cannonball idea (his back still hurt). After a short walk along the stream he worked his way around a smaller upper pool to the base of the second and much higher water fall.

Looking up the rock face, there remained only one option. He just had to see what adventure awaited him over the rim. Despite staying well to the side of the falls to avoid wet slippery rocks, it still proved a tricky climb. A good portion of the way, there were roots and brush to provide hand and foot holds, but not always. Sometimes he was forced to plaster his body against sheer rock, while other times he scrambled frantically to find his next foot or hand hold. At all times he felt the distinct thrill of fear in his gut, until he finally scrambled over the top of the ledge. Laying flat on his back for a few seconds, he allowed his heart to slow its beating, and let out a long, final sigh of relief.

Standing up he peeked out over the edge. He found he could see everything in the valley two hundred feet below. Further out, past the lower fall and ledge, he could see camp, and tiny versions of the horses. When he turned around however, he discovered another almost completely different world. His eyes followed the mountain stream through a whole new series of small pools and cataracts. He discovered he stood in the entrance of another still higher canyon. Much narrower, and strewn with boulders, it took some scrambling along the stream to discover still another small lake. Almost surrounded by high cliffs and snow caps, no breeze could disturb the surface of the pool making it a perfect mirror. A long narrow fall from the glaciers above, seemed to be the lake's source.

Following the falls upward with his eyes, Mamzer saw what he took to be patches of everlasting snow. He wasn't surprised, he knew snow remained in the high places year round. Then a snowbank moved! Rubbing his eyes in disbelief, he gazed up at the white patch again . . there, it did it again!

Completely forgetting his duties, Mamzer started climbing and scrambling up the mountain once more. Moving quickly, he came across a narrow path which he followed. Soon well above tree line, he occasionally found a tuft of white hair that got caught in low-growing course brush. Here and there he found a profusion of small round droppings. Then he caught a whiff of a familiar smell–goat! Moving fast as he could along a very steep slope, he became all the more determined to at least catch a glimpse of his quarry. The goats however were very shy and not about to be caught by anything on two legs. They easily stayed comfortably ahead of him. He followed the path along the mountain until it came to a place where the steep slope completely fell away and became a sheer cliff. Drawing close he saw the path did indeed continue, but on a small lip of rock only inches wide. Fresh from completing a tight rope act, one of the goats turned to look back at him from the other side of the narrow path it just traversed.

Pure white except for two short ebony horns, dark beady eyes and a touch of black on the end of his nose, it became clear how the creature could be mistaken for a patch of snow from a distance. The Billy gave Mamzer a real ornery look and issued a challenge to step out on the narrow ledge and follow. But as he looked at the rock shelf the trail followed, narrower in most places than the width of his foot; he knew he would never be able to walk that path–or at least he didn't want to. The goat snorted at him in disgust and turned back up the trail going still higher up the mountain.

Giving up on the idea of catching up to the goats, but glad he at least got to see one, he turned and looked down over the valley and the pools far below. From this high place the water in the stream appeared to be a liquid aquamarine crystal, flowing over millions of precious stones. The small lake flawlessly mirrored the peaks and sky. He tried to imagine what it would look like on a clear night, reflecting the moon and stars.

For as long as he possessed memories, he remembered gazing at these distant peaks and desiring to climb to the heavens. What he didn't understand is that despite having finally ascended to the clouds, why did the longing only grow more intense, almost insatiable? Now, with the whole world laying at his feet, why didn't the longing feel satisfied?

A question popped into his head, stilling his heart. "When you smell baking bread, does the fragrance make you less hungry, or more?"

Spoken as a quiet whisper, the many possible answers and implications to the question, took his spirit by storm.

His racing thoughts however were interrupted by a high-pitched scream that suddenly caught his attention. He looked up to the sky to watch an eagle soar, then fold its wings and dive. The raptor's target was a marmot that had foolishly dared to venture too far from its hole. The fierceness of the attack triggered a sense of panic as he remembered his main responsibility for the day, watching over the hobbled horses.

Frantically, he scurried down the mountain, leaving the high valley behind, never to visit it again. Getting into a hurry while treading down narrow mountain trails–is *never* a good idea. So only after a little bit of luck, a lot of huffing and puffing, and a few close calls, he reached the canyon rim at the top of the high falls. To his relief he could see the horses grazing peacefully by the deep pool, far below.

In the scramble down from the high valley, and an even scarier climb down the cliff beside the upper fall, he realized he'd worked up a pretty good sweat. So he stripped, threw his clothes to the shore below and prepared to dive into the lower-most pool. Looking over the edge this time, convincing himself to jump would require quite a bit more persuasion now that the icy waters were an unforgettable part of his experience. After several games equivalent to one for the money, two for the show–always chickening out before getting to go, he finally jumped. Descending through the air he changed his mind and did his best to flap his arms and try to scramble up an invisible ladder. Failing to escape gravity's grip however, he hit the pool's surface, shocking his system. Despite his best efforts, he kept sinking deeper into liquid crystal. Once again the water felt so cold it burned, but as he waded out to shore, it seemed to have scrubbed his skin free of sweat, even of fatigue.

Shivering and dripping wet, he crossed to the nearest bank to retrieve his clothes. A couple of the feral horses, velvet noses dripping from the mountain pool, looked at him as if he were crazy. The boy decided they had sound reason to doubt his sanity. He shrugged as he walked past them to base camp to prepare for Brannan, Brónach, and the brothers to return.

T *wo*

"Names are everything. The man who could call a
spade a spade should be compelled to use one.
It is the only thing he is fit for."
~Oscar Wilde

The next night Brónach spoke up at the campfire.
"Brannan, son, I think it's enough. I don't think
we should thin the herds too much, we have
more than enough for a good profit, and some fine
animals to be sure. But, we have also been here three
days without incident, and I don't want to press our luck,
or chance angering the Irijah."

For the first time in his life Mamzer disagreed with
his grandfather. He had absolutely no desire to leave
the mountains and go back to the farm, at least not yet.

"Also" Brónach continued, "I think we should
release the black stallion. A warrior like him, I doubt
he'll ever be trained, but he will ensure the quality of the
breeding if allowed to stay here in the mountain valleys.
I think he deserves his freedom."

Mamzer's heart skipped a beat, at the mentioning of
the black being released. He'd been wondering what might

happen to the proud horse if he refused saddle or harness.

Brannan didn't answer for a few moments. At last he flatly responded, "One more day, but we keep the stallion, he's worth as much as the whole lot I think. Though I agree, he'll never be tamed."

"All right son, one more day, although I think the risks outweigh the reward. But Lad," here he looked at Mamzer, "While we are out tomorrow, you'll need to break camp and pack for travel. It's in my gut we have been in this place too long, and I would like to at least put a few miles behind us before we rest."

The next morning after watching the riders depart, Mamzer did as instructed and began packing things away. Because of the nature of the trip, they hadn't taken the time to hunt, so they carried mostly jerky. Mamzer decided a good hearty stew, made with fresh meat, would be appreciated–especially if they would be traveling after an already hard day. There were several large hares making this canyon home, and he was pretty accurate with a sling and stone.

The sling is the main weapon used by the Irijah, or so he had been told, and with deadly results. Then again, *they* could sling stones weighing ten to twenty pounds. Mamzer, however found he was very accurate with a stone about the size of a child's fist. Not as devastating as the small boulders centaur's used as projectiles but sufficient for a rabbit, maybe a man, with the right shot.

Within a couple hours he actually managed to stun a few Coney's for his stew. By late morning, they were simmering over a low fire of mostly coals. Brónach had taught him that, "Very dry wood," he told him, "burned down to coals, is far better for cooking lad, and there is much less smoke to draw attention to our presence here."

While leaning over his pot for a little taste test, he heard a twig snap off in the trees, and then silence. Mamzer suddenly felt the little hairs on the back of his neck stand up.

"Hello in the camp!" A deep voice called out from the trees. This was the polite greeting before walking into some ones' campsite and catching folks by surprise. "Mind if I come in and set?"

Mamzer's mind raced while he thought about how to answer. In the end he gave the polite response. "Come on in, I have food and drink to share."

The person who stepped through the trees wasn't who or what Mamzer expected, not a man or even one of Irijah's centaurs, but rather one of the sons of Dun.

"Well now, that's right neighborly." The stranger's reply came as he boldly walked up to the fire and stood there grinning. He was about four feet tall, with thick dark hair everywhere but on his bald head. His eyes were bright, set beneath bushy brows, and his large nose barely escaped the jungle of his beard which contained crumbs from breakfasts or suppers past. Over his thick body frame he wore a heavy leather tunic studded with metal rings. A well cared for axe, with a thick handle and black iron blade was tucked in his belt where it could be easily reached. Mamzer also noted a short bow strapped to the stranger's back.

Looking at his sling laying over a log a few feet away, the boy suddenly felt terribly outgunned.

The man of Dun saw where Mamzer glanced and he looked at the boy and grinned, as though he could read his thoughts. "I'm passing through these parts doing a little prospecting. Wouldn't ya know it, I lost my supplies down a shaft in a cave a few miles from here. What is it folks say, be thankful for bad luck, cause you could have no luck at all? Anyways, I smelled the fire and the stew, and I must admit I'm a mite hungry. Could you spare a bite of bread, maybe just a touch of the stew? It smells awfully good."

Mamzer replied, "I'd not turn any man away from my fire hungry, sit and be welcome."

"That is the answer of a gentleman, and a downright courteous lad. Thank you kindly." Mamzer pulled a

42

trencher out of a supply pack, and tossed it to the Dun prospector, along with a small loaf of dark bread.

Famous for their appetites, the man of Dun leaned over the pot and dished out a generous portion, then ripped in half his small loaf and used it as an utensil for scooping up the stew. Chewing thoughtfully he looked around the canyon and asked, "Where's the rest of yer horse boys? You're a likely Lad, and a great cook, but surely they didn't leave ya out here by yerself?"

Mamzer's natural caution warned him this was a probing question, and so he answered, "Oh, I'm not alone, several of my family, older brothers, uncle and father, they're just across the canyon, they could be here in a shout if I needed em."

"Really?" he answered. "Ain't it strange they took their horses and gear for such a short trip?"

Mamzer started to sweat, likely he was in a fix, but he didn't have a clue as to how to handle it. What did the man want? Surely not his money, they'd almost none with them. Of course *he* might not know that.

"We were hunting treasure ourselves, hoping to find perhaps some gold in the streams, we haven't found any though. My Uncle is real sad about that, our family is out of money."

The prospector grinned as though guessing the intent of Mamzer's lie. "Oh, there's lots of treasure to be found in these hills, and not just gold. Now take horses for instance, my people have a lot of mines in the desert mountains further south. Strong horses that can pull ore cars and wagons, well now, they're almost worth their weight in gold."

With this comment, the Dun looked up and grinned again, not a very pleasant grin. It wouldn't have been pleasant even if the teeth were white rather than a jagged, dull yellow. "Mind if I have a bit more of that Coney stew? It sure is tasty."

"Help yourself." Mamzer responded nonchalantly. The Dun leaned over the pot and filled the ladle, but rather than slapping the food on his plate, he flicked it expertly at Mamzer hitting him in the face and eyes. Mamzer jumped back in surprise and tripped, falling back over the log that also served as a bench. On him in a second, the Dun gave the ra`ah no chance to recover. Mamzer quickly found himself on his back, his opponent sitting on his chest, and a cold blade across his throat.

"You can go ahead and yell if you want to boy, I know the rest of your lot are out chasing more horses as they have done for the last couple days. Holler for help if it will make ya feel better, but don't try anything else. If you did I might have to cut your throat, and I don't want to do that, because you really are a likely lad. If you behave yourself, no harm will come to ya. Now, . . your word, will you behave yourself? If so I'll let you up."

Another deep voice spoke from a few feet away, in the trees somewhere, "Aw, go ahead and slice the boy's throat and get it over with, we don't need him."

"No," the Dun spoke thoughtfully, "I recognize the old man on the red horse at least. He's a cavalry officer from the early wars against the Dagon. Back then, a mighty dangerous fighting man, expect he still is. He might overlook the taking of feral horses, but I think if we harm the Lad, he won't rest until he finds us. He's no one I want for an enemy, . . so no, if the lad here will give his word to behave, I'll let him up, and as I said, no harm will come to him."

The voice of still another man of Dun piped up, "At least tie 'im then, and blindfold as well. He doesn't need to know any more than he already does."

"Well, I guess no harm will come of that. Sorry Lad, but at least you'll live." The Dun lifted Mamzer as if his weight were of no consequence, spun him around and put him back down face first in the dirt. His hands were pulled behind his back and tied tight, so tight the ropes bit his flesh. Then a dirty rag, with something slick on it that smelled awful, was pulled over his eyes.

44

"Sorry for the rough treatment Lad, if ever you come to my own home I'll treat ya better. Even my partners here, . . . ah, the bit about cutting your throat, that's just to scare ya. Ya see we really do need horses and our people pay well for them, to bad yer horse boys won't sell 'em to us. To hard on 'em they say. But I don't see how working in a mine is any more shameful then pulling a farmers plow or tote'n packs."

Spitting out bracken he got in his mouth from the face plant, Mamzer warned his captor. "My uncle, and grandfather will come after you, and it is a long way to the desert mountains. Release me, and I'll say nothing about this, you can just go on your way."

The Dun didn't respond directly, but rather barked instructions, "Gather the horses boys, and take the mules and pack animals as well. Be quick." Then in a softer voice he spoke to Mamzer, "Figured they would chase us, but there's more of us than there is of them, and I expect they won't want to follow where we're going. Now you lie still there Lad, and as I promised, don't try anything and you won't be hurt."

Mamzer heard the surprisingly light footfalls of the Dun as he moved away, and then he heard the rattle of cookware as packs were snatched off the ground. Mamzer felt the frustration of trying to piece together what was happening by sounds. Most of what he heard he couldn't quite make out. The screams of the black horse were unmistakable, and when followed by howls of pain and cursing, he gathered they took the hobbles off the stallion and lost control. Within a half hour he heard no sounds at all, except for the natural sounds of the mountains. For a long time he lay on his belly and tried to work his hands lose from the ropes, but the Dun adventurer knew what he was about in tying the knots. After not hearing a sound for several minutes, a quarter of an hour that seemed like an eternity, Mamzer decided to risk movement. Curling first into a ball he managed to roll to his knees and shuffle in the general direction of his fire until he bumped into the log where he'd been sitting. Then lowering his head down level with the bark, he used the rough surface to scrunch up and finally remove the blindfold.

Able to see again, he confirmed the Dun and his companions were indeed gone, but the packs were still there, although they looked as though someone had rummaged through them. Next to the pot Mamzer had been cooking in, he saw a cleaned trencher, a small loaf of bread and a note, written with charcoal on a piece of hide. A small leather bag with the top drawn closed and tied with twine sat on top of the little pile.

After a short search to find a rock with sharp edges, it still took him the better part of two hours to cut through the ropes. Walking over to the message the Dun adventurer left behind, he picked it up and though he struggled with reading, he eventually managed to sound it out, "Sorry about yer treatment Lad, ya do make a fine stew. I know it ain't much, but it's all the coin we have. Thot it might take some sting out of yer folks anger. If ever we meet again, I'll treat ya better."

"He obviously doesn't know Brannan." murmured Mamzer, as he peeked inside the pouch and saw several silver coins. Working his way down to the lower pool, he washed his face, knowing he could do nothing now but wait. And it would be a looong wait. Brónach, Brannan, and the brothers were not expected to return until late afternoon. Time crawled painfully slow. He knew he was really going to catch it, and he'd much rather just get it over with. He looked up to the mountain heights beyond the falls and seriously thought about climbing up to the high valley and peaks once more. . . perhaps making himself a new home with the mountain goats.

After what seemed like an eternity, Brónach, Brannan and the brothers road back into camp, this time with a smaller prize of only three mares and two foals. Mamzer dreaded telling his uncle, still he tottered fearfully forward and started to cry out, but the words froze in his throat. Brannan's face slowly turned from surprise to dismay, moving on towards rage. "What happened boy? Where are the horses?"

Mamzer's answer came out as a stammer, "I was watching sir, but while I cooked..."

Fury filled Brannan's voice as he bellowed, "Where are they BOY?!"

"A small band of the Dun jumped me, left me bound and blindfolded and then took the horses. . . I didn't see where." Suddenly Mamzer wished he hadn't managed to free himself, if Brannan found him still tied, perhaps it would have made it easier to understand there wasn't anything he could have done. Looking now though at his Uncle's face, he rather doubted it.

Without a word Brannan wheeled his horse and flew back through the canyon to the gate, followed by the brothers. Brónach walked his horse over to Mamzer and reached down his hand. "Take my arm boy, and let me pull you up behind me. There's going to be a chase and I won't leave you here."

They rode through the canyon gate and Brónach took a moment to close it so the horses they just captured would remain in the canyon. Brannan dismounted and started searching for a trail that would indicate where the Dun were headed. Brónach turned to Mamzer and asked quietly, "About what time did the raid take place Lad, can you remember?"

"Yes sir, it was mid-morning."

Brónach hollered out at Brannan, "There's no point in searching for their tracks. I know where they're headed, and we'd best move fast if we're going to catch em."

Brannan looked up from a confusion of tracks, and barked back in frustrated anger, "What are you talking about?"

"I'm talking about where they're headed, I already know. Think man, the Dun don't ride, and these horses weren't broke for riding anyway. They're too smart to try and walk across the plains home, we would catch up to them in a few hours. They wouldn't have done this unless they knew of a place where they felt safe, someplace where we wouldn't want to follow."

Brannan's seemed to come completely unhinged, for Mamzer while experiencing his wrath many times, never heard his uncle raise his voice this way against his own father. "Well get on with it then! Where are they?!!"

"A few miles, through that pass to the East, is a series of caves and caverns. I've never seen them, but from all I've heard they would be a natural place for the Dun to seek refuge."

Brannan leaped to his saddle and tore off in the indicated direction, followed by the brothers with Brónach and Mamzer bringing up the rear. Sure enough as they breached the rim of the saddle the tracks were quite clear that the horses had been brought this way. By length of stride it was possible to tell they were being led at a leisurely pace, not driven at a run. The raiders weren't in a hurry, and no efforts were made to conceal tracks. This spoke of the confidence they felt in their escape.

Late that afternoon, the tracks led to a cave in the side of the mountain. The entrance was sandy, level, and large enough for a horse to enter, but too low for a horse with a rider.

Brannan dismounted and started to hack a pine limb with his sword, intending to make a torch. Brónach watched for a moment and let him hack away, hoping the exercise in futility would at least be a sound vent for his anger. Speaking softly from behind, Brannan's father tried to speak some sense to his son. "You're not going in there."

Drawing back his sword to swing with all his might in an attempt to cleave the branch, Brannan spit the words through clenched teeth, "Yes I am."

Brónach reached out and grabbed his arm. "Son, listen to me, I know of these caves, they are a maze with many entrances, and a network that goes for untold miles. We don't have the equipment needed to go into such places. Lose light in there, and we will all be dead. Besides, no one in their right mind is going to take on a party of Dun in caves. Caves are their domain, and you can bet they will have set all manner of traps for any who dare follow. They're masters of that sort of warfare. One by one you will lose your sons, a couple of them mere boys, and in the end perhaps your own life. Is that a price you are willing to pay? Come now, we really have lost little more than our labor, and maybe some of our pride. It's time to cut our losses, and head for home."

Brannan angrily pulled away from his father, sheathed his sword and started back to his horse. He stopped right in front of Esh and looked up at Mamzer. In a fury he reached out and grabbed the boy by his tunic and lifted him bodily from the horse and threw him into the dirt. "You are not a son, you have no place riding with the Capall. Especially after letting those half men steal our horses. This is your fault!!" Brannan then kicked the boy in the stomach lifting him back up off the ground. He went to kick him again but Brónach embraced his son in a bear hug and pulled him away. Brannan however continued to hurl accusation and obscenities that all struck home with greater impact than any blow or kick could have.

It was a hungry, dejected party that finally rode back through the gates of home three days later, with only a few horses to replace the lost pack animals. In the small sack however, they did find some silver, even a few gold coins, not as much compensation as they would have received from the market, but still a pretty good return for their labors.

Despite this, Mamzer still experienced Brannan's wrath for the remainder of the trip. Over Brónach's

49

objection Brannan insisted that since the Mamzer allowed the horses to be stolen, he certainly didn't have the right to ride back, even double. So Mamzer walked, every single step of the way. One foot in front of the other for untold thousands of strides; each and every step adding to his growing burden of accusation and shame. Finally the accumulated weight crushed his spirit leaving it broken on a trail of tears.

Three

Ruarc the first Monarch of Jeshurun was a son of Rapha`. Twelve feet tall, head and shoulders taller than any of his people, truly a giant among giants. After being named king, the Irial and sons of Dun combined skills and resources to arm Ruarc as no other for war. With a silver helm resting on his great mop of red hair, the king came equipped with incomparable chain mail and shield, making him a virtual walking, talking, living tank. Wielding a battle axe two strong men could barely lift, Ruarc scared the sheol out of his enemies and all but the mightiest of foes. Most opponents, (unless they lacked good sense) after one glance the king's way, converted from warrior to long distance runners, leaving nothing behind but a cloud of dust.

In the poor light of early dawn, the King of Jeshurun saw no sign of activity in the Dagon garrison before him. With all the spontaneity of a wildfire, Ruarc's personality proved to be the perfect match for his unfettered copper hair and beard. So, it came as no surprise to any of his captains when the king's hasty assessment of the situation called for action. "This will be easy Jireh, they suspect nothing. I see no evidence a watch has even been set, we should strike now while we have the advantage of surprise."

Next to the king straining to see, stood a large centaur, one of the sons of Irijah. A gold torc with a white stone in the center marked this particular centaur as the Shophetim of Jeshurun. For nearly fifteen hundred years the Shophetim were leaders, prophets, and judges for Jeshurun's five tribes. For over five hundred years, Jireh presided as the nation's prophet/judge. He would also be the last as the Age of the Shophetim reluctantly transitioned to the reign of kings.

Jireh's eyes moved from Ruarc to the faces of the great captains standing near and surrounding their king. Old, even by the reckoning of the Irial and the sons of Dun, the seer somehow needed to persuade the tribal leaders present–especially the king, that his cautionary urgings were based on hundreds of years worth of experience. Not one of these men had drawn a breath when he first received the call to be Jeshurun's judge and deliverer.

In the hundreds of years he served as Shophetim aggressive neighbors selected the land for invasion close to forty times. Several times managing to pass through the Keys and subjugating all the people.

Unique among all nations, called to be a land ruled by laws nurtured in each man's heart, somehow the rule of law kept degenerating into everyman doing what seemed right in his own eyes. After so many invasions, the people decided enough is enough, so they decided to trade freedom for security–they started clamoring for a king. Jireh remembered the day well, he called the five tribes together and warned them all to be careful of what they wished for. Ignoring his warnings the people cast lots, (a divine roll of the proverbial dice) and Ruarc became king. The growing regret of this selection remained heavy on the Shophetim's mind as he looked into the eager king's eyes and again tried to counter his impulsiveness.

"That is what bothers me my King, the Dagon knew we would be coming. To overwhelm this outpost and establish a garrison here would be an affront they knew we could not ignore. Would you provoke an enemy, then not keep watch for a response? I tell you, the Dagon know we are here. They are watching us now, even as we are watching them."

Mereah, the Rapha' Crown Prince and Ruarc's only heir spoke up from just behind the Shophetim's shoulder. "Do you think we should start preparing for a siege Jireh, we don't have much in the way of siege weapons, . . . they will take time to build." The son had the king's strong face, but the queen mother's blonde hair, which he wore braided. Mereah was sixteen, and while this was considered an adult among the Rapha`s, his beard still remained quite thin, so he kept it trimmed short.

"Aye," quipped the king, "Time is something else we don't have. The garrison has plenty of water, and food– we have sun, scorpions and sand. If it's to be a siege, we won't last three days."

Jireh acknowledged the facts grimly, "No, you are quite right, we must attack. We must not precede however, under any illusions that we will catch the enemy by surprise. Once our main force draws closer than two hundred yards, we can expect long bow bombardment. Perhaps catapults at around one hundred and fifty yards."

Turning to address the captain of Jeshurun's cavalry, Jireh advised, "You won't want to waste your horses in such a charge, Korah, hold your men back until we have secured the gate, and if necessary, prepare for a counter attack, just in case the battle goes ill and the army is forced to retreat."

"What are you talking about, what retreat?" The

king scoffed. "My army will not retreat, can we just get on with it?"

Jireh remembered wincing back when the lots selected Ruarc as king. This wasn't anything against Ruarc particularly, only that he was one of the sons of Rapha` specifically. The Rapha` have the shortest life span of any of the seven races–they reach adult physical maturity in about thirteen to fourteen years, but only rarely do they live past the age of fifty. Having so few years many of the big titans such as Ruarc realized that they didn't have much time to spare. Knowing their time was short, they tended to act a bit hasty.

Again the Shophetim tried to calm him down, "Patience O King, we'll attack soon enough, but we must make some preparations. All attackers will need some form of shielding against archers. Can the Rapha` prepare anything special, to deal with the gate?"

Mereah grinned, "Leave that to me. Lithos and I have been working on something special, just for the occasion."

At four and a half feet tall, Lithos appeared barely higher than the king's knees. Ruarc made a point of looking down at the Dun captain to make a playful jib, "I don't think anything special will be required, simply send Lithos ahead. He doesn't even need to duck as he walks underneath the crack at the bottom of the gate."

Lithos shot the king a smoldering glare, "There are times when being of smaller stature is an advantage O high and mighty King. For example, my people will be quite happy knowing that when we cross several hundred yards of open ground, the Rapha` will be there to offer Dagon archers much more inviting targets."

The cheerful banter between the king and his Dun commander went in one of Jireh's ears and out the other. He continued to gaze at the garrison, a quizzical look on his great bearded face. Speaking almost as much to himself as the group of Jeshurun captains assembled, Jireh muttered, "They knew we would be

54

coming, why were they so confident? Well, can't be helped, we'll just have to respond when the enemy reveals what's hidden in his robes."

Turning to the Irial Captain Ragnhildr, Jireh asked, "What is the effective range for your archers?"

Just as the chieftain started to respond, the front gate to the garrison slowly creaked open drawing the attention of the entire army to see who or what would walk out.

Jireh gave a low whistle, "King of heaven! Now that explains a great deal." Framed in the opening stood a tanniyn, a wingless serpent. Thought to have been exterminated during the land's conquest well over a thousand years ago, the dragons inspired many a fairy tale, and more than a few nightmares. Jireh didn't have a clue as to how the Dagon found the means to bring the creatures back from extinction.

The tanniyn would be intimidating enough by themselves, but when the Jeshurun forces saw one mounted by a warrior bearing shield, bow and lance, a murmur of panicked dismay swept through their ranks. The fear only grew as the scaly serpent and it's rider moved through the gate only to be followed by another, and another, . . .

The king turned to the Shophetim, grinned, and tightened the chinstrap on his helmet. Despite his soldier's dismay, the king didn't seem to be at all alarmed. "Wonderful plans Jireh, can we get to fighting now? All this talk hurts my head." With that, the king hefted his axe and charged. His son Mereah let out a whoop and took off after his father with Lithos right on their heals.

Jireh yelled at the top of his lungs after the already charging king, "Ruarc, if the Dagon are removed from the citadel remember the ban!" Shaking his head in disgust he knew it to be quite likely that Ruarc hadn't heard a word he said.

Reacting quickly, (though not fast enough to stop

the king) Jireh grabbed Ragnhildr, "Rally the Irial and follow the king. When within effective range, stop your advance and unleash an arrow bombardment over the king's head. Keep it up until just before our forces engage the enemy, is that understood?"

The captain looked quizzically at the Shophetim as if to say, "Do you really need to ask? Of course I understand!" just before running off to join his men.

Turning then to Korah, the cavalry captain, Jireh shouted out further instructions, "Take the cavalry to the west and fall on the Dagon flank, but not until they are already engaged. If attacking the tanniyn, use your horses' superior speed to keep a safe distance and attack with short bows. I will bring the centaurs up the center to support the infantry and help protect the archers."

Korah started to run to get his horse, but the cavalry captain stopped and looked back long enough to ask, "What are those things?"

Jireh gave the Capall officer a somber look, "A creature not seen in Jeshurun for almost fifteen hundred years. Be careful, teeth and claws are not their only weapons; 'ware the tail."

Jireh joined the other centaurs at a dead run, having only seconds to bark instructions and to take stock of the army's present circumstances. In all, he counted ten tanniyn and riders emerge from the gate to form a battle line. Then Dagon infantry poured out of the garrison like angry ants and quickly flowed to the front of the ranks. The surging whistle of a volley from longbows made the Shophetim look up and mutter, "Too soon Ragnhildr, your Archers are well out of range."

From a distance of close to three hundred yards, in most cases he would have been right. Whether from better weapon design, or the skill of the Irial, the deadly rain started finding targets. But only a few volleys were possible with Ruarc and his guard foolishly forging ahead so rapidly and engaging the Dagon center so fast the Irial were forced to cease firing lest they strike the king. The sons of Dun in the infantry could hardly be expected to match the Rapha's long strides, so to no one's surprise, they were treated to a generous helping of the king's dust.

Jireh could only shake his head at Ruarc's recklessness. The Dagon infantry moved quickly to surround the king and cut off his support. The only way to reach Ruarc now involved trying to break through the thick ring of swords that quickly engulfed him.

Addressing the few centaurs, Jireh barked simple instructions: "After more than a millennium, Jeshurun has its first king, I would prefer it be at least a few more years before having to find a new one. We must do what we can to deliver him from his own foolhardiness."

Meanwhile, Ruarc kept striding forward. The combined craft of Irial and Dun smiths provided him with impenetrable armor, while his great axe both cut and crushed his foes. Unfortunately the Rapha` in his guard were not as well equipped. It is not easy to fell a giant, yet many of the sons of Rapha` were already wounded, some severely, from dart, arrow and sword.

The enemy infantry fled from the face of the king, and from his son Mereah emboldening them both. Jireh thought this to be a design of the enemy rather than an act of cowardice. For while Ruarc and Mereah advanced ever deeper into the enemy lines, in their zeal they didn't notice they left even the Rapha` in their guard behind. Soon the father and son team became an island in a sea of blades.

At first the enemies plan seemed to backfire, as Jireh noted the Dagon dead started to pile up like wheat sheaves, around Ruarc and Mereah. "Maybe the king's right after all." he thought, "Soon the infantry will break through the lines in support of the king, and this battle just might turn into a rout."

Then a tanniyn and rider charged through the Dagon

57

ranks, engaging a giant from the king's guard in combat for the first time. Everywhere else, the fighting stopped. Warriors on both sides held their breath and watched. Instinctively everyone knew the results from this combat would likely determine the outcome of the whole battle. If a giant couldn't handle one of the dragons and its rider, . . . well, a long bloody day for the army of Jeshurun would be in the forecast.

From twenty feet the attacking rider hurled a short javelin that penetrated deep into the Rapha's shoulder. Then in two swift bounds the tanniyn closed the distance between combatants and the dragon pounced on its victim. Jireh shouted out encouragement, "Stand the creature up, attack it's belly!"

The instructions were lost on the giant who couldn't hear because terror plugged his ears. Backing away from the assault, panic neutered the Rapha's sword swipe to a feeble blow that merely glanced off the dragons armored scales. The horror and fear in the young giant's eyes were visible to all, before the tanniyn's fangs and claws sank deep into soft flesh dragging the screaming son of Rapha` down.

Then to the horror of the Jeshurun army, the tanniyn started to feed. The Dagon infantry roared in triumph and approval, as the great head lifted with a prodigious chunk of bloody meat from its still screaming victim and started gulping it down. The men of Jeshurun became unnerved, the Dagon emboldened, and they renewed their attack with a frenzied vengeance.

Then a second Rapha` fell, and the Jeshurun advance screamed to a halt, ground gears into reverse and started backing up. With the infantry breaking ranks Jireh knew the day would be lost unless a bold strike could somehow turn the tide.

Jireh tried to get the attention of the captains, but found it almost impossible to be heard above the battles confusion and tumult. In the end he resorted to charging frantically towards fleeing soldiers screaming orders to stand their ground. He might as well have tried to hold back a fleeing tide.

At that moment, Ruarc proved his worth.

Striding forward toward the largest of the tanniyn, feeding from the carcass of a slain Rapha`, the king bellowed a challenge. Lifting its gory head with blood staining yellow fangs red, the serpent charged, just as its rider hurled a dart. Ruarc swatted the javelin aside but still the attack accomplished the purpose of occupying the king's defenses and giving the tanniyn the split second it needed to get inside his guard. A half stride before reaching its quarry, the creature reared high on its back legs for a three-fold attack of talon, tooth and claw.

The fallen Rapha` of the king's guard had panicked and reeled backwards from this same attack, but not Ruarc. The tanniyn drew too close for the king to effectively wield his axe, so instead of backing away, the king drove in even closer, slammed his shield under the tanniyn's throat and pushed the dragon higher in its stance on its back legs. This caught the creature's rider by complete surprise and threw him from the monster's back into the dirt. Then with a blow that started high but from behind his back, Ruarc swung his great axe as an uppercut down from his shoulder, to his knees and then back up into the monster's soft underbelly.

The serpent's rider climbed up out of the dust just in time to see his tanniyn die and hear its screams. Extracting his blade from the creature's belly, Ruarc then gave its rider a big grin and issued a challenge to come and finish the combat. The Dagon rider, however, demonstrated a great deal more discretion than valor as he turned and fled for his life.

The dragon's death screams did more to stop Jeshurun's flight than all of Jireh's angry threats, warnings and admonitions. Pausing long enough to look back, the infantry watched as their king roared his triumph over one of the serpents. Once again they rallied to his support.

The momentum now completely shifted, another tanniyn rider fell, this time to a Irijah sling stone. The riderless dragon, now unguided became more of a threat to the Dagon than the soldiers of Jeshurun.

Observing that development, Jireh barked orders to Korah's cavalry, "Target the riders!"

Striking swiftly, staying well clear of the dragon's teeth and claws, the Capall rode to within the effective range of their short bows and shot a few more of the riders out of the saddle. With leaderless tanniyn trampling their own soldiers, their advantage rapidly evaporating, the Dagon fled in a panicked route through and around the garrison and across the Cnámh plain.

FOUR

"But fear no more! I would not take this thing, if it
Lay by the highway. Not were Minas Tirith falling
in ruin and I alone could save her, so, using the weapon
Of the Dark Lord for her good and my glory"
~J.R.R. Tolkien
The Two Towers

The Anak Anbhás stood on a small rise watching the tattered fragments of his army come reeling across the Cnámh plain.

With all trace of human warmth absent from his acidic rasp, he protested "I risked much on this gambit. Too few of my soldiers from a sizeable force are going to survive the day. Several tanniyn were also lost–all for a ruse?"

Next to the Anak stood one of the Watchers, a demon named Skandalon. Lacking vocal chords, the Watchers projected their communications into the minds of those who would know their voice. The humanity that still existed in Anbhás experienced these communications like an acid poured inside his skull.

"Concern for your soldiers? I'm touched. If I didn't know better I'd accuse you of being sentimental. You need not concern yourself, in the end you will only have lost about half of a diversionary force. The slaughter of the tanniyn is a great loss, but more and deadlier are being bred.

The pursuit of your army, however, must soon end; the fools did not stop for water while they were in the garrison. Already the horse soldiers are turning back. The emotional saps among the Capall will not allow harm to their mounts. The Dun make up the main force of the infantry, and while capable trench fighters, they are not effective in pursuit. They were left behind hours ago. If thirst does not end the chase, darkness soon will. If you are truly concerned, I can give you a small persuader to use, to convince the dogs to turn tail and run back home."

"For a price." The thought popped in Anbhás head before he could check it. The Anak knew when dealing with such dark messengers, nothing ever came free. Any "persuader" Skandalon might offer would come at a steep price. He didn't say this, but felt a thrill of fear for just thinking it. The Watcher he knew to be capable of projecting his thoughts, but it remained unclear to Anbhás whether or not the demon could read them as well.

"For a price, of course." A perfect echo of his previous thought popped into the Anak's mind, this time a projection with a voice that mimicked his own, casting further anxiety in the Anakim shaman's heart, and thoughts, "Can this demon read my mind?" Images of a cat toying with a mouse filled Anbhás mind as he pondered the answer to his own unspoken question.

The Watcher's next telepathic communications began uncharacteristically gentle, even soothing, the sarcasm barely detectable. "I am sorry for your loss of course, but let me tell you about your risk . ."

The gentle soothing tones were instantly replaced with acidic vitriol, *"You* risked nothing!" The demon's thoughts screamed in the Anak's mind causing him to flinch and shrink back: "You fight for a worthless scrap of land. The Watchers help only as a way to spit in Elohim's eye. Don't speak to me of risk. Try defying an El capable of creating or destroying a world at his word.

"Elohim *did* destroy the world once, remember? Do you know why? Because my kind were remaking this world, this Tebel and its peoples, in *our* image. It promised to be the ultimate revenge–to corrupt the pathetic, weak, fleshy usurpers, before Elohim could give them dominion!

"I will tell you a secret Anbhás, I will reveal Elohim's weakness. Oh yes, even He has one, otherwise our cause would be hopeless. He actually loves the pathetic creatures he placed on this planet. And whenever an opponent cares about something, that is a weakness that can be exploited. One day, it will be the death of even Elohim, the mighty Power.

"How do you best hurt the one who is Almighty? By taking away from his heart, and then hurting the ones He most cares about. We corrupted the children of His image into ours. We took their women and bred spawn in our likeness. We stuck a fork into the apple of Elohim's eye, the children of his image, and we bled from them all life and joy. They became so corrupt, Elohim had no choice but to destroy the very thing He loved, in a pathetically desperate attempt to save it."

Suddenly Skandalon reached out his shade arm and reached into the Anak's skull, dropping Anbhás to his knees in agony, his hands covering his face. The voice of the Watcher was like an ice pick being dragged across the inside of his skull, the pain so great he couldn't even scream, let alone respond.

"Don't forget, you are still flesh, I can cause pain such as even your depraved mind can't fathom. The risk is mine, all you risk is failure and displeasing me. Let me tell you why this pathetic little strip of land is so important. The Watchers have already succeeded in corrupting most of the re-created world of Elohim. He has placed all his hope and trust now in this pathetic land and the people of Jeshurun. The power whose other name I will not utter established them as a land ruled by law, a light to stand against darkness. The Watchers will empower you to snuff out that light like a candle. If you fail, you will die and know unimaginable torment. Then another shall take your place, and there will always be another to take your place. My offspring are legion."

The Watcher suddenly realized the Anak was still writhing in the dust in agony. His mind-crushing assault continuing through his entire rant. After releasing his invisible grip the agony quickly subsided, and in a few moments the Anak recovered enough to rise and stand. In a weak and much more subdued voice Anbhás whispered, "What I meant to say my lord, is that with the sacrifice of the tanniyn and so many soldiers, how am I to arrange another attack?"

Skandalon's response became less severe, but not any less sarcastic, "I told you fool, the soldiers you lost will be replaced ten fold. But with what was accomplished this day, the next battle is already won. The idiots believe the key to their defense is found in narrow openings through the high plateau wall to the North. The true key to Jeshurun's defenses, is the courage and heart of their newly appointed king, and today I have given *him* to you. The loss of a few reptiles and the rabble you named an army is nothing compared to this. This alone should be enough to earn your undying loyalty and service, but I will give you more besides."

The Watcher removed his veil and fixed the Dagon Anak with a glance that despite the desert heat froze what remained of his human blood, "Your soul was worthless at any rate, and a very small price to pay for all the help you receive in exchange. Soon the Anakim, your people, will control the land once more, and you shall be their shaman king–if you do not fail or displease me."

~

Striding through the wide open garrison entry, Ruarc and his captains saw the last of the Dagon fleeing out the back gate. All manner of plunder lay scattered everywhere, as though the enemy intended to flee with as much as they could carry, and thought better of it.

Jeshurun soldiers upon seeing all the wealth laying on the ground started a mad scramble to pick up as much and as fast as they could. Jireh quickly recognized the danger from greed, as it took just seconds for the first squabbles over loot to erupt.

"Ruarc," the Shophetim shouted, "Get them moving again or run the risk of losing your own army from self-destruction!"

But the king just stood there staring as though dazed, so Jireh turned to Mereah and the captains. "Mereah, we can't delay here, every soldier of the enemy that escapes today will be back with a new force tomorrow."

The King's son, instantly grasped the wisdom of this, and started barking instructions to the captains, "Tell the men to leave it, all of it, no time, . . we must pursue the Dagon."

In the chaos and confusion, Mereah didn't have any greater success that Jireh in getting anyone's attention, so after a few moments of desperate frustration, the Prince placed a great horn to his lips and gave it a mighty blast. With every eye now on him, the young Rapha` simply grinned and charged out the back gate, while the men of Jeshurun looked on stunned.

Jireh shaking his head muttered, "Truly the apple ever falls close to the tree." Then without a word he leaped in pursuit of Jeshurun's Crown Prince.

Lithos, not about to be left behind sprinted through the opening. For a moment, Korah, Capall's captain nursed a humorous mental picture of the entire Dagon army running from three men. Then he realized the Dagon would eventually realize this and turn to fight. His mount rearing slightly, he urged it to turn broadside to his men as he cried, the cavalry motto, "First to fight!"

"First to victory!" came the thunderous response, as a hundred horse charged out the gate, joined by all the remaining centaurs. Most of the sons of Dun and Irial also headed for the gate but were log-jammed in the exit.

Just a glimpse of the treasure left behind however, proved to be all that Ruarc needed to cool his battle fever. So he grabbed a few remaining among the Rapha`, Dun and Irial and ordered them to remain, "Idiots, we need to secure the garrison! Now spread out, search the buildings, take alive anyone you find, if you can, and bring 'em to me."

Originally built by the Dun, the fortress strategically guarded the only source of fresh water on the entire Cnámh plain. Most of Jeshurun's enemies were to the south and the desert plain the preferred invasion route. So many battles historically were fought there it also received the name Gleann Anbhás, or valley of violent death. Others named the place simply the valley of dry bones (Cnámh means bone).

Because the Dun were the designers, only so many places in the citadel even permitted a giant's entrance. A quick visual scan allowed Ruarc to locate the two or three buildings built to accommodate a person of his stature. A few long strides took him to the first building where he believed he hit the jack-pot.

He walked into a dining hall recently converted to a

temporary temple. Not much to speak of in way of ornamentation, in addition to simple benches of various sizes and heights, he located an altar, fire pit, and a bronze statue of the god Dagon from whom these peoples took their name. At close to thirteen feet tall, the idol's dragon head leered at Ruarc through large garnet orbs. Dark and blood-red in the poor light, the god's eyes would likely flame to life when offerings were set on its blazing altar. A humanoid body, with arms hanging at its sides, the god Dagon's outstretched hands were palms up, in order to receive living sacrifices.

Up close, Ruarc's eyes were drawn to an amulet clasped to a gold chain around the god's neck. The amulet formed a gold circle with a large ruby filling the center. The talisman seemed to have a faint red glow, as though a light radiated from within.

Suddenly, Ruarc remembered Jireh's warnings about treasures of the enemy and Elohim's ban against taking Dagon plunder. Forcing himself to turn away, he circled behind the idol, and spotted another door leading to a back room. Backtracking to find some kind of light, Ruarc grabbed a candle off Dagon's altar, and lit it by blowing life into some warm coals from the brazier. In two strides he went back through the door into an inner storage room. Here Ruarc's eyes really grew wide; the room was filled with plunder. Alive about thirty-five years, he knew he could live two or three more lifetimes and never see this kind of wealth again.

Ruarc might be a king, but merely the first king of a loose knit confederacy of tribes and peoples and so far, no one would confuse him with a rich man. What he did receive from the five tribes he considered a pittance, far less than what he thought appropriate for a monarch. After all, he lived in a tent, not a palace; the people paid no taxes and he didn't have a treasury or any accumulated wealth. What the people expected, he considered outrageous–they wanted him to fight their battles and risk his neck, while living on an income considered paltry even for a peasant!

But here before his eyes was sufficient wealth to set him up to live as a king indeed, even as the kings of other nations. The wheels in Ruarc's mind started turning. All this wealth, and Jireh would have him destroy it, . . no—worse than that, he wasn't even supposed to touch it! Before setting out, Jireh specifically banned taking any of the wealth of conquest or victory from the Dagon. Ruarc agreed at the time, but now in the presence of all this treasure, the ban suddenly made no practical sense. The more he thought about it, the more good things he could think of that could be done with all this gold.

Besides, he reasoned, this could easily be plunder from Dagon raids against the peoples of Jeshurun! Elohim couldn't have intended its destruction, it should be returned to the people!

Leaving the Temple, Ruarc got the attention of one of his lieutenants, a tall Irial archer. "Quillan, any news of my son or the Shophetim Jireh?"

The Irial officer looked up to answer his king. Quillan was over six feet tall, but the top of his head was barely over the king's belt buckle. He looked up into Ruarc's grinning face, his bright green eyes framed by his great red beard. "No my King, your son and the Shophetim still pursue the enemy, Prince Mereah is very valiant I think he is loath to give up the pursuit."

Ruarc turned aside in thought and inner debate, then finally seemed to make a decision and so turned his attention back to his lieutenant. "Listen, I want to be informed as soon as there is news, in the meantime, I want you to send to me as many of my people that you can find."

After watching the Irial officer run off to carry out his instructions, he strode back inside the converted temple. The amulet still glowed red on the idol's chest. After turning to walk away several times, Ruarc in the end walked over to take a closer look at the image of Dagon.

He had to admit the craftsmanship far exceeded the skill and attention to detail in most other idols he had seen. However, it was the amulet around the god's neck that continued to draw his eye. A single beautifully cut ruby with a circumference similar to a medium sized apple, formed the center. Nothing in his whole kingdom even came close to matching its beauty or value. Set in a perfect gold circle, light from within the stone cast a crimson glow on the idol's front.

Then he discovered that a tanniyn, one with wings and more lithe like a snake, appeared to be trapped inside the gem. Truly perplexed by this mystery, he wondered how in heaven did they carve this image inside the stone? Taking the ruby in hand, he felt a surge of power which surprised him so that he quickly let go, and the pendant dropped back against the idol's chest. Now even more intrigued, he took it up once more. He couldn't put it down again, instead he lifted the pendant's chain over the serpent idols head, and somewhere a demon laughed as Jeshurun's king took the bait.

~

Jireh the Shophetim, paused from his exertions to wipe the dust and sweat from his brow. Turning his head, he saw a back trail of Dagon dead stretching for more than fifteen miles. He hoped to ensure precious few of the Dagon would live to reach the southern coastal city from which they came. Unfortunately a lack of water and soon a lack of light would put an end to pursuit of the enemy. He worried the delays back at the citadel looking for plunder rather than replenishing their water supplies would in the future cost them dearly. Korah the cavalry captain and the Rapha' prince

69

Mereah, stood beside the Judge of Jeshurun.

Jireh's mouth felt so dry, he could barely speak so Korah became the temporary spokesman for the centaur who was known as the voice of Elohim. Pulling down a piece of fabric that acted as a filter for the dust, the captain's voice remained husky from a coating of grime that almost made him choke. "Mereah, it is enough, the horses cannot continue, they've had little water since the battle began at dawn. Every step they take raises a cloud of bone dry dust. We have to return to the garrison."

Jireh finally managed to spit enough filth from his throat to add his voice to Korah's appeal, "The good captain is right, if we continue on we will start losing more than horses. My own water is long spent, it will be dark soon, which will only serve to encourage our enemies. And, the further south we go, I feel a growing presence, . . I cannot yet name it . . . but I discern an evil power . . . a power I don't believe we have a name for at this time. We should halt the pursuit, and be content with today's great victory."

Mereah drew the back of his filthy tunic sleeve across his sweaty brow, which merely succeeded in adding to the smears and dark stains that he already wore like a veil.

The young Rapha` grinned when he looked at the sweat and grime coating Jireh and Korah head to hoof. The centaur's many years were normally only partially displayed by streaks of white and gray that peppered his chestnut colored beard. Now his whole front, including the facial hair and features looked as though painted a chalky bone gray.

While the captain's face looked a bit cleaner where protected by the fabric covering, the dirt around his eyes made it seem as though he wore a bandit's mask. Mereah chuckled at the sight, oblivious to his own ridiculous appearance.

He lacked the energy for his usual hearty laugh, so

he started to make a wise-crack about how everybody looked. When the words wouldn't come, he realized he was to tired to speak. In the end the Rapha` prince simply lifted his great ox horn to his lips and gave it a blast, signaling the withdrawal.

An hour after sunset, some troops started to straggle through the south gate. The information given to king Ruarc was that Jireh, and Mereah his son, along with many of the Irial, some of the Rapha`, Capall Cavalry and all the Irijah continued their pursuit of the enemy.

With the garrison secured, the nation's ruler remained busy preparing the financing for his new palace. Jeshurun's king would dwell in a tent no longer. Flames from the makeshift forge the Dun set up filled the garrison courtyard with garish light. Worker's shadows danced on citadel walls as they filed in, bringing plunder for cleansing in white hot flame. The king watched anxiously as a couple of the soldiers placed articles of gold in the furnace to be melted down. Waiting for purification, sitting next to a pile of gold, sat Dagon the bronze idol. Its gem stone eyes were removed and sat in the king's purse, along with an amulet that once hung around the idol's neck. A deep, low voice interrupted Ruarc's dark thoughts, "And just what are you up too, O King?"

Ruarc stiffened as a man caught with his hands in the proverbial cookie jar. From all reports, the Shophetim shouldn't be back, not for at least another hour. Apparently the reports were wrong, for the voice of Jireh was unmistakable.

Turning, the giant king faced the centaur. With the body of a great war horse, and the muscular upper torso of a small giant, Jireh remained one of the few creatures in all of Jeshurun capable of even coming close to looking Ruarc in the eye. With strong arms crossed over a broad chest, and despite the coating of dust, he maintained the very air of a teacher reprimanding an errant student. Ruarc struggled to answer, but instead just stammered, until the centaur grew impatient. "Well? Answer me."

Finally the king stopped stuttering and answered, "I am sanctifying these articles of gold and silver and bronze, refining them by fire so that they may be used in El's service."

"And tell me Ruarc, did you not understand Elohim's command – not my command – Elohim's command, that nothing of the Dagon's wealth or treasure is to be taken?"

With the Shophetim far away, Ruarc felt confident in his defiance of the ban. But now, with Jireh standing there, a torc around his neck representing the authority of Jeshurun's Judge–worse yet–all the authority of Jeshurun's God, suddenly the king didn't feel nearly as self-assured. Instead he resumed the stuttering and stammering of his previous responses, "But nothing has been taken for myself, or for anyone else. These items are being sanctified by fire for El's use."

Reading guilt and shame all over the king's face, Jireh continued his interrogation. "Tell me something O King, has the El of Jeshurun suddenly become impoverished?"

As an act of defiance, and perhaps as an escape from Jireh's fiery gaze, Ruarc turned his back to the Shophetim and resumed his tasks. "I don't understand what you mean Jireh, please don't speak in riddles."

The temperature of the furnace wasn't the only thing rising, as Jireh reacted to the king's disrespect. "I mean you must have somehow come under the impression that Elohim has suddenly become poor–so poor that He needs an offering from Dagon's loot. Ruarc, it is dangerous to take treasures of the enemy. You may have indeed intended their use for good, but whatever you take from Dagon's hand will end up taking you, and will seek to work our enemies will. I see you are going to melt down the Dagon idol, and it needs be destroyed;

but was there not an amulet? A red stone, with a light emanating from within? The amulet is called the Zilliah, the Red Shade. This thing is particularly evil and also needs to be destroyed, but you lack the power to do this. Where is it?"

Ruarc's turned back suddenly stiffened and he paused several seconds before responding. "It wasn't here. I never saw anything such as you described, it must be the Dagon took this thing when they fled and abandoned the citadel. But come now, chastise me no more, tonight you must preside over the sacrifices to El."

Deep in thought, Jireh grimly looked at the king, saying nothing. Ruarc grew increasingly uncomfortable as he felt the eyes of the Shophetim boring through his back. Finally he turned as if to face the music once more. With eye contact re-established, Jireh pronounced his words of judgment.

"Do you remember the proverb, spoken by our people? 'With no king in Jeshurun everyman does what is right in his own eyes.' A world where every man does what is right in his own eyes is chaotic, void of law. This is why you were made king, to enforce our laws. A king can't do whatever he wants, I'm sorry to disappoint you. You are not Jeshurun's first king, there has been a king in Jeshurun for well over a thousand years."

Ruarc grew increasingly frustrated and spit back at the Shophetim, "There you go speaking in riddles again! You know very well I am the first king, you placed the crown on my head yourself! What king besides me ever ruled this land?"

"I'll tell you who, the same King who ruled long before your coronation, and in fact rules even today. Jeshurun is ruled by Law Ruarc, always has been. Any monarch who will not first be governed by the law, is not fit to rule. I tell you plain Ruarc, if the law is not king, a tyrant eventually will be."

73

Ruarc frowned at Jireh, "Why wouldn't El approve of my taking of this treasure and bringing it to Him as an offering? Surely you don't think I wanted anything for myself?" Ruarc's face took on a look of unearned hurt and offense, "And IF I did, what of it? Does Elohim find some kind of virtue in keeping the King of Jeshurun in poverty–or living in a tent like some kind of desert nomad?"

Jireh rolled his eyes and his voice raised an octave as his frustration grew. "Think man! It is not that our El does not want *you* to have things. It is just more important to learn not to allow *things* to have you! There is no one for whom this is more true than for a king. Controlled by a love for gold, and the ruler becomes susceptible to all forms of corruption. I see your preparations to melt this Dagon idol, can you tell me another idol hasn't already taken its place in your heart? Have you become corrupted O King?"

Although the laws of Yahweh Elohim have no amendments against self - incrimination, still Ruarc stood silent before the nation's judge.

"Obedience is the sacrifice our El requires above all other things, for this alone is the sacrifice that reveals your heart. In your sacrifices of gold I see lies, greed and deception. If I see these things, what do you think El sees? Ruarc, the king of Jeshurun must be in submission to Elohim, even as his subjects are in submission to him. Hear me now, this is your last warning, whatever evil you have taken to your heart, let go of it now, or one day your kingdom will be removed from you and given to one who will listen and obey El's voice."

The centaur tried to reestablish eye contact with the king, but, Ruarc merely looked at his feet, more like a chastised adolescent than giant or king. The expression of hopeful expectation on Jireh's face got crushed by the king's silent response.

Jireh muttered "So be it." Then turned his tail to the

king and swished it as though shooing away a fly.

Ruarc became frantic. "Jireh, you can't leave, the whole army is expecting you to pronounce the blessing over tonight's sacrifice."

Jireh trotting towards the gates shot back, "And you need your position propped up by my approval which will be evidenced by my presiding over the very same sacrifice. You have chosen other counselors; you will have to be content with whatever support they can give."

Then the Shophetim stopped abruptly. There in the shadows, listening to everything being said, stood Mereah, the king's son. Jireh stared at the young Rapha` a moment when suddenly the eyes of the seer turned white and seemed to lose focus as a startling vision took him far away. Several awkward, silent moments later, his spirit returned from some distant place, and he looked the young giant in the eye. Reaching out, he grasped the prince's arm as tears flowed down his face and gathered in his beard.

Mereah had never experienced this behavior from Jireh before. Alarmed, he asked in a hushed voice, "What is it Jireh, what did you see?" The Rapha` prince loved and respected the Shophetim almost as much as his own father, and his angry departure was unsettling. Even more disturbing to the young giant however, was the mournful look in the centaur's eyes. If he could have somehow forseen the centaur's response, he might not have asked, for the prophet's answer proved dire.

"I saw the armies of Jeshurun scattered and fleeing to the hills, like sheep fleeing because they lacked a ra`ah. I saw the corpses of thousands of our people, and the circling of a mist covered hill, by scores of carrion birds. Among the many voices, I heard, . . the ravens calling your name."

The Rapha` princes' jaw dropped at the ominous pronouncement, and his eyes revealed deep feelings of shock and betrayal. Jireh himself was deeply grieved by what he saw, for the prince possessed a great heart and would himself make a worthy king. "I know not if this thing I saw must happen or may happen if present choices and circumstances do not change. But remember this, the content and nature of the heart and spirit is what determines whether one's end is glorious or ignoble."

With that, Jireh departed, ignoring the protests and pleadings of the king. Never again did the Shophetim visibly support Ruarc as Jeshurun's Monarch.

Five

If of all words of tongue and pen,
The saddest are, "It might have been,"
More sad are these we daily see:
"It is, but hadn't ought to be."
~Francis Brett Hart

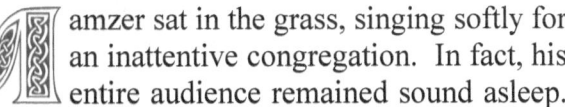amzer sat in the grass, singing softly for an inattentive congregation. In fact, his entire audience remained sound asleep. He envied them, he hadn't slept a night the whole way through in weeks. So despite the realization that if he too were sleeping, he'd miss the glorious morning sunrise coming over the mountains, he grudgingly decided appreciation for beautiful sunrises declined in proportion to the increase of his sleep deprivation.

Still, despite his blurry eyes, something about the rising of the sun on clear mornings, made those distant peaks more clearly defined than they would be all day. So, sleep or no sleep, he loved the quiet clarity of early morning sunrises so much that he would be willing to give them up only for a day or so.

Looking over the still sleeping sheep, he continued to serenade them with an ancient song of his people.

I lift my eyes to the hills
From the highlands will come
the One who will be my help
My helper has made the heavens.
Why should I be afraid?
Though our enemy prowls like a lion
Or spews venom like a serpent,
He who keeps me will not slumber.
Behold, He who keeps me
Is ever vigilant, He never sleeps
He stays as close, as the shadow of my hand.
The One who establishes the world's foundation,
whose laws direct the paths of the stars;
shall also direct my steps,
Yahweh shall direct my going out
and my coming in, now and forevermore.

Ancient Songbook - 131

Mamzer first heard the song in one of the religious gatherings that took place in the village Joktan. Although never actually allowed to attend, sometimes he would go with the family, and sit outside the building, so he could listen through a window.

Once he make the mistake of asking why he couldn't enter into the gathering with the others? Without their saying a word, he found himself being shouted down by silent glares in an unanimous family response. But after a couple more minutes, aunt Mara decided to dispel any possible confusion as to the intent or the message communicated by the everyone's cold, non-verbal reply. "Because the Assembly excludes anyone, who is a mamzer, or in any other way unclean."

When younger, he didn't even know what being a Mamzer meant, it was just the name he'd been called from his earliest memories. All the name meant to him is that exclusion from community applied to him personally.

The term unclean however, he understood better. Mamzer knew a man forced to live on the edge of town, the villagers required him to call out everywhere he went that he was unclean. And as if his words weren't warning enough, they also forced the man to wear little bells on his ankles, like a sheep or a goat, just to re-enforce his humiliation.

Wrapped in rags, the man seemed to be missing some of his fingers. He also wore a veil, but despite his best efforts to conceal his face, Mamzer could see that it seemed to be disintegrating. In times when he felt less than kind, he thought the ringing bells and warning cry's were hardly necessary. Most times the stench of decaying flesh gave ample warning of the man's approach or presence.

The ra`ah recognized the revulsion on people's faces whenever they saw the man because he saw similar reactions in Aunt Mara's and Uncle Brannan's eyes, or for that matter, the eyes of half the village when they looked at him. In addition to Mamzer, dark names–unclean, outcast, excluded–took root in his heart.

Thus condemned, he remained outside the holy gathering, allowed only a window by which he could look and listen in.

He didn't get much from the reading of the law. For one thing it was usually read in a tongue he didn't understand. For another, nothing existed in either the reading, or in people's lives that he witnessed that helped him make a connection of value for life. But he loved the music and songs, memorized them quickly, and sang them often, although usually just to the sheep.

True, he didn't understand the meaning of the songs all that much, still they spoke to a place in his soul, not generally reached by intellect. Somehow they gave him hope, that even he would one day be made clean.

With the last stanzas of his song ushering the pink

and gold of the sunrise through a sanctuary of linen and pale blue, Mamzer retired to his simple shelter. Nothing more than a sheep hide lean-to, it provided a place where he could keep a couple wool blankets to roll into when cold, or sleep on when warm. He stayed awake at night now, experience teaching him no other time presented a greater danger from predators. Even in the daylight, he slept lightly. He couldn't do otherwise, awake or sleeping, the safety of the sheep remained solely his.

Nothing brings on the feeling of being alone more than duties shared with a friend, who shares them no longer. If a person loses a valued partner, the one time mutual responsibility now only serves as reminder of loss.

Peeking past the folds of his simple shelter, his eye drifted over to a low mound of fresh-turned earth. His loneliness felt like a scab forming over a re-opened wound, that piled upon countless other old but never healed cuts, still seeping with blood and infection. Loneliness joined hands with mourning and served as a constant reminder of his recent pain to go with a life filled with loss.

Mamzer became a ra`ah at age ten, a little over five years ago. The first night Brannan left him to spend the night in the pasture alone watching the sheep he remembered being terrified. But in the early evening Brónach showed up with a dog.

In the culture of the Capall, nothing associated with dogs could be considered complementary . Out of the hundreds of proverbs passed down through generations of Jeshurun families, none called people's attention to a dog's virtues. Hard workers were told to look to the ant for inspiration, while only lazy people—or the immoral— were compared to dogs. Canines were among the few creatures of the Capall who suffered from a lower status than a ra`ah.

"This is Jax," Brónach made the introduction. "He's

a pup from a farm out west of Joktan. Watching a flock is a big job, with lots of responsibility. A dog will be a huge help. Plus, it can be plenty lonely out here by yourself, a lad can always use a friend. Usually a boy your age is given his first horse about this time, but . . . with the way Brannan feels, that's not likely to happen. Jax here is the best I can do for you, son."

Mamzer almost said "Thanks, but no thanks."

Shaggy, with floppy ears, the fur on Jax's ears hung down making them seem much longer than they really were. Tri-colored, and weighing about sixty pounds, even Mamzer knew a mutt when he saw one, and in his private thoughts he gave Jax a different name–Useless.

It took about one night to find out he couldn't have been more wrong. Jax was smart. Really smart. When Mamzer talked to him, he'd cock his head sideways and look at him as though to say, "Not only am I listening, I'm thinking," and most important, "I understand."

It took the dog all of five minutes to figure out he had a job to do, and how to do it. If a ram or ewe started feeling contrary and began to wander off, Jax would worry 'em right on back and then give 'em a lecture about not being properly appreciative of his benevolent protection.

Sleeping outside at night on the prairie, with naught but a piece of hide over your head and sheep for company seemed pretty scary for a kid who hadn't even reached puberty. Jax immediately proved to be mighty comforting company. He'd curl up with the boy and help him keep warm. In a dark night, with almost zero visibility, the dog's big ol' ears and nose proved to be the perfect alarm system. Mamzer could actually sleep at night, knowing Jax would stay alert, and wake him if trouble came along.

It took less than a day for the boy to revoke the name of "Useless" and to give him a new title, "Best Friend." Shoot, only friend would've been more accurate. Except for Brónach, all the people Mamzer knew treated him with contempt.

Maybe that's why the two of them made such a good pair. A dog, and an ugly one at that, didn't have much value among the Capall. Nobody seemed to think much of the boy or the dog, and so their worth went pretty much unnoticed, making them an almost perfect match.

In a week, Mamzer could give Jax complex verbal instructions, and the dog would carry them out perfectly, to the letter. In a Month, verbal instructions were no longer necessary, like a true friend, the closeness of their bond seemed so strong that they knew the other's thoughts somehow.

For five years they worked together, until just a few weeks ago.

That fateful night he and Jax were sleeping by a fire of small sticks and dry sheep dung. First the dogs head and ears picked up, and then he gave a low growl. When he jumped to his feet and barked. Mamzer remembered asking "What is it boy?"

Then he heard off in the dark, a snarling snapping growl, and as the sheep began to scatter, Mamzer could make a pretty good guess as to the cause of their panic–wolves!

Jax jumped up and started in the direction the sheep were running away from. The ra`ah showed pretty good reflexes and agility when he leapt and tackled his partner, and then looped twine over the dog's neck and tied him to a stake. He knew as a general rule, wolves feared and shied away from man; they wouldn't hesitate however, to attack and kill a dog.

Taking a small stick, about the width of his thumb out of his meager fire, Mamzer walked through the sheep in the direction the sounds came from just moments before. Behind him, he could hear Jax going nuts trying to get loose. His first thoughts were he'd better do this quickly because the thin line wouldn't hold for long. Then he saw them, about twenty–five feet away, at least a half dozen eyes were reflecting the light from his small torch. A chill ran down his spine when he realized one set of eyes had started walking closer.

Looking into those cold calculating eyes, all thought of intimidating or scaring the wolves off flew right out of his head. Mamzer knew whatever occupied the mind behind those orbs wouldn't be scared of nuthin'.

Suddenly white teeth flashed and he heard a low growl, warning him—leave the sheep to us and nobody gets hurt. In the pitch black, seeing only glowing eyes and snapping white fangs, every bit of common sense the boy possessed screamed to be smart and take the wolves' advice.

Then the anemic flame from his small stick torch went out. As the last trace of light slowly blinked out, he reached to his belt to draw out his flint knife. Then something hit him from behind. Few predators are as effective as wolves at working together as a unit. Clearly, one wolf came forward for the purpose of being a distraction and holding his attention, while another quietly moved to attack from behind. Fortunately, the lack of light affected the wolves vision almost as much as Mamzer's. After the flame went out, the boy shifted his position slightly, so while the attacking wolf's front claws shredded the back of his tunic, leaving long red streaks down his back, the most menacing attack missed its mark. Snapping jaws failed to clamp onto the back of his neck, and succeeded only in leaving a gash along the back of his skull.

He went down and the large canine's momentum carried it right over his head to hit the ground and roll in the grass. Wincing from pain, acting mostly on instinct, he scrambled to his knees and thrust the knife forward managing to catch the wolf with a glancing blow just as it charged back in. Yelping it jumped away, but two more pounced into the fray to take its place. Mamzer would likely have been shredded right then, had the cavalry in the form of Jax, not arrived.

Rather than pulling forward and trying to break the line, the dog wisely turned his rump around and backed up. With a lot of pulling and wagging his head back and forth, he eventually managed to work the rope over his big ears and out of the loop. Crossing the distance to his master in seconds the mutt threw everything he had into the lead wolf just as it went for his boy's throat. Sixty pounds at full tilt with the added advantage of surprise bowled the pack leader over, and Jax went straight for its neck. Then two more wolves joined the fray and for a second Mamzer could only watch in horror as a furious mass of snarling teeth, claws and fur formed a swirling vortex. Somewhere inside the snarling tornado, Jax fought for both their lives.

Without much thought of the likely consequences, Mamzer jumped on the pile and sank his blade deep in the side of one of the wolves, and slashed the haunch of a second. And just like that, the fight ended. The pack leader jumped up and out of the fray, barked a command to the others, and they took off. Three more wolves, taking advantage of the confusion, having already nabbed a couple young lambs, ran out from the midst of the flock carrying their prey to rejoin the others.

In the wild, a predator can't afford injury–injury almost always leads to death. Mamzer had wounded at least two, one seriously, and the pack leader simply counted the cost too high. They got what they came for, and so lit out.

Looking down at Jax, the ra`ah realized the dog couldn't get up. Dropping to his knees to be close to his friend's side, he ran his hand gently over the furry head, where he discovered a mangled ear, and several other wounds that dampened the dog's thick fur with blood.

Picking Jax up, he walked a good mile cradling him in his arms. The sheep were pastured so far from the farm house because for the most part the horses were given priority and kept where they could be more easily be protected.   He didn't arrive at his grandfather Brónach's cottage until a couple hours before first light.

Unable to use his hands to knock, the boy kicked the bottom of the door several times while hissing, "Grandpa, open up, it's me, Mamzer."

When the door opened a few moments later, Brónach held up a lamp looking just a bit dazed and confused, "What in the world are you doing out this late lad?"

But as soon as he noticed Jax he seemed wide awake and alert, and his voice changed from one of sleepy confusion to a voice of authority and concern. "Bring him inside son, lets take a look while you tell me what happened. Why don't you set Jax down on the cot over there?"

Mamzer gently laid his friend down while his grandfather lit a couple more candles and lanterns to create as much light as possible. Speaking gently while kneeling beside the dog, Brónach made a quick assessment of the damage. "There's a kettle over by the fireplace lad, if it doesn't have water, fill it and put it on, we're going to need lots of hot water to bathe these wounds. You'll also find on a small hook there on the wall, and some sheers. I'll need those. I'm guessing that Jax took exception to some wolves or perhaps a wild cat's plan of having mutton for dinner?"

Mamzer after all the frenzied excitement of the moment finally took a second to pause and emotionally absorb all that he'd experienced. He suddenly felt his throat get a big lump in it, and his eyes mist up, so it took him a few more seconds to respond. "I tied him up, hoping this wouldn't happen, and he managed to get loose. He didn't fight to save the sheep, he fought to save me."

While listening, Brónach continued to bath the blood and dirt from several bloody patches where there were deep puncture wounds or scratches. After a moment's thought he commented, "I've argued for a long time, if we aren't going to bring the sheep into the fold each night, we need to build one out where they are. Then when I was told you would be in charge, . . well lad, I lost that fight too. It's not that I don't think you're capable, it's just that with our living out on the edge of the prairie, so close to the mountains, it mean's being a ra`ah is dangerous work. It's a man's job, despite the disrespect our people have for shepherds.

Now lad, see those rags over there? I need you to tear 'em into strips for me."

Mamzer did as he was told but asked the first chance he got, "How is Jax, is he going to make it?"

At first it seemed Brónach ignored the question, for he responded with something almost completely off-topic. "You know when I first saw Jax, I almost kept looking, he appeared so . . . ridiculous looking. Then I looked in his eyes, and that goofy grin, and well I could tell he would be a great helper for you. I also saw a loyal heart . . . I won't lie to ya son, Jax is badly hurt, and he's lost a lot of blood. More than anything else, I'm worried about this bite here on the throat, a major artery was damaged . . . I've been able to slow the bleeding, but so far I can't stop it. Jax lost a great deal of blood in just the time it took you to get him here.

"When I picked Jax, it was for something I saw inside him. I knew anything looking to hurt you would have to go over his dead body. Son, I'm really sorry, I really hoped it would never come to that. But I'll also never regret my choice."

Mamzer kneeled beside the cot carefully stroking Jax's furry head. Avoiding the mangled ear, he chastised his friend, "Dumb mutt. I didn't want your help, that's why I tied you up. Why couldn't you at least this one time have actually done what you were told?"

"Because if he did, you would be on the cot torn up, instead of him. Lad, I don't know if Jax is going to make it. If he doesn't, don't let your grief over your loss, diminish his sacrifice. To not help lad, would have torn 'im up worse than this. Now, I need to put some balm on some of your own cuts and scratches, I'll warn ya, it's gunna sting a bit."

An hour later, Brónach emerged from the small backroom that served as his bedroom. Mamzer was sitting on the cot in the main room, sleeping, with Jax's head in his lap. The dog's breathing seemed very shallow, and he didn't have much hope Jax would make it through to the next day. His greatest concern however came from the attack itself. Such aggressive behavior against a human in his experience seemed quite unusual for wolves. He remembered watching a man die after being bitten by a mad wolf that foamed at the mouth. It was a horrible way to die. Earlier Mamzer said he'd wounded a couple of the animals with his crude knife. Brónach decided to track and hopefully capture one or examine a dead one. If these wolves were mad, and Jax died quickly from his wounds, he worried that the dog might prove to be the lucky one of the pair.

Six

Nahor, didn't like it. An uneasy premonition persistently gnawed at his gut. So before turning in he checked on the garrison sentries. He inspected the south wall last. Everything appeared to be fine. All was quiet. The watchmen were alert and fulfilling their duties. Still, he didn't like it.

Only about a month ago, the Jeshurun army took the small fort back from the Dagon. He strongly suspected that in all probability his edginess would prove to be for nothing. It seemed impossible that the enemy could raise another army. At least not so soon.

Despite his head's sound reasoning, he couldn't get past his gut telling him . . something's amiss . . something just didn't feel right. More to himself than to the close by Night Watch, Nahor muttered, "I'm too old to be spooked by quiet. What would I expect it to be? Nothin' capable of making noise lives in the Cnámh any way."

But, there it was again, every once in a while he swore he picked up the smell of chalky sand being stirred up. This time addressing the Watch directly he asked, "Any of you boys smell dust?"

The Watch collectively stared at Nahor, not daring to vocalize what they were thinking, their Watch

Sergeant must be crazy. What'd he expect to smell in this hell-hole on an ocean of sand?

Still muttering Nahor continued, "Aye, I know what ye lads be thinkin', nothing but dust in the wind. Then again, it could be something–or worse, a lot of something's–moving under the cover of darkness, not wishing to be seen or heard."

The Jeshurun military operated with a very simple command structure, and each of the five tribes functioned independently but cooperatively. Each tribe had a chieftain or captain over their own forces, which they divided into smaller units of one hundred directed by a lieutenant or command sergeant. Placed in charge of one hundred Dun infantry because of his toughness and instincts, Nahor had used his wits as well as his blade to survive quite a few campaigns. Right now experience whispered a warning to his sub-conscious, something ain't right.

The Dun have excellent night vision. but heavy cloud cover blocked all the light of moon and stars, so that Nahor couldn't see a thing. Not to be deterred, the sergeant hoped that by simply looking harder, he could somehow see better. Detecting nothing, he began to relax just a bit. Then he *heard* something. Something, vaguely mechanical. . . the creak of a wheel. . . he wasn't sure, but something.

Placing his hand on the shoulder of a young Dun sentry, he whispered, "Lad, I want you to do sumthin' for me. I want ya to wake the Cap'n, tell 'im that sumthin not wantin our knowin' about 'em, is coming across the plain. On yer way back, send up an archer with a torch and fire arrows."

Peeking between battlements, the sergeant renewed his vigilance. Then he heard another muffled sound, and whispered to no one in particular "Aye, come on then, I know yer out there."

Lithos started up the wall, taking two at a time, the sound of his armor and weapons jingling. Nahor gave him a puzzled look, "It's after midnight, ya should have been in bed. Now don't tell me ya sleep in that stuff?"

The Dun Captain was a walking armory. Over the iron ringed coat he wore a thick leather jerkin and a host of leather utility belts. Each belt held braces of long knives, short sword, axes, short bow and arrow, and a wicked war hammer. That list of course didn't include his "hiders." Nahor knew all that iron weighed considerable, but didn't seem to affect the Cap'n in his movements at all. Lithos grinned, and kept his voice down as he explained, "Couldn't sleep, an' sumthin about tonight making me uneasy too. What'cha got?"

The sergeant pointed toward the darkness, "I'm hearing muffled sounds, there to the south, about three or four hundred yards or so. Could be nuthin', but it sounds too much to me, like something trying hard to sound like nuthin."

Lithos joined the watch in giving the night a hard look, but effort alone couldn't penetrate the gloom. "We drove the Dagon out only a few weeks ago, not possible they'd raise another army and be back so soon. Not after the thumpin' they just got. I'm tempted to chew ya out for disturbin' my sleep fer nuthin', Nahor."

The sergeant answered the jib dryly, "Yeah, I can see by yer chain mail jammies ya were sound asleep. El knows you need yer beauty rest–if for no other reason than to preserve yer downright cheerful dis-po-sisition."

Hearing footfalls, they turned to see the dancing light of a Dun sentry carrying a torch back to the walls. Right on his heals came an Irial archer, an unlit fire arrow on string. Lithos trotted down the steps to stop them from bringing the torch up to the battlements. "Lads, if somebody's out there, we don't want to give 'em a focal point for targeting. After I get back up on the wall, light yer arrow down here, outta sight, and launch it for maximum height and distance over the south wall."

Once back up the steps, and looking in the direction

the sergeant indicated, he heard the familiar twang of a long bow and the fire arrow shot out like a bright orange flair. When it reached a height of about a hundred feet it began a gradual descent. Nothing became visible by the arrow's illumination until just before coming to earth two hundred and seventy five yards out–its descent stopped short by the chest of a very surprised Dagon infantryman. Light from the fire arrow increased as the enemy soldier's garments caught fire. His screams of pain were silenced quickly by a dagger across the throat. Then several of the Dagon threw sand on the fallen man to extinguish the flames–but not before giving Lithos enough light to see a mass of troops carrying ladders. Knowing the gig was up, the Dagon went ahead and charged.

Lithos looked down at the Dun sentry and Irial archer at the bottom of the battlement steps and barked simple orders, "Dagon infantry! Hundreds of em, they got ladders. Send archers up here, but first bring me the torch."

As the alarm spread through the garrison, Lithos did some quick figuring, with the enemy crossing about three hundred yards of mostly level ground but carrying ladders and battle gear – possibly a ram, the first wave of the Dagon infantry would reach the walls in two, maybe three minutes. By his calculations, this was likely a full two to three minutes before any help would arrive.

Turning to Nahor he pronounced his grim assessment. "Gird yer loins laddie, it'll be just the three of us for a couple minutes, to defend a good hundred feet of wall."

The sergeant grinned, and while he didn't "gird his loins," he did tighten the chin strap on his helmet. Without being told he ran to the end of the wall where a large lever was connected to several clay vessels placed at about ten yard intervals.

Pulling a short bow, Nahor fired a couple arrows off into the dark. In such poor light the odds of his hitting anything were extremely remote. But with a couple of minutes to kill, he just hated not having something to do.

Lithos' calculations proved dead on. The Dagon front runners started reaching the wall in about two and a half minutes, and ladder bearers were there in a little more than three. With a sizeable party gathered at the base of the garrison defense, and after a few moments of Dagon commanders barking instructions, the scaling ladders were lifted up and dropped against the wall.

Lithos frantically waved his arm in signal to Nahor who put everything he had in throwing a lever, spilling black oil all along the wall and on the attackers. Using a torch, Lithos lit another fire arrow and then shot it into the oil soaked ground at the Dagon's feet. As the oil ignited and the flame spread along the wall, several of the soldiers below became living torches and ran screaming back through their ranks.

Lithos drew his war hammer and took advantage of the enemies turmoil by throwing down ladders, a couple of which were already burning. He quickly brought two of the ladders down but as he went for a third, a long and lithe troll sprang from between the battlements. Although at least seven feet tall, it seemed likely that Lithos would actually be larger and heavier; for the troll was all limbs, and his short body not even as thick as one of the captain's thighs. Two red orbs were the largest features on an otherwise very long narrow face. Well adapted to provide sight in a world of darkness, the orbs fixed on Lithos and held his attention.

"One things certain," the Dun Chieftain thought, "I've got a new definition for ugly." Lithos almost never finished his thought because while fixated on the glowing red eyes, and the pathetic long face, the troll used his lengthy arms to swing an iron shod cudgel in an attempt to crush his skull. Chastising himself for being careless, he just didn't expect an attack from almost ten feet away, he ducked. Not quite quick enough. The blow skipped off the top of his helmet with a clang. Glancing blow or not, his bell got rung and he felt a bit dazed.

The troll swung the metal shod end around until revealing a metal spear point on the other end of the staff. This end the monster intended to plant in Lithos' face. Then the Dun weapon master's almost constant training kicked in. The staff thrust at his face struck air as Lithos spun sideways, dropped and rolled. Battle hardened by more than a century of combat, he had an almost automatic response to attacks by a larger, or much taller opponent. Getting close helped to negate the trolls reach advantage while maximizing his own attack capability. The Dun Captain understood, no matter how tall his opponent, its legs must still touch the ground, and no one, man, giant or troll, can fight if they can't stand.

As the troll rewound his long limbs and weapon for another strike, Lithos came out of his roll, and crushed the monster's toes with his war hammer. Dropping the cudgel, the brute started jumping up and down on one leg, screaming and holding its crushed appendages. Now swinging the hammer into the knee of the good leg, Lithos left his enemy without a leg to stand on. With his opponent now flat on his back, the final strike planted the sharp spike side of the hammer's head into the downed troll's helmet.

Unable to extract the hammer, he fought against panic as another Dagon soldier leaped from between the battlements. Attempting to buy time, he tried to pry the weapon loose with one hand, while throwing the dead troll's cudgel at his newest opponent with the other. Forced to give up on the hammer, he started to reach for a broad sword, knowing he'd run out of time. All his frenzied efforts proved unnecessary as an arrow flew just over his head, and buried itself in the eye slit of the Dagon infantryman's helmet.

Lithos looked up in time to see Quillan, a young

Irial lieutenant notch another arrow and follow several other archers through the entry to the southwest corner tower. Lithos then caught the collapsing Dagon warrior and quickly threw him back over the wall dislodging another attacker. After he threw the ladder down into the still-burning oil, the Dun warrior collapsed against the wall with a sigh of short-lived relief.

Still more Dagon tumbled over the wall, but now re-enforcements stormed up the steps to the battlements, and Irial archers were firing long-bows from the higher corner towers. In short order the Dagon were dispatched, and only the garrison defenders remained on the walls. Then, to Lithos' dismay, the Dagon left the burning ladders and their dead and fled from the fortress.

Puzzled, the Dun commander muttered, "Can't be *that* easy."

It wasn't.

With light discipline no longer a concern, the Dagon started lighting fires about three hundred yards out. While still too early to tell the size of the attacking force, from what Lithos could now see in the dancing firelight, it appeared to be sizeable.

After liberating the garrison from the Dagon weeks ago, Ruarc the king left only a token force behind to defend it. The reasoning seemed sound. Considerable time would be needed to raise another army after suffering such substantial losses.

Apparently not.

With only about a hundred Dun regulars, a handful of Irial archers, and only two Capall cavalry–to serve as messengers–it seemed clear the citadel would not be able to hold for long. Not if the enemy possessed a force at least as large as the one they'd just driven from the fort a few weeks ago. It seemed unlikely to Lithos the Dagon would return with a smaller force . . so what if it proved to be even larger?

Retrieving his war hammer from the troll's skull, he

went to the stables, hoping to find the cavalrymen. Both of the messenger riders were still sleeping in hammocks, oblivious to the alarms that sounded throughout the keep. The term cavalry-*men*, as it turned out, proved to be a misnomer: these "men" were little more than boys, or young men in their teens.

Roughly Lithos flipped them out of the sack, dumping them on the hard-packed dirt floor. Both riders came up ready for a fight. The largest even made the mistake of taking a swing, but Lithos deftly caught his wrist and threw him back to the floor with a flying mare. The smaller, younger man quickly realized who he faced and backed away.

Lithos grinned, ignored the young man groaning on the ground as he congratulated the other now standing at stiff attention. "Smart lad. Much smarter than yer partner here." He gave the one on the floor a gentle kick in the ribs just in case the young'un didn't realize who he was talking about.

"And, because yer smart, I'm givin' ya a special job, can I count on ya lad?"

Without giving a verbal response, the young man puffed out his chest, and answered with a swift crisp salute. A sure signal the boy felt more than ready for a man's responsibility.

"Good man," Lithos rewarded respect with respect, and from that point on he would treat the adolescent like a man, unless his behavior merited otherwise. "I need you to gather yer gear and saddle a horse son. I've got a very important message that needs to be got to the king."

The cavalryman lowered his jaw and tilted his head towards Lithos in such a way that the Dun Captain could see his focus, so he continued. "Tell the king the Dagon have returned with what I believe to be a larger force. We'll hold for as long as we can, but we won't be able to buy much time. Should the garrison be over-run, look for us to fall back to the Keys until the army can arrive, but they'll need to hurry. Ok lad, repeat that back to me."

Now Lithos understood why this young man was selected for this particular duty, his sharp mind enabled him to repeat the message back perfectly.

"Good job son, now just one more thing before you go. When you get to the keys, a small force of my people are at the entrance, working on the defenses there. Let em know to expect us coming across the plain sooner rather than later. When we come, it's likely the enemy will be hard on our heels."

The courier started gathering his few belongings quickly and Lithos knew he would be ready to travel in minutes. "Be sure to take plenty of water, you'll be well out of the Keys before finding more. The Rapha` city of Flann is a way to the West of the Capall plain and the road to Bethel. I believe you'll find the king there."

Turning to look at the other young man, still on the ground, sitting on his rump, Lithos extended his hand and pulled him to his feet. "You'll need to get ready as well laddie, I'll be needin' you shortly I expect. Sorry to be so rough on ya."

Striding out of the stable and back across the inner courtyard, Lithos trotted back up the steps to the battlements on the south wall. Walking along the wall he came to the bloody corpse of the troll he had dispatched just moments earlier. Kneeling down, he looked at the face sticking out of a gruesome, crushed helm, and remarked, "Mr. Troll, yer just about the ugli. . . ." His insult got cut short as boney fingers shot out and wrapped around his throat.

Eyes bulging, his immediate reaction, a futile attempt to grab the troll's wrist and extract the boney fingers from his neck. Realizing this wouldn't happen before he passed out, the Dun weapon's master fumbled a bit but drew his short sword and lopped off the offending arm. He then grabbed the creature by its course shift, hefted him above his head and threw him over the wall into the still burning fires below.

"Come back from that!" Lithos challenged and resumed walking along the wall, until he reached the place where the watch sergeant stood gazing intently over the battlements. Nahor somehow sensed the Dun Commander's presence and spoke without ever taking his eye off the enemy.

"I don't like it Cap'n, they gave up way to easy on that first assault."

"Aye," Lithos tried to see around the sergeant but his bulk filled most of the gap between the stone battlements. "I've been givin' that some thought myself, and the only thing I can figure is that they hoped we'd be caught napping. Their instructions must have been to high-tail it back if they didn't catch us with our pants down. What'cha say we head up into the corner tower? I think we'll have a little better view up there."

A low entrance led to a narrow stair that climbed up inside the square walls and onto the top of the tower. A few of the Irial archers were there watching for another attack. Nahor walked to the battlements and pointed out toward the Dagon. "Ya probably need to look at this cap'n, see those two big contraptions? I've watched 'em spend the last few minutes bringin' 'em forward. Ever see anythin' like that 'fore?"

Lithos' gaze followed out to where the sergeant pointed. Although several watch fires and torches were lit, there wasn't quite enough light to make out just exactly what the devices were.

"Can't say I ever have. Almost wonder if they ain't some kind of 'pult, but I've never seen em' built like that before. Ya notice they seem to know the quality of our archers, see how they got the machines sittin' just out of range. That's all right with me, if they are catapults they'll never hit anythin' but sand from way out there. Hold on, wait a minute–what are the black-hearted devils up to now?"

It appeared that the Dagon were laying out something in front of the big machines. Then huge trolls pulled heavy

97

lines through some form of block and tackle, lifting massive weights on the end of a pendulum, a good twenty-five feet in the air. When the ropes were let go, the weight dropped and swung through the machine center sending the non weighted end flipping violently over the top. Long lines and a pouch, almost like a sling were attached to the non weighted end. As this swung out in a high arch over the crest, it released some kind of ordinance.

"Definitely pults, . . of some kind, pretty ingenious ones at that." Lithos murmured, "Wouldn't worry about it though, . . have to be over three hun'rd yards out . . can't possibly hit anything."

Then he heard the whistling sound of something heavy flying through the air. A clay container hit just in front of the wall, spraying its liquid contents, much of it splattered all over the structure as well. The sputtering flames from the ignited oil exploded back to life when it made contact with this new liquid, and engulfed the whole wall in flame.

On the heels of the clay firebomb came a solid sling stone, and it too hit just a few feet to the front, and after a bounce slammed into the wall with great force.

"King of heaven!" Nahor exclaimed.

Looking over the side of the wall, Lithos could see the south gate in flames, while the stone that the second new-fangled 'pult just threw weighed at least fifty pounds. "Well that explains the quick retreat; why waste men trying to go over a wall when you can just knock it down?"

The watch sergeant dropped into a crouch and looked up at Lithos with wide eyes, "I've never seen a pult that could throw more than a hundred and fifty yards, and *those* threw a lot smaller stones. What are those things?"

Lithos dropped down behind the protection of the battlements in a crouch to talk eye to eye with Nahor. "Aye. I don't rightly know, but them contraptions are gunna grind us into dust. I'll tell ya something else, the Dagon are quite happy we dropped the oil at the front and lit it. They lost a few men, but it made the wall an easier target and we provided the igniter for their fire bombs. Question is, how long will it take to adjust the trajectory of the thing."

Popping back up to look between the battlements, the sergeant noted grimly, "Not very long." Despite the distance and the dark, they could see clearly that trolls were being used to roll the death machines forward. "The pults are on wheels."

Lithos gave instructions to the Irial in the tower. "They're moving in closer, shoot some fire arrows and see if they're in range."

Turning his attention back to the watch, "Nahor, you'd best get the lads away from the gate. That seems to be the target."

The sergeant acknowledged the wisdom of the order with a simple, "Aye." And started down the stairs.

Dropping back down behind the protection of the wall, Lithos knew he would have to think quickly. Having been constructed by his people, he knew the walls were strong. Still, with the strength of bombardment that the Dagon's machines offered, the wall would be breached before morning. Frustrated that he knew so little about the strength of the enemy, he tried to calm down and figure things out. "Alright, first off, they wouldn't come with a smaller force than what we drove out a few weeks ago. Second, even an army the same size means we're outnumbered ten to one. Third, those big pults are capable of bringin' down these walls in a hurry, and without 'em, we don't have a prayer. Alright, so what do we do?"

Making simple calculations in his head, Lithos figured it was about twenty miles to the protection of the keys. His people were hardy fighters . . nobody would ever confuse them with falcons or race horses. Mereah, the Rapha` prince once told him that "Watching the sons of Dun run was like watching a turtle race."

Out on the Cnámh, and badly outnumbered, nothing would prevent the enemy from engaging their small force while sending out equal numbers to their flanks, or even the rear. If they were going to make it, they would need a head start, plus a small force left behind to keep the enemy occupied.

The debate over, with no other options available, Lithos decided, they were leaving–*now*. To hesitate further only meant death, buried in the rubble of the garrison or slaughtered out on the desert sands. Either way their carcasses would add to the already prodigious pile of sun-bleached bones found on the Cnámh plain.

Standing once more to observe the effect of the fire arrows on the enemies siege weapons, he quickly discerned it was very little. The machines could be protected by a fire resistant coating of some kind, or perhaps shielded by metal plates. Regardless, without some form of catalyst it would take days to ignite 'em with arrows. Just as this thought occurred to him, one of the sling stones from the 'pult hit the garrison wall. The stone exploded into fragments, as a second quickly followed. The wall held–this time–but he could feel it shudder through the soles of his feet. It couldn't take too many more hits like those.

In one sense, however, the archer's fire arrows were having an impact: the Dagon found them irritating enough to change targets. The trolls were changing the angle of the 'pults and with a slight thrill in his gut, he realized they were now targeting the very tower that he and the bowmen were standing in.

After just a couple minutes, it appeared they were set to make another throw. Speaking to the Irial he warned, "Best get down lads, I think we're the target now."

The pendulums dropped and in seconds they could hear the stones hissing through the air. This time they were lucky, the stones flew over their heads. Lithos didn't think they would miss twice.

"It'll take 'em a few minutes to adjust their aim boys, go ahead and rain fire on em until you see they're lifting the weights. If it were me though, I wouldn't still be here when those weights drop.

"I'm ordering the infantry to get out and high-tail

it for the keys, but I gotta ask something of the Irial that's gunna be hard: I need ya to keep firing for a bit, to give the infantry a head start across the Cnámh."

With Quillan in command of the archers, they were a well-oiled machine. In the time it took for Lithos to make his request, his Irial had already fired two rounds of fire arrows. The lieutenant paused just long enough to respond to the Dun Captain's request, "Don't worry about a thing, the Dagon will not realize the garrison is abandoned until your men are well away. We'll see you at the keys."

Lithos gave Quillan a hurried salute, and ran down the tower steps. On the way he grabbed Nahor by the shoulders, and hollered, "Pull everyone off the walls, tell 'em to grab only what they can carry. Make sure they got water–and get out, head for the keys!"

The sergeant nodded, and without a word started moving the defenders off the walls. A minute after they started the exodus, the Dagon launched another round. The two rocks struck almost simultaneously, and the front of the south corner tower seemed to almost explode and crumble. Lithos looked up anxiously at the tower. Most were long gone by the time the stones hit, but a few bravely remained at the back of the tower and were ok. Before the dust cleared another round of fire arrows were launched and streaked towards the enemy.

Having found their range, the Dagon only needed to reload. In a little more than two minutes another volley flew through the air. This time the Dagon launched another clay vessel, followed a fraction of a second later by some kind of fire ball. Lithos screamed, "Quillan, get yer archers out of there!"

Not everyone made it. The vessel shattered and sprayed black pitch everywhere, and when the fireball hit, everything ignited and exploded. Lithos averted his eyes as about five Irial archers that were too close to the tower became engulfed in flames.

Attempts to roll them on the ground or beat the flames out with fabric were in vain; something about the nature of the black goo resisted all attempts to be put out once lit. Cries for help from the stricken were soon replaced by pleadings for mercy and the ending of their lives. The agony of the Irial dilemma tortured their faces. Life was precious–sacred–and so they were torn between the desire to end their friends suffering and the fear of playing God. In what seemed like hours, but really proved to only be a minute, the mercy of shock followed by death silenced the anguished cries of the Irial. The brimstone flames however continued to burn for several more minutes.

With no time to grieve, Quillan responded by moving his archers to the other corner tower, and renewing the attack. If the enemy readjusted their aim by targeting the other tower, by the time the pults found their new range, Lithos knew the archers would have already moved on.

So the enemy bombardment continued, while the Irial did their best to stay a step ahead. Not wanting to waste the archers' efforts on their behalf, it took less than ten minutes for the last of the Dun to exit through the north side gate and head for the keys.

Lithos went to find Quillan to give final instructions. He found him just as the archers released another volley, this time from the courtyard, a short way behind the south gate. "Well, there's one good thing about the enemy's fire attacks." The Irial lieutenant looked back at the Dun warrior as if he'd lost his senses.

"Sure," Lithos continued, "the walls remain intact, plus no need to fire the buildings and supplies to keep them out of the enemy's hands.

"I wanted you to know, the last of the infantry is out the south gate, I would like some of the Irial to take water skins and follow. The Dagon will notice a reduction of arrows, but can only guess as to the why. With luck, they'll believe it's men lost to the success of their bombardment. The rest of us will all leave together, in about another half hour. By keeping a good pace, we should make the keys a little after dawn."

While Quillan selected about half of his archers to send them out the gate, Lithos went to the stable. Relieved that it hadn't yet caught flame, he found the remaining Capall messenger rider. The young teen was already dressed, packed, wide-eyed and smelled of fear. "Alright lad, now it's yer turn. I need ya to ride hard to the keys. You should get there well ahead of even those who left awhile ago . . tell em' the garrison is overrun. We're all coming in, most everyone should be there by dawn. Tell whoever's in command they should prepare a counter strike in the event that the enemy is in hard pursuit as we come across the flat."

The young rider seemed ready, down-right eager in fact to leave the garrison, more than half of which now burned uncontrollably. The young rider mounted quickly and Lithos opened the gate for him, and the archers that were also ready to make their break for the keys.

Moments after their departure, some form of rapid movement charged the gate slamming into it, so that they just barely got it closed. Looking through an arrow loop in the gate house, Lithos saw five tanniyn with riders. Having failed to crash the gate, they now elected to pursue the Irial that exited the garrison just moments before.

Flying out of the gate house, he ran across the courtyard and grabbed Quillan's arm. "We're out of time, we all have to go, *now*."

In response to the question in the Irial lieutenant's eyes, Lithos offered a one word explanation. "Tanniyn. We must hurry, in moments they will be on your archers."

Abandoning everything except weapons and water skins, they charged out the gate and out onto the desert sands. In moments they started coming across the evidence of a running battle, finding occasionally an arrow that missed its mark, or perhaps the shaft of a broken lance.

A mere five minutes out, they came upon the first body. Not much more than a crimson stain on the sand remained of what they could only guess to have once been that of one of the Irial. As Quillan and the archers under his command sorted through the gory carnage, trying to find something among the remains that would allow identification, Lithos could read the horror on their faces.

The Dun Captain believed the Dagon used the tanniyn in battle primarily to tap into all men's greatest fear, the primal fear of becoming prey. He remembered hearing sailors describe having their ship sink, and while floating in the water watching sharks take their shipmates, one by one. No question known to man holds greater potential for horror than the simple thought—am I next?

Quillan tapped Lithos on the shoulder and pointed. About twenty-five feet away, seven feet off the ground, a pair of eyes reflected the red light cast by the flames from the burning citadel. Then the eyes blinked, and a tanniyn charged in, seeking to sate a seemingly unquenchable thirst for blood.

Several bow strings sounded in chorus as the quick reflexes of the Irial were put on display. Several arrows were in flight before the creature took more than a couple steps—but to no effect. Either the missiles bounced off the tanniyn's scaly hide or were caught in some form of shielding, meant to protect the rider.

"They learned." Lithos thought grimly, referring to the last battle with the Dagon when Capall Cavalry used short bows to shoot most of the riders out of their saddles.

Lithos drew a broad sword, took a wide stable

stance and braced himself for the charge. As the tanniyn raced close, several of the Irial broke from the ranks and started to run. At the last second the great dragon veered to lunge after one of these and snap them up in its great jaws.

The Dagon were not the only ones who learned from their last encounter; the Dun Chieftain not only knew the tanniyn's weak spot, he learned the best plan of defense: to attack. While the dragon focused on its prey, Lithos dove past the creature's flank and came up from underneath, driving his sword up to the hilt in the soft underbelly.

Then something slammed into him and everything went black.

Seven

haken awake moments later by Quillan, Lithos looked dazed and confused so the lieutenant explained, "When you stabbed the serpent, it thrashed about so wildly you were struck and knocked out almost immediately. I am loath to rouse you so soon after such a blow, but to delay is to die. Can you walk?"

Lithos took a moment to knock sand out of his ear, and off the side of his face. "The Dun have exceptionally hard heads, and mine is harder than most. I'm fine."

Quillan grinned, "Yes, sons of Dun do have a reputation for hard-headedness it's true."

Lithos glared at the Irial Lieutenant knowing he implied something very different by the use of the same term. He climbed to his feet without further comment, but rather than fleeing south right away, he strode over to the tanniyn to gather a little intel on the enemy. The great lizard wore a simple collar with thin rods that stuck out about three feet. Attached between the rods, he saw a leather curtain with several folds, forming a very flimsy looking shield wall. Lithos grabbed the apparatus and shook it, quizzing Quillan, "What do you make of this contraption?"

"Quite ingenious really," the Irial officer replied. "If the leather were to be stretched tight, an arrow would pass through and continue straight to the target. But because of the folds, the arrow either changes course, or gets caught and so stopped completely. Ineffective in stopping a centaur's sling stone perhaps, but as effective as metal shielding for stopping arrows, at a fraction of the weight."

"Aye," Lithos mused, "The Capall will have to find a way to counter this defense. Come now, we have to get this information, plus a drawing of that siege weapon they're using back to the king."

Without further words, they started running, at a pace that left no energy for talking. In an hour they found another body, badly mutilated. By his stature and armor they reasoned it must be one of the Dun. Dun mail is extremely tough, consisting of mostly iron rings that's much to heavy for archers or cavalry. While not even the teeth or claws of the tanniyn can effectively pierce iron mail, this dragon arrived at a particularly messy solution, it put all of its weight on the soldiers chest and squished him into jelly. Soon they started finding more bodies, of both the Dun and Irial, and occasionally they heard chilling cries of terror further ahead. A few moments later, they spotted light from what appeared to be torches ahead. In another half hour they recognized the main body of the remaining Dun and Irial. They were using torches in intervals of about ten feet to form a protective ring against the tanniyn. Two or three of the serpents seemed to be circling the firewall, waiting for the flames to burn down and so create an opening. For the moment all their focus remained on the soldiers hiding behind the meager flames. Lithos knew however, if his own small band were spotted, the dragons would be upon them, and quickly. Using hand signals, the Dun Captain urged the Irial with him to drop to the ground. "This'll never do, we've got to keep moving."

Quillan tried to search the Dun Commander's face for non-verbal cues as to what he had in mind. He tried to minimize the use of words, but found it difficult to read the hooded face in the dark. Finally he gave up and responded, "Aye, but what do we do about the tanniyn?"

"Been giving that some thought, and I think I've got an idea . . . ever hear of an ant lion?"

The lieutenant's face brightened, "I believe I understand, what do you want the Irial to do?"

"Prepare some fire arrows, and give me a few minutes to get buried in the sand just in front there. I've got a surprise or two for them serpents. Once yer arrows are lit, get ready, them dragons are mighty quick. They'll be here in seconds."

Lithos crawled out about forty feet, and chose a spot directly between the archers and the tanniyn. He scooped out a depression in the sand, displacing a few dry bones through his efforts. Climbing in his little hole he covered his whole body minus the face with sand, hoping the tanniyn in the dark, if it did see his ugly mug, would think it just a rock. He barely completed his camouflage when he heard Quillan ignite a torch.

"Ware, two come." The lieutenant hissed, just loud enough to give the Dun Captain warning. Less than two seconds later, he heard the foot pads coming across the sand, and he started to tense his inner springs to snap shut the trap. His timing had to be perfect. Then he heard the impact of two large clawed feet strike the sand just two feet away and he flew up out of his depression coming out perfectly under the serpent, catching it between strides. Rather than stick his blade straight into the dragon like a pin in a cushion, this time he made a long slash across the soft underbelly even as he dove clear of the tanniyn's death throes.

Soldiers who fail to learn from mistakes in combat don't last very long. At a hundred and fifty years old Lithos proudly told anyone who'd listen his mama didn't raise no fools. If knocked unconscious by the dragon's thrashing, as happened with the first encounter, he would be an easy kill, for the second.

To deal with the other one, he pulled a round clay

vessel from his cloak. Quillan's archers fired two flaming arrows which got stuck in the leather folds of the dragon's shielding. With expert aim, Lithos hurled the pottery vessel and it shattered, splashing its liquid contents all over the shield. With flaming arrows already in place, the whole shield quickly engulfed in flames, along with the tanniyn's rider. The creature reacted as any might with flaming objects on their back, and started rolling in the sand, crushing its' master and exposing the belly. Not likely to miss their chance the Irial quickly fired several more arrows in the heart area of its' soft underside.

Lithos now turned his attention back to the first dragon, quickly noting the serpent's gyrations and death throes. Trampled in the midst of the serpent's black blood and spewed gore, he saw the remains' of the tanniyn's rider.

The third tanniyn seemed to have disappeared into the night, so with the way clear they ran to rejoin the band of Dun and Irial who had fled the garrison earlier. Stepping between the now mostly extinguished fire arrows that formed the ring in the sand, Nahor stepped forward and grasped Lithos' arm. "Pretty piece of work Cap'n."

"Aye, but we're not done, there's at least one more out there, so tell the men to keep a sharp eye. And we've got to keep moving, we've got maybe two hours before dawn, and at least three hours before we reach the keys."

Without a word the watch sergeant turned and barked orders to the infantry and archers to grab their gear and move out. It took less than two minutes for about eighty Dun and a handful of Irial to once again start sprinting across the sand.

The lighter, longer legged Irial soon moved to the front of the formation. The shorter legs and heavier armor of the Dun required a great deal more sweat and effort just to keep up, and so they brought up the rear.

Lithos and Nahor acted as rear guard, and did their best to hurry their soldiers forward.

After keeping a brisk pace for about an hour, a thin trace of light started outlining the eastern hills. Nahor, gasping for breath haltingly observed, "Be light soon"

Then they heard wolves howl, the distinct cry of a pack on the hunt. No words were spoken, but Lithos gave Nahor a grim look. Wolves did not live on the Cnámh plain. Nothing natural did. Without speaking both Dun leaders knew this to be another device of the enemy. Without needing to be told, Nahor barked the order to quicken the pace–an order met by a collective groan from the already spent Dun.

Without slowing, Lithos started giving his sergeant instructions, "The enemy intends we panic and leave our backs turned while running. In about five minutes we're going to need to stop the men and establish a rear guard. It's likely whatever the Dagon sends after us is fast movers . . not heavy infantry."

Wishing to save energy, Nahor simply nodded and kept running. But at the appropriate time, he called for a halt, and for the command to be passed ahead to the Irial. It took a few minutes for the word to pass through the ranks. As the last of the men came to a stop, many welcomed the chance to catch their breath. A few of the soldiers made the mistake of drawing great rasping lungful's of air, filling them instead with the bone dust stirred up by hundreds of booted feet.

Many of the soldiers looked back to Nahor and Lithos. It took the two of them a moment to realize the rest were watching something else. Looking back to the south in the increasing light they saw the long shadows of perhaps a hundred wolves. Bred for size, and cunning, the canines were perfect pursuit hunters. Several long limbed trolls, very similar to the one Lithos fought on the wall back at the garrison, kept a tight grip on the predator's tethers.

Lithos calmly gave the order "Cover Retreat

Formation." and Nahor bellowed it out for all to hear. Quickly the Irial established a line with gaps for the Dun to pass through while they faced the enemy and covered the retreat; about thirty yards through the Irial lines, thirty of the Dun did the same, with the remainder of the Dun fighters and then the Irial passing through the new front. The next group through also went thirty yards and turned to cover the retreat for the rest. By constantly repeating this pattern Lithos hoped they could make an organized, quick and strong defensive retreat back to the Keys.

Quillan dropped back to join the Dun commanders. "This formation will work as long as the enemy doesn't send forces to our rear and take a stand between us and the Keys. If they do that, we'll have no choice but to fight."

Lithos acknowledged the presence of the Irial Commander, "Aye, let's hope they don't think of it. Haven't heard of trolls being particularly good tacticians. The wolves are smarter. But how about you remaining with the forward formations just in case?"

Quillan immediately acknowledged the wisdom of this suggestion and returned to take his place with the foremost units which at the moment were the Irial.

With increasing light the archers could see the wolves with troll keepers closing to less than three hundred yards, so they released a barrage of arrows. The trolls responded by releasing the wolves.

Crossing the space gap in mere seconds, Lithos shouted in warning, "Soldiers of Dun, watch yer backs!" Barely in time the Dun turned and the warriors in front knelt and locked shields, while the rest took positions with lance and broad sword from behind the protective wall. One or two wolves leaped over the barrier, and were met with pikes and quickly dispatched. Unfortunately, just as quickly they learned. For just a moment they paced back and forth at a short distance looking for an opening.

Much to quickly they figured out that it would be relatively easy to just run around the wall to attack the unprotected archers at the rear of the formation. Lithos watched the long legged predators run around the flanks forcing him to turn and issue a new command, "Shield Ring!" and then mutter, "I hate wolves."

Like a well-oiled machine the flanks popped up and turned in. The archers raced to take positions in the center and the back ranks of the Dun completed the ring. Not quite fast enough, a couple of Irial were caught by the pack while the circle was still being formed. Screams of agony were quickly silenced by savage snarls and ripping flesh.

Once the circle was closed however, the Irial struck back, firing arrows with deadly accuracy, slaying all the creatures squabbling over the bodies of fallen comrades. Wary now, the canny predators trotted away to a safer distance, and resumed watch.

Quillan approached Lithos and Nahor standing in the formation center. Wryly he quipped, "Trolls are not very good tacticians it's true, clearly wolves are. I know the tanniyn inflict greater shock and fear, but the wolves are faster, smarter, and there are far more of them. I think I prefer the great lizards."

Nahor while acknowledging the wisdom of the Irial lieutenant's statement, voiced his own thoughts, "I'd rather not have to face either one just now. But why are the trolls out there just waiting?"

Lithos was quick with the grim answer, "They've accomplished their purpose, they've got us stopped. Now they mean to keep us here so the main force can draw up and squash us like bugs."

Turning to face the North, the Dun Captain could see the high cliffs from the plateau, and he could just make out the crack in the wall that marked the entrance to the Keys.

"We've got about five miles to reach the keys lads. I suggest we keep our circle, shuffle forward like a turtle with centipede legs and get on home. If the Dagon bring forward that big pult of theirs, our shield wall won't do us much good.

112

We've got to keep movin."

And so the shield ring slowly, but steadily moved toward the keys. It took mere moments for the enemy to respond. Several trolls showed amazing speed as they used their long limbs to run almost as fast as the wolves and easily ran a big circle around their turtle formation attempting to cut off their escape.

Looking to the South in the early morning light a huge dust cloud created by a massive army no longer concerned about concealing their movements or numbers, lumbered across the desert plain. It was unclear whether or not the turtle could win this race, but by remaining in the formation, it would be at least two hours before reaching the keys. And now they were surrounded, and while they had no choice but to press forward, it seemed certain that at some point they would be engaged in combat, and unless it was decided quickly, the main body of the Dagon army would catch up and then, . . it would be all over. All their carcasses' after being picked clean by vultures, would make each and every one the latest contributions to the valley of dry bones.

Eight

"And the heart that is soonest awake to the flowers
is always the first to be touch'd by the thorns."
~Thomas Moore

Mamzer woke up to a silent house.
Brónach must have left early this
morning while he slept. Judging by the
light it appeared to be nearing midday. He started to
jump up in a panic, the sheep were alone with no one
watching! Then a weight in his lap caused him to
freeze, and remember all that took place the night
before.

Wide awake, Jax lay with his head still in the boy's
lap, his sad eyes looking up, watching him. Careful to
avoid the dog's mangled ear, and his many other
wounds, the young shepherd stroked his friend's damp
furry head, and whispered, "Everything is going to be
ok."

Jax picked up his head and gave one of his
trademark grins that always convinced Mamzer the dog
could talk. Alarmed by the dogs very weak shallow
breathing, a shudder of fear shot through his stomach

with a thought, Jax seemed to be waiting until he woke up; because he refused to leave without saying goodbye. With just enough strength remaining to give the boy's hand a soft kiss, the only friend Mamzer had in the world lowered his head, the light of life left his eyes, and Jax was gone.

The ra`ah wept, mouth wide open in anguish, sobs so deep within they actually made no sounds. His heart, throat, and chest . . . were all in a vise that squeezed everything out but grief.

Then he heard uncle Brannan calling his name, and Mamzer could hear the rage in his voice. For a few moments he sat on the cot, holding Jax, holding his breath, hoping that his Uncle wouldn't think to look for him in Grandpa Brónach's cottage. But then he quickly realized the consequences would be far worse if Brannan thought he were hiding from him. So whatever the charges, once again he found himself in deep trouble, and he decided the best thing to do would be to just get it over with.

He stepped out of the cottage, with Jax's blood staining his cloak and walked numbly, like a zombie across the yard toward his uncle. Brannan became aware of him when he came within ten feet and spun around and fixed on the boy with a steely glare. It took a full minute for Brannan to control his rage enough to even speak. "Where have you been boy, and why aren't you watching the sheep?"

Mamzer started to open his mouth, he tried to tell his Uncle that he and Jax fought off wolves, and that Jax gave his life, but looking at the fury in his Uncle's eyes, the words got caught in his throat and all he could manage in response was to stammer. This failure to answer became interpreted by Brannan as defiance or admission of guilt; either one needing to be dealt with swiftly. Two quick strides closed the gap between them and a sweeping backhand took Mamzer off his feet depositing him in the dirt.

"Torin checked this morning. He saw no one watching the flock. He also said all the signs showed wild animals attacked and killed several sheep." Brannan reached and pulled a leather strap from inside his cloak.

"And now I find that you spent the night here in my father's house and weren't watching the sheep at all." Brannan slapped Mamzer across the face with the strap raising a welt and drawing blood.

Torin and Cavan came out to make the coming beating a public humiliation. "I hope you enjoyed your night in a nice comfortable bed, because before I'm through, I doubt you'll be able to sleep for another month."

Mamzer curled and rolled exposing his back but protecting his face. The lash continued to fall tearing first his cloak, then his tunic and finally his back and shoulders.

After a few seconds Mamzer went into something similar to a state of shock, with everything blocked out of his mind, except pain. Time seemed to stop, and searing agony became his whole world, until suddenly the crack of the lash stopped. It took a few seconds for this new development to register, but when it finally set in, he rolled over to see what caused the change. Looking up, he saw Brónach standing there, with his hand firmly grasping Brannan's wrist, the strap removed from his hand and laying in the dust.

In a tense moment and struggle of wills, Brónach put into words what his smoldering glare tried to communicate, "How long will you make this boy pay for your mistakes?"

Now it was Brannan's turn to stammer for a second as he recovered from the surprise and the implications of the question. "This *boy* left the sheep unattended last night and wild dogs or wolves ravaged the flock. He has to be punished."

Calmly Brónach began cross examining the judge,

jury and prosecutor's case, "When Torin checked on the flock, did he see the dog Jax? Before you started beating the boy, did you look at him, perhaps see any signs of scratches, or blood? Did you ask the lad *why* he left the flock, or if he knew anything about animals attacking the sheep?"

Suddenly what seemed an air-tight case was beginning to appear as though based on purely circumstantial evidence. "Well, no, but it was obvious, I found the Mamzer here, I can only assume sleeping in your house while he left, . ."

"Yes, the lad slept this morning in my cottage, and so did the dog. They both fought a wolf pack last night. If not for the dog, the boy would likely be dead. When I left early this morning the dog nearly was. I attempted to track the pack all morning, afraid they may have been affected with madness. I lost their trail when they used a water course to conceal their tracks. I will tell you this–they were a canny lot, and large, not the normal grays that come down sometimes from the mountains. These headed south, towards the Dun Mountains. The lad did as well as any man could have under similar circumstances."

Brannan objected, "But if what you are telling me is true, he left the herd unprotected to tend to a dead dog, no one with any sense would have done that."

Brónach answered with words dripping with sarcasm, "Well the dog seems to be the only family the lad has, can't hardly fault him for that."

With that, the trial over, Brónach stooped over and lifted Mamzer out of the dust and helped him back to the cottage. Lifting Jax out of the cot, he helped the boy lie on his belly and started peeling back the fragments of his course robe and shift. Using a cool clean cloth he bathed the bloody stripes and applied a healing balm. Emotionally and physically spent, the boy fell asleep before he could finish. He then picked up Jax and deliberately walked past Brannan and Torin on his way back to the sheep pasture, where he decided the dog's final resting place would most appropriately be located.

~

Lithos barked orders to get the turtle formation moving again, and they made all of another fifty paces before the enemy attacked. The wolves charged toward their formation and almost on cue the outer ring of Dun infantry dropped and locked shields. The canines apparently didn't learn from the first encounter because once again they leapt over the shield ring. Their obvious intent, go after the Irial archers who lacked armor and heavy weapons. And this would have been a great tactic against many peoples, but the Irial proved to be such deadly archers that many of the wolves were shot right out of the air. The few wolves who made it through now found they were in cramped quarters where they were unable to effectively use their speed to any sort of advantage. These were quickly impaled on Dun pikes.

Lithos began to feel a bit smug about how easily they'd dispatched the wolves, when it dawned on him – it is never that easy. Turning around quickly, he noticed all the Irial were focusing their firepower in the direction that the wolves just came from. But from the opposite direction, several more of the long lanky trolls were charging. The wolves were just a diversion!

"Quillan!" Lithos barked out his warning and the lieutenant rallied the Irial to meet the newest threat. Again, rather than fight in the face of the shield ring and the heavily armored Dun, they used their long metal shod cudgels to pole-vault over their heads. Several of the archers turned to face the new threat seconds too late and were quickly struck down. But here the enemy demonstrated their cunning: the blows they struck were meant not to kill, but to maim and cripple. Knowing the wounded wouldn't be left behind, they intended to further slow the Jeshurun retreat.

Lithos grabbed several of the Dun to assist the Irial, and the trolls were quickly dispatched–but not before wounding about ten of the archers and close to twice that number of the infantry.

Satisfied their delaying tactics were accomplished, what remained of the Dagon forces retreated to just out of bow-range, and took up their vigil once more.

Quillan approached Lithos and Nahor with a grim look on his face, understanding full well the implications of the enemies' actions. "What do you suggest we do with the wounded? We lack materials for any kind of liter, and the enemy is counting on our not leaving anyone behind. But my friend, we may have no choice."

The forehead of the Dun Commander became knotted from deep concentration. "Aye, but first, we must deal with these trolls, they regenerate. I doubt we have the oil to burn 'em all, but we gotta try."

Quillan looked off in the distance, and noted grimly, "They come."

Lithos looked in the direction the Irial lieutenant was staring, and he could see the main body of the Dagon army coming across the plain, kicking up a massive cloud of bone dust. "We've got about an hour at best, before they get here. They'll be at the Keys in two. That gives us little more than an hour to get there first. If they catch us on the plain, no one survives."

After that grim pronouncement, made as much to himself as anyone present, the Dun Captain turned to his sergeant, "Nahor, get every able-bodied soldier paired up with another, we'll two-man carry the wounded, double time pace. We can't be delayed any more. Those not carrying the

119

wounded will have to be rear guard."

As soon as the Jeshurun's started across the plain, the wolves and remaining trolls also leaped into action. Rather than attack the back-peddling rear guard, they simply used far superior speed to run past and out-flank, attacking the Dun who were occupied carrying the wounded. At least a couple were a tad bit slow in putting down their wards and drawing their weapons. And while the infantry mounted an almost immediate counter-attack, the list of the wounded continued to grow.

"We'll never make it at this rate," growled Nahor. "If we stand and make a defense the main body of the Dagon army will be upon us, and we all die. The only way any of us reach the Keys is if we forget defending ourselves, and just run for it."

"Aye," acknowledged Lithos, "but with our backs to the wolves and trolls, they'll pick us off one by one and we get slaughtered that way as well. If I'm to die, I'd much rather keep some semblance of honor, look my enemy in the eye, and not show him my back. Quillan, any chance the Irial can keep the wolves off those carrying the wounded?"

To tired for a vocal response, the lieutenant simply nodded.

"All right then, let's get em movin."

As soon as they started making for the keys, once more they were attacked. Despite being surrounded and outnumbered, the weapons of the Dun and Irial actually gave them the advantage. All things being equal, they would have won this fight, handily. Unfortunately all things were not equal. Fatigue started to set in, and as the sun climbed ever higher, the heat started becoming a factor. The Dagon army coming across the plain were clearly gaining ground, their large drums beating out a quick march cadence and adding to the overall sense of panic.

Lithos considered forming another shield ring in

preparation for a last stand, but just before giving the order, he heard another sound growing louder and coming from across the plain. Not from the direction of the enemy however, but from the North, the direction of the Keys. Hardly daring to believe his ears, the Dun Chieftain turned to see about thirty Capall cavalry charging across the Cnámh. At first Lithos thought Korah led the charge, but he quickly realized, "Can't be, way to young, . . . but as like to his father as a mirror image."

Fifty yards out, after a sharp command, the columns divided. Another command and all the menacing lance points lowered in unison. Breaking around the ring of Dun fighters the long columns fanned out wide into battle lines that left wolves and trolls alike to scramble out of the way or end up on the end of their spears. Eoin, Korah's son charged up through the infantry ranks and threw sand in a sudden stop in front of Lithos.

Lithos looked up at the young commander and started sputtering, trying hard to overcome his dismay at the unexpected deliverance. Finally the Dun Captain sputtered, "Yer such a purty sight Lad, I could kiss ya."

Eoin laughed, Oooh, tempting offer, I'd have to insist you shave about a hundred years of beard, maybe remove some of the bird's nest, . . also the food you're saving for later."

Ignoring the joke, Lithos interrupted, "What are you doing out here lad, not that I'm not glad to see ya.?"

"My father sent me on patrol almost three days ago, to inquire as to the needs of the garrison and to scout for signs of Dagon presence. We were camped on the other side of the keys early this morning when one of our relay riders came through with your message. We gave the messenger a fresh horse, and water and sent him on to the king at Flann. I see the garrison is already lost, how can the Capall best be of service?"

For a moment Lithos did nothing but frown at Eoin as he gave the matter a lot of thought. When he heard the young officer say "The garrison is already lost" he couldn't help but wonder if this wasn't a veiled accusation. Self doubt echoed the thought and he also wondered if more should have–could have been done to preserve the fort.

Just as quickly as the resentment cropped up however, he dismissed it. There just wasn't time for sleights, real or imagined. Right in front of the commander's eyes he realized, a solution to his biggest problem sat mounted on horseback. "I need fifteen of your riders who are willing to yield his mount to get our wounded to safety . If we're gunna reach the keys before the main body of the Dagon army, we've got to be able to move a lot faster than a crawl."

After a moments thought, Eoin responded, "I'll have the men put their ponies on a string, and one of the boys can lead 'em, less of course, the Dun know how to ride?"

Lithos frowned at what he perceived to be another mild jib, "You know we don't ride Cavalryman, and there's isn't time for more jokes. The Dagon army will be here in minutes, when they arrive, we'd best be long gone!"

It took little time to place two wounded soldiers per mount, and then with a swat on the rump, they rode out. As soon as it became clear to the enemy the nature of the new plan, wolves set out to attack the horses weighed down carrying the wounded. The Dun are about two feet shorter than most men, but more stout, and Dun infantry wears much heavier armor than Capall riders. With all the extra weight it became quickly clear that the horses carrying wounded Dun warriors would have a difficult time pulling away from the swift long-legged wolves. This meant the remaining riders were required to provide escort. The only positive being that with wolves snapping at their heels, the mounts on ambulance duty ran much faster than they might have otherwise.

Relieved to see the wounded safely away, Lithos got

the remaining soldiers in another guarded retreat formation and raced for the Keys, making much better time.

After only a half hour it became clear however, the main body of the Dagon army kept gaining ground. They were so close that the tramp of thousands of heavy boots keeping time with cadence drums created the sound of a coming storm in their ears. The Dagon themselves were blurred into a black cloud mass by the heat waves coming off the bone dry sand. The effect seemed to wrap the whole massive army in a ghostly supernatural haze.

Of the Jeshurun forces left, only the Capall cavalrymen now on foot were at all fresh or rested. The sun and heat became oppressive, but the dust proved far worse, for it rose up just high enough to get sucked in their mouths whenever they gasped for breath. No one seemed to have the strength for the final sprint.

From a thousand yards out Lithos could see a strong force of most likely Dun infantry moving into the narrow opening of the Keys. As a tribe the Dun lived in these southern desert mountains and they learned out of necessity the skills needed to mobilize quickly. He knew that the defenses were already being strengthened and supplied. Once they reached the narrow pass, they could hold off a much larger army almost indefinitely. Every man's safety seemed so tantalizingly close, and all the men started tottering faster towards the Keys like thirsty cattle picking up the scent of water.

As he stumbled forward, Lithos caught a faint sound in his ears, even above the roar of the marching army in pursuit. He knew he'd heard the sound before, and that it was important. Exhausted, dead bone tired, it just didn't register what he seemed to be hearing–until too late. Then it hit, a forty pound stone struck one of the Dun bringing up the rear of the formation, and much of his upper body got separated from his legs. The projectile continued to cut through the ranks killing or badly maiming a half dozen soldiers.

Turning around, he could see the Dagon used massive trolls, the size of small giants to pull their sling-pults to within two hundred and fifty yards. He never heard them coming because of all the racket coming from the main body of the Dagon army. Looking up, he could see more ordinance from the second pult already in the air and would hit any second.

"Spread out! Spread out!" Despite his urgent warning, the men were just too tired to respond quickly. Even the carnage from the first stone was stared at dumbly, as though the soldiers were in a drunk stupor. Few heeded the warning and so a clay flask hit in their midst spraying oil. A Dagon archer sprinted forward and launched a fire arrow. With their center engulfed in flame, the sound of the Dagon soldiers marching boots was drowned out by Jeshurun's anguished cries and screaming death.

An orderly retreat disintegrated instantly. Nothing more remained for the men but to throw away heavy weapons and equipment and to run for their lives. Lithos couldn't have stopped the panicked rout if he wanted too. He didn't. Everyone, including the Dun Commander found themselves in full survival mode as they sprinted across the desert sands. Putting wings to their feet, and adding to the over-all sense of panic the wolves returned seeking turned backs as easy targets for the kill.

His mind gone blank, the eyes of the Dun Captain registered that horses were riding to meet them but at that moment, putting one foot in front of the next demanded all his focus. So it was, he missed seeing the valiant last ride of Eoin, Korah's son.

Galloping across the sand, fifteen riders rode right through the Dun' ranks, driving the wolves back with their spears, in an attempt to cover the retreat. The sons of Capall who earlier gave up their mounts for ambulance duty, jumped back into the saddle as their horses were returned to them. With the full patrol reunited, they acted as the rear-guard for what remained of the troops from the garrison.

Then the sling-pults threw another round. Nothing could be done to stop the munitions once they were in flight so more men were going to die. But, Eoin reasoned, they could ensure the most recent rounds fired would be the last. He gave the order and the sons of Capall charged. The trolls who were bringing the big siege engines forward dropped the heavy hemp tow lines and took up their weapons.

There are many different species of trolls, and the breeds come in all manner of shapes and sizes. Remnants of the Drochshaol, the age of sorrow, these particular trolls were massive descendants of subverted giants.

Bred for brawn rather than brains, the behemoth's were not particularly known for their cunning. Completely dependent on brute strength, hefting great clubs, stone axes or even an occasional crude mace, they charged, intent on crushing the puny attacking insects.

They soon learned–too late–that the battle doesn't always go to the strong, but often to the swift. All attempts to swat the swarming cavalry pests hit nothing but empty air. Rather than engaging the trolls, the cavalrymen merely made several passes casting lances and firing short bows. Soon, the disfigured giants were walking, roaring pin cushions. Moments later, they were no longer walking, or roaring, just bleeding their life back into the sand.

And then, Eoin, Korah's son got an idea, a *brilliant* idea. In order to use the weapons in a final assault on the retreating Jeshurun's, they were placed well in front of the main army, so why not . . . "You men, take up the lines, use the horses, and drag these machines into the Keys, the Dun will know what to do with 'em."

And so they strained and pulled the contraptions on

125

their great wheels across the sand. It appeared as though none of the Dagon were swift enough to prevent this valuable capture. Then one of the Dagon riders on a tanniyn road forth and issued a challenge. Eoin instructed his men to ride on, he would meet this threat, and so he did.

Charging straight towards one another, in a deadly game of chicken, a mortal collision seemed certain. Moments before colliding, the Dagon rose above his shielding and threw a lance. His aim true, the accuracy deadly, but while his spear went straight to target, the target was no longer there. Swerving at the last second, Eoin dropped his body to the side of his mount and fired an arrow from under his horse's neck as he passed. His arrow struck just below the helmet, driving through the Dragon Rider's neck.

Riderless, the threat eliminated, Eoin started to ride back to help his men with the capture of the sling-pults. Then still another tanniyn and rider appeared, but larger than any they'd seen so far. This one road forth almost casually, as if in no hurry, or in no danger. Eoin hesitated, but quickly decided this threat must be faced. Unchallenged, dragon and rider would remain free to come up from behind and attack the still retreating infantry. So, he charged.

Korah's son would never be seen again. No one in Jeshurun actually saw him die, but sons of Dun who watched from the trenches in the Keys say they saw a big explosion of fire out on the Cnámh plain, just ahead of the main body of the Dagon army. And while the Capall cavalry succeeded in bringing the sling-pults to the Dun in the keys, not even the horse of Eoin, Korah's son ever returned to run free on Capall's grass plains.

Nine

"Fear not, I have redeemed thee, I have called thee
by name, thou art mine."

~Isaiah the Seer

Laughter and dinner conversation drifted
through the house and out of Brannan's open
window. Travelers to such a remote area on
the Capall grasslands were rare, so any visits were
treated as a special social event. The visitor in this case
seemed to be a man of some importance, heightening
the drama and formality of the whole affair. For such
an important occasion, not all of the household enjoyed
enough prestige as to participate in the festivities.
Mamzer, as usual, found himself on the outside looking
in–literally.

He could sit outside the window and listen, just as
long as he didn't get caught. Likely, he would present
an enigma to the visiting dignitary. His simple coarse
clothes would identify him as a slave or household
servant, but his facial features sure as a fingerprint
proved his identity. The boy could only be a son of
Brannan, or a close relative at the very least.

In Mamzer's case however, the distinct odor of

sheep would deny the face and agree with the garments, the boy must be a ra`ah, a shepherd; and among the peoples of the Capall, personal status doesn't come any lower than that.

The yammering chatter of jackals prompted him to bring the sheep in from the fields to the safety of the fold. Jackals by themselves aren't much of a threat, although they wouldn't hesitate to go after a young or newborn lamb. It's the company they sometimes keep that's the real problem. Scavengers and followers of larger predators, the smaller canines generally are content to live off others scraps. So while he knew he would get an earful about being scared of jackals, he just couldn't chance losing a ewe or lamb to wolves or worse, again. Still smarting from the welts received in his last beating, losing any more animals would come at a price greater than what he could afford to pay. Brannan may be contemptuous of sheep and shepherds, but he could be absolutely brutal about losing anything of value or profit. Even so, something beyond the economics of loss fueled an anger so disproportionate, he just didn't dare to trigger another episode.

Without his grandfather's intervention, he couldn't be sure it wouldn't have been fatal. Mamzer remembered looking up to see the strong arm that stopped Brannan's stinging lash. The ra`ah guessed Brónach to be a man in his seventies, but he didn't really know. One thing seemed sure: Old or not, Brónach wasn't anyone to mess with and on that day, even Brannan stood mute, transfixed by the old man's smoldering eyes.

Mamzer didn't remember much from the conversation that stopped the beating. But as he lay in a cot in his Grandfather's cottage, he overheard another somewhat heated conversation taking place outside between Brannan and Brónach.

"You insist on keeping the boy in a servant's status, and I reckon that be your right." Brónach seemed to be trying hard to keep his voice down, in contrast to Uncle Brannan's loud rage. "But does it occur to you that even as a servant the boy has shown his quality? In your hurry to punish, did you even see the claw and teeth marks from the wolves? This boy faced a pack of deadly predators with sticks and stones, creatures that would strike fear in the heart of an armed warrior. Can you name one servant or hired hand in the entire household that wouldn't have turned tail and ran, leaving the sheep to fend for themselves? Can you see this boy, really see him? Or has your own guilt and pride darkened your eyes that much?"

The ra`ah's memories of the incident still replayed in his mind. He did not quite understand all that Brónach said, but his words succeeded in at least getting Brannan to back off a bit. Still, with signs of another predator returning, Mamzer refused to take any chances.

Peeking through the window of the earth and sod home, Mamzer could see a stranger sitting at the place of honor at the family table. Even seated, the boy could tell the man was tall, with a strong jaw and face barely concealed by trimmed dark blonde moustache and beard. Piercing gray-blue eyes suddenly met Mamzer's as though the man's senses were so finely tuned as to know when he was being watched. Not a hint of alarm appeared in the man's eyes, just mild curiosity when he discovered the ra`ah observing him. The eyes moved on without betraying to anyone else in the room the discovery they'd made. Mamzer breathed a sigh of relief.

A quick assessment of the stranger brought on a guess that the visitor appeared to be a soldier of considerable rank. Under a green, light-weight wool tunic, which would remain cool under the piercing sun of the Capall plains, he wore a gleaming shirt of chain mail. Not crude rings sown into leather, or even linked iron rings, this protective coat was likely forged by the sons of Dun. Long strands of strong bronze wire, were woven almost as threads of fabric. Costly, but much lighter and more flexible than iron, the bright armor offered no openings for blade or dart. To light for heavy infantry, this type of mail wouldn't stop a heavy iron blade, but would be well suited to a cavalry officer among the Capall.

The quality of the gleaming armor, only hinted at the quality of the man. His presence seemed to project an air of professionalism and authority, with courage the light of his eye. Riding for several hours and miles, it somehow seemed by his command dirt and dust were refused permission to rest on his clothing. He kept his dark blonde beard trimmed, every buckle polished, no detail seemed to miss his attention. The weathered face spoke of long years in the sun and field, and of a captain who endured hardship with those he led. Mamzer's immediate impression– "That is a man I would follow."

Hearing the voice of Brannan his Uncle caused his ears to perk up, "So Captain, I deem the need must be great for you to ask me to pay such a high price to meet it. My sons are among Capall's finest. I would not spend a drop of their blood lightly unless the need be urgent."

Mamzer saw the stranger's face flinch in pain at Brannan's words, and the boy made a guess that the captain did indeed know something about paying a high price. It took a moment for the man to regain his composure, but when he spoke, his voice remained calm and assured.

"Please, there is no need for rank or title, this is *your* home. My name is Korah, and a name I would count as an honor of friendship for you to use; and yes, the need is great. A few months ago the Dagon overran a small garrison on the Cnámh plain. The king responded and the enemy driven from the desert plains in a great rout. As it turned out however, the initial offensive proved merely a feint, made to gauge our strength. A little more than two weeks ago the Dagon returned, with perhaps ten times their previous numbers. The south desert garrison once again became overrun, and what is left of the soldiers stationed there took refuge in the narrow passes and ravines, known as Jeshurun's Key. There, the king and the rest of the Jeshurun army is presently holding the Dagon back. We are able to compensate for the enemies' vast numbers by holding the narrow canyon passages, but still, every one soldier of ours lost, . ." For the briefest moment pain flashed in the captain's eyes, but only Mamzer saw it. "Even just one, is more precious than a thousand of the enemy."

"Mara, can you pour the good captain a little more wine?" Brannan didn't wait for a response from his spouse before interjecting, "My father Brónach, once occupied the position you hold now, . ."

"I knew your father, as a great man and officer in fact he . . ."

Feeling irritated at a perceived interruption, Brannan likewise denied Korah opportunity to finish his statement regarding his relationship to Brónach. "Then you understand that I would have at least a limited understanding of warfare, or at least the use of light cavalry in battle. What you are describing sounds like a defensive engagement. The Dun are what's needed for fighting in trenches, that's hardly the place for mounted warriors. I am familiar with the Keys, those narrow passes would restrict cavalry as much as it does the enemy."

"Yes, I admit, the use of cavalry at the moment is limited. Nor can I promise that your sons will not have to take a turn in the trenches on the front lines. But you must understand, Jeshurun has been driven from the desert plain with great loss, including many from among the sons of Capall." Mamzer noted a distant misty look in the captain's eye as he continued.

"I am in need of young recruits to train for mounted combat to replenish the ranks. It is vitally important to maintain the cavalry's strength because if the enemy

131

manages to break through the Keys, then it is a short journey through the southern mountains and plateau to the Capall grasslands. And, to be frank, defensive engagement or no, every able-bodied man is needed."

Mara piped up, "Is it that serious captain? Jeshurun now has a king, a mighty Rapha`. What need exists that requires the sacrifice of my sons?"

"I have personally witnessed Ruarc's might, great as he is, he is still one person, while we have never faced an army of this size before. Sheer numbers alone would make our circumstance perilous. But I'm afraid it's worse than you know. Some as yet unidentified power drives them, and so the enemy comes on, heedless of the price. Also among the Dagon there are riders on dragons, the tanniyn. This is a terror few are willing to face. In combat the tanniyn devours the wounded and fallen. This actually slows the enemy's advance but strikes absolute fear in all our soldier's hearts."

Mara's shrill high-pitched voice piped up once again. "Such a story by no means encourages me or my husband to send our sons to their deaths, Captain." By the icy way she spoke the word, Mamzer understood Mara refused to honor the man as requested and use his name.

Patiently Korah responded. "Yes ma'am, I understand your concerns. I have . . . three sons of my own." Momentarily the captain's voice quivered, but he continued after a short pause. "Believe me when I tell you I know the cost of what I ask. Yet if we fail in the southern mountains, then the enemy will breach the plains of Capall and all our homes overrun. No price is too high to prevent this from happening. Everyone is called to make the sacrifice. The king himself has his own son involved in the battle, Prince Mereah is among the most valiant of warriors. Believe me, everyone is doing their part. The alternatives are unthinkable."

The ra`ah could hear a slight rising, wheedling tone in his father's voice, and he recognized it from negotiations with other men in the village; a voice used while striking a deal for a horse or a sack of grain. "But the king must be very rich, surely he must have many wives and sons. As you can see, I am but a poor farmer, my sons are all I have."

Mamzer saw a light of recognition briefly flash in the captain's eyes and it seemed obvious to the boy that the officer had seen similar negotiations as well. After a moment's hesitation, he changed his tack, no longer emphasizing responsibility, he began to describe rewards that were perhaps greater than risks.

"It is well spoken that a man's sons are his ultimate treasure, this is true be he peasant or king. However, when a man is poor, he desires better for his sons, better than perhaps he can provide of his own means. I was once the son of a poor farmer, even as you, placed in service as an armor bearer for one of Capall's greatest captains. On the battlefield there is no significance of rank or title . . . courage, prowess and skill, these are what determines how far a man can advance. The king's need is desperate and any who rise to the occasion and meet that need cannot help but win his favor and the favor of all Jeshurun."

Brannan wiped some grease from his chin with the back of his hand and politely burped before responding, "Of course my sons and my family will do our part captain. But surely you must understand my reluctance to send them into such dangerous circumstances. However, when you have met my sons, I believe you will see that they are more than equal to the challenge and would be a source of pride for any father. Allow me to present to you my boys, beginning with my eldest son, Torin."

Torin entered the room followed by his brothers almost as on cue. Looking upon them, even Mamzer couldn't help but be impressed. All of Brannan's sons had indeed grown tall and strong, especially Torin. When he walked into the room Brannan's heart visibly swelled with pride. Torin was even taller than the captain and carried a strong confident bearing.

Korah stood and clasped the hand of each of Brannan's older sons and found their grip strong and confident, and they each boldly looked him in the eye. "Yes," he thought to himself, "Young men such as these will indeed go a long way towards meeting the people's need." What he spoke out loud was for Brannan's ears and heart.

"Magnificent, you have great cause to be proud, such sons would truly be a treasure to any man. But tell me, there are only four here, I have heard you have five sons." As he spoke this, Korah looked into the ra`ah's eyes through the window.

Mara's face flushed red for a moment, and Brannan's eyes flashed briefly in anger. "My Lord is mistaken, I have only four sons."

To the thousands of wounds in Mamzer's heart, Brannan just added one more. Once again, he knew he didn't count. All his life he'd been declared an orphan. Yet in his heart, the ra`ah knew he counted for far less. Orphans can have dreams; they may not know their father or mother, but they can imagine who they were, and that they were once wanted, if not loved. Mamzer entertained no such dreams or illusions. He knew his place to be far worse than not being loved. As far as aunt Mara and Uncle Brannan were concerned, his very name meant illegitimate, rejected, denied, despised, and now not even worthy of mention.

Then it struck the ra`ah that perhaps this captain represented an opportunity, a way out. What was it he said, "On the battlefield there is no significance of rank or title?" A man who met the need of his people, as the captain said, he could not help but catch the attention of the people, even of the king! However something else, even more important came to Mamzer's mind. A law existed among the People of Capall that only sons rode for their families in battle. If a servant, slave, or orphan, were pressed into battle they first must be adopted as a son. The wheels in the ra`ah's mind began turning, "What if?"

With that, a plan began to form in the boy's head. If he'd thought it through a little more carefully, perhaps, he would have realized the risks. But even so, he likely would have gone ahead with his plot anyway. There is no courage to match that of a man, or even a boy who has nothing to lose.

Moments later, the ra`ah walked into the small hall where the captain feasted with Brannan, Mara, and their sons. Korah noticed him first and rose exclaiming, "And who is this?"

Brannan turned and saw the boy walking towards him, the shock on his face, turned first to anger, and soon moved on to rage. Mara turned white, while the sons of Brannan quickly jumped from their chairs and started shouting angrily.

"Sorry to disturb your meal *uncle*, but I heard jackals and feared they were following wolves, so I brought them back from the pastures until I received further instructions."

The captain excitedly jumped right in, "Oh ho, so you were hiding another son, a boy but soon to be a man, and as the other boys, his face is a mirror image . . . ."

Korah realized that as he spoke concerning Mamzer being the image of Brannan, that Mara glared at him and at Brannan, and in her face there was a mixture of shame and rage. Brannan wore the surprised bluster of a man caught in a bold-faced lie, as he blurted out, "What are you doing here? How dare you interrupt our meal?"

Torin grabbed Mamzer by his coarse shift and started dragging him towards the door. "I will put the ra`ah back with the sheep father, and later I will discover the truth about his ferocious jackals."

"Wait!" The captain spoke with a voice of authority, a voice used to being obeyed, "I want to see this boy."

"My Lord," Brannan pleaded, "This boy is not a son of mine, the resemblance you see is of a long lost brother who fell in battle years before. Mara and I, we care for him despite the trouble he causes and the bread he takes from the mouths of our own sons, poor as we are. He is far too young to participate in the battles, the ra`ah is of little use but we do allow him to care for the sheep."

"Come here boy, let me take a look at you." Korah grasped Mamzer's shoulders and looked him in the eye, where he saw a sharp wince from pain. His eyes were then drawn to welts on the back of the boy's shoulders and neck, the torn flesh not completely covered by the shabby tunic. Looking more closely at the young face he saw a partially healed welt on his cheek, likely from a leather strap. "Your kindness to the boy is evident." Korah's eyes captured Brannan's, and he spoke sternly. "I trust your kindness will be seen and rewarded."

Mara interrupted, "El sees all we give and He will give us our reward."

"Yes Lady, I am sure of it." Korah's voice dripping with sarcasm, continued, "But here now, this is also a worthy Lad, surely there is more suitable work for him than watching sheep? He is not yet of age for battle, but he would make a fine page or armor bearer. That is how my service began. As the son of your brother, fallen as you say in battle, surely the boy is worthy of being redeemed in this way?"

"Captain," replied Mara, "You don't know the boy as we do, he is completely hopeless. If he was anywhere near our army he would be more of a danger to them than the enemy! It is only at great loss do we even allow him to watch the sheep. No, believe me, the boy is not ready for such undertakings, so we must protect him and decline your offer. Now, if you will excuse me, I will take the ra`ah and find him provisions for his return to the fields and his duties."

Turned forcefully by Mara, Mamzer's eyes met

briefly with Brannan's. With a look, Brannan warned him this wasn't over and he would be dealt with later. While walking past Torin and the brothers, he realized he would be dealt with by them as well.

After they left the house, Mara spun him around and slapped his face hard enough to draw blood on his lip and cause little lights to flash in his eyes. She spoke in a low voice of suppressed fury, "Don't you dare think it is not understood what you tried to pull with that little stunt in there! Listen you little Mamzer, you will never, never, ever take a place of honor among MY sons. NEVER!! Now get out of my sight!"

After slapping him again, the ra`ah watched Mara turn sharply on her heals and rush back into the house. Despite her words about provisions, he knew nothing would be given that night, especially not supper. There was nothing for it but to ignore the rumblings in his stomach and try to make himself as comfortable as possible in the barn. He knew it would be a very long night, followed by a cold, dark morning.

Entering the barn, devoid of light from the moon or stars, Mamzer started a search for a lantern. He was startled by a gentle voice, "It's not you she hates you know."

"Brónach? Is that you? Who are you talking about?"

"I'm talking about Mara, it's not *you* she hates."

Mamzer with his face still stinging from the slaps struggled to make sense of what he just heard. He finally responded simply, "Well, she sure has me fooled."

"Son, some families have legitimate secrets, and some families have secrets where everyone knows the truth; but they keep pretending no one knows their secret. Mara knows you are not the son of a lost brother. It is true Brannan lost a brother; my youngest son in combat with the Dagon.

"But my youngest son, the one Brannan named as

your father, never married and I am sure he never had a son. But if he had, by the laws of our people Brannan would be required to raise you as if you were his own, not treat you as though illegitimate. No, Mara's fury is directed at you, but only because she doesn't know how to unleash it towards Brannan, your real father. I have watched this family tip-toe around the truth for far too many years. Truth faced can bring healing. Truth ignored or buried brings nothing but hurt. It has hurt you most of all, I think.

"Now don't act surprised, you don't need to pretend you didn't know. For you the truth I know is very painful. A father should love his son; no one knows this more than a son who is unloved. But you must understand you represent something, to every member of the family. To Mara you represent betrayal of fidelity. To Brannan you represent his own weakness. To Torin and the brothers you represent family shame. They too have heard other families talk. You see no one else believes the lost brother story either."

Together the two sat in silence, the weight of the words spoken crushing the words that needed yet to be said. A tear slid down the ra`ah's face, and he was glad for the dark's concealment. Brónach at last got up and walked up to the boy, and placed a gentle hand on his shoulders.

"I told you what your father, brothers, and Mara see when they see you; they see their own shame and pain. That is what *they* see. Now let me tell you what *I see*, and far more important, what Elohim sees. A man's eyes and sight are limited, he can see only circumstances, physical characteristics, flesh and bone. Elohim sees all these things, but He also sees beyond them. The One we also name Yahweh Yireh is a power who sees the heart. This is something we all must learn to do, and how I wish my stubborn son would learn this lesson."

Now it was Brónach's turn for his voice to crack

with emotion, "You never met your grandmother. She died a few years before you were brought to us. Her death I believe to be a part of the hurt that seems to have hardened your father Brannan's heart. Oh how I loved her, now *she* had eyes to see. When I first met her, she seemed so young, and beautiful, and I a man already getting up in years. She looked beyond my years to see a heart that loved her, a heart that saw her worth.

Elohim gave me eyes to see her. My Zerah came from among the coimhthíoch as our people name outsiders and foreigners. But looking at the place of a person's birth, that is to see only flesh, only circumstance. I learned to see what El sees, and not just with your grandmother. I see your heart as well, even as the One who is true sees it. It breaks my heart your own father will not, but I will tell you now, that Yahweh Yireh the One who sees, He knows your heart, He understands that it is broken." Brónach was silent again for a long time as he struggled with memories of his love now lost, his own heart still broken. "The sacrifices Elohim most cherishes lad, if we offer them to Him, are a broken heart and spirit. Such a sacrifice, he will never reject or despise. Don't you ever forget that."

After a moment of heart-rent silence, Brónach continued, "A man should not love a women so much and be asked to stay so long after she has departed. I do not know why Elohim keeps me here so long, but it has occurred to me that perhaps I am kept here for you my son."

Brónach struck a spark to tinder for a small flame, by which he lit an oil lamp. "It is time; I have a few things I must give to you. First, what is your name?"

Confused by the question the boy stammered "Mamzer, but everyone also calls me the Ra`ah. You know that."

"Yes, and both names are meant to bring shame. But did you know you once possessed a different name, a name given at birth by your mother? When you were

139

brought home the few things sent with you were discarded. This blanket you were wrapped in, lovingly woven, a household servant rescued it. See here, in the corner? A name has been stitched, I assume it must be the name your mother gave you. It is not Mamzer, or Ra`ah, it is Riordan. That is a name that can mean king's bard or poet, or even king's song. That is a name a man could wear, without shame I think. If a person is to overcome their past, they first need a new name."

Pain and frustration broke through in the ra`ah's voice, "But how can I ever escape my past? Everyone who knows me reminds me daily who I am, and who I am not, and who I can never hope to be!"

Brónach lifted the lamp closer to his face so that the boy could hear more than his words, "You can do nothing about the names that the people of this world give you until you can change the names you give yourself. In your heart, can you tell me you haven't also called yourself such names as Mamzer or worse? Your mother gave you a name, it is a good name, and one you can embrace until perhaps one day Elohim may give you another. Now, I must give you something else. Come with me."

Leading the ra`ah into the stalls area of the barn, Brónach walked to where his own horse was stabled. "I know you have met many times, but tonight it is important that I formally introduce you to Zaquen Esh. At one time the name was just Esh, or flame in the old tongue. But he has added much gray, so now I call him Zaquen Esh, the aged Flame. Thirty-seven years ago, Esh time and again proved to be one of the greatest chargers in all Capall. Now he is over forty, and has been far more than a horse to me, Esh has been my friend for more than half of my life."

The ra`ah knew the horse well. The charger's true age he could never guess, but he always knew he was indeed old. Yet, despite the age, and the gray hairs now mingled extensively with the deep roan red, hints of the power and muscle that marked Esh as a mighty stallion of Capall were still evident. Looking in the horse's dark eyes, the ra`ah could still see his fire, intelligence and life.

"Now remember what I said about seeing as man sees. Esh is old, even by the standards of the horses of Capall. But he has wisdom to go with those years, and perhaps the patience to teach a new rider. Esh has born me well in times of peace, and in war, Capall has seldom seen a finer charger. He has saved my life several times, and now I am asking of him one more task; to teach you how to ride. Perhaps one day he will save you, but at the least I think, he will keep you out of trouble."

"But," Mamzer protested, "I will not be allowed to ride, not unless . . . "

"Once before have I been a Goel, a Kinsman Redeemer. By giving you Zaquen Esh I am exercising a right. Brannan is too proud and stubborn to claim you as his son. I am not. By giving you my horse, I am claiming you as my own. You will bear my name, and my family crest. As for your name, I give you back the name your mother gave you at birth. I shall call you Riordan, now bear the name with honor."

Stunned, unable to speak, Riordan buried his face in Brónach's chest and clung tightly. Years of anguish, rejection and shame breaking through the floodgates and finding release.

"Aye boy, I will take away your reproach. I only wish I'd done it years ago, but I always thought Brannan would finally do the right thing. Now everything cannot change at once. You will still need to watch your father's sheep for a time, until new chores can be found reflecting your new status. The authority of the house has already passed to Brannan, and he may resist any changes, but in this at least he will not deny me."

Just then, there was a stirring and commotion

outside. Brónach and Riordan went to a window in the barn and looked out as the Captain Korah mounted a large black mare. Brónach whispered softly, "I know this man."

Speaking from the saddle, Korah relayed his final request, though it sounded pretty clear there wasn't much room for refusal, "All the new recruits are gathering outside the village Joktan, on the North Plain. As agreed, in two days please have your two eldest sons join me there. I will train them for about a week in the basics of mounted combat. Much more time is needed, but our need is pressing. I'm afraid their training will have to be completed on site in the Keys. I promise to train them well enough to give them the best chance for survival I can. While it's true the enemy is stopped in the mountain passes, this advantage may not hold for long. Do not delay in sending your sons, the survival of our Nation hangs in the balance. Farewell."

Everyone watched the captain quickly disappear in the dark night. Brónach placed his hand gently on Riordan's shoulder. "I know that man, Korah is a worthy captain . . . once he was my armor bearer. Perhaps if I . . . but no, you are not yet ready for this fight, but other battles may be in your future. For now, let us find a better place to sleep than the barn, a place more befitting an adopted son of Capall."

Ten

The next morning, Brannan, riding crop in hand, went looking for the ra`ah in his usual place in the hay loft of the barn. He wasn't there. Finding the sheep still in the holding pen, he knew that Mamzer hadn't rose early and left for the pastures. The longer he looked, the more his temperature rose until the rising mercury stained his neck and face red. His riding crop making an ominous, thundering crack across his palm as he stormed across the farm towards Brónach's home.

Watching from the window of his little cottage, Brónach felt certain the crop must be raising welts on his son's palm, but with his anger so intense, he just couldn't feel it. Looking back at Riordan he advised, "You'd best slip out the back boy, and head for the pastures. I'll bring the sheep along to ya in a bit."

Riordan rose from the cot prepared for him the night

before. Sensing his grandfather's concern, the boy walked over to take a peek from out of the bottom corner of the window. Fear started to gnaw at his gut when he saw the expression on Brannan's face.

"Go on lad, you'd better let me deal with him. I don't always advocate running away, but occasionally time and a little distance is the best response to wrath."

Riordan did as instructed, slipped out the back and chose a path leading through a cut, taking him behind a hill until he was no longer visible from the house. But even when well out of sight, he heard the eruption when Brónach told his son what he'd done. When the yelling started he couldn't help but pick up the pace after another surge of fear shot adrenaline to his feet.

His pace slowed once out of earshot, and his eyes were drawn to his new tunic. Brónach gave it to him last night to replace the scratchy burlap shift he'd worn for years. Over his heart he now wore a patch bearing the family crest. This simple coat of arms came in the form of a distinct round buckler divided by a cross into four sections. In the upper left corner was a white scroll against a cerulean field, a symbol of the Covenant of law Elohim made with His people; in the right a rearing white horse against a cobalt night sky filled with stars. This symbolized the Capall's belief the horse was their gift from the beginning of creation. In the bottom left, a blue star over pearl linen. Shortly after retaking the land Capall and his sons, one of Brónach's great grandfathers (Riordan lost count of how many greats there were) saw in a vision that his family would be marked and guided by a star. Finally, in the bottom right, the unopened bud of a desert rose. This particular rose of exceptional fragrance and beauty would remain closed for decades, until just the right amount of rain and temperatures created ideal climatic conditions for the bud to open. Because the bud remained closed, the flower represented the true destiny of the family line as not yet fully revealed.

Brónach warned him everything wouldn't change

all at once. But losing the scratchy burlap garments–
that certainly seemed to be a welcome change. Not
getting a regular beating, that would be a nice change
also. Maybe everything wouldn't change all at once,
but he decided he sure liked the changes already made.

Even so, once again he found himself headed into
the fields and at least for a while he would remain a
ra`ah. And yes, to be a sheep herder is regarded as a
disgrace, but he really didn't mind that his occupation
would remain the same. Riordan actually found
roaming pastures among the sheep most of the time to
be relaxing, even peaceful. With plenty of water and
grass, the sheep didn't wander too much anyway, giving
him plenty of time to think. Plus, it felt good to take
genuine responsibility for their safety and welfare; he
liked being needed. And they really needed him – the
sheep looked to him for protection; as critters go, sheep
aren't too bright, but they're smart enough to know
they're not very high up on the food chain. Wolves,
most of the great cats, many large birds of prey, and far
worse things enjoyed munching the little mutton
morsels.

Sometimes, just checking to see if the sheep were
paying any attention, and while their heads were down
grazing, Riordan would try to sneak away. For a few
moments, the sheep would continue grazing but when
they noticed he'd moved, they would give an alarmed
bleeting cry and fly after him.

With so little love from his family and such
devotion from the sheep, he found he came to truly love
the wooly fuzz balls. His brothers or father could not
distinguish one lamb or sheep from another, but Riordan
knew and recognized them all–and could call them by
name.

In those times when they stayed together in the
fields for several nights, he discovered his singing had a
calming effect that helped put them to sleep. One night
while composing a song to serve as a sheep lullaby it

struck him, "I can't believe it, Cavan is right, I am becoming their mama."

Later that morning Brónach rode out on Zaquen Esh driving the sheep before him. Looking down from the old charger's back, Brónach flashed a rather sheepish grin.

"Well I can't say that was one of the most pleasant ways I've ever spent a morning. But while Brannan has agreed to leave you alone, I think it perhaps best you stay out here with the sheep for a few days. So, I brought you a fresh bed roll and something to eat."

Swinging his leg over Esh's rump, he dropped down onto light feet. "Also I needed to keep one more promise." Intertwining the fingers of his hands that were lowered to his knees, he offered a step and boost for Riordan to climb to the big red horse's back. Age did little to reduce Esh's height of over sixteen hands, and getting up on his back would prove a real challenge for Riordan.

"I have to be getting back lad, but as I promised, Esh is yours now. As a son of Capall, you should have been astride a horse from birth, so you're more than a mite behind in your education in that area. I figured you can start learning now while out here watching the sheep. Esh will prove a good teacher. Just remember the most important lesson of all: a truly great horseman is a partner, not a dictator. Esh is old, but not dumb or senile. If you love and respect him, he will return your affections.

Sitting high on the horse's back, Brónach could see by the gleam in the boy's eye that already the love was there, and that very soon a bond would be established. Running his hand under Esh's chin and gently patting the velvet on his nose Brónach talked to his long-time partner directly. "For forty years now old friend you have given me everything you had, no man could ask for anything more. But one more thing I need to ask;

146

this is Riordan, my adopted son–he's young, he needs to learn how to ride. Even more important, he needs to learn how to be a man. I'm counting on you to help me teach him."

Esh nuzzled his chest in response, "Thanks, I knew I could count on you." So after sharing a bite of carrot, Brónach offered another farewell and started back towards the cottage.

Now this was a big change, for the first time ever, he watched over the sheep from the back of a horse. So out in the pastures while the sheep grazed, Riordan learned to ride.

Brónach proved right, Esh couldn't have been a better or more patient teacher. The sons of Capall used a simple saddle and blanket for riding, without reigns. The rider learned to guide his mount by pressure from the knees. Esh always seemed instinctively to know where Riordan wanted to go anyway, and even seemed to work at keeping him in the saddle. Only a few times did he fall, which from the height of Esh's back could have been a serious problem except that the prairie grasses were almost waist high, so the falls felt pretty well cushioned, almost fun.

A week later, with the older brothers away training with the captain, Riordan became enlisted to make a trip into Joktan for supplies. The sheep were brought back to the fold, and Riordan riding Zaquen Esh rode into town, leading two pack horses.

Slipping off Esh's back, he tied the horse's lead to a post and pulled out a soft clay tablet that served as his shopping list. Stepping away from Esh and trying to decipher the writing, Riordan didn't notice the approach of three young men, all a few years older than himself.

Snatching the tablet from Riordan's hands and throwing it to the ground, the leader of the little gang, a young man named Meribah, looked into Riordan's face and said with a sneer, "What is a Mamzer doing riding a horse? Although to call that creature a horse is an insult to all horses!" Meribah's friends laughed and jeered.

"Mamzer, don't you know riding a horse is illegal for such as you? I think we need to take this animal away, he must be stolen!"

"Yeah," another jeered, "nobody lets a ra`ah have a horse, they're confused by the smell of sheep!" All three of the boys started laughing and shoving the boy between them until he eventually spilled into the dust. When the boy's treatment of Riordan started getting rough, Esh went nuts, almost breaking his neck trying to pull loose from his lead.

One boy tried to catch Esh's lead rope, but a flying hoof almost took off his head instead. After that all three boys were focused on trying to secure the horse and temporarily forgot about Riordan, who they left lying in the street.

Riordan quickly sized up the situation in his mind. All three of the boys were older, and stronger. A beating and humiliation seemed to be what they had in mind, and they were trying hard to make good on their threat to take Esh away. That he could never allow, and a cold fury started to rise up inside.

The three tormenters, however, made two mistakes; first they turned their backs on Riordan, and second they tried to take away his most treasured gift.

Riordan got to his feet. Two long strides brought him up behind the boys who were focused on avoiding flying hooves while trying to catch the big red horses lead. The ra`ah grabbed Meribah by the shoulder, spun him around and looked him straight in the eye, "My name is Riordan, I am the adopted son of Brónach, a son of Capall, and Zaquen-Esh is *my* horse."

With that Riordan swung his foot into an unprepared Meribah's groin. As the youth doubled over in pain Riordan's open palm caught his nose as the head lurched forward. This caused the nose to break and Meribah to fly backwards spraying blood.

Forced to fight for respect against Torin and the

brothers from almost the time he could walk, those battles were always against older, larger, stronger opponents. Maybe he didn't win many of those fights, but he learned from every last one of them. All that he learned, he made use of now.

The other boys were completely caught off guard. After all, it wasn't supposed to happen this way. They figured the kid would get scared, plead for a while, then they'd have some fun while they roughed him up a bit. It didn't occur to them the younger boy would strike first and with such fury. While they watched in shock as their leader went down to the dirt, Riordan put all his might into a haymaker to the chin of the second boy, sending him into the dust to join his companion.

The third recovered from his surprise and blocked Riordan's next blow. He soon found however, the little ra`ah very adept about dodging all the punches he threw back. But he only needed to keep the younger, smaller boy occupied long enough for his friends to recover. The first was Meribah, who with blood streaming down his face, hit Riordan from behind with a tackle that took his legs out from under him. Then all three boys jumped on the pile and a beating started to commence.

A few feet away, Esh still screamed and pulled at the lead rope, If he got lose, somebody would get hurt. Nothing but fury and death could be seen in the red stallion's eyes. His years were forgotten as he strained to come loose and come to his boy's aide. But the harder he pulled the tighter the lead got, until in his wrath he came real close to choking himself to death.

Across the street, Torin, given a bit of time off from training, along with several other recruits, witnessed the fight. He knew Meribah and his friends, couldn't say he much cared for them. He also grudgingly admired Riordan's spunk in the way he took the fight to the older boys. The whole household felt Mamzer to be a shame to the family, however, pounding on a younger brother is an older brother's exclusive right. Besides, judging by the fury of Meribah's response to having his nose broken, Torin knew this beating could become fatal. Finally, no son of Capall could abide the mistreatment of a great warhorse like Esh. After a few moments' hesitation he started to step across the street, perhaps more to defend Esh's honor than Mamzer's.

Further up the boardwalk, behind a corner of a building another observer–a woman, hid in the shadows. Most of her thirty-four summers were spent enduring a life-sentence at hard labor where bread and water would seem a feast. The cumulative effect of hot sun and scarce nutrition all worked to age her well beyond her years. Once she radiated a deep quiet beauty, now lines of worry and pain marred her face. Long ago, her golden tresses were replaced by dirty, scraggly, premature gray hair.

She made a promise once, she said she would stay away . . . but how could she hide and merely watch from the shadows? She could see what the boys were doing to her son. She also heard the name they called him. She knew full well the pain caused by a label, and the name Mamzer cut her even more than him. Her immediate reaction–an urgent need to help as his cries of pain once again stabbed anguish into her own soul.

A cynic would ask just what could she do? The woman, aged and malnourished, couldn't have weighed more than eighty, ninety pounds soaking wet. The question of what could she do never entered her head however, she stopped only to consider; would too much be revealed by her rushing to help the boy? Would people guess her connection? Despite the damage of the hard years and the wrinkles, someone might still notice that the boy mirrored her face. She stood for a moment and breathed an anguished prayer, then did what only a person of her heart could do, she started forward to rush to Riordan's aide.

Neither Torin's or the woman's effort's to help proved necessary. Aid arrived much sooner. Two massive hands pulled two of the boys off the pile and lifted them so that their feet dangled two feet off the ground. After having their heads knocked together, the pair were tossed aside like outgrown children's rag dolls.

Meribah rose to his feet and turned to face an angry centaur (something no one in his right mind wants to do). But this was far worse, Meribah's eyes grew big as plates as he recognized the gold torc and white stone around the neck of the Shophetim, and Judge of all Jeshurun. Shocked, he uttered the name "Jireh" just before a sweeping backhand took him off his feet and deposited him in the dust several feet away.

One of the other boys proved sufficiently recovered to get up to his knees and mutter while holding his aching head "Jireh, you choose to help this Mamzer?"

The Shophetim glared and responded angrily with a deep booming voice, "A mamzer is he? Well if that is so, who is guilty of sin, this one or his parents? The boy's conception couldn't be an act of his own I assure you, so where is *his* sin that he should be scorned so?" This challenge Jireh issued so loudly that the whole town felt the shame of it. "But as for you, you thought to prey on one you deemed helpless, as though by this action you could relieve your own cowardice. Your actions, because they were a conscious choice reveals your true nature to be that of cruel knaves and cowards. This mamzer as you called him showed more courage in his smallest appendage then you have in your whole bodies. Now I suggest you crawl on out of here before I get really angry."

Dismissing the boys by turning his back on them, Jireh with a gentleness that seemed impossible of one of such strength, picked a semi-conscious Riordan up out of the dust, and held him in his arms. Torin crossed the street and picked up the now filthy tablet, and tried to calm a still enraged Esh.

Jireh looked at him with penetrating eyes, "A little

slow to come to the Lad's aid, weren't you? Take your father's instructions, recover the pack animals and see to the provisions for your family."

Torin hung his head, and simply said "Yes sir."

With that the centaur went over to show Esh that Riordan was alright, then placed the lad on his back, and together they took him home.

Eleven

"Perfect love casts out fear."
~John the Apostle.

Mereah watched his father Ruarc brood darkly in front of a small fire in his tent. The battle went badly that day and after several hours of furious combat, the mouth of the Keys fell into the hands of the enemy. Forced to withdraw through the next pass, all that remained of the dispirited Jeshurun army hid in trenches and holes. Another couple of days like this, and the Dagon would break through completely to the Capall grasslands where they would be able to take advantage once again of far superior numbers. Nothing would stop them from marching freely through the heart of the nation.

Protected to the north and east by high mountains and the impenetrable Negev forest, any army seeking to invade Jeshurun first must come across the Cnámh plain. Sailing vessels were not yet well enough developed by most nations to form effective invasion fleets. And so, before Jeshurun could be conquered the Keys must first be unlocked.

Each of the Key's three canyons narrowed to a bottle neck that could be plugged by a small force without danger of being flanked. For the last several days the Dagon hurled every weapon in their arsenal against their defenses. The invaders suffered heavy losses while managing to inflict very little harm. No small part of the Jeshurun success could be credited to the use of the sling pults captured from the enemy. The sons of Dun quickly engineered a clay vessel with a wick, that would shatter and ignite upon impact. When combined with withering fire from Irial archers on the heights, the enemy became thoroughly dispirited long before reaching the trenches.

The Dagon, however, changed tactics today. From first light their forces were arrayed in a huge battle line, two thousand combatants wide, at least five thousand deep. Mostly hidden by their defenses, the Armies of Jeshurun huddled down in the canyon mouth and braced for attack. But the Dagon Army never moved, they just stood silently watching, waiting, as though mere spectators in the day's drama.

After an hour with the enemy never moving to attack, Jeshurun's fear and anticipation became palpable. Suddenly the enemy parted ranks to let a man mounted on a tanniyn slowly, almost casually, pass through.

That an Anak proved to be the driving force behind the recent military advances made by the Dagon surprised no one. The rumors were whispered around watch fires for weeks, with fear providing all the credibility gossip and hearsay needed. Born from an evil breeding program, created through the union of a

154

mother of flesh and the Nephilim, the fallen ones; the Anakim were the design of demonic messengers called the Watchers. Spiritual half-breeds, not belonging to any realm, neither Sheol or the world, the Anakim were given wholly to the service of destruction.

Both the Anakim and the Nephilim were present when the peoples of Jeshurun entered the land. Though widely believed that they were all destroyed, it now appeared rumors of their demise were greatly exaggerated. The evidence approached right before their eyes, riding upon a tanniyn.

The Anak carried no visible weapons, seemingly content to wield a very short staff or perhaps a scepter, with some form of red gem at its head. Mereah watched him come forward slowly, and sensed the fear in the trenches as he heard "Anak" being whispered among the Jeshurun warriors.

Lifting the scepter over his head the Anak started chanting in an unknown dark tongue. The gem on the scepter started glowing. Suddenly a red ball of light, like a flare shot into the sky almost to the clouds where it exploded, sending crimson fragments to the four winds.

"Jeshurun, can you hear me? Where is that giant of a coward you call king? I would speak with him. But if he lacks the courage to come out of hiding I will speak with his craven dogs hiding in their holes. Lay down your arms and come down, and you will live. Yes, you will be slaves, but your heart will still beat, and you will preserve the life blood of your people – all of you, except of course your king and his heirs. Their heads will be placed on pikes so that their folly may be displayed for all to see. Decide quickly, for I have invited many guests to a banquet. Once they arrive, I doubt that they will suffer being denied their promised feast."

The Anak's icy voice seemed to have its desired effect. Fear of whatever hell he planned to unleash seemed by itself enough, but his very words burned ear and mind as with acidic vitriol in oppressive demonic overkill. Jeshurun's finest ducked down and hid in the dirt at the bottom of their trenches.

He turned his dragon mount so that he could see behind him, watched for a few seconds, then made the turn a complete revolution and so faced the Jeshurun lines once again. "Too late fools, my dinner guests have already begun to arrive."

A black cloud appeared on the horizon, moving toward their lines as though racing before a fast wind. But there wasn't any wind, not even the slightest breeze to counter the oppressive heat.

Then dismayed murmuring spread through the Jeshurun lines as the soldiers noticed a gathering cloud of dust well behind enemy lines betraying still another massive advancing army. Terror raised from below.

"What manner of Devilry is this," Mereah muttered.

One of the Irial archers from his position high in the rocks suddenly called out, "Ware the skies!"

Looking up Mereah at last realized the black cloud could only be a mass of birds, and after drawing closer he could see that they were carrion fowl, black vultures, ravens, crows, and even some species of shrike, eagles and hawks. When their flight came directly overhead untold thousands of the dark birds–so many the whole valley found itself cast into shadow–started a swirling vortex of gory anticipation over their next meal. The Anak's message proved to be not very subtle, everyone got the point: they were all going to die and become the main course for these foul birds' banquet.

Then Mereah's heart skipped a beat, the source of the dust cloud became visible, and at first he thought reinforcements were coming to their aide. For among the advancing army's ranks were men, Irial, Dun, even a few Irijah and sons of Rapha`. But rather than attack the Dagon, they passed right through their ranks.

Something wasn't right, they were not moving

naturally, but haltingly, with jerky slow movements. In the trenches hope turned to dismay as it became clear while indeed soldiers of Jeshurun, they would not be allies against the Dagon. As these soldiers crept closer, their gaping fatal wounds became apparent, but none of the horrible injuries were bleeding, just crusted over with scabs, dried blood and maggots. Some of the advancing army lacked limbs, and with dismay Mereah realized some even lacked heads as they'd been decapitated.

The stench of decomposition reached the noses of the soldiers in the defenses as a very effective first attack. But the worst blow came when the advancing force drew close enough for the defenders to recognize the faces of many former comrades and family.

Through the years thousands of Jeshurun soldiers had fallen in battle on the plains south of the mountains. The Cnámh sands concealed an almost limitless number of dead for the Anak to animate. More than just an unspeakable horror to see fallen brothers and friends now marching against them; long held religious laws and beliefs regarding the touching of dead corpses meant that all of the Key's defenders by this fight would be made unclean. The Anak's clear message? The fate of every man is eventual decay, while the stench of decomposition spoke his promise that we're all worm food. With such cold hard realities, the Anak meant to chill their hearts and wring from them any hope.

Lithos, looking down at the advancing undead army murmured, "He can't be serious. This is an army that can barely walk, how can they be expected to fight?"

"The Anak harbors no illusions that these animations can defeat us, but that is not his purpose." Mereah watched the progress of their un-dead foes and felt the advance of revulsion climb from the pit of his stomach and up his spine.

"This isn't done because it poises a serious threat, but there is just enough of the corpses left to be recognized as the bodies of family and friends. We will have no choice but cover our noses and pray that the face of a loved one, a father or brother or friend will not be among the ones we are forced to strike down. He believes killing our bodies will be easy enough once he has crushed our spirits."

Jeshurun began their defense with missile attacks. But the Irial archers quickly discerned this was pointless; a perfect head shot didn't even give the dead a reason to pause.

Lithos muttered under his breath, "Maybe this is going to be even *worse* than I thought."

Then a centaur threw a ten pound sling stone with such velocity that a walking corpse almost disintegrated. This brought a cheer from the men in the trenches, and several more stones were slung. Then came the horrible realization; even then the dead wouldn't stop; torsos separated from legs were now dragged by arm and hand, and they just kept coming.

Puzzled by something Mereah asked, "Lithos, why haven't the sling-pults been brought into the fray?"

The Dun Commander turned his head and spoke over his shoulder, "We ran out of the clay vessels in yesterday's assault. More are being made but haven't arrived. I'm sort of wondering if the Anak knew that somehow when he planned this attack."

Mereah nodded solemnly, "Or perhaps intended we waste the last of our armaments against this gruesome diversion, . . we need to go to the trenches."

Soon enough the animated dead reached the defenses and the fighting became hand to hand, or hand to severed limb.

Then the birds struck. Not at the animated dead, but at the living. Even a slow and clumsy opponent can find an opening when a fighter is distracted by raptors and carrion birds attacking with wing, beak and talon from above their heads. First a son of Capall, then one of the Dun fell, and it soon became clear not just the birds were invited to the feast. As unlucky soldiers fell wounded, the dead fell upon and devoured them while their victims screamed. Worse still, if killed quickly, the Jeshurun dead were animated almost immediately and so joined the attacking un-dead forces. In this way, the enemy ranks actually grew the longer the battle continued.

Lithos took on a decomposing Rapha`, that tottered towards his position. Using his normal attack protocol against a much larger opponent, he used his hammer to smash the huge foot. When the un-dead giant didn't jump up and down howling while holding his toes, the Dun commander looked up and muttered, "Uh-oh."

Slow, clumsy, yes the undead certainly were; but also relentless, and impervious to pain. Lithos jumped out of the way of a swinging club, but wondered how long he could continue the evasive dance, so he shouted out at Mereah, "I've a foe three times my height, and completely impervious to pain. Any suggestions?"

Thick in the heat of battle Mereah already discovered that several of the dead when struck with his mace were sent flying, but they kept returning to the fight, "I'm trying to answer the same riddle my friend, but so far haven't found any solution. Just how do you go about killing a foe already dead?"

Drawing a massive iron sword he began removing limbs, but even so the dead kept coming. So beset by enemies, the young Rapha` realized he would never be given the opportunity to think of a solution, all he could manage was to continue fighting.

Irial archers from their positions above the fray were the ones who stumbled on the answer to their deadly dilemma. Harried by birds of prey, they first lit torches to keep the dive bombing fowl from attacking their heads. This inspired someone among the Irial to see how the dead reacted to flame, and they lit a fire arrow. Soon after this they discovered they could ignite the dead. Watching the archers turn some of the undead into non-living torches, Mereah realized they'd found their solution to this riddle at least. Pulling away from the fight Mereah called to a group of Rapha` held in reserve, "Quickly, bring torches and oil."

Having accomplished his purpose and upon seeing the undead set ablaze by Jeshurun's defenders, the Anak withdrew the power animating the dead and let them simply collapse into heaps. Then the Carrion Birds descended. The living retreated as the vultures and crows screeched and squabbled over the scraps of fallen comrades. Everyone looked away rather than watch the birds go about their gruesome business.

And the Anak laughed. With all the warmth of a hyena celebrating a fresh kill he continued to laugh hysterically. The sound of his laughter actually grew in volume as it echoed and bounced off the narrow desert canyon walls. Soon all of Jeshurun tried to bury their heads and cover their ears as eardrums threatened to split and hearts filled with despair.

Then with a outcry that sounded like a scourge given voice, the Anak called out encouragement to the feasting fowl, "As I promised, an overflowing profusion of foul flesh! Death can always be found in abundance, and this is just the first course. Soon, ah very soon, more meat . . . fresh . . sweet–dead meat."

The putrid banquet continued, accompanied by hideous ear-splitting laughter until mid-morning. Then suddenly the birds lifted off and claimed perches on the tops of the cliffs, leaving the valley in complete silence. Being watched from above by so many vultures and crows, all salivating in anticipation of their next course, threw a ton of weight to the already oppressive dread of impending doom.

Out of the shadows the Anak rode forward once again with no escort, challenging any who dared come out of hiding to oppose him. The tanniyn he rode looked different from the others, a bit lighter-bodied; with longer limbs and neck, likely close to forty feet from nose to tail. Sleeker, faster, the longer more narrow head while less heavy, allowed for even more serrated dagger teeth.

Now that the Anak could be seen more closely, Mereah guessed long ago he'd spawned from an Irial mother, but really couldn't be considered anything living now. The hood of his black cloak was thrown back, revealing long flowing sable hair and milky white skin. It occurred to Mereah "This Anak must have a hatred for the sun light because apparently he'd seen precious little of it."

The eyes were the worst–just empty, dark sockets. If the eye is the mirror of the soul as the proverbs say, the soul of the Anak could only be a black hole from which no light emanated or escaped.

All Jeshurun watched as the Dagon shaman raised his scepter high, and howled incantations in a dark tongue from a long forgotten age. The words may have been from another time, but the results were very present and deadly. Starting as a lowly dust devil, a swirling dust storm grew in height and power in response to the growing resonance of the incantation. Soon the roar of the wind drowned out even the chanting voice as the dust devil grew into a swirling funnel hundreds of feet high. The sand thrown by the twister would take the flesh off any mortal so all of the Jeshurun camp cowered in holes or fled to find shelter. Some did not move fast enough, as the twister hurtled through the center of their defenses, Capall cavalry, Dun infantry, even sons of Rapha` from the king's guard were pulled into the vortex and carried up hundreds of feet. Some were carried to meet their creator many miles away. Far worse for Jeshurun's crumbling morale, friends and companions fell screaming for hundreds of feet, only to be crushed before every ones' watching eyes.

Then it went dark. Not just dark–a complete absence of light. As the vortex continued moving deeper into the Keys, Lithos shouted as loud as he could in order to be heard by Mereah who hunkered down right beside him. "What sort of devilry is this, does the Anak think us children afraid of the dark?"

"What reason does any man have for loving the dark, if not to conceal their actions?" Trying to be heard above the wind's roar, Mereah called out, "Jeshurun, beware, an attack will follow this darkness!"

When the winds died, eery silence remained, amplified by darkness. Unable to see a hand in front of their faces, the Jeshurun's found it impossible to find and return to defensive positions they'd abandoned because of the twister. For several minutes the defenders stumbled and crashed around. In the resulting confusion, cursing, and panic, the approach of thousands of iron shod boots went unnoticed.

The black lifted suddenly. In its place a thousand Dagon soldiers a mere ten yards away. With defenses in shambles, the enemy took full advantage of Jeshurun's complete surprise. A slaughter commenced, another feast for the vultures seemed a certainty.

Korah's two surviving sons saved what remained of the day and kept the battle from becoming a complete rout. Leading the cavalry in a thunderous charge, lances down, they swept through the advance parties of the enemy, giving the Jeshurun forces in the center time to regain their composure and positions.

The cavalry were held in reserve for this very reason; but Ruarc the king realized this to be a temporary gain at best and that soon the enemy would sweep back into the canyon. Orders for immediate withdrawal back through the second canyon were given with the remaining sons of Korah and Capall cavalry acting as the rear guard. This allowed the army to take up new positions at the second narrow choke point that acted as a gateway for the next pass, deeper in the heart of the Keys.

Using long spears, from the backs of swift mounts, the Capall were able to strike, yet remain out of the enemies reach. Using a series of rapid assaults, then retreating before the Dagon could retaliate, they drove their enemies mad with rage. Their rage led to mistakes which the cavalry were quick to make the enemy pay for. In this fashion, the retreat continued in a fairly orderly manner and there seemed to be some hope that the day would not be a total loss. Then the Anak made his presence felt yet again.

Once more, total darkness descended on the cavalry and the retreating troops. Not even the most sure footed horse will chance movement when it's pitch black. Their long slender legs are the source of their great speed and power, but also the source of greatest weakness and frailty. Since a break in the leg could easily cripple, or even lead to death, movement of the swift cavalry slowed to less than a crawl.

Then the darkness lifted once again. Unhindered by the dark, the Dagon soldiers were now within an arm's length of the horses that had driven them insane with rage for the last hour. Retribution came, swift . . . brutal. Riders were dragged from their horses and hacked to pieces with cold iron blades.

Some riders managed to break away, but not without heavy loss. The Anak then unleashed still another deadly weapon, as a fireball dropped in the midst of the retreating riders. Twenty five men and horses were kindled with sorcerer's flame, filling the air with the stench of burning flesh.

The swift actions of the cavalry saved the main army from annihilation by covering their retreat. But now unless someone protected the withdrawal of the horse soldiers, they would all be lost. Both the sons of Korah reached this conclusion separately. When their eyes met they knew they were in agreement about what must be done. Korah's oldest remaining son ordered the riders to retreat back behind the newly established lines at the head of the valley. Then to buy them time, the brothers turned, clashed their shields together in solidarity, and rode straight on to attack the Anak.

The demon vassal recognized the charge for a real threat; he knew the metal of his foes. Korah's sons were raised from infancy on horseback, and except for their father, there were no more deadly riders in all of Capall, and that meant the world. Their horses were direct descendants of those bonded with their fathers. Not as strong or as swift as the days of the First Age, but still the mightiest of their kind.

The Dagon forces collapsed back to form a protective wall for the Anak. The brothers lowered their lances, and singing a song of death and woe, passed through that wall leaving impaled bodies in their wake.

Their lances shattered on the Anak's bodyguard, the brothers pulled short bows from holsters attached to their saddles, and while still at a full gallop, fired with deadly accuracy at the tanniyn's soft underbelly. Korah's sons were capable of bulls-eyeing a tick on the wagging tail of a small dog while at full speed. Something as large as the dragon—no way they would miss. Except they did miss; with a wave of his scepter a powerful gust of wind suddenly kicked up and blew the arrows off course.

Drawing fresh lances from a large quiver behind their saddles, the brothers split up, one to the right, the other to the left. Simultaneously, they thrust their lances not at the dragon, but at the rider, trying to kill the head of the snake. The tanniyn with speed very much unexpected for such a large bulky animal twisted its torso; the head tried to rend and tear the rider who went to one side, while the great tail swung around to strike at the other. The sudden movement likely saved the Anak's life as he twisted away from the spear thrusts. The horses needed no guidance from their riders as they used speed and agility to avoid the

164

dragon's attacks of teeth and tail as they sped by. Wheeling as one, Korah's sons now faced the Dragon broadside, and charged once more seeking to impale its soft underside with long pikes.

The Anak grew weary. The animation of the dead required so much in payment of strength to the Watcher to whom he served, he needed to dig deep and somehow find the strength to respond. Looking at the bright spears drawing down on him, he knew the death of his dragon mount could easily become his own. Raising his scepter while speaking in an ancient tongue, he called yet again on the aide of the Rashama, the familiar spirits. As always help came at a steep price, increasing the soul debt, but providing assistance once more. The sand in front of the charging horses lost its firmness, transforming the consistency to that of powdery snow. With their long slender legs sinking deep, the horse's great speed became frantic attempts to get free. Losing the advantage of speed and agility, Korah's sons knew they were in deep trouble. They urged their mounts on, but as they feared, their struggles were quickly ended. The tanniyn's tail with a force that could crush stone, swept through both horses breaking their legs and necks, while sending their riders flying from their backs. Stunned, the wind knocked from their lungs, recovery for Korah's sons would require several minutes–minutes they would not have. Instead, great talons impaled the small of their backs, pinning them to the ground and breaking their spines.

The second born, now Korah's heir, gazed helplessly while the tanniyn devoured his younger brother. All the time the Anak laughed riotously, reveling in the bloody carnage. All Jeshurun watched from new defensive positions, transfixed by the horrible price of self-sacrifice before their very eyes.

But then Korah's heir showed he would not bow or give in to despair or fear. To the astonishment of the whole valley, and the fighting men from both armies,

Korah's son started to sing. At first his voice was weak while he started an ancient song of his people; as he continued to sing his voice grew stronger;

Yahweh, you have created me
You have called me by name,
I am yours

Though I pass through a blood red sea
My El shall walk with me
Even a river of death
shall never overcome thee.

Though I walk through Sheol's fire
Still I will not be scorched, nor burned
And the flame, intended for harm
Will only purify my soul!

Yahweh knows and calls me by name,
Jeshurun tell me, whom shall I fear?
I shall walk now in His freedom,
And Into the kingdom of His glory.

As the son of Korah sang, his voice carried even to the ears of Jeshurun's soldiers at the head of the valley; his song of hope echoed off the canyon walls. The Anak screamed in absolute rage and the tanniyn pounced on him, not to consume, but to rend and tear, and so in great fury tore Korah's last son to pieces.

Mereah winced as he watched the carnage and wondered how this news could be told to Korah. So much loss, the captain lost his wife giving birth to their third son. His first son fell in battle on the Cnámh plains, just a few days ago. Now his two remaining sons, the last light of his life, were also gone, sacrificed on the altar of Jeshurun's need.

The voice of the elder son in song kept replaying in his mind. Such courage, laying in his own blood, back broken, helpless, and yet he sang. In that voice everyone heard victory, even triumph. The fury of the Anak came in response to the song. By refusing to give in to despair, Korah's son effectively denied him his victory. A small thing? Perhaps, but even such a small thing still required great heart. Such courage could sow the seeds for still greater deeds.

Mereah knew down in the canyons, the Dagon sat in their camps reveling in their victory. While in the last pass, the very back of the Keys, the army of Jeshurun waited in their defensive positions with hearts full of fear and despair. Tomorrow, another assault would be coming and unless the men found their courage, the battle, perhaps even the nation would be lost.

Replaying the day's events in his mind, and now looking at his father, brooding and bitter, he saw neither hope nor courage. Without a word as to the establishment of the defenses, Ruarc turned on his heels and returned to his tent. In addition to his father's behavior, the prince didn't have a clue as to how the king's guard managed to salvage the pavilion during the days route, but there it was.

Soon Mereah knew, a strange red glow would emanate from the sides and bottom of the tent flaps. Now at a time when the king needed to show courage and strength the most, his new pattern seemed to be, retreat to his tent and hide. If the soldiers did not find encouragement from their king, where would they find the strength and will to face such a relentless enemy?

The song sang by Korah's son replayed in his mind. Even in death, courage and strength resonated from that voice. Without more deeds of such courageousness, all would be lost. The son of Korah found his victory in song. Considering this, a plan of action started to form in Mereah's mind. Slipping away from the lines, he went to put on his armor and gather his weapons.

Twelve

Jireh the Shophetim brought a half-conscious Riordan home. Brannan didn't know how to respond to the situation of his un-named son brought in obviously hurt, and it seemed clear he lacked the courage to show or even feel concern. Not surprisingly Brónach took Esh's lead and walked the horse and his boy back to his own quarters while Brannan merely watched. Jireh walked beside Brónach past the main house to the small cottage, and the way the two talked it seemed clear they knew one another, and were even old friends. Riordan heard little of the conversation except for the centaur's explanation that the fight broke out when a group of older boys challenged the boy's right to ride a horse. With a soft chuckle, Jireh said the lad responded by challenging their right to challenge. The Shophetim further said the boy fought like a lion, and he should be proud.

Riordan could hear the truth in his grandfather's voice when Brónach responded "I am proud, any father would be."

Mist came to his eyes as he tried to remember if anyone ever said they were proud of him before. Brannan, however, remained in stunned, muted silence, and then the boy passed out and remembered no more.

When he woke the next evening, his ribs were wrapped tight with bandages and he could feel swelling on his hand and left eye. Brónach was standing at the foot of the cot when he woke. "Don't try to rise, you were pretty banged up. A couple ribs were cracked, and all we can do about those is wrap 'em real tight and let 'em heal. Moving, I'm afraid to say, is going to hurt like all the depths of Sheol. The Shophetim said you gave a pretty good account for yourself and showed real courage against steep odds.

"Even Torin gave witness to the fact that you fought bravely and that Meribah will think twice before he challenges your right to ride. His nose will never be straight again, and it took quite a bit of effort from what Torin heard to get the bleeding to stop. Your brother said it's pretty funny to see him around training camp with almost his whole face a black bruise. Your father couldn't say so, but he is my son, I saw pride in his eyes too." Brónach sat down at the boy's side for a few moments, no words were spoken, or needed. The words of affirmation and approval from Brónach, however, brought a glow to all of Riordan's insides, temporarily easing the pain in his ribs.

"After a few days of rest, you are going to be returned to the pastures to watch the sheep. Mostly because until your ribs heal, I doubt you could do any other work. You need to do something however, because we really don't want you to get fat and lazy. Zaquen Esh will go out with you, but I think it will be too painful to ride for a time, so I brought you this."

Brónach pulled out of hiding from behind the cot a

wonderfully carved wooden harp. The wooden body provided a sound box for twelve strings attached to a U-shaped swan neck. "You were named Riordan by your mother, the king's poet or king's song. It occurred to me that a young man with such a name should have an instrument to give support to his voice. This . . once belonged to your grandmother. It occurred to me that it's time the swan regains it's voice."

Once again Riordan sat there stunned, his voice not finding sufficient words to express his gratitude. A look into his shining eyes, however, and Brónach could see thanks deeper than any words could express anyway.

"I bought the harp for your grandmother from a merchant in the the Irial city of Bethel. The carvings tell the legend of Eala Amhrán, a princess from the age of Drochshaol. According to legend, one of the Nephilim, or the fallen ones, a demon named Oros approached Bearach the King of Irial demanding Eala as a bride. Afraid to refuse the king consented, but she did not. So the demon caged her inside a high tower until she had a change of heart.

"In despair she cried out to Yahweh Elohim, and she was transformed into a swan, with a song so powerful it burst her bonds allowing her to fly from the tower. Only a legend I know, but more than one legend has truth as its foundation. Anyway, the best instruments are almost always made by the Irial.

"You can play for a bit, but you slept all through the night and day, and now it is time for me to go to bed. I know you won't be able to sleep without at least plunking a bit, but a serenade by someone just learning an instrument is not likely to help anyone's sleep. So please play softly if you don't mind." With that Brónach rumpled the boy's hair, and left the room.

That night, he could hear the lad's attempts to pluck at the strings quietly, and found it wouldn't

170

be so hard to sleep after all. "Well what do you know," he murmured before going to sleep, "The lad's pretty good."

~

Riordan sat in the pasture, watching the gentle breezes blow the high grasses of the Capall prairie like endless green ocean waves. It was indeed two weeks before he could ride Zaquen Esh, and he used the time to work on mastering his musical instrument. He found both the horse and the sheep to be a very receptive audience. His playing seemed to calm them as much as his singing did. Alone with his thoughts, he found the solitude on the grasslands to be a place of rest for his spirit. In the stillness and quiet, he often heard a small voice, that made him pause and wonder. He recognized it from other times in his life, and had wondered for a long time about its source. Could it be just his imagination? Would the Mighty Power of his people bother to talk to a mamzer, or for that matter a ra`ah? But here, in solitude and quiet he heard the still, gentle, whisperings more and more clearly. He began to respond to the voice on the wind through song. When he sang, despite the seclusion, he no longer felt alone.

While Riordan worked on a lively new tune, Esh's head suddenly came up from grazing, ears erect and alert. A quick snort seemed to be some form of warning, or perhaps a challenge. His Grandfather recently told him, all riders must learn to pay attention when his horse is trying to tell him something.

Esh snorted another warning and trotted a couple steps looking intently west. Riordan slowly rose, carefully put down the harp, and searched with his eyes in the direction the horse was looking, while feeling blindly with his hands for his sling. Speaking softly to Esh he asked, "What is it boy?"

The Aged Flame quietly nickered as if to reply. Though entrusted with a horse, he still hadn't been given a short sword or spear, just a knife and a sling. The sling as a weapon wielded by boys, seemed to have safety as its chief virtue. Pretty hard for young-uns to hurt themselves with such a simple weapon, most folks reasoned. No one kept statistics of course, but if they actually counted the number of youngsters who beaned themselves in the noggin while learning to use em; slings might not have enjoyed such wide-spread parental seal of approval.

With practice, a sling is pretty safe. Riordan swung the rock around and hit himself in the head only once or twice. The damage done to a notch in a large cottonwood he used as a target gave some testimony as to the proficiency achieved through countless hours slinging rocks. He constantly practiced, what else did he have to do? Especially after the incident a few months ago, back in the mountains, when the Dun horse-thief sidled into camp, armed to the teeth. Riordan never forgot that sinking feeling in his stomach of being over-matched.

Out here alone with predator magnets to watch after, he wondered if maybe the sling was his only weapon because Brannan hoped he wouldn't survive an assault from a serious . . . before he could finish his thought, Esh's head popped up from his grazing once again, but this time he reared and screamed defiance as his front hoofs assaulted the air.

From the stream bed Riordan could find unlimited ammo for his sling, and so he reached down for a little pile he'd made near his campfire. As he dropped a stone the size of a child's fist into the leather pouch of the sling, a deafening roar made him jump. Just to his left a lion thundered and the sheep all fled past him to the right. Esh raced to face the predator screaming a challenge. In a panic, Riordan charged after the horse. A stallion of Capall is a formidable foe when fighting with teeth and hooves, he'd already seen that. But can he take on a lion? And perhaps even more important, is the lion alone? As he ran after the horse, he got his answer, the one he was afraid of. As the sheep all ran away from the roar, they rushed unwittingly straight to the real danger. Several lionesses had lain hidden while an old male circled around to the other side of the flock, with the purpose of driving the terrorized sheep frantically to an ambush.

Completely baffled, Riordan fought against the feeling of total panic. "Do I help Esh, or do what I can to save the sheep?" With a sinking heart, he chose and ran to try and save the sheep, hoping Esh would prove capable of saving himself.

Running upstream against a wave of wool fleeing in the opposite direction, Riordan only got through with great difficulty. One lioness had already grabbed a ram by the throat, and started the slow process of choking its life away. Several more were chasing ewes, and likely would catch them quickly; then the slaughter would commence–unless he did some thing. Swinging the sling above his head, the ra`ah released his stone with cool accuracy towards the lioness with her jaws clamped on the throat of the young ram. Hitting the lion just behind the front shoulder, likely cracking a rib, she let the Ram go. That was the good news. The bad news . . . she looked at him and in lion-ese clearly said, "You're next."

Dropping another stone into the sling's pouch, Riordan knew he would not be able to get off a shot in time. The lioness would cross the twenty yards between them in less than two seconds. Quite sure he'd hurt the lion, but only enough to make it real mad, a perfect head shot would be needed to kill it now. The odds of that happening were astronomical, provided he even got off another stone.

The lion crossed the space between them and pounced just as Riordan started to twirl the sling above his head. Looking into the lion's mouth and enraged eyes he saw his own death. He reacted instinctively–he closed his eyes, threw his hands up over his face and ducked. As he braced for impact, he prayed fervently the big cat would make it quick. Bewildered that he wasn't immediately torn to shreds, he found the courage to peek between his fingers. The lioness lay dead a few feet away with a large stone smashed into her gaping maw.

Riordan slowly straightened up and turned his head to look over his shoulder. There stood Jeshurun's Shophetim coolly placing another stone in his own sling. The lions quickly decided they'd seen enough, and were already in full flight, hoping to find easier prey.

The boy turned to face the Shophetim Jireh, "That's twice you've pulled me out of a tight spot. You seem to have a way of turning up when I am in trouble."

The centaur chuckled, "That's not too great of a coincidence on account of the fact that from what I hear, you are almost always *in* some kind of trouble."

Suddenly the light of remembrance hit Riordan's face, and he exclaimed "Esh!" Turning back he fled towards the old stallion standing about forty yards away. The lion who started all the trouble lay trampled, and dead in the grass. There were scratches on his flanks with a touch of blood, but otherwise Esh seemed unhurt.

The centaur walked up behind Riordan, "It seems this old stallion is the real lion here. I knew him to be a warrior back in the village the way he fought to get free so he could come to your defense. Had his lead rope broke, I believe he very well may have killed those boys."

Examining the scratches on Esh's flanks more closely he remarked, "We'd better clean these, they are not deep, but sometimes lions claws are very dirty and even shallow wounds can cause nasty infections. Now let us check on the sheep and see what damage and hurt may have been done there."

Riordan quickly found the sheep that one of the lionesses had grabbed by the neck. The young ram lay very still, alive, his eyes wide with fear. "Quickly now, this one may yet be saved. The lion kills by taking the throat and choking its victim to death." Lifting the young rams head gently the Centaur examined the wound. "See here, the windpipe is crushed, he is suffocating. Do you have a small knife? Hand it to me, run down to the stream bank and bring back a hollow reed. No questions, quickly now." When Riordan returned with the reed, the centaur made an incision just below the place where the lion clamped down on its throat. Taking the reed, Jireh inserted it into the incision he made.

Amazed, Riordan asked in a puzzled tone, "The ram can breathe through the reed?"

"We can hope so . . for a while . . and we can hope that just perhaps renewed pressure in the wind pipe will cause the portion that is collapsed to open again. Now let us check on the others."

They found one old ewe with its throat slashed, already growing cold. There were a few others with scratches on their flanks, but they would recover. So for the next few hours they worked together doing what they could for the wounded animals. Riordan observed with amazement the centaur's knowledge of medicine, healing herbs, and of just the animals themselves. He would never have guessed a centaur would know much of anything about sheep. But then again, what did he really know about centaurs, especially Jireh the Shophetim?

After caring for the animals, Riordan went to examine the slain lion that Jireh killed with a sling. The creature's face had been pushed back inside its head, a large rock now in its place. Astonished, he lifted the bloody stone; it had to weigh close to twenty pounds!

He could not even guess at the strength required to hurl such a thing for any distance with a sling. The Irijah chose weapons readily available to them on the mountains where they made their homes. Slinging stones were an obvious choice. Riordan once heard it said that a centaur is able to sling ten to fifteen pound rocks with accuracy for over one hundred yards. Hurled with astounding velocity, whatever the chosen target, it usually got crushed.

Studying the centaur carefully for the first time, Riordan realized just how formidable Jireh would be. Brannan and Brónach were both well over six feet tall, but the tops of their heads would be just over the top of Jireh's front shoulder flank. From there the human portion of his waist began. The fleshly upper body, all knotted with muscle, rose almost four feet above the horse shoulder to the top of the head. Riordan speculated that Jireh must be over nine feet tall. The color of his hair, full beard, and horse portion were a rich chestnut, except for white stockings over the fetlocks. Over the years his hair and beard were slowly filling out with gray, but he still looked pretty spry for someone rumored to be over nine hundred years old. Strapped to his back were two stone hammers, with heads made of super hard black volcanic rock. Each weighed over twenty pounds and were attached to gnarled oak handles a yard long and thicker than a man's fore arm. The hammers could be wielded with ease and great power in each hand. Such weapons would be considered crude compared to the craft of the Dun or Irial, but extremely effective in such powerful hands.

Looking up from the ram he was attending, the centaur saw the boy looking him over. Dark set eyes under heavy brows returned the lad's gaze, and Riordan felt a probing of his heart and spirit. He could not long withstand the gaze before having to look away.

Jireh spoke, and for the first time Riordan took in the resonance of his voice, "The windpipe is opening again, and soon I will be able to close the incision in his throat. This one is very fortunate indeed. You may not think your attack against the lioness did much, but it prevented her from finishing the job. Most likely you saved this ram's life. You might consider this: you have two dead lions here, and their hides are of value. Even if you don't sell them, they make a distinct wrap for sitting around a fire at night. I can tell you this, not many ra`ah's are wrapped in lion's skins, but for you it would be appropriate. Shall I show you how to skin a lion?"

Walking over to the male lion killed by Esh Jireh examined him closely, and called Riordan over, "Come here and look at this lad, I won't diminish Esh's accomplishments, but I want you to see something. Look at the condition of this lion's teeth, and then look at his side, anything jump out at ya?"

Riordan almost asked if Jireh thought him blind, because upon close examination the lion looked half-starved and several of its' teeth were missing, "It's really old I think. Is that why Esh could kill it so easily?"

"Well despite its' age I doubt it was easy. I think at least a few of the missing teeth Esh kicked out, but definitely this great cat is old. Still, killing even an old lion is no small feat. Lions on occasion allow old males like this one to hunt with the females, although they aren't allowed to feed until all the others have eaten their fill. This is done because they can provide the useful service of scaring prey, and getting them to run into an ambush."

The centaur stayed with Riordan for a few days. The lions and the dead ewe were skinned, and their coats preserved. Jireh taught the boy how to track, how to use the sling more effectively, and never seemed to fail to have an answer for any of the boy's pressing questions. At night, under an endless expanse of lights, the centaur taught him how to navigate using the position of the stars as guides. He gave the constellations names, and Riordan looked at the heavenly bodies with new wonder.

In the morning Riordan woke to find Jireh already preparing a fire, and breakfast. "Good Morning, I wondered if you planned to sleep through to the next day."

"If I did, it would be your fault for keeping me up all night gazing at the stars."

The Centaur chuckled at this, but then got serious and looked with his deep set eyes at the boy and again Riordan felt the gaze searching out his spirit and soul.

"Have you wondered why I have watched the sheep with you these past days?"

"Yes, now that you mention it, I have wondered why the Shophetim of our people would take the time to help a ra`ah watch sheep."

"As you say, I am the Shophetim, for all of Jeshurun, I am also the ear for El, I hear His voice. When I hear, I obey. A few weeks ago, the voice of El spoke to my spirit, commanding me to go look for one of the sons of Capall. I knew the purpose of my search, but not who I searched for, only that he would be one of the sons of your people. The exact person, Elohim would have to reveal to me, . . and I would know him when I saw him.

"I journeyed across the plains and felt led to Joktan, and wound up where Korah trained new riders for the cavalry. I went into their camp and saw many fine young men there, none finer than your older brother Torin. When I saw him, I thought to myself, surely this one must be the one Elohim has sent me to find. But Elohim listened to my thoughts, and spoke directly to my mind and spirit."

At that point Riordan interjected, "I sometimes hear a voice like that, a quiet voice . . . usually only during the night watches . . . how did you know it was Elohim speaking, and what did he say?"

The Shophetim's forehead wrinkled up in thought, "How indeed do I know it's His voice, . . in some ways it's in much the same way your sheep know it is your voice when you speak, . . . they know *you*. I know it is Elohim's voice because I know Elohim, I don't know how else to explain it. But as for what did he tell me? Well, in a way I was rebuked. I looked for a man called by Elohim for a purpose, but I wasn't searching using Elohim's eyes. I used only my own. After a gentle rebuke, Elohim instructed me not to look at outward appearance, but rather the heart."

Riordan then piped in, "That's what Brónach told me, about Esh. He looks old on the outside, but it's what's inside that counts."

"Brónach is a wise man, and you have more in common with your old horse than you might guess. But after Korah released the recruits to go into Joktan and blow off a little steam, I felt I should follow. I saw you for the first time when you decided to take the fight to those other boys in town, rather than be bullied. From that moment, something leaped in my Spirit, and I knew you were the one Elohim sent me to find."

Riordan sat there stunned, unsure of how to respond. Was this good, or bad?

"Aren't you curious as to why I was sent to find you? Ah, never mind, I'll just go ahead and tell you. One of the reasons I came is that I have been instructed to show you this."

Jireh pulled a long object wrapped in a cloak, from a pack he kept by the fire. Removal of the cloth revealed a sword. In Jireh's hands it seemed just a short sword, but its actual length proved to be more than half that of a tall man. A bluish blade, almost translucent, that allowed light to pass through, gave the blade an appearance of being cast from precious stones rather than metal. Longer than the width of two hands at the grip, the blade's two sharp edges seemed all the more menacing because they seemed magically formed. A sapphire gleamed from its setting in the pommel, and rubies were placed in the ends of both cross guards.

"This," Jireh's voice whispered as though revealing a mysterious secret, "is the Riail dlí, first wielded by Jephthah the deliverer. Forged by Yahweh Elohim and fused with the Nomos, the very same law and life-force that governs the universe. For centuries have the Shophetim guarded this blade. We've kept it hidden for over a thousand years, not since Jachin, Jephthah's successor has it been wielded. It has been allowed to pass into legend, until the time of our people's greatest need. As I told you I am the ears, the eyes, the voice of El for our people. But not for much longer; the time of the Shophetim is almost past—I am the last. I am old, and soon I must go the way of my Fathers . . . soon the blade must find a new home, as it will be needed once again."

That last statement raised so many questions in Riordan's mind that his thought processes short circuited for a moment. Finally he babbled the only question that the answer wouldn't hold absolute terror for him to hear. "You don't seem old Jireh, and what will Jeshurun do without you to stand in the place of El as judge?"

"Age is something that for all peoples is very relative. A Rapha` who has lived fifty years is already old. At fifty a centaur is still in human terms a toddler. I became Jeshurun's Shophetim when I'd seen five hundred summers. For over four hundred years have I been the ears, eyes and hands of Elohim for our people. To the Ancient of Days I am a blink, but to a young human such as yourself, I am indeed very old. But I cannot allow you to change the subject that easily. It's El's will that the Age of the Shophetim give way to the Age of Kings, with Ruarc as the first king. Ruarc is great, even among the Rapha`, and a very great warrior. But giants spring up quickly even as a flame kindles, they also expire quickly, much too soon to really grow in wisdom. With Ruarc's selection for the throne,

Jeshurun's mightiest warrior became king. But Ruarc cannot rule long. Lacking understanding, he has already made an awful exchange. He traded his reliance on Elohim for self-reliance and a controlling voice of fear. In his heart he knows even his great strength is not sufficient. The love, joy and laughter that once was so much a part of his soul, is now replaced with a gnawing dread.

"The fear that fills his heart has opened his soul to the Rashama, though he doesn't know the identity of the voices to whom he has given his ear. Despite their promises to the contrary, listening to such spirits only brings death and destruction and could very well bring about the destruction of Jeshurun.

"Our people must have a new king, a king who will not depend on his own strength, but the strength of Elohim. In His wisdom, Elohim has chosen to replace the mighty warrior with a ra`ah, a simple shepherd."

Riordan gave the Shophetim a confused look, "If you are making a joke, to be honest, it's not very funny. I am as you say a ra`ah, I am called Mamzer by my own family. Until recently I didn't even have the right to ride a horse, which among the Capall means I barely qualified as a human being. Becoming a household servant would be an upgrade to my status. Could you kindly explain by what miracle I would ever become king?"

Jireh looked gravely at Riordan for a moment and gave a perfectly honest answer, "No . . . no I can't. Now that I've actually said it . . . well it does sound crazy, even to me! But let me say this, it seems impossible because it is not within your power to ever make this happen, This task however is in the hands of the one named Elohim, his very name means mighty covenant, a promise that cannot be broken, to bring his creation and his children into His own image. From the time you were born, He laid a foundation, working a forge to prepare your heart, to make you the man you are called to become. Understand, you always can choose, which means you can reject and resist His hand in your life, but then His destiny of good will also be lost to you."

Years of pain fueled an angry outburst in response, "He's been working in my life? In what way? Was it His will I be born in sin, outside of a marriage covenant? Was Elohim working through my father when he used the lash to tear my flesh? Was He working when my mother abandoned me to be raised by a woman who would hate me, and brothers who would hold for me nothing but contempt? Did He command the people of the village to cut me with their words and names, and with the sneers . . . the whispers? Is that how Elohim works?!"

The centaur reached his massive hand down gently and rested it on the boys shoulder. "No, Elohim is responsible for none of those things. There is an enemy at work in this world that seeks to maim, crush and destroy our spirits and souls. Yet Elohim is a redeemer. That which has been done for hurt and destruction can be turned, and used for good. I am Jireh, named by the One who sees, and I tell you this; He has seen all that has been done, he has seen the cut of the lash, he also sees the wounds . . . though many and deep; He sees the longing of your heart, and he hears your weeping in the night. Suffering is used by our soul's enemy to crush and bring despair. But when a life and heart is yielded to Elohim, that same suffering becomes a forge-tempering strength; it creates a hunger, a yearning for the hand and knowledge that heals.

"Your heart and spirit is broken and crushed, this is evident to all. This has brought an inner weakness and uncertainty; but weakness can be our greatest strength. Come with me a moment and I will show you." Walking among the tall grasses and flowers of the prairie clearly looking for something, Jireh stopped when he spotted a butterfly, with blue wings outlined in black.

"Tell me, who is stronger, you or this butterfly?"

Riordan rolled his eyes as the answer seemed so obvious he found it embarrassing to be even asked. Such a question did not even merit a response.

"I see by the roll of your eyes you think I'm asking a stupid question. All right then O mighty one, I want you to test your strength against this insignificant insect. Catch it and crush it." The boy just looked at the Shophetim as if to ask, "Are you crazy?"

"No I mean it, go on, crush it now."

So Riordan tried to crush the butterfly in his hand. But whenever he made a grab for it, the insect always flew just out of his reach. After several minutes of chasing the creature around the meadow, the centaur called out. "Well come on, crush the thing and be done with it!"

"I can't! He's always just out of my reach!"

"Surely you're not going to be bested by a puny insect!"

"I . . . I just can't catch him! I'd like to see you try!"

Laughing from deep within one of two stomachs, Jireh cracked "Oh no you don't, I'm not the one foolish enough to be trying to catch the thing in the first place!"

"But you told me to!"

With tongue in cheek and a chuckle, Jireh responded, "Oh sure, and if I told ya to jump off a cliff I suppose you'd try that too? C'mon lad, I was just making a point, and I have, so give it up." Riordan stubbornly persisted, partly because he didn't want to admit that he was licked, and partly to prove a point of his own.

"Come on now lad, give it up, and come here." Riordan came back huffing and puffing and dropped in the grass.

"A part of what it means to have wisdom is to know when what we are trying to do isn't working. Physical strength rarely determines the outcome of any contest. The unseen factors are more important, such as skill, heart, and courage. But, in this case you were bested not

183

because of your opponent's strength, but rather the butterfly's ability to harness and use a strength far greater than its own. He rides upon the Ruwach, the breath of God. The eagle also shares this trait, soaring on Elohim's breath to unimaginable heights. If you learn to do the same, the Ruwach will take you to places beyond your wildest dreams.

"And make no mistake, the task to which you are called requires great strength, far more than you possess. You must find the strength that is not like that of Ruarc, or even strength such as mine. You must rely on the Ruwach, the strength and power of Elohim."

The centaur brandished the mythical sword so that its translucent, cobalt blue blade transformed to bright sapphire in the sunlight, "You will begin by yielding your life and learning from the Riail dlí."

"What can I learn from a sword? Does it speak?"

"In many ways yes, yes it does. But here, take the blade." Riordan took the two-handed grip in both hands, and raised the weapon between his eyes and the sun, confirming that indeed the blade was transparent.

Laughing the ra`ah remarked, "It feels almost like a toy, there's no weight to it at all!"

"I simply cannot believe you just called the mightiest talisman of our people a play-thing. I will try hard to forget you ever said such a thing." Dropping his stern manner, the seer pronounced his judgment, "As punishment for such a bone-headed statement *you* have to make supper. Take the blade and slay one of your sheep."

Fascinated by the beauty of the sword, Riordan responded without taking his eyes and focus off the blade, "Jireh, my father would *kill* me, if I killed a sheep without his consent. We already lost . . ."

"Trust me boy, strike that lamb over there, with a mighty swing, if you strike true the creature won't feel a thing."

"But Jireh,..."

"Do it, now, and strike with all your might!"

Riordan approached the lamb as it looked up at him

with somber innocent eyes. The sheep only knew him as their protector, he knew every one by name, every one of them knew his voice. The ra`ah looked back to the Shophetim and pleaded, "I can't."

Understanding his hesitation Jireh urged him to strike, "Lad, if you hesitate or don't hit a vital area with the power to kill quickly, the creature will suffer. Strike hard, and strike true."

Riordan raised the blade and closed his eyes. Unable to watch, he swung the sword with all of his might as instructed. The blade struck the lamb passing through so easily that the momentum carried him completely around, spinning him hard to the ground. Jireh let out a long booming laugh, and held his sides to keep them from splitting. Still chuckling a few moments later when Riordan picked himself up, the centaur asked "Well, how long before supper is ready?"

To Riordan's utter astonishment, when he looked at the lamb before him, it remained completely untouched.

"You seem to have missed boy, you'd best try again."

So Riordan drew back again for a mighty swing, and this time he did not close his eyes. Once again he swung with all of his might and watched the blade pass through the lamb's neck. Once again the blade passed through so easily that his momentum carried him around and despite being more prepared, he still tumbled into the tall grass.

Still laughing and now forced to wipe tears of merriment from his eyes, Jireh reached down and roughly pulled the boy up by his tunic. Riordan looked at the lamb, and once more it showed no signs of being struck with the blade.

"Jireh, I don't understand, I know I hit 'im that time, I watched the blade pass . . "

Composing himself Jireh explained, "Son, I hope you don't think this a cruel joke, but sometimes the burnt hand teaches best. The Riail dlí is a two-edged sword, its blade is forged from the same laws that bind all creation. Precepts from the heart of El our God, those laws are meant for judgment, but also for healing and life. Therefore the first edge cuts, but the second edge heals."

Riordan looked at the blade with renewed awe. "A sword that heals the wounds it inflicts." For several moments the boy just looked at the weapon in wonder. Then a new thought occurred to him, prompting an obvious question. "But what good is a sword that heals as it cuts? How would I be able to fight with this?"

The brows of the Shophetim raised in astonishment at the intelligence and thoughtfulness of the question. "You must understand that Elohim formed the Universe from a foundation of law. Those laws govern and flow through all of creation, and they determine everything from the beating of your heart, to the rising of the sun, even the celestial dance of the stars. The Riail dlí is forged not with human hands, nor is the blade a product of any craft known to the children of the Creator. It is formed from the Nomos itself, infused with law, the same substance from which Elohim formed all of creation. Nomos law brings judgment and this is the sharpest blade this world has ever known. But the purpose of the law ultimately is to heal and restore. It heals because it must, it cannot violate its own nature.

"However, the purpose of the law is to also discern the intent and motives of the heart. This lamb is innocent of malice. The law discerns this and therefore heals as it cuts. But if the blade strikes a creature of evil intent, its nature is also discerned, and for those not judged innocent, there can be no healing. The blade discerns evil, dispassionately judges it, and often brings death. The essence and foundation of law is truth, and in the Law there is discernment, but never mercy. For this reason the bearer must also use discernment as to the use of the Riail dlí. It must never be wielded lightly.

"But as for the question of whether the sword can be

186

a weapon? Understand this–the cutting edge is truth.
There is no shield or armor that can resist it. Therefore
it is a weapon against which there is no defense.
However, as a weapon the Riail dlí is limited. As you
have seen, it is a blade that cannot be used against the
innocent."

"Why would anyone ever use a sword against the
innocent?"

"Now my friend, you are thinking like one called to
be a servant of the true King. Why indeed?"

"Jireh, why are you giving this blade to me?"

Riordan popped the question in so quickly it seemed
to catch the seer by surprise (something not easily
done). He delayed the response as he considered the
enormity of the answer.

"A few years ago, I offered the blade to Ruarc, at his
coronation, to help him rule. He failed to recognize its
value, and therefore chose other weapons. I am Jireh,
the Shophetim of Jeshurun, and the power to see has
been given to me . . . and I see that Ruarc's choices will
soon bring his end. For good or ill, he is king, and
consequently his end will also be the fall of many and of
much that is good, endangering even our Nation. This
blade, if you choose to accept all that it represents, will
need to be wielded by one who recognizes its value and
will use it for the healing and restoration of Jeshurun.

"Ruarc, the name means sudden squall, and I'm
afraid his reign will pass just as quickly. Another storm
is coming. When it arrives, you must be ready to stand
in the gap, and prevent the destruction of our people.
But it is NOT for you to bring down Ruarc yourself.
The king resists Elohim's hand, and so His purpose is
not being realized in his life, but the calling and
anointing of Elohim is never retracted; such gifts are
without repentance. If by your own hand you strike
Ruarc, it will be the same as striking Elohim Himself;
something that if you do it, will only bring death and
destruction to yourself and your whole house."

The two watched the sheep now in silence for several minutes. Riordan obviously needed to process a great deal, and the wheels of his mind were spinning crazily. Finally he asked, "When will these things you speak of concerning the king, when will they take place?"

"Many of the preceding events are already in motion. For just a few more days will you remain a simple ra`ah. Although, even in this do I see the hand of Elohim, for I have seen a vision of Jeshurun scattered on the hills. They were very much like sheep without a ra`ah. When Ruarc falls, a shepherd I think is just what our people will need.

"But now, I must ask you, will you indeed accept this task? This commission and call of Elohim does not leave you without choice. You may refuse, even deny it. If so, another will be raised up, and you may walk in your will as your own master. If you accept this task, it will require of you submission to the hand and will of Elohim. Acceptance will mean hardship and danger. In time, Ruarc himself may very well try to kill you, and you will live much of your life on the run. You shall know hunger, exposure, thirst, heartbreak and pain. Many of those you will be called to aide will return your charity with hatred and contempt."

Jireh paused allowing the truth of his words to sink in. "I do not want you to think you are invited to walk a pleasant, flower-strewn path. You must count the cost, and the cost is high, your very life." The centaur turned his gaze toward the sun now climbing higher on the horizon.

"The cost is high, but so is the joy. The road you are asked to walk is hard. But let me ask you, what is more important, how easy the road or its destination? The easiest road in the world is a waste if it does not take you to a place you want to go.

Riordan stood and turned with his face to the

West. At the horizon he could barely see the snow caps of the mountains.

"All of my life I have longed to journey the miles to those mountains that are so close, yet they might as well have been a million miles. Not many days ago I finally made the trip. What I found there exceeded all my dreams, but the beauty of the place only made my heart long for something more."

The boy turned again to face the centaur, "If I take this call from Elohim, will I–this time, find what I've been searching for?"

The Centaur paused as he considered his response. "I think in the end all men find what they are looking for. The tragedy of most people's lives is that they search for nothing, or for so very little and so always find it. Its not that they want too much, its that they want far too little. My heart tells me however, if you take the path before you–while it may break your heart– in the end you will find what you seek. All men do."

Riordan expressed his last and hope and concern, "Will you walk with me, or will I remain alone?"

Jireh smiled, "Our paths will go together for a while. But when I am no longer able to be there, when darkness seems impossible to overcome, you may not be able to see your help–do not be afraid–He who is your help can see you."

Jireh then removed from a pouch at his waist a small flask of oil; he walked to Riordan and poured the oil on his head. "This oil represents the anointing of Elohim that will be on your life, and when the consequences of the choices of Ruarc are complete, it is an anointing on your life as king of all our peoples." With that the Shophetim of Jeshurun laid his massive hands on the boy's head, and began to silently pray. After a moment he pronounced a blessing.

"In His heart Yahweh Yireh, the One who sees the wounds, many and deep; He who sees your pain, also sees your healing, but not today. The wounds, the weakness, the brokenness, the pain, these will keep you on the search for your greatest strength. But just as Brónach has adopted you and redeemed you from shame, hear now the voice of the Adonai from His Shophetim, Today I call you my son, today I have adopted you, no longer will you be called Mamzer, forsaken, rejected. But the name of Ra`ah will forever be yours, though it's meaning I will change. A ra`ah you shall always remain, for you have been called to be a shepherd to my people Jeshurun."

Thirteen

"Without vision, the people perish."

~Proverbs

Mereah walked through the various camps behind the defensive lines. Fear covered the camp with a death shroud. In many ways, that the army survived the day at all seemed almost a miracle. But if the men in the camp experienced or witnessed any type of miracle, it didn't seem to impact their morale. In horror they all watched as the tanniyn dismembered and devoured the sons of Korah. In the trenches the soldiers were able to shield their eyes, but covering their ears could not shut out the Anak's laughter.

Within two hours of the retreat, the Dun were already constructing defensive trench works. A series of pits and booby traps were made ready for the next assault, and even now they worked to improve the defenses. Mereah admired their efficiency, but the preparations were almost mechanical, lifelessly performed by repetition of habit. The case could easily be made that this gave tribute to the quality of their training, but not to their present state of morale or courage. Even now an oppressive power or spirit seemed to sap everyone's courage and strength clear away.

The Dagon enjoyed such a tremendous numerical advantage that fresh soldiers could be brought in for the fight at night as well as the day. They'd taken advantage of this fact now for weeks, and so were able to keep tremendous pressure on Jeshurun's soldiers, who slept most nights in the trenches and rarely received more than a few moments rest. He knew all the men were exhausted, and they say that fatigue makes cowards of us all. But what the Rapha` prince sensed this night was a fear born out of more than exhaustion . . . the Jeshurun army showed all the signs of a people who'd lost hope. As they were preparing the trenches Mereah read despair in their faces, and the expectation that they were really digging their own graves.

Although the enemy inexplicably allowed their retreat through the narrows and into the last of the keys, somehow the assault continued. An oppressive presence–a malicious spirit–hung in the air as an invisible mist. Mereah nervously cast a glance towards his father's pavilion to see the strange red glow still casting shadows from under the flap.

But no attacks were forthcoming this night, and almost all the line troops were too tired to leave the trenches, so once again they just collapsed from exhaustion and tried to sleep fitfully in their holes.

Desperate to understand the day's events, he tried to find something, anything positive that he could take away from the day's combat with the Anak. The Jeshurun ranks contained Rapha`, Dun, Irial, Capall cavalry, a dozen Irijah, all with their own strengths, all mighty men. Yet against the powers used against them today, no one possessed the ability to respond.

In the old stories, Elohim always sent a deliverer, a

Shophetim empowered by the Ruwach, the very breath of God. Spiritual power is what would be needed to combat the powers of the Anak. If only Jireh were here! But the seer was absent, and somehow, so to his father Ruarc. "That only leaves me." The thought frightened the young Rapha` to death. He didn't feel any power, only a raging sense of despair and powerlessness.

With a sense of desperation, Mereah turned to the last course of action left to him–he started to pray. "Ah, Elohim, I know I'm not telling you anything you don't already know, and I'm ashamed to say I'm only turning to you as a last resort, but things went pretty badly today. Your people . . . we don't have the power to fight this Anak . . . perhaps if our Shophetim were here, or . . my . ." Mereah couldn't finish his thought, so he moved on. "I don't know how to fight this battle . . . but if we don't find a weapon, or some way to respond, even before the rising sun, your people will be finished . . . overrun."

Sitting in silence, waiting for he knew not what, a sign perhaps, a voice, something to tell him the El, the Mighty Power of his people heard his petition. Several minutes that felt like hours later, he despaired and lost hope that there would be any response. He didn't have a roof over his head, but if there were, the giant seemed sure his request had bounced off.

His mind replayed the day's events. No matter the starting point, he kept returning to the last of the combat, when the sons of Korah faced the Anak. Suddenly it occurred to him maybe fear itself could be a device, a weapon of the enemy. Then it hit him, and a light from some where in his spirit came on; the older son of Korah, wounded, helpless, laying in the dust—he wasn't afraid.

Mereah hoped to pass through the lines undetected, but now he felt the need for self-chastisement, "What in Tebel were ya thinkin? You do realize yer a giant and not a sneak-thief?" The muttering started when the young Rapha` realized he'd already been spotted by the Watch and his presence reported to Lithos.

While he tracked the approach of the Dun Captain his mind scrambled for something to say, . . something that didn't make it sound like he'd completely lost his mind.

Lithos stood close to five feet high, rather lofty for a son of Dun. But he seemed almost as broad of shoulder as he was tall. Mereah thought if it were possible to condense a powerful giant into a five-foot frame, Lithos would be the result. Armed with every imaginable weapon hanging from utility belts strapped across his back, chest and waist, Mereah knew the weight of all the entire arsenal was nothing to the Dun warrior. Time and again he proved himself capable of marching for days with packs seemingly larger than himself. He seemed the proverbial ant walking off with the picnic melon. Try to take the melon from this ant however, and he became a wounded badger.

When within range of a whisper, the Dun Captain asked dryly, "Out for a stroll?"

"Lithos my friend, say nothing, nor try to hinder me, but I am going to the enemy's camp."

"Hmmm, and what do you think the king would say to me afterwards when he finds out I watched his only son and heir walk right down to the Dagon camp to be killed? I have lived too long and survived too much to end my life roasting on a spit or worse. And make no mistake, your father Ruarc would have me roasted alive."

"I hear you friend, but unless I tell the king myself, he will never know you failed to hinder me, but regardless, I must pass."

Lithos stood in a trench, so it came as no surprise that the giant's face remained several feet above his own, even though Mereah crouched down about as low as a son of Flann can get. A late night shouting match would be the last thing the Dun Captain wanted right now, especially concerning a subject matter sure to anger the king. He'd experienced the Rapha` Prince's impetuous nature before, but it was late at night, and he felt dead tired. "Don't make me come up there." he hissed. Looking up into his friend's face, he recognized the stubborn look in his eye. "Yep, he's going to make me go up there."

Resigned to the fact it would be up to him to stop this foolishness, Lithos started to climb out of the trench.

Recognizing the Dun Captain to be every bit as stubborn and determined as himself, Mereah hissed in whispers revealing his intent. "My friend, listen to me, we are at a crossroads for this fight, our army, our people, and this battle. Tomorrow, if we fail, we are lost, . . this war–our people and nation overrun. I don't know why the enemy has called off the attack this night, but I know that our forces are completely demoralized. Only a bold stroke will rally their hearts and give them back their courage."

"So, this bold stroke is for you to walk down to the enemy camp and assail it single-handedly?"

Here Mereah got a little sheepish, and turned away from Lithos' piercing gaze, "Well no . . ."

"Well that's good because if I thought my Prince was going to attempt something so foolhardy I'd . . ."

"I'm going to go down and sing to them."

Temporarily forgetting the need to keep the noise level down, the Dun Commander shouted, "You're going to do what??"

"Lithos, you saw what happened today, if the Anak rides out to meet us again in the morning, we are finished. Yet at the close of the day, I saw the first real victory over the Anak, from the sons of Korah."

"Victory? You call being torn to pieces victory?"

"I did not say the Anak is vanquished, but the son of Korah purchased an important victory nonetheless. Did you not feel the power when he sang? His victory? To meet fear and despair with a song. The Anak's attacks were meant to break much more than bone, they were designed to crush spirits, and so allow desperation to fester and grow. I have realized that fear, . . despair, these are our enemy's chief weapons. That is why the Anak became so enraged by the son of Korah's song . . . he wasn't afraid! He looked malice in the face and sang of a power that casts out fear. In the morning, when the assault is renewed, unless we can find just such victory, . . victory over the despair and fear that is filling their hearts, our people will once again be overrun. But this time, the Capall are too decimated to strike a counter blow with the cavalry, and so there will be nothing to hold the enemy back for another retreat. The army will be destroyed, and the Dagon will march freely across the plains, all the way to Bethel."

"My Prince, you are going to your death."

"I am going to show my people they can find courage to overcome despair. If I do not, who will?"

Lithos kept the thought "Certainly NOT your father" to himself. What he said was, "Well, I can't allow you to walk down there alone to your death."

"Please don't try to stop me, I would not want to raise my hand against a friend."

The Dun warrior reached to his waist and pulled a battle axe from his belt, and for just a brief sickening moment Mereah thought their dispute would come to blows, but the Weapon's Master looked up at his prince and grinned, "Who said anything about stopping you? I said I can't let you walk down there alone, so I am coming with you."

"Lithos, this is my fool's errand, and I can't ask anyone else to throw their life away."

The Dun chieftain shook his axe as an extension of his index finger as though scolding an errant soldier,

"You didn't ask me to, but you are right, I have been puzzling things myself, through much of the night. The Dun in my command started quickly on defenses, yet I could see in their hearts the fear that it is all for naught. Listen, can you hear anything in the camps but silence? It has been that way all night; no laughter from a bold jest, no voices lifted in song, not even from the Irial. The laughter and joking from the Dagon camp, however, even from across the canyon reaches my ears. It is the sound of soldiers confident in tomorrow's outcome. If something isn't done to change this, the battle is lost, and we all will be dead. So, if it is just as well with you, since we'll all likely die anyway, I might as well die doing something insane." The Dun Chieftain tightened the chin strap on his gleaming helmet. "After you, my Prince?"

The moon, covered with a shroud, left the darkest of nights for the unlikely pair's stroll. Creeping down to just outside the enemy's camp, they sat down to wait for the dawn to begin their serenade.

Fourteen

Riordan woke to the sun's light painting the eastern clouds various shades of peach and gold. Jireh stood nearby, facing the coming sun. Riordan gazed at the Shophetim's back and wondered if the centaur slept standing up, since he never seemed to lay down.

Jireh's deep resonate voice broke the silence, "There is much yet I must teach you concerning the Riail dlí. Start on some breakfast, and while you are preparing I will give you further instructions."

The boy tossed aside the blankets he used to ward against the night chill. After stretching out morning stiffness, he moved over to the stone pit to rekindle coals from the previous night's fire. The prairie did have a few small groves of trees, especially by the quiet stream that flowed nearby. Still, with wood so scarce the fire needed to be supplemented with dried sheep chips. As the ra`ah attempted to breath life back into the gray coals, Jireh continued.

"The blade is sharpened with truth, and as you have seen, the edge will cut through anything, but the innocent and blameless it heals as it cuts. Other powers also inhabit the blade, and you should become aware of them."

"What other power? Do you mean magic?"

"I mean nothing of the kind, at least not in the way many understand the term! Magic is a tool of our enemies such as the Dagon. By invoking rituals and incantations, sorcerers such as the Anakim attempt to make spiritual powers do their bidding.

"You are not called to be a wizard, but a Ro'eh, a prophet king. Understand this: a Ro'eh is much different than a sorcerer of dark arts. You must never think there is anything you can do to force Yahweh Elohim to do *your* commands. Never! A Ro'eh listens, discerns, hears, and then obeys. Instead of controlling spiritual powers, the Ro'eh seeks to be controlled by THE highest spiritual power. Do you understand this difference?"

Jireh's passion on the subject overwhelmed Riordan so he didn't reply, but since Jireh seldom paused long enough for the boy to respond this hardly seemed noticeable. "A Ro'eh does not employ magic, they are however equipped with powers and gifts to be used for El's purpose, working within His laws."

Riordan looked up from some flour cakes about to be baked on hot stones, along with some side meat of lamb to make a sandwich. "What is a Ro'eh, and what kind of powers and gifts are you talking about?"

"A Ro'eh is one who does three very important things, they hear, they see, and they obey. I am a Ro'eh. Ruarc the king once was actually a Ro'eh, but now instead of obedience, he walks in folly. This is why at times he becomes so enraged, and at other times despondent. Nothing grips the heart with despair as much as having been one who once could see, but now is blind; being one who once could hear, but now is deaf. Carrying the Riail dlí, you too will become a Ro'eh. Mourn Ruarc, but take warning; do not repeat his folly.

"The powers and gifts I speak of all flow from the gifts that were imparted by Elohim at the beginning of creation. Seven children he created, all dissimilar, with different but complementing strengths. Each of the seven were given a specific portion of creation that would be their area of dominion and stewardship."

Riordan excitedly interrupted, "I have heard this legend! That is when Capall our first father was given the gift of the horse!"

Jireh's long eyebrows lifted, and his deep dark eyes pierced Riordan with a glare, "Legend? And what do you mean by that?"

Riordan now responded with all the confidence of one dancing on what he knew to be thin ice, "Well, I mean a myth, an ancient tale that . . ."

Jireh's brows furrowed deeper and higher, "A myth?" Riordan could now feel the ice breaking beneath him. "If by myth you mean a story that explains the unexplainable, but everyone knows has no basis in fact, then the story of Capall receiving the horse as a gift is not a myth! The man in the moon, that is a myth in that sense, but I am not talking about any myth with that understanding. Many of our people thought the Anakim and the tanniyn were also *myths*. Yet in this last invasion of the Dagon, who should be leading their armies but an Anak, riding a dragon. Not a winged one, not breathing flame just yet, but obviously the legend has at least some roots in fact. Over time, much knowledge, details, understanding, and some facts are lost. What is left we call myth. The myth I will tell you is not some fantastic story everyone knows to be hogwash, but truth that is condensed over time. Many details are lost perhaps, but the essential truth remains, even as a seed grain after the stalk is long gone."

"I'm sorry Jireh, I didn't mean to upset you."

"It's alright boy, you only repeat what you have been taught. My task is to teach you better. But don't you dare dismiss what I tell you as the fairy tale type of myth or legend. Time has a way of clouding the extraordinary out of the realm of the feasible and possible. This is especially true of men and giants whose span of years is so few. A span of seventy years seems very long for a man–a lifetime. When a centaur reaches seventy the Irijah call it puberty. The area of my people's dominion is the mountain realms, and like the mountains, our lives and memories endure.

"Capall experienced incredible joys from the hands of Elohim. These stories he passed to his children, who in turn passed them on to their sons and daughters. A few hundred years seems an eternity to a people so short-lived, and beyond their understanding. If left outside of human experience, the incredible deeds of Elohim become myth and legend. People whose lives are but a blink are left to wonder, did El really do these things?

"I am a centaur. Much of what has passed into legend for man I have beheld with my own eyes. For you the fable must become reality. And the only way for this to happen is for the myths and legends to become confirmed in the experience of your life. Are you ready for Elohim to work in you, as he worked in your ancient father Capall?"

Riordan looked Jireh in the eye, and he knew he could not lie, so he searched his heart to know the truth of how he should respond. All of his life, the works of El were something their God did a long time ago. The possibility that he might see the mighty power at work in his life, and the lives of his people . . sent a thrill through the boy's spirit. After a few moments, he answered, "I never dreamed that Elohim would work through me, even as Jephthah and Jachin in days of old, but I would welcome the chance."

"Then learn from the Nomos law. Be filled with the Ruwach breath of God and be prepared for the myths and legends to become a part of your living experience and life."

Not sure even now if he'd been given a clear answer, Riordan asked one more time, "I understand not using magic, but what are these gifts you spoke of Jireh, and can I learn their use?"

Jireh appeared to be pleased by the question; the inquiry proved the boy to be actually paying attention. He only wished he could give him a better answer. "I don't know, lad, not completely. When the peoples separated themselves from Elohim's control, they also separated themselves from what He called them to be. So much good . . never realized. So much knowledge . . never comprehended. So much of what they actually did know–now forever lost."

"My father walked with Jephthah when the peoples of Jeshurun were liberated. He also knew Jachin, his successor and the first Shophetim. My father told me that one of the workings of the Riail dlí would be that as the tribes submitted to the authority of the wielder, their Gifts of Dominion would gradually be restored. I wish I could be of more help on that score lad, but the blade hasn't been used for well over a thousand years, long before I was even born. The Shophetim have merely been caretakers until such time as instructed by Elohim. So we have waited, watching for the one who shall once again wield it.

"But remember this, all that has happened in this world has happened within the parameters of the Nomos Law. Nothing is forgotten, all can be, and will be revealed. The Riail dlí is forged and infused with Yahweh's law. The one who wields the blade–once attuned to the Nomos–scenes from the past and visions of the future will become known to him. But only in the stillness and peace of your heart can you hear the voice of the one whose heart outpouring established the governance of the earth, moon and stars.

The unlikely pair sat in silence for a few moments; Jireh wondering if he dare say more, Riordan trying to process all that he had heard. At last the centaur broke silence for one more question, "You haven't by chance noted anything different in your ability to communicate your wishes to Esh–since you have received the Riail dlí I mean?"

Riordan's blank stare seemed to ask, "What are you talking about?"

"No?" I thought you might have noticed something different. One of the gifts given to the sons of Capall was a mental, an almost spiritual connection with the horse of their bond. At least the surviving histories from the First Age indicate this. No matter. Time will reveal much and make many things clear. Come now, I have talked long and given you a lot to digest. Far too much thinking before breakfast on an empty stomach."

Fifteen

"A dreamer is one who can only find his way by moonlight, and his punishment is that he sees the dawn before the rest of the world."

~Oscar Wilde

Mereah and Lithos sat just outside the enemy camp. The sun would be up soon. Having spent so many hours in the night watches, neither one needed a cock crow to know the hour. The Dagon outer watch were gathered by a blazing fire turning flesh on a spit, all the while laughing and jesting–sometimes arguing in their own dark tongue. The Rapha` Prince and Dun Captain both recognized the smell of the roasting flesh as being that of horse. Mereah thanked the Mighty Power that one of the sons of Capall were not present; he doubted they would be able to contain their outrage.

They decided to wait until just before dawn to carry out their fool's plan and begin to serenade the enemy. Using cover of darkness, the unlikely pair managed to simply stroll down to within a stone's throw of the enemy watch fires and sat down.

They hoped the dawn's light would strengthen

them, and prove a time when the Anak's dominion over his forces were perhaps relaxed. Their presence never suspected by an enemy who thought all of Jeshurun's Army lay up in their holes licking their wounds, and likely trembling in fear.

Mereah, as best as he could understand their crude language, gathered that a general expectation seemed to be that when the Dagon next attacked, they would have to avoid being contaminated by the Jeshurun forces wetting themselves. This was followed by a lot of laughter and jeering.

Looking at the gray on the horizon, Mereah whispered, "Time to begin my friend. Lithos, I am about to reveal myself. I think it may be better if for a little longer you remained hidden. This will be the sign that Lord of Hosts will be with us: after I begin singing, if the enemy invites me to go down to their camp and sing another song, then we will know they are given into our hand." By not waiting for a response from Lithos, he missed the rolling eyes commentary about the foolhardiness of what they were about to do. The Rapha` Prince stood and strode forward a few paces to begin the serenade.

Starting in a low base originating deep in his diaphragm, his voice then resonated in the young Rapha's massive chest. Mereah chose fittingly to sing a song celebrating a great victory from the days of Jephthah the deliverer.

I will sing unto Yahweh,
His name is highly exalted!
Yahweh is my strength and song.
Today He will be my salvation.

Hear me O Jeshurun
Yahweh is our El, Mighty is His name.

He casts my foes away
Into the depths of the sea
All those who trouble my people
They will not be seen again
Jeshurun remember
Yahweh is our El, Mighty is His name.

~The Five Books of Law

As he sang, he stood and his form became visible to the Dagon Watch. The enemy camp started laughing, "What's this?" A Jeshurun dog drawn to the smell of fresh meat? Another voice chimed in "Well what do ya know, the dog wants to sing for his meal! Come and join us, we have ways to make a man or giant really sing!"

Mereah took just a second to look back at Lithos and flash him a wink and a grin. His singing continued as he moved forward to accept the Dagon invitation, his steps dogged by a chorus of jeers and laughter. As he drew near their watch and cooking fire, the Rapha` wore a big ol' grin on his face and casually tossed something into their fire. This was done so subtly that it almost went unnoticed. Despite the fire's heat a sudden chill came over them all when they realized a giant had indeed come down, and at their invitation! Jeers and taunts stopped. Eyes doubled in size. Taunting what they assumed to be a demoralized, defeated foe seemed a great jest, but who could have guessed the gigantic fool would actually answer the call?

No one moved, which proved to be a fatal mistake. Had they reacted immediately, they might have escaped. They delayed a few precious seconds to long, shocked by Mereah's bold response to their challenge. As the watch fire burned brighter, and hotter, the implications jolted them (albeit too late) out of their stupor. As if they needed another clue that something bad was about to happen, the fool of a giant suddenly dropped to the ground and started rolling away. As they reacted by jumping up and scrambling to get away from the fire, it exploded. The horse carcass they were roasting became consumed along with most of the Dagon within a few yards of the fire pit. Only a troll walked out of the inferno alive. He took a few frantic seconds to locate Mereah and then charged. In absolute rage, heedless that his course garments were ablaze, the troll came on swinging an iron studded cudgel.

Mereah pulled a javelin from a quiver strapped behind the cloak on his back. A mighty almost point-blank throw drove the short spear through the troll's throat, silencing his screams of pain and rage. With all that uproar, the entire Dagon camp quickly became aroused. Soon he would be facing enemies almost without number.

The young Rapha` took off a forty pound iron ball attached to a twenty foot chain, from an equipment belt around his waist. Starting with a few feet of chain, he began swinging the ball in a circle around his body, letting out a few more feet with each revolution. When the first attack wave of Dagon soldiers arrived, the giant let the chain out to full length, changing the height of the ball's orbit from waist high to just over two feet above the ground. Ten Dagon unwittingly ran into the ball chain's kill zone around the Rapha` and were instantly cut down. Then several more cautiously entered the deadly ring. Countering their efforts to dodge the lethal ball, Mereah deftly changed the pitch and height of his swing. The Dagon who entered the killing radius were inflicted with snapped limbs, broken necks and crushed skulls.

Finally a second rock troll came forward. Ducking under the swinging ball, the troll thrust a cudgel up to catch in the chain. To not have the cudgel ripped from his hands would take strength, to stop the chain's orbital path would require incredible power. Watching the ball entangle around the troll's cudgel, Mereah knew his enemy's might. Rather than further test the monster's potency, he let go of his end of the chain, pulled another javelin, and threw it at his enemy. The great creature threw up its arm to block the throw, and the spear thrust all the way through its forearm. Bellowing with rage, the troll snapped the end of the spear off, threw it back at Mereah, then charged. Mereah hastily pulled his sword, but realized he wouldn't be ready in time to meet the attack. As it turned out, his growing panic proved unnecessary; the troll fell dead almost landing at his feet, an arrow sticking out its eye.

Lithos casually notched another arrow as he walked forward to join his friend. "I decided you'd had your fun, and it looked like a good time to enter the fray."

"My Thanks, Lithos, and my apologies for indulging in all the 'fun' and leaving you out. But I believe that Troll doesn't appreciate your interference."

The Dun Captain fired his arrow at the next wave of the enemy. "Well the creature can lodge a formal protest if it wants, but my buttin' in t'wer for its own good Mereah. I believe its pain to be largely due to your singing. I merely ended its misery."

The Rapha' let out a long, hearty laugh, "If my singing causes the Dagon such pain, my friend I intend to give them more than they can stomach, or perhaps I should say, stand to hear." And with that, Mereah started back with his singing, while the Dun warrior dropped his bow, pulled an axe, and joined him in song.

So it came to pass, Mereah, with sword and shield, and Lithos, battle axe in one hand, war hammer in the other, walked down to meet the next wave of the enemy and so walked into legend. The Dagon in their wildest dreams would not have foreseen an attack this crazy, or one of such fury.

Lithos, in stature not much higher than Mereah's knees, still proved to be extremely formidable: compact

. . indestructible, like an armored snapping turtle armed to the teeth. He also possessed an unmatched understanding of armed combat. Mereah remembered a young giant in camp that once thought he would make sport of the Dun Weapon's Master. The youngster quickly learned a lesson concerning leverage, as his legs were taken out from under him. Before he could recover, Lithos plopped down on his chest and put a blade tight to his throat. The now older and wiser giant still gives the diminutive warrior a wide berth while passing him in camp.

Jeshurun's crown prince observed that many of the Dagon were learning the same lesson. Seeking to avoid combat with a Rapha`, dozens rushed to dispatch Lithos. Only after several lay dead or dying with severed limbs and crushed helms did they learn how deadly the Dun warrior could be with axe and hammer. Both weapons would be heavy to wield with two hands, but Lithos handled each tirelessly, and with incredible power.

The Dagon did well to avoid Mereah however, the Rapha` Prince was one of the few giants to carry a sword. A bronze blade longer than a man, crafted by the Dun, it brought death to all it reached, and when wielded by the young giant the reach was long.

His singing however proved the most potent weapon of all. As Mereah sang, the light of courage illumined his countenance. What's more, his face and eyes revealed absolute mind-boggling peace, despite the odds. Nothing strikes more terror in the heart than an opponent who is completely unafraid. Either they have nothing to fear, or nothing to lose. Whichever is true, it's bad news for their adversaries. When both are true however, look-out, there isn't a deadlier combination. For the first time a crack rapidly spread through the impenetrable wall of the invader's confidence.

The Dagon camp hadn't set up any defenses. No need. They were the aggressors. The enemy they knew to be defeated, crushed, completely demoralized. No attack from the Jeshurun forces would be coming, or expected.

The Anak, deep in the center of the Dagon camp, sheltered in a black tent, slept while recovering from his exertions the day before. His enemies were all but defeated, of this he felt sure. He could sense their spirits completely broken, their hope crushed.

However, animating the dead, the calling of carrion birds, conjuring the wind elemental and fire balls, the magic's all cost something. The Rashama never give anything away. All the powers he wielded came at a steep price, and such masters never fail to collect.

The spell cast to defend against the sons of Korah proved to be the last straw. Changing the structure of the sand underneath their great charger's feet pushed the Anak beyond all limits. Let the enemy hide in their holes for a day longer. When recovered, he intended to finish the task before him. In order to rest however, he could no longer maintain the dominion spell over his forces. It would not be needed. The utterly demoralized Jeshurun army, lacked the spirit needed to mount a counterattack.

In his fitful sleep, the Anak dreamed he heard the shouts, screams, and the clashing of blades on shields, sounding almost as if battle were joined. Knowing this to be impossible he continued to sleep, albeit fitfully, disturbed by a terrible nightmare. Once again he heard the voice of the horse soldier singing . . but no, the voice wasn't quite right, it seemed deeper somehow . . .

At the head of the valley, Dun sentries listened to the clash of arms. Whispers were that the king's son Mereah, along with the Dun Captain Lithos dared to actually go down to the enemy lines, but no one knew their purpose. Now the echoes of battle were unmistakable. Considering the insanity of the deed (brave or not), the soldiers kept expecting the clash of arms to end at any minute, and be replaced with shouts of gleeful triumph from the enemy. And yet, more than twenty minutes later, they still heard the ringing of sword and hammer falling on helm and shield–followed by the anguished cries from the wounded or dying. Rather than triumphant celebrations from the enemy, those with the sharpest ears swore they could hear a deep voice, a glad voice . . . singing.

Nahor, the Watch Sergeant finally called one of the Irial to be a runner. "Now lad, listen to me, I want you to be careful, but I must know what is taking place down by the Dagon camp. Look for Captain Lithos, and Prince Mereah. Find out what is happening, and report back to me, double quick. Can you do that?"

Primarily used as a message runner, this would be the closest the young-un ever came to the enemy. A grin splitting his face from ear to ear, the young Irial answered by nodding and turning to run. Watching the youngster leaping over defensive works, as he flew down the stony valley, Nahor shook his head and wondered if he'd ever been that eager.

Turning to a Dun infantryman the watch sergeant gave another order. "Tell the lads to get their weapons, and send a message to the Irial. We may need some archers."

"What about the king? Shouldn't he be informed? His son is down in the midst of the battle."

"Aye, but the king is in a fey mood, and likely as not will do nothing. Perhaps we can save the prince and the captain if they're still alive, but only if we act without delay. Now go! Hurry!"

A few moments later, the sergeant watched as the young Irial messenger returned, eagerly running back up the canyon with his report. In the short time it took the runner to reach the enemy camp and come back, a couple hundred Dun infantry were already armed, along with close to a hundred Irial archers. The few centaurs left in the army also arrived and were champing at the bit to join the fight. Also, several of the Capall Cavalry were drawing close to the lines, eager to avenge the loss of their valiant captains from the day before.

The Irial Messenger leaped over the trench works and raced up to Nahor, reporting excitedly, "Captain Lithos and Prince Mereah have brought a great slaughter to the Dagon, and they fight still. They stand now back to back surrounded by the enemy, but also by heaps of the slain. They are singing, even as they fight!"

Nahor turned to face the troops to ask "Shall we join 'em boys?" The words never really got out of his mouth, as he turned, the centaurs were already charging past and the infantry was on its way. Watching his formally demoralized troops now eagerly charge down the valley slope, the sergeant grinned, shrugged his shoulders, tightened the strap on his helmet, and unsheathed his axe as he too headed down the mountain.

Ruarc the king emerged from his tent for the first time since yesterdays disastrous retreat. He appeared to be haggard with massive dark circles under his eyes, the look of a giant who hadn't slept for days. In fact, he *hadn't* slept–at all. He listened instead to a whispering voice of fear that kept him awake all night. His heart filled with dread for the coming dawn, he pushed back the flaps to his tent and cursed the light. Brooding in the darkness, meant that even the early morning light required his eyes to make a painful adjustment (the king usually kept the tent dark these days). Using his fists to try and drive exhaustion from his eyes, Ruarc watched in dismay as hundreds of his troops abandoned defensive positions to charge the enemy lines.

"Where are those fools going?" The first time he asked the question it came as a low astonished murmur. Then it became a loud bellow, "Where are my captains? And can somebody tell me where those fools are going?!"

Mereah and Lithos stood back to back in a ring of enemies. After several minutes of intense combat, a temporary lull in the fighting gave everyone a minute to catch their breath. At the moment, the combatants merely glared at one another, much like roosters paused and circling so they can have the time to stare and bluster. Both the Dun and the Rapha's extremities were inflicted with multiple wounds, but nothing they knew to be mortal. They also knew that the next attack wave would likely be the last, and their end.

"Lithos my friend, if I must meet my end at the hands of the Dagon, this is the end I would have chosen. It has been an honor to have you join me in this, my final song."

"A finer Prince our people may never see, and I will always love ya, but will you forgive me if I don't lay down and croak just yet?"

The Rapha' chuckled, "That sounds to me like a request for another song." And so Mereah stood to his full height of eleven feet and bellowed out a song louder than any before.

"Check that," Lithos mumbled, "death might be preferable to what you call singing."

The Dagon charged with single-minded focus, hell-bent on destroying the prince and the Dun Captain. Because of their concentration on the two singers, they did not see their own danger until too late. A short fifty yards up the canyon, centaurs slinging stones with the velocity of a cannon found a target-rich environment. With the Dagon packed in so tight together, each stone they slung dropped dozens. It helped immensely that the centaurs in this desert canyon were able to find lots of ammo; the Keys had plenty of rocks. Close to fifty Dagon infantry died before awaking to their peril. By the time they turned to face their new enemy, a rain of deadly arrows from Irial archers began to fall. In their zeal to get at what they believed to be a pair of melodic fools, many of the Dagon grabbed weapons only and not shields. After all, the attackers were only two Jeshurun dogs. Lacking shields, they could do nothing but throw up their arms, close their eyes, and pray they weren't hit. The Dagon weren't nearly as effective prayers as the Irial were archers, so many more died. After another deadly volley of stone and arrow, aided by the confusion of their uncertainty, the enemy broke and fled.

Without the imposed will of the Anak to drive them, the Dagon will to fight dissolved. As the last of the enemy fled, Mereah and Lithos in exhaustion just sat down in the dust. Then they watched as the Irijah, Capall cavalry, Irial light infantry and archers flew past in pursuit of the enemy.

In feigned bewilderment the Rapha` looked at his friend and asked, "The Dun seem to be absent from the pursuit my friend, why do you think that is?" A moment after posing the question the Watch Sergeant Nahor ran past with a century of Dun infantry. "Ah, now I remember, those absurdly short legs aren't much good for running are they?"

A sharp whap with a war hammer would be all the response Lithos could manage.

The Rapha` back in the Jeshurun camp eagerly looked over their shoulders, hoping to receive the order to pursuit a clearly fleeing enemy. However, none dared defy their king's command against joining in the attack.

Ruarc stood on a rise and stared down in an attempt to determine the outcome of the combat. The voices of fear that now whispered in his ear advised caution; beware of enemy tricks. This could be an attempt to get his army to abandon the defenses and run into a trap. Other voices told him any attack that put the enemy to flight, should have been ordered and led by him.

Whoever led this attack, if they survived, would be seen as a great hero. He'd been the hero for his people once. A new champion would be a threat to his throne. The voices of fear he listened to advised he jealously guard and keep all that should be considered his.

"I will ask ONE MORE TIME, who ordered this attack?!" The Rapha` still in camp merely looked at their shuffling feet. A voice from somewhere in their midst spoke quietly, "No one knows my king, but the enemy flees."

"I can see that imbecile, but the enemy is more than fifty, a hundred times our number. They are not fleeing, they are leading those idiots into a trap! Listen to my vow, may the Mighty Power do to me and more if the person who led this attack still lives when the sun has set!"

As he turned and looked back down through the valley, Ruarc knew he could not risk sitting safe behind the defenses. If the enemy was truly fleeing, and he'd no part in the battle, his hold on the throne would be in jeopardy.

Turning to face what remained of the Army, Ruarc growled, "Alright, we will join the attack, but stay with me and be wary, I tell you there will be a trap set. It's up to us now to do what we can to save the fools who disobeyed my orders."

The trap Ruarc feared never materialized. Without the will of the Anak driving them, the Dagon fled over the ground they captured the day before, and kept on fleeing until they left the Keys altogether arriving back at the Cnámh plains. There a new will exercised dominion and they stopped their flight. There also the forces of Jeshurun wisely chose not to follow. The Irijah and Capall cavalry recognized the danger of the flat plains and the enemy siege engines that were recaptured just the day before. They called for a halt to the pursuit and waited for the Dun infantry. When they arrived, Nahor immediately began restoring the

215

defenses at the canyon mouth and once again they locked Jeshurun's Key.

After walking past miles of the fallen enemy, the king arrived at the restored camp amidst the active reconstruction of defenses. Because he'd no part in the victory or its outcome, his heart slowly became filled with fear and rage. Appearance is all important to one whose chief value is keeping power, and in his imagination Ruarc saw every whisper and glance as being directed against him. His only perceived choice? Discredit the value of the day's victory, since he'd no part in it. Then, he must learn the identity of this new hero, and remove the threat to his throne.

His fear poured fuel on the smoldering flame of his anger, until just before sunset he called his leaders and captains before him.

"You fools may believe we have achieved a great victory today. You are wrong. All we have succeeded in doing is to further anger our foe, and make him more determined. The Anak still lives, and the enemy will be back, in greater force. This lunacy will end in the death of us all. Because of this I require the blood of the one who ordered the attack. It must have been one of my captains, so tell me, who was it?"

No one answered the king, choosing instead to stand silent. Most didn't know how it all started; those who did were not about to tell Ruarc. Their silence made the king's rage boil over. "Very well," The king drew his great battleaxe, "I am sure you have heard the saying heads will roll, well it's going to be your heads rolling, until one of you tells me who led the attack."

A great commotion of shouts and cheers suddenly erupted as Mereah and Lithos walked last of all into the camp. The pair were quite a sight. Tearing up cloaks for bandages, they'd doctored one another's worst wounds; but they simply lacked enough material to cover all their gashes, cuts and abrasions. Observing the encouraging cheers coming from almost the entire

216

camp as the pair walked through, the king could now take a pretty good guess as to who the instigators were. The pair walked into the midst of the captains and before the king, and simply collapsed sitting down in the dust.

"So glad you two could join us." Growled Ruarc, "We were just discussing who ordered the attack that brought this great deliverance today."

Missing the cue of the king's anger, and unaware of the king's vow, Lithos spoke up, "My King, I am 150 years young and have survived countless battles with the Dagon; but I could live twice the years of the Irijah and never see braver deeds than those of your son this day. No people could ever have a braver, mightier prince." Then with a grin the Dun Chieftain added, "Now if only we could learn him to sing."

Missing the point of the joke, in quiet rage Ruarc asked, "So, Mereah is responsible for leading this attack?"

Finally recognizing the tone in the king's voice, Lithos remained silent. It was Mereah who responded. "Yes father, I am responsible. Lithos is innocent in this matter. When he saw I would not be deterred, he joined my foolish mission in an effort to keep me from harm. Nothing, not the enemy, or even my singing deterred him from his task, but I am the one who went down to the Dagon camp. If in this I defied your wishes then I stand ready to face my punishment."

After a pause Mereah cracked a small grin, "Though I may need a little help to actually stand."

"Fool!" The king raged, "I vowed this day that the person who led this attack would be dead before the sun sets, which will be in just a few moments. This is not victory, what you have done is assure the death of us all, any chance of negotiating peace with the Dagon is now lost!"

Mereah knew he'd pushed his body beyond exhaustion. Even after accounting for this, he still couldn't make sense of his father's thinking, so he asked, "Father, what makes you believe peace could be won through negotiation with a people driven by such reckless hate?"

In response Ruarc raised his battleaxe and started moving toward his son, sitting in the dust in the midst of Jeshurun's Captains. Mereah made no other move than to go to his knees, lower his head, and give his father the king a clean target.

It was Lithos who stood and drew his own axe, and ran his thumb along the notched iron blade. "My King, I started this day intending to be guardian for my Prince, and this will I do–be it to protect him from the Dagon or a king's foolish pride. Do not try to touch him, or I swear I will cut even you down."

Ruarc looked into Lithos' smoldering eyes and saw no fear. Not even of the giant who the people once declared the mightiest warrior in all of Jeshurun. Then the Dun Commander no longer stood alone. A centaur stepped forward until he was standing next to Lithos. Then Ragnhildr the captain of the Irial, moved to a position just behind Mereah while putting an arrow to string. Then all the officers came forward and formed a wall between father and son.

When the Jeshurun soldiers heard about the king's judgment, murmurs of dismay and protest spread through the camp and grew into angry shouts of defiance. Ruarc quickly realized he could not do anything to Mereah. In the end, with no other option, he belted his axe, and returned to nursing his fear in the dark confines of his tent. Adding to the list of things he already feared, he added now his son and his own people.

Mereah watched his father turn his back and depart to his pavilion. A single tear ran down his cheek, as he mourned. His father lived, yet still seemed very much lost to him and to his people. Mereah did not exactly know what caused the falling out between his father and Jireh, but the prince mourned that his father no longer seemed to be the king and warrior he once knew. Now his ears seemed to be hearing other counselors. Not for the last time, he wished Jeshurun's Shophetim were here. But if that couldn't be, the prince knew he would do anything, face any foe or obstacle, if it would bring his father back to him.

Then Mereah remembered the bravery and sacrifice of the sons of Korah. Would it be lost in the memory of all but a few, the true source of the day's victory? Today he received praise as a hero, but he didn't feel like one. Not if the measure of what makes a person a hero is the extent of their courage. He'd never seen greater courage than when Korah's son faced a certain horrible death absent of fear. The refusal to surrender to despair, and meet bitter spite with a song–planted the seed in Mereah's heart that proved to be the source of the day's victory. This thought stirred hope in his heart, a hope that the story of his son's courage would bring at least a small measure of comfort to a bereaved cavalry Captain.

Sixteen

From high on a rocky crag, Mereah looked down on the Dagon spread out across the southern plains. Since being driven from the mountain pass back into the valley, the enemy chose not to make another assault. No need, they could afford to be patient. They were in an easy position for supply and reinforcement. The counterattack that drove the Dagon from Jeshurun's Key would prove a deadly mistake if the army of his father were to carry the fight to the plains. So presently all the Jeshurun forces could do–would do, is continue to watch from the heights as a deadly standoff carried on day after day. Meanwhile, the enemy only grew stronger and resupplied, while Jeshurun's soldiers neglected their homes, farms, crops and families.

Mereah however, felt most concerned about his father, some force he didn't understand worked to change or control him. How could he counter what was happening without some idea of his adversaries power or identity? His father's reputation was that of a great warrior, a ferocious fighter, the lion of his people: yet he seemed clueless as how to fight against the unseen powers that worked to keep his heart and spirit under siege. As despair withered his father's heart, Mereah no longer felt capable of facing his own fear.

At one time, the Rapha` Prince knew his father would never have done the prudent thing of hiding here in the shelter of the rocks and ravines. Giants aren't known for their wisdom anyway, but the passion and fire in his heart would have compelled the king to stride down the hill, face the enemy, and challenge him.

Instead, the proud warriors of Jeshurun sat in this desert pass called Jeshurun's Key and waited. The cynical amongst them whispered they actually cowered. A new disease of the spirit spread throughout camp, the virus of prudence brought symptoms of apathy and infected passion with a slow death.

A break in the Dagon line opened, and abruptly the Anak that led the attack days before rode forth. Immediately alarms went off in the princes' spirit. Murmurs ran up and down the Jeshurun line when the soldiers on the front drew back in fear, as word of the Sorcerer's appearance spread.

"All right, what are you up to now?" Mereah murmured out loud to no one in particular.

It took a few minutes for the Anak to get well beyond the Dagon lines, and so within earshot of the Jeshurun's position. Stopping a hundred yards from the first line of defense, the Anak just sat there looking the army over for what seemed an interminable amount of time. Finally he greeted the troops with his now familiar laugh, a laugh that grated the heart and burned the spirit.

One of the Irijah decided he would take no more. Stepping out from the defenses the centaur slung a chunk of granite the size of a man's head towards the Anak with such velocity that it appeared to travel on a line like a taut rope. The stone crossed the distance in less than a second, and for a brief instant hope swelled in Mereah's heart. A perfect shot! The small boulder would be deadly even to the Anak! With only a millisecond to spare the laughter ceased, his scepter flashed up, and stopped the missile in mid-air. The

221

stone hovered for a few taunting seconds before being shot back at the centaur killing him instantly. The murder happened so quickly no one understood what had taken place until the son of Irijah collapsed in a bloody heap.

"So, perhaps some of the Jeshurun dogs wish to fight after all!" The Anak called out. When no one else stepped forward he taunted, "I name you vermin and flies! Flies because you hover up there afraid to come down, just like the flies on the roof of my tent! But look now, I am not without mercy or compassion, even for vermin or flies! I have decided that all of you need not die, and that it is time to end this useless conflict."

Lithos came up beside Mereah, "I don't know about you my prince, but I find it comforting that this Anak has such compassion for us flies."

"I don't think we are going to much care for where this compassion is headed." Mereah murmured.

With acid voice the Anak continued. "Send a message to your king that I name craven, that he meet me in single combat. If by some miracle your beloved king of cowards should prevail against me, my army will lay down all arms and serve your people. But, when your king dies in this combat–and he will, if your people will lay down their arms, they will be shown mercy. You will serve as household slaves for the peoples of Dagon. Not much of a life I grant you, but at least you will live. Even your fearless leader would tell you to be a live dog is better than to be food for worms. Take this message to Ruarc, who I know cowers in his tent, that I will expect an answer when I return at this time tomorrow. Tell the sniveling dog I said not to disappoint me!" With that, the Anak turned and rode back through the Dagon lines.

Puzzled by the offer, Mereah watched the Dagon shaman ride away, "Lithos my friend, perhaps you can help me discern the motive behind this offer? The Rapha` as you know are known for acting first, thinking

222

later, but even to me this offer seems foolish. Why would an army with clear advantage risk certain victory on the chance of single combat?"

Lithos noted grimly, "You've seen yourself what this sorcerer can do. He hopes your father can be goaded into gambling on a contest that he cannot win."

"Assuredly that's true," murmured the prince, "and yet, . . yes, the Anak is powerful, still he would be risking much in combat against the mightiest of Jeshurun's warriors. Perhaps his confidence is overconfidence. This might be a real opportunity. We now understand that the Anak's chief weapon is fear. If a mighty warrior would but face the Dagon shaman without fear . . ."

Lithos dismissed the thought out of hand. "The Anak challenged the *king*, just in case you've something else in mind. There was a time when your father would have boldly answered this challenge. I don't see it happening in his present state of mind."

So caught up in his own thoughts, Mereah hardly heard a word Lithos said. In truth, he knew answering this challenge would indeed be the king's responsibility. But if the king wouldn't give this challenge answer, perhaps his son?

Keeping his thoughts to himself, Mereah turned and used long, purposeful strides to move in the direction of his father's pavilion. Lithos, his short legs churning trying to keep up shouted after him. "Hey, where are you going, and you'd best not be thinkin' what I think yer thinkin' . . ."

~

Ruarc gave his son a heated look that

smoldered with anger, and through clenched teeth quietly said "No."

"Father, this challenge must be answered, I merely wish the honor of representing our people . . as champion . . . ."

Mereah's words were cut short as his father roared, "I said *NO*. This offer of combat is a ruse, a sham . . . and only offered by an opponent with no doubt of the outcome. Why else make the offer? You have seen this Anak about his work, same as I. He seeks to remove the head of the snake, that is all this challenge is about and I for one will not throw my life away so foolishly . . . nor shall you."

"But father . . ."

"GET OUT Mereah!"

A chalice sailed past the young Rapha's head as he hastily exited the tent. Lithos sat on a rock by the entrance his chin resting on his chest as though asleep. When Mereah came through the tent flap, without looking up the Dun Captain muttered "Well, *THAT* went well."

Mereah looked down at his friend, "You heard eh?"

"Aye, along with the whole camp. I must say that while I hate to agree with the king, it is best for now to let the challenge be met with silence."

Mereah considered this for a moment, then declared, "I am not afraid of the Anak, and whether it be in single combat or when our armies once again clash, someone must eventually face him. My father is king, but it is not uncommon for a king to choose a champion to fight for the people in his stead."

Lifting his head so that he could look the young Rapha` directly in the eye, "And I suppose ya planned to sing to him?"

Mereah grinned sheepishly. "Seemed to work the last time."

"Only because the last time most of the enemy ran holding their ears, begging ya to stop. My prince, I love

224

ya, but ye can't carry a tune in a bucket. And as brave as that stunt proved to be, I don't think either one of us has a song to match that Anak's hate. The sons of Korah taught us both that a song can be a weapon against fear. We both know on horseback either one would have been the equal in combat to any warrior we have in camp. Still, *they both died.* I don't think there is a weapon in our possession at this time capable of killing the Anak, so until one presents itself, I see no alternative but to wait and plug our ears to his taunts."

The young prince stood staring off into space and spoke almost as if to no one in particular. "I dare not defy my father again . . I . . . I . . . wish Jireh were here."

Mereah lost focus on his thoughts at the sound of riders. He turned to watch Korah the Capall Captain lead a string of fresh recruits into camp. Watching the cavalry officer give orders to dismount and care for their horses, Mereah murmured, "If I want to confront the Anak in combat my friend, I may have to stand in line. At any moment a very brave captain of our people is going to start looking for the last two reasons he has to continue on in this world. Will you join me? I need to tell a good man how his brave sons died. We may have to restrain him as gently as we can–challenge or no–lest the good captain ride out to meet the slayer of his sons."

Seventeen

"Too long a sacrifice can make a stone of the heart.
O when may it suffice?"

~Yeats

Korah lay flat on his belly on a high rock outpost frequently used for observing and tracking the enemy's movements. As part of what had become a twice daily routine, the Anak rode out, offered his challenge, and in infinite and increasingly creative ways, questioned the manhood and courage of the Jeshurun army. Particularly the king's.

Korah tried more than once to charge out to meet the Shaman's challenge, but each time Mereah or Lithos restrained him. One or the other kept watch over him at all hours of the day and night. At one point an exasperated Prince tied him up until he gave his word not to ride down and answer the Anak's taunts. Korah usually knew better than to respond to the taunts of a thug. This was different, with so much more at stake. That demon massacred his sons, fed them to his tanniyn, and now paraded the crime in front of his face. Every day his son's killer mocked Korah's incalculable loss with his challenge. Every day, it seemed as though the vile butcher rode out to display his bloody hands so they may be rubbed in the father's face.

226

Drawing back from the rocks' edge, Korah stood up and started down the now well beaten path back to camp. Rounding a bend he almost ran into Mereah, his gigantic shadow, leaning against a huge rock. The Prince's eyes were filled with sorrow for his ward. He understood how much it tormented the good captain *not* to ride out and answer the Anak's taunts. And so, he watched the officer like a hawk, seeking to prevent a righteous–perhaps foolish–act of vengeance. Never did a man have a larger, more benevolent jailor.

A slight smile cracked the Rapha's face, "I trust I won't have to restrain you again good captain?"

"My given word is not enough?"

"Yes. Yes, of course it is. I am sorry my friend, I regret being the one who gave the order to have you bound–I hope you know that." With a slight chuckle the Rapha` continued, "Lithos suggested I merely need guard your horse . . . that a son of Capall would not attempt armed combat on foot. Forgive me captain, but I don't think the good Dun understands the size of your heart, or the depth of your grief."

After a moment's pause with no response Mereah continued. "My friend, I believe you are wise enough to know watching our enemy and listening to his mocking will only bring more pain to your heart, so I thought perhaps you intended another purpose?"

Korah turned for a moment and gazed back in the direction of the lookout perch. "I am observing the enemy, and their means of supply. I estimate their numbers to be ten, maybe fifteen times our thousand."

"My observations would agree with your count. As you know this is the reason the army withdrew to the Keys. You are not thinking we should resume our attack back down on the Cnámh plain?"

"No, I am thinking this is the desire of the enemy and the true reason for his ruse of a challenge. I believe that whoever answers the challenge will be betrayed by some treachery, and slaughtered before our eyes. The

Anak believes that our anger at this will at last draw us down to the plains to fight, where we will have no chance."

"That is likely the truth, so surely you must understand then why you can't be allowed to answer the Anak's taunts?"

"Mereah, I may have a death wish, but I do not wish to just throw my life away. Not without first destroying the demon spawn who stole my sons from me. But please hear me, while watching our adversary, it has occurred to me there may be a way to make the size of our foe a disadvantage."

The Rapha` Prince chuckled, "Oh, that our people could have such a disadvantage my friend."

"I hear you, but such a vast army under the right conditions does indeed have a major weakness. In the desert they can get mighty thirsty."

Mereah's eyes lit up as he realized the implications, "And just how my friend, do you suggest we increase our enemy's thirst?"

Korah grinned, "Go to my perch and look for yourself. The dust cloud from the supply caravans betrays the effort required to sustain an army of that size in the desert. The Anak doesn't see a need to conceal this, because locked up here in the Keys, we have no chance to attack his supply."

Mereah nodded, "I think I understand where you are wanting to go with this my friend, but, please, continue."

"As you know, mounted cavalry is of limited use in a defensive engagement such as this. But think on the mischief we might cause running free behind the Dagon lines."

Mereah's face broke into a wide smile as he recognized the genius of what the captain just suggested. "The Anak wishes to use the challenge of personal combat to lure the army away from our defenses. But I propose we use this combat for a diversion of our own; while the enemy is distracted, mounted cavalry should be able to break past the enemy's flank, and out to the open plains. The enemy does not have any units fleet enough to catch the Capall, or engage them in combat. Once past the enemy's flank, light cavalry will be able to swing to the rear and strike his line of supply. How long can an army the size of the Dagon's last without water? Two, maybe three days at most?"

Mereah looked at Korah thoughtfully, trying to read his mind. "I see two minor flaws with this plan, my friend. First, the Dagon will surely respond by sending a strong force to secure the former Dun garrison out on the Cnámh plain, keeping the Capall from water; and second, you realize, of course, that whoever volunteers for the diversionary combat with the Anak–that it's likely to be a suicide mission?"

"Agreed. So an important part of the cavalry attack involves a raid on the garrison before it can be re-enforced, take all the water we can, then salt the well. Regardless, the well at the garrison is able to provide only a small portion of the water needed to sustain such a force.

As for combat with the Anak, I am the one who must accept his challenge. I concocted this scheme, I can't ask another to go to their death to make my plan work. I am also the one with the least to lose."

Mereah said nothing in response to this, but rather walked a few paces and stopped to observe the Dagon ranks. For several minutes he stood with his arms crossed over his chest, thinking. Korah waited patiently for Mereah as he considered everything carefully. This tendency to think things through, set the Prince apart in many ways from the general fiery and spontaneous nature of most of the Rapha`. When at last he spoke, it seemed at first an attempt to change the subject. "I was little taller than a man when Jireh made my father king. All of Jeshurun had gathered, and all of the peoples gave their reasons why one of their leaders should be king–as though their lobbying should help Elohim make up His mind."

Korah wasn't sure where Mereah was headed with his thought but softly responded, "I remember the day, very well. I have no desire to be named king."

"Would you be surprised to learn that neither did my father? When Jireh as the Shophetim searched for the one to be anointed as Jeshurun's king, do you know where he found him? While the whole nation argued and campaigned, hoping to be selected, they discovered my father hiding among the tents and baggage. I do not believe Elohim selected my dad for the reasons most people believe. Not for his height or strength; would El Shaddai, the Almighty be impressed by such things? No, I think He hoped that one who thought so little of his own worth and strength would learn to rely on a strength that is greater still.

"I like your plan captain, but in truth there is a reason that I have not already chosen to defy my father and go down to face the Anak myself. I still have hope the king will realize this task is his. If he realizes that it is not possible with any strength he possesses, perhaps he will turn to a higher power. It would be his salvation, I think. So for just a little while longer, I ask you to wait . . . I know this causes you horrible pain, I know you need to avenge your sons, and we shall. However, I still have hope that my father may also be saved."

Eighteen

Riordan woke up to the aroma of breakfast. Jireh kept him up late again the night before, but at least he had graciously allowed the lad to sleep in. Not wanting to leave the warmth of his covers and shelter to brave a cold morning until it became necessary, Riordan kept his eyes closed hoping the discernment of the Shophetim did not extend to whether or not a poor ra`ah still slept.

In his mind he reviewed the night's lessons which began at sunset. Jireh asked "Spending so much time out in the fields, you must have noticed the sun's journey north and south on the horizon each season?"

"Of course, and I noticed the changing positions of the stars through the night, except for the guide star, whose position in the north never seems to change. I still fail to understand what any of those things have to do with the Riail dlí or the gifts of Elohim."

Remembering his answer, Riordan also remembered Jireh's patience as he explained the basics of understanding the mastery of the blade he now carried, "The changing positions of stars and the sun reveal all the heavens are governed by natural laws that can be discerned from observation. More than just laws over the changing positions of the sun or stars, there are laws

231

that govern all of life. For example one inescapable rule determines that an object cast into the air must return to earth unless the return is in some way hindered. To foolishly ignore this fact results in death. Ah, but what would be possible if there were ways to suspend the law temporarily, or lessen its effect?

"The Riail dlí is forged from the Nomos, the source of all law; its name translated means Rule of Law. I believe it may give the wielder dominion over natural law. But before a person dares suspend or change these laws they must understand their nature and purpose. Ignoring or altering any of them may have disastrous consequences.

"Ancient texts tell us that the seven races were created as vessels to nurture the image of Elohim. The seed planted there developed only by knowledge and understanding. As the races grew in maturity and understanding of Yahweh Elohim's laws, they grew in stewardship and dominion of Tebel, our world."

Riordan responded in mild protest, "Well if that's true, somebody didn't get it right because this world sure got messed up."

Rather than getting angry Jireh just laughed, "It did indeed." Then he suddenly turned very serious and solemn. "In fact one of the ancient kings used a powerful talisman, a scepter to change just one of these laws, and almost catastrophically destroyed the world. "

Riordan suddenly got excited, "I remember this story, you're talking about the great flood!"

"I am indeed, but to call it a flood is close to making an ant hill out of a mountain. Far more than heavy rains that caused localized flooding, this event saw landmasses sink and subterranean floodgates burst open shooting massive amounts of water into the sky. Continents broke up and rapidly changed position resulting in waves miles high sweeping across the land. The devastation so complete, entire civilizations disappeared without a trace, washed clean from the earth by the wrath of God.

"Lad, I'm telling you all this because you absolutely must respect and come to understand the power of the Riail dlí. Dominion is among the most powerful of gifts ever given to the children of Elohim. Its proper exercise can bring healing to the world, but misunderstanding or abuse of the gift will mean certain destruction.

"At this very moment the soldiers of Jeshurun battle one of the largest armies they've ever faced. But it is not the size of the army that concerns me most, it is the Anak who leads it. The Anak is learning to call on powers that were instrumental in the destruction of the First Age. Against such powers, iron blades will not suffice. I am afraid the enemy will break through our defenses in a matter of days.

"If the Dagon invade Jeshurun, I don't want you to fight, I want you to flee to the mountains. I will come and find you there. Under no circumstances are you to engage the enemy. Any attempt to use the Riail dlí without understanding the potential consequences to natural law, could be devastating."

"But what if I . . ."

"There is no but or what if, do *not* use the blade, is that clear?" Jireh towered over the ra`ah, arms crossed and scowled in an effort to drive an important point home.

Suddenly Jireh looked up and stared off into the distance, "Someone is coming. Riordan, I needed to leave you soon regardless–but my presence here with you now might cause some to ask questions. I will find you again before long. For now, and for your own safety, keep the presence of the Riail dlí and the contents of our conversations secret. Farewell my young friend."

Quickly, the Shophetim gathered his few things and with a wave cantered over a small hill and quickly disappeared. Riordan meanwhile hastily wrapped the Riail dlí in a blanket and got it out of sight. A few short moments later, Brónach walked over a small rise leading a couple of pack horses laden with supplies.

"How are you lad? Hope you haven't been too lonely out here by yourself." Even as he spoke, a quick scan of Riordan's camp revealed he'd not been by himself, but Brónach said nothing about this.

"Are you going on a journey Grandfather?"

"No, no I'm not–but you are."

"Where . . . where would I be allowed to go? Is my father sending me?"

"Yes lad, he is. Your two older brothers serve with the Jeshurun forces about three to four days' ride south of here. The army has blocked the passage of the Dagon army in a series of canyons called the Keys. All the men are in a tight spot, where it's very difficult to keep them supplied with food and water, so your father wanted these items to go to your brothers. They left in a bit of a hurry; so these supplies should help them get through the next couple weeks or so."

"Does Brannan know you call him my father?"

"No lad, such honesty must remain just between us. Go on now, get your gear together, you'll want to be able to get going fairly soon." Brónach followed Riordan into camp and watched as he rolled up his bedroll. He casually asked, "So why was Jireh here? And if you don't mind my asking, what business does the Shophetim of Jeshurun have with a simple ra`ah?"

With an amused look on his face, Brónach watched the boy's face pop up and his jaw drop. "Now don't be surprised Lad, hoof prints are very different from one another. As a warrior of the sons of Capall you're going to need to learn to read their sign. A casual look around confirms that a large draft, or heavy war horse, maybe a centaur, has been visiting your camp, possibly for several days. But this particular print is very distinct, like a man's signature, one I have seen before; the day Jireh brought you home from Joktan for one. I'm not angry boy, just curious."

"Yes he came here, a few days ago, he saved my life–*again*. Several lions came for the sheep. Esh actually attacked and killed one, the one that started the excitement by roaring. Then I noticed that all the sheep ran from the roaring lion over to where several other lions lay waiting."

Brónach listened thoughtfully and murmured softly, "Hmmm, I have to think there's a lesson somewhere in that."

Riordan looked puzzled, "A lesson?"

"Yes, an old toothless lion, no longer able to hunt, roars. By running from the roar, you run into the real danger. There is a proverb among our people that Conri, the enemy of souls is like a roaring lion, seeking whom he may devour. Isn't it interesting that the roaring lion is old and toothless, and that the real danger lies in running where fear tells a man to go. Son, I've learned through the years of all the weapons used to defeat us, fear is among the most powerful. Run in the direction that fear dictates and it's likely the wrong direction and the most dangerous. I think we would all do well to remember that. Any way lad, finish your story."

"Well, a lioness grabbed one of the sheep by the throat, so I hit it with a sling stone, but succeeded only in making it real mad. It charged and I tried to get another stone in my sling, but wasn't going to make it. The lion pounced, and as I braced myself a stone the size of my head went slinging by, hitting the lion and plucking it out of mid-air. Jireh went after those lions and they didn't want anything to do with him after that, so they took off."

"They were smart. Remember when we went into the mountains, lad? I told you I didn't want to do anything to anger the Irijah? They combine the strength of a small giant, with the speed and mobility of a mounted warrior on heavy horse. To have a centaur as a foe is a serious matter. And in your case, to have one as a personal bodyguard seems to have come in quite handy. How's Esh?"

"A few minor scratches. Jireh showed me how to make a salve to treat them. He even knew how to treat one of the sheep; its windpipe got crushed. Somehow he knew what to do."

"Centaurs live long, lad. With a life span measured in centuries, they have the opportunity to forget more knowledge than a man will ever have the opportunity to learn."

After a short pause Brónach continued, "You know what son, I'm not going to press you to answer why he was here. I could see some discomfort on your part when I asked, and it could be he asked you not to tell. But know this, if the Shophetim of Jeshurun takes an interest in you, you need to understand that despite your humble beginnings, Elohim is calling you to great things. All packed?"

"Yes sir."

"Good. Now lad, I want it clearly understood that you are only there to bring your brothers' supplies. I know there are some in the cavalry not much older than you, but don't let yourself get pressed into service. I just don't think you're ready for combat. You've only just started learning to ride. Deliver the supplies, and head straight home. You will have other opportunities soon enough, likely too soon to suit me."

Brónach laced his fingers together and lowered them, offering Riordan a place to step up and mount more easily. "Keep heading south lad. Keep the Irijah mountains always to the east, and ride until you reach some low desert mountains, hopefully in about three days. Then ride west until you find a heavily–used road that splits a dry gorge. Take the road south again until you come to a place where the world seems to fall away. The path basically drops through a large ravine and series of canyons, called the Keys. You'll find the army and your brothers there. It's a hard ride, but I'm hoping you can make it sometime after dark on the fourth day. You'll need to get riding. Luck to ya lad. I'll be waiting for you here when you get back."

Waving goodbye, Riordan felt a growing sense of excitement. The last few weeks offered more opportunities to travel and see more of Jeshurun than he'd seen his whole life. But this excursion wasn't nearly as exciting as the journey looking for feral horses. This trip across the southern plains confirmed his belief that the steppes of Capall were an endless sea of rolling grassy hills. Very little to see, very little shade, and a sore backside to remind him he'd yet to get a rider's seat.

Right around sunset, Riordan reached a small stream cutting through the grass sea with some cottonwood and poplar growing along the banks. The spot offered a little bit of shelter, and a source of wood for a small fire so he decided to stop for the night and make camp. He and the horses enjoyed a long, cool drink from the stream, and then he gave Esh a much appreciated rub-down before letting him enjoy a fine grass supper. Turning his attention to the two pack animals next, he removed the packs and ensured the pack straps weren't causing any rubbing or discomfort. Hobbling them both, he released them to graze. Right about the time he got a fire going, the crimson sunset gave way to an endless expanse of stars.

Laying out his bedroll beside the fire, he placed the Riail dlí just beside him. The combination of a warm fire, a cool early summer night, and a small stream to provide a constant lullaby ensured Riordan's entrance into a dream world quickly.

Nineteen

The grass started to change a couple hours after he started out the morning of the fourth day. By mid-day he saw almost as much sand, brush and rock as grass. While he still didn't see any sign of the Dun Mountains, because of the change in terrain, he decided to go ahead and veer west. He hoped that traveling on the edge of the prairie would be easier on the horses, and that he'd still be able to find the road south that would take him through to the Keys.

He saw no one. Not a sign of any of the sons of Dun, although he passed through an abandoned village. A short time later he passed a farm that looked to belong to a family of the Capall. It also seemed deserted. This puzzled him for about an hour or so, until he realized that if the Dagon broke through the Keys, all these settlements and farms would be attacked and destroyed. Every invasion for the last thirteen hundred years or so came from the south through the Keys. Seems like the folks in the southland at least knew the value of learning from history.

By mid-afternoon, he reached the road heading north and south that eventually split the Dun Mountains.

After turning onto the packed dirt path, the hills and plateaus came into sight within an hour. It seemed to take forever to cross the last few hot, dusty miles to where the highway began to descend into a wide valley. Because of its southerly direction he never really escaped the sun and it only got hotter as he lost elevation.

A short while before sunset he passed through another settlement. The buildings were constructed from mostly stone, which would suit the Dun just fine. With such small amounts of wood, practical dwarves simply used the most readily available material. They sure didn't have to look very hard to find stone for building in these parts; not much in way of water, or trees, but plenty of rocks.

The doors were all halved so that the lower part could be used by the Dun, but still be able to accommodate an occasional human or Irial by opening the upper door. Riordan guessed if you were from among the Irijah or Rapha`, you pretty much needed to remain outside.

He saw only one of the Dun on the street, and he sat on a low bench in front of one of the buildings. After exchanging cautious greetings and comments about the heat, Riordan found himself already out of town. As the sun set he reached a deep cut, the ravine that dropped down into the first of three narrow canyons.

Descending steadily now, Riordan passed through the first of three choke points, places where the gulch narrowed to an easily defended bottleneck. With the sun down, he resorted to picking his way through almost pitch black darkness. The high rock walls and stone formations offered all manner of threat in his imagination, as did every sound. Riding past abandoned defensive works, he passed through the narrows until the canyon walls fell back again to create a large bowl; just how large seemed impossible to tell in the dark.

Crossing this canyon also, once again he passed

through abandoned defensive works, but his eyes and nose detected evidence of a bloody battle. Some of the corpses of the enemy hadn't yet been buried or burned, and they presently were providing nourishment for crows working overtime to fill their stomachs.

Going through a graveyard after dusk is never enjoyable, but passing through a recent battlefield full of exposed corpses in all manner of grotesque contortions and mutilations went far beyond giving him the creeps. When the grisly sights combined with the horrid croaking from Ravens with other carrion birds in the pitch black, additional gruesome images assaulted his already vivid imagination. The young ra`ah suddenly found all manner of rationalizations as to why he should turn around.

Only one thing is more hair-raising than being alone in a black eerie place; ironically its the feeling that *you're not alone* in a black eerie place. Riordan imagined all manner of ghastly creatures sneaking up from behind, and kept looking over his shoulder. The absence of moon or even starlight meant of course he couldn't even see the packhorses whose leads he held in his hands.

He couldn't see anything on his backtrail, but he could feel blazing glares burning holes in his back. Reason finally tried to talk sense to his fear. "Of course I'm being watched, you idiot" he muttered, "The army would have posted sentries all through the canyon. Just don't do anything stupid."

Passing through the second lock into the final and largest canyon, he came to the first visible sentry outpost. A watch fire strategically placed made it impossible to pass through the checkpoint, even in the dark, without being detected. Riordan let out a deep sigh of relief that his long ride through the dark ravine was finally over. The night monsters that stalked him all mysteriously retreated back into the shadows.

One of the sentries, a man of Capall, his right hand

resting casually on his sword hilt looked first at Riordan and then at Esh,. "Things must be more desperate than I thought if they're sending us boys mounted on half-dead 'orses. Where'd ya get that bag of bones anyway son?"

Riordan started to answer when a commanding voice spoke from behind the sentry. "That bag of bones, sergeant, at one time proved to be one of the greatest chargers Capall has ever known; the man he bore, one of our greatest captains. Please show some respect."

Riordan looked up and he saw a man leaning forward in his saddle. Even in the dark he recognized the cavalry officer who'd come to his home a few weeks ago and recruited his older brothers for the war.

The captain's smile flashed white in the dark night, "How are you lad? I see your uncle is allowing you to ride. Has he decided your worth is for greater things than tending sheep?"

Thinking once again he was being challenged, Riordan hastily responded, "My grandfather Brónach is my Goel, my redeemer, Esh is my . . is his horse. He gave him to me."

Dismounting, Korah approached Riordan and reached out to gently pat Esh's nose. "I wasn't challenging your right to ride lad, from what I hear that's a dangerous proposition. No, but close to twenty-five years ago, I was sent by my father to be the armor bearer for a mighty Captain of Capall. He rode a blood-red stallion, that showed quite a few years, even then. But I could never forget Brónach, or his charger. How are you, Esh?"

Esh nickered softly and gladly accepted Korah's embrace of his neck. Anyone watching would have thought it a reunion of old friends.

"And your grandfather, is he well?"

"Yes sir, he is the one who sent me with these supplies for my bro . . . I mean, cousins."

If the captain noticed Riordan's verbal slip, he didn't

show it on his face, he simply gave the Watch instructions, "Sergeant, this lad has family camped among the new recruits and trainees. Would you mind leaving your post for a moment to show him the way?" Korah walked back to his horse and climbed back in the saddle. He started to turn to ride back towards camp, but thought of one more thing. Looking back at Riordan he asked, "After you deliver the supplies to your . . . um . . . cousins, lad, will you be staying on in camp? I could always use a page or an armor bearer."

"No sir, my grandfather is expecting me back."

"I understand. I know you don't need me to tell you this lad, but stay close and learn from your grandfather all that you can. He was a great captain, and an even better man."

"Yes sir, I know that, and I will sir, learn all I can that is."

"Good lad. It's already late, likely you don't need me to tell you, but it would be best if you spent the rest of the night here in camp. You've only a few hours before morning, and you and Esh both need a rest. Good luck to you, son."

The watch sergeant drew close to the head of Esh and took hold of the simple halter. "I didn't mean anything by what I said about the 'orse lad," he looked up at Riordan with a sheepish grin and a wink. "I was just ribbin' ya. No offense?"

Riordan met the sergeant's eye and replied with a grim look on his face, "I'd be more worried about apologizing to Esh. He's killed men for less."

The sergeant guffawed at that and started leading them through the camp when Esh quickly jerked his head, freeing himself from the man's hold and nipped him on the shoulder. "OOWW, he bit me!"

Riordan grinned, "Don't look at me, I warned you. I'd say ya got off easy."

Keeping well clear of Esh's head, the sergeant led Riordan through the Capall camp. Many of the mounts they passed were young stallions who issued challenges to Esh, and he responded like an old veteran to still wet-behind-the-ears colts. With a flash of worn teeth the old horse let them know they still had a lot to learn, and that he could still take em."

Reaching the far side of the Capall encampment, the sergeant turned to Riordan. "This is where the rookies and new recruits are camped. Your brothers will be somewhere here. It shouldn't be too hard to find 'em, ask around. I don't know exactly where they are, I don't keep track of recruits. I don't see many right now, but in this type of engagement, cavalry's not much use. They may be down in the trenches standing night watch. Luck to ya lad, but I need to get back to my post . . . not that there's much danger of an attack coming from that direction."

Riordan thanked the sergeant and rode on, and after a few minutes of looking he found a small pavilion with a posted standard bearing the family crest, but his brothers were not there. He removed the supplies from the pack horses and placed them inside the tent. Then he removed the blanket saddle from Esh, and gave all the horses a good rub-down.

Looking over Esh's sway back, he noticed several of the men in the camp moving toward some sort of disturbance down toward the south entrance of the Keys and the Jeshurun defenses. Bored and tired of waiting for his brothers, Riordan decided to walk further on to see what the excitement was all about.

Considerably smaller than the Dagon camp, it still required twenty minutes to walk through—especially with it still being pitch black. With only an occasional torch or watch fire for light, he still managed to get turned around a couple times (he wouldn't ever admit to himself that he got lost). After stumbling in the dark on several occasions, or tripping over tent lines, he finally found his way past the pavilions to draw closer to the actual defenses.

The last southern opening of the Keys, best he could tell, appeared to be about two hundred yards wide, with high rock walls on the East and West. Trenches ran from rock wall to rock wall and were defended by sons of Dun and men. Large wicker barricades were placed just behind the trenches to provide concealment for the Rapha` and Irijah. Behind their respective positions stockpiles of stones and oil filled clay jar-firebombs sat prepared to provide ready munitions. Irial archers meanwhile occupied positions in the rocks above. Any of the Dagon forces would have to cross a long, exposed stretch of open sand flats before scrambling up through loose scree to reach the opening of the Keys and the defenses.

Every eye seemed to be focused on something happening, or about to happen in the desert plain below, and so no one noticed as the ra`ah crept through their ranks. Curious about what seemed to be happening below, Riordan decided the safest way to get closer to the action and the least likely way to raise suspicion would be by simply joining the Capall soldiers down in the trenches.

In just over an hour the first morning light broke through mountain gaps to the east, and he heard an acidic, vitriolic voice rising from down on the plain. Finding an open spot in the defenses and peering over the side of the trench, Riordan saw the Anak and his tanniyn for the first time.

"Dogs of Jeshurun, I have led the Dagon in conquest of many nations; some were brave, many more were cowards. For me to name you cowards, especially the craven you call king, would be an insult to all cowards. You are vermin and cockroaches, hiding in excrement holes. Even the flies crawling on your stink are a higher life form. What's more, your god must be the Dung beetle, no other would claim you. I am running out of patience, oh worshipers of excrement and eaters of Dung. If your craven king does not come down to face me by tomorrow's sunrise, I promise I will come to *him*. My promise of mercy will expire, and before tomorrow's sunset you will all be worm food. No, I will not see to your burial, but your stench has become so vile, even the buzzards won't have you."

The longer he listened to the Anak's rant, the madder Riordan got. He was just starting to look for footholds in the trench wall to climb out and charge down to hurl a few insults of his own, when a strong hand grabbed the back of his tunic at the neck and yanked him back hard; throwing him into the dirt. Torin stood looking at him from across arms folded at the chest, his eyes full of accusation.

"Alright Mamzer, what are you doing here?"

Cavan, from just behind Torin's shoulder chimed in, "Yeah Mamzer, and who's watching the sheep?"

Riordan started to scramble to his feet while trying to explain his presence. "Grandfather . . . Brónach, and Uncle Brannan sent me with supplies, for you, but I didn't find you in the camps so I came here."

Grabbing his tunic, this time at the throat Torin lifted Riordan back up to his feet. "You didn't seem to be looking very hard for us Mamzer, and you aren't a very good liar. What did you think you were going to do after you got over the side of the trench? I know even you aren't so stupid as to think you would go down and face that Anak? Do you think I want to face the King of Jeshurun and have to tell him that yes, the little mamzer ra`ah that made a laughing stock of our whole nation is a servant of my household?"

Riordan, while gasping for breath replied, "Did . . hear what . . Dagon said? The insults he makes . . against . . people, . . against Elohim."

"We have been listening to them every day, twice a day for several days. We are all under strict orders from the king NOT to respond. But Mamzer, if you went down to face the Anak, our only hope for victory would be that he die from laughing too hard. Hear me, you will not even think of going down there again. Do you understand?"

Torin tightened his grip on Riordan's tunic even further, so a nod had to do for a response. The matter settled, Torin released his grip and shoved him backwards.

"Now as to the matter of your presence here. You will lead me back to camp and show me these supplies. If I find that you have lied, and have left my father's sheep so you can get a look at the battles, you will not be battling the Anak; because I will personally stake you out on ant hill and watch them fight the buzzards for your sorry carcass. Now turn around and get back to camp."

~

Korah stayed on his lookout perch long after sunrise. Finally getting up to leave, he jumped down to the place where Mereah waited below. "My prince, I don't think we can wait much longer. Always the Anak's words are meant to divert from his true intent. But, I think his purpose in delay has been accomplished. Tomorrow morning if the challenge is not at last answered, the demon will keep his word and attack."

"I agree." No further comment seemed necessary on that point, but the Rapha` Prince needed to bring up one more matter, yet dreaded it, "A response to the Anak's challenge must be made. And as much as I know and understand your need to be the one to make that response, there is no one to take your place and lead the cavalry my friend. Our plan will call for much independent action once the Capall are outside of the Keys and out on the desert plain, . . you know there is no one else."

"Also, I have waited for my father to respond to this challenge . . . as he will not, I must. I know this is sudden, but can you have your men provisioned and ready to ride before the Anak returns tomorrow morning to issue his last challenge?"

"We will be ready."

"Good, and so will I. I am not the warrior my father is, but I am a Rapha`. I will wear death on my brow, and meet this Anak with a song. I doubt our enemy will cower in fear, but at least I don't think he will laugh."

Korah looked into the eyes of the Rapha` prince, with a tear of love and respect softly tracing his face. "No, my prince, the Anak is many things. Fool is not one of them. He will not laugh."

"I want to thank you for your service Korah, few understand the depth . . of your sacrifice for this land, so I wish to thank you personally, and to say farewell. It was truly an honor to know you. I don't expect to see you again, but pray for me, that perhaps in my attempts at creating a diversion, I may strike a fatal blow against this demon before he, as he certainly will, ends my life."

"What fortune tomorrow morning may bring, no man can say, but my heart tells me for good or ill, tomorrow's events will decide the fate of our people and the outcome of this war. I will pray to Elohim, and at least a part of my prayer will be that I will see you my prince, and my friend, once more."

Looking up into the early morning sky to hide the enormous tear on his own face Mereah responded, "Then we are in agreement in our prayers, dear captain. Surely Elohim will hear."

Mereah watched Korah move through the morning light back to where the cavalry were camped to make his preparations. He'd sensed all along it would come down to this. He'd just paid his respects to Korah, what–if anything–should he say to Lithos? If he gave the Dun Commander even a hint of his plan, his friend would either insist on going with him, or try to go in his stead. Neither could be allowed.

Lithos had a massive heart buried under all the

247

weaponry, and iron mail. Perhaps in time room in that great heart would be found to forgive his going away without saying a word.

Meanwhile, his thoughts veered toward what his father's response would be when he learned of his conspiracies. Wisely he Dismissed the idea of telling him the plans directly. Of one thing he remained certain, the long journey down onto the Cnámh plain to meet the Anak would be a one way trip. That meant just one more goodbye. He couldn't leave without saying *something* to his father. But what? How could he manage another farewell without giving his intentions away?

Twenty

Mereah reluctantly pushed back the entrance flap to his father's tent. His eyes went to the strange red glow that always betrayed the king's location these days. Realizing that his son watched, Ruarc concealed the Zilliah, the red shade inside his cloak. However, even with the red light extinguished, the evil presence still remained.

"Didn't any one ever tell you that the Rapha` are not like Irial or the Sióga? We make lousy sneaks and spies. What is it you want, Mereah? Don't hide like a rat in the corner, come in and tell me what you want."

"The Anak has been breathing threats again this morning."

"I heard them. He breathes threats every day, why should today's lies be any different?"

Mereah passed through the flap and drew closer to his father. "I believe that on the morrow he intends to move at last, the ruse of his challenge has served its purposes."

Ruarc looked at his son through dark eyes. "You tell me things I already know Mereah, so I am not impressed with either your knowledge, or your wisdom. But I know you are not here to cool my poor tent with the breeze from your flapping gums, so I will ask you again, *why* are you here?"

The young Rapha` looked at his angry father and lost what little remained of his hope and courage.

Several seconds passed before he could stammer a response, "I . . . I . . . came to say goodbye father, just in case the Dagon attacks, and things go ill for us in battle, I . . . . thought I should make my peace wi . . ."

Ruarc cut off his son's goodbyes with a harsh interruption. "Since you are too squeamish and cowardly to speak your true purpose, let me help you. You intend to make a play for my throne. You have once again conspired behind my back to attack the Dagon. This time the partner in your conspiracy is not that idiot Lithos, but none other than my dear Cavalry Captain Korah. Do you think me a fool? Do you think me blind as well, or that I don't have eyes outside of this tent? You are the only *fool* here." Ruarc made a quick motion with his hand and his two personal guards stepped out of the shadows to grab Mereah's arms from behind.

"So, after proving the hero once again, and so the people clamor to name *Mereah* king, what did you intend to do with me, your daddy? Would my death have been swift or slow?"

"Father, I know not who has whispered these lies into your ear, but I have no desire to . . ."

A sharp backhand silenced Mereah, "Now you think me an imbecile in addition to a blind fool. I fear there will be no hero to face the Anak in the morning. Such a pity; without the diversion, I'm afraid if our dear captain does attempt to break free from the keys, he and his cavalry will simply join his sons and be numbered among the slaughtered."

With a nod from Ruarc, one of the king's guard struck Mereah from behind, causing him to lose consciousness, "As for you, my son, I will keep you alive, perhaps until such time as I can find a way to turn your death to an advantage."

~

Riordan woke up in the middle of the night, or at least very early in the morning. Lying on his back, while gazing up at the stars, it took a few moments to reorient to his surroundings. In the end, movement all through the Capall encampment finally jogged his memory. The Anak promised an attack today–unless his challenge was answered. Suddenly wide awake, he rose to see if the Capall were preparing for battle.

Standing beside Esh, he saw riders saddling their horses, and placing packs with supplies behind. Despite his lack of experience the ra`ah realized the packs indicated more than a drill or skirmish. Saddlebags and bedrolls meant only one thing, the cavalrymen didn't have any intention of returning later that day, or even the next day. The presence of additional pack animals and baggage reinforced the hunch that they were preparing for a possible extended campaign.

The tent where his brothers slept remained quiet, as did the tents of all the new recruits. Evidently, whatever the cavalry's plan, it was considered too dangerous or too important for troops so young or inexperienced.

It took some convincing for Torin to accept Riordan's staying through the rest of the day yesterday in order to get an early start this morning. Esh had quite truthfully traveled hard for several days and needed rest. So he remained in camp, even if it meant spending an uncomfortable day trying to stay out of his brother's sight and avoiding his wrath.

He'd slept outside the tent simply because his brothers wouldn't allow him to sleep with them inside. That's ok as far as he was concerned, Esh had always proved to be better company. And besides, after spending so many nights under the stars, to be inside a tent would have given him the uncomfortable feeling of sleeping in someone else's house.

As he watched the cavalry make their preparations, something stirred inside his spirit. That quiet voice whispered once more, get ready because something very

251

important is about to take place. Reaching down, he quietly picked up his saddle and gently placed it on Esh's back. The use of a Capall saddle meant there weren't any straps or buckles to make much noise for his brothers to hear. Having so few things to pack up and roll into his bedroll, he could be ready to ride in minutes. Then a thought popped into his head: what if he were to fall in at the back of the column of riders? He still remembered what the Captain Korah said weeks ago when visiting their farm . . something about rank or status meaning little in battle, just valor and courage.

A plan started to form in Riordan's mind. He led Esh over to stand beside a large rock so he could climb on easier and throw his leg over his few belongings behind his saddle. He pulled the Riail dlí just slightly from its old and worn scabbard, just enough to see the gray blue of the blade. Rather than try to continue to conceal the sword in his bedding, for the first time he belted it openly on his hip. He'd just finished adjusting the belt which required much of his concentration, when a voice startled him.

"And just where do you think you're going Mamzer?" Torin stood there, glaring over crossed arms. "Did you really think a ra`ah on a broken down old horse could slip in with Capall cavalry unnoticed? Even if they didn't notice you were just a boy and your horse is older than Tebel itself, the sheep smell would have given you away. I myself am not riding with the cavalry, but am assigned to the trenches, so there is no way in Sheol you are going to ride with them. Not today—not ever."

Torin stepped forward to take Esh's halter and physically remove Riordan from the saddle. With no time to think, or consider the consequences of what he was about to do, Riordan simply acted. He urged Esh to jump forward while planting his foot in Torin's chest; shoving him to the ground. He then tore off through the camp as fast as the aged flame could take him. With

252

much of the camp now stirring to life, a son of Capall riding hard didn't present any cause for alarm—yet. Riders, especially the younger ones, were often used as couriers in camp, their business often proved to be urgent. Eventually cries of alarm to "stop the fool" spread through the camp, but Riordan managed to always stay a step or two ahead. Until half way through the camps he raced past one of the officers, who hesitated a moment, then decided to give pursuit. While only a few seconds delay, it gave Riordan and Esh a pretty good lead.

Calls to stop him finally outraced Esh, and so were heard by several Dun in the outer defenses, but the horse and his boy were charging fast. There wasn't time to climb over the walls of the trench, and they wouldn't have been physically able to stop him regardless. At least, not without killing Esh. So they mostly watched in fascination while what they took to be a bag-of-bones, half-dead nag leaped over their heads. Strengthened by some unknown power, the red horse cleared the width of the trench easily and continued on down the embankment towards the Dagon camp. A few of the Dun recovered from their surprise and took aim with bows until a urgent commanding voice ordered, "Hold your fire!"

When they turned to look they saw Korah, the cavalry captain riding hard in hot pursuit. His own horse leaped over the trenches only to pull to a sudden stop, a few yards down the slope, spraying sand and gravel for several feet.

Korah spent most of the previous afternoon and evening waiting for Mereah. It wasn't like the Rapha` prince not to show up, and he worried through all the possibilities about what could have happened. His strike force remained on full alert since yesterday afternoon. Finally he felt no other choice remained but to give the early morning order. It looked as though the task of being the diversion and facing the Anak would fall to him after all.

By now, he knew his lieutenants would be bringing the cavalry down for their attempted break out of the keys to get behind the enemy and attack their lines of supply. Food would be a secondary target, but if they could cut off the Dagon water supply . . . but where could Mereah be? While having a pretty good hunch, he didn't dare risk going to the king's pavilion to confirm his suspicion.

The Anak would be coming out soon with what he expected to be the last issued challenge. Appropriately enough, he would be coming forth with what by all appearances looked to be a red dawn. If the Rapha` Prince did not show, Korah speculated on the chances of the cavalry breaking past the lines without a diversion. He quickly ruled that option out, but he did have every confidence in his lieutenant's abilities to lead the cavalry in his stead.

About the time he completed this last thought, he became distracted by the sound of a horse charging hard through the camps. Turning in the saddle he saw Riordan just as he cleared the tents and pavilions. He immediately recognized the ra`ah, riding hard on his grandfather's old red charger.

"Now what is the lad up to?" he murmured. Then it struck him, "The young fool is looking to break out of the Keys? But to what purpose . . . he wouldn't . . ." As Esh flew past he realized, "You know, I think maybe he would." The captain dug in his heals and with a shout gave chase. His first thought, "This could ruin everything."

His second thought, "How in Sheol can that old bag of bones still manage to run so fast?"

He started yelling to the men in the trenches, but most of them were half asleep, or just now waking. No way anyone there would be capable of stopping the lad, and he still trailed by several lengths when the big, gray-flecked roan leaped and cleared the trenches. Calculating time and distance starting from the time Esh made the leap over the defense works to when he himself would get there, he realized he wasn't gaining any ground on the old charger–just eating his dust. He didn't have even a prayer's chance of stopping the lad, short of driving his mare beyond her limits. Korah felt compelled to make a split-second decision. His choices were, continue to chase the horse and his boy in the faint hope he could catch him before he gets too close to the Dagon camp, or . . . The debate in his mind grew intense. To let the boy go would be to abandon him to certain death. But that old red horse could still run; it didn't seem likely he would catch him until they were practically at the Dagon lines, if at all. Korah suddenly noticed a couple of the Dun had short bows and were taking aim at the boy, or the horse, so he barked out the order to hold their fire. As he cleared the trenches himself, he grudgingly made the decision and pulled his mare up short letting Riordan go.

Because of his hesitation, catching the lad in time to bring him back now would be impossible. How could he rescue the situation? It may not be the diversion that he planned, but it surely looked like there would be one, nonetheless. But he couldn't abandon the lad to face the Anak alone . . . before he could ride after the boy, he first must give instruction to his lieutenants. Turning his horse quickly, once again he urged his mount into a full gallop back to meet the line of Capall cavalry already working its way through the camps.

Clear of the defenses, and no longer hearing pursuit, Riordan slowed Esh to a trot. They had to pick their way very carefully down a slope of sand and scree, and the boy was determined not to give Esh any cause to stumble, hurting one or both of them. They reached the level plain about the same time as the sun breeched the horizon to his left.

About two hundred yards away, waiting like a sentinel of the dawn, the Anak sat on his tanniyn. He urged the dragon forward about twenty-five yards and stopped, deciding to let Riordan come to him, if he dared.

Cold fear settled in the pit of his stomach. Yesterday, when the shaman was hurling insults against Jeshurun and Elohim, he got so mad, he wanted to fight the demon–right then. Now with his anger cooled, he found himself actually facing the Anak, his adversary mounted on a tanniyn, it didn't seem like such a good idea after all. He knew he'd run out of good options; he didn't dare go back, yet to go forward would be certain death. And so the debate raged in his mind even as sweat began to trickle down his brow, "Don't be an idiot. What did you think would happen by coming here? Turn around, now, and you might make it back without getting killed."

Fear seemed to be giving him prudent advice. Yet still he remained frozen in place. More than anything he wished he could see Jireh trotting down the slope to join him. He doubted the Shophetim would be afraid of anything—ever. Then he remembered the Riail dlí, the blade now strapped to his side. He reached for the sword and when he touched the handle he received such a shock that he yanked back his hand. The sword, it was alive, active–aware.

He remembered Jireh telling him, that Yahweh had forged the Riail dlí from Nomos, the rule of law that flowed through all of creation; so why should he be surprised to discover that the blade would be a living thing?

He took the handle into his hand and once again felt a surge of strength. While he still felt afraid, at least he didn't feel like he would pass out. The Riail dlí began to exert a calming effect and a strange peace settled in his spirit. He remembered Brónach's warning about the roaring lion, and about not going in the direction fear dictated.

He took a deep breath, gave Esh a gentle nudge with his heels, and together they slowly started forward.

Twenty-one

"Yahweh is my light and my salvation–whom shall I fear? The LORD is the stronghold of my life-of whom shall I be afraid?"
~The Shepherd's Songbook ch. 21

Mereah sat on a stool in his father's tent. Under guard, his hands tied behind his back, only his thoughts remained free. Concern about his father's sanity weighed heavily on his mind. For the last several weeks a large wedge worked violently to split them apart, seeking to separate the king not just from his son, but from all the people. Only now however did Mereah realize that the relationship with his father had so completely deteriorated. All night, Ruarc the king seemed possessed, tormented by fits of madness. At times he wept like a child; other times he raged, grabbed whatever he could get his hands on, and threw it about the tent. He screamed obscenities and shook his fist in the air as though responding to the taunts of an unknown antagonist. Then all of a sudden, he went deathly quiet, and he fixed Mereah with a deadly stare.

Spittle trickled from his mouth, catching in his beard; evil, obscenity and death flared in his eyes. As he watched the demented display, Mereah felt certain of another presence, that inhabited the body of his father like a tent. Something unspeakably evil. Immediately after completing his thought, Ruarc, or whatever hostile power occupied the king's soul, fixed its eye on the young giant. It seemed as though the evil entity had discerned Mereah's startling discovery. Although an idiotic grin transfixed his father's face, the vehement gaze sent chills down the prince's spine.

Almost casually, the king reached over and took a long lance from a rack by his tent wall, and threw the spear straight at Mereah's chest as he screamed, "The crown is mine, you can't have it you . . you bloody son of a . . ." One of the prince's guards pulled him aside just as the lance buried its head in one of the tent support posts.

The king staggered back and collapsed into his chair. He dropped his face to hide in outstretched hands as he wept uncontrollably. Unseen tormenting voices hissed taunts of accusation about this his latest horrible and cowardly deed. Legions of affirming voices confirmed shames accusal, shriveling the king's soul and dragging it down into the burning flames of his own personal purgatory.

The two Rapha` guards looked at each other, nodded, and while one untied the prince's legs, the other sought to remove the bonds from Mereah's wrists. One of the guards whispered, "We must get you out quickly my lord, before the madness passes."

While waiting to be freed the prince asked "How long have these fits been coming upon my father?"

The guard who untied his hands replied, "For about two Months, but lately with more frequency. Mostly at night, and every night this week."

"Can nothing be done?"

"If our prince has a suggestion, we would be glad to

259

listen. Attempts to reason with the king are pointless.
When the fits strike, the only wise thing to do is flee
until the rage is passed."

"Are you not worried what your king's reaction will
be when his fit passes, and I am gone?"

The other guard responded to this question, "Yes
Sire. But we also have hope, as often happens, that the
king will not remember much at all from this night.
Also we believe as you, the Anak and the Dagon are
coming and, someone needs to lead our people . . . it is
clear the king cannot."

Mereah rubbed his wrists, chaffed by the ropes,
"Thank you my friends. I believe you are right, battle
will be joined today, and I must go to meet it. Promise
me, if the fighting breaks past the defenses, you will
protect the king. Make him flee from this place, and get
him to safety."

"What about you my lord?"

"There will be no need to worry about me after this
morning my friends. Against my father's orders, I go to
face the Anak." Mereah believed his response to be
sufficient explanation. There wasn't any need to worry
about his safety, because after the morning's combat, he
didn't expect to be alive.

After the guards expressions indicated they caught
his meaning, Mereah grinned despite his fear, "But
please, again I ask of you, if the fighting gets past the
trenches, . . . get my father out, don't worry about me."

~

Riordan crossed the distance to within twenty five
yards of the Anak, and stopped. The shaman's very
presence burned his spirit like acid. Buzzards circled
overhead, as though summoned to emphasize Riordan's
fate. Flies, the size of the end of a man's thumb
swarmed around Esh, threatening to take a few pounds

of his flesh and drive him mad.

The Anak sat on his tanniyn and looked down his nose at his opponent. "Am I a mongrel that Ruarc sends a boy without even a stick to fetch me? This insult will only result in his death being much slower. For this affront I will strike all life and hope from his soul–I will dismember his son and bath in his blood while he is forced to watch. Then we shall see if the craven's whelp still wishes to sing. I will be merciful and allow you to live so you may go and tell him this."

Fear reached an icy hand into Riordan's chest and squeezed all courage from his heart. His mind raced, "Did he just tell me he was letting me go? A way out! Take it you idiot!"

But he didn't follow the reasonable voice of sanity screaming in his mind. Instead he reached for the handle of the Riail dlí. Once again–felt its life repel his fear. Slowly the words came. Even he was surprised, as he spoke, it seemed the words came from someone else.

"The king has not insulted you. He has not sent me but remains in his tent. I have come of my own accord. I am nothing, as you have said. I have not come because í think I am anything at all, I know I am not. Who I am really doesn't matter, the one who came with me . . . He is the one who matters." For the first time Riordan dared to look the sorcerer in the eye, "I advise you to be afraid."

"The Shaman's laughter spit out a wave of venomous contempt, "The one who came with you? I can only assume you mean the walking bone bag that carries your sorry carcass to a slow agonizing death."

"Ah, you understand that to insult the horse of a son of Capall, is to insult his rider. You have a talent for taunts, and insult, but I have come not because you have taunted me, my horse, the armies of Jeshurun, or even Ruarc the king. No, I have come because you made a fatal mistake. I am here because you are a flea who has dared challenge Yahweh Elohim, the one whose word created the stars, and formed all of creation upon a foundation of law. It is not by any strength of mine that you shall be destroyed, but by the power of one who speaks a word and out of the darkness a universe of light explodes into being."

The Anak lifted his scepter and the jewel at its crown began to glow blood red. "Boy, my tanniyn has not feasted on flesh for a few days. I can't feed him that over-ripe carcass you call a horse—no self-respecting buzzard would even touch him. That leaves the worms . . they're always hungry, and the fly's who aren't too picky. You're tender flesh however, a dragon might enjoy, provided I cook it first." With a flick of the scepter a fireball launched straight at Riordan and Esh.

For the second time that morning Brónach was struck with a surge of energy that staggered him, and almost knocked him down. Reaching out to steady himself against the wall, he tried to remain calm while he sorted things out. Earlier, he could feel Esh and Riordan in a race that felt like they were running for their lives. Now, Memories flooded back to him of combat; combat while riding Esh when they both were young, fighting the Dagon. He knew beyond doubt that Esh along with Riordan were engaged in deadly battle even now, he didn't know how he knew, but he did. Earlier he felt Esh in a race he knew the old charger must not lose . . . so he willed and lent his own power to the effort. Together, their strength combined, increased, multiplied. He couldn't quite see with Esh's eyes, but he could feel what his old friend felt, he even sensed the approach of the fireball, and willed Esh the dexterity to dance away . . .

He sensed with every fiber of his being that this fight, the young boy and old horse couldn't hope to win. Without the ability to see what was happening, he didn't have a clue how to lend his battle-hardened experience to Riordan, but somehow he knew the horse would know what to do. The problem wasn't a lack of wisdom, or fighting experience. For Esh the problem would be his age, and finding the strength to accomplish all that needed to be done. So gathering all the potency left to him, Brónach again imparted power through a mystical bond to Zaquen Esh, the Aged Flame.

The fire ball hit so close, the hair on Riordan's head singed and curled. He didn't have any idea how Esh managed to get out of the way, but the horse did so without any command from him. Of the two, Riordan knew that only the horse possessed combat experience, so he hoped Esh would know what to do—because he sure didn't. It's likely a good thing the ra`ah didn't know that a tanniyn with an Anak rider was a foe even the old charger hadn't faced before.

A deadly dance commenced with the horse staying close enough to the dragon so the Anak couldn't unleash any more attacks of magic. Remaining so near however meant staying in striking distance of the dragon's teeth, claws and tail. Esh, with a strength and swiftness Riordan couldn't fathom, managed to stay just out of the tanniyn's reach while maneuvering to keep within striking distance of the reptile's exposed flank. Twice the war horse avoided tanniyn attacks and managed to bring his young rider into position to use the Riail dlí. Unfortunately, Riordan lacked the experience and the skill to take advantage and effectively strike.

After yet another wild swing and complete miss by Riordan, the dragons tail swept around threatening to crush Esh. With a supernatural display of power the old horse leaped in the air and vaulted the deadly strike of the monster's tail. Most sons of Capall are practically born on horse back. Riordan however, had learned to ride only a few short months ago. Esh's leap caught him off guard and even as the horse lifted into flight over the deadly strike, the inexperienced young ra`ah flew from the saddle and landed in the dust and gravel several feet away. Worse yet, the shock of sudden impact sent the Riail dlí flying from his hand.

Laying in the dirt, all the air forced from his lungs, Riordan couldn't move, couldn't breath, but his eyes worked. Likely he wished they didn't. He saw a tanniyn with a wicked grin made from rows of razor sharp teeth, choose to ignore Esh and close in on his own crumpled and helpless form. He closed his eyes, tight. The dragon screamed in anticipation while the Anak laughed in contempt over the whelp's fate who so audaciously dared defy him.

Then in a red blur of fury, Esh charged between Riordan's prostrate form and the dragons. He opened his eyes, and attempted to scream a command for the horse to flee. With the air not yet returned to his lungs he couldn't manage even a whisper. It wouldn't have mattered. Esh would never have obeyed any command to abandon his place as the boy's protector regardless of who gave the order. He reared and screamed defiance. Esh met claw and teeth with striking hooves. Defensive maneuvering and avoidance were no longer possible. To do so would be to abandon protective positioning of his boy. So as he engaged the serpent's teeth and claws, the charger remained vulnerable to the mighty tail as it swept across and broke Esh's back legs.

Esh struggled valiantly to rise. His head and shoulders lifted upwards, but the back legs dragged uselessly. Intent on finishing the job it started, Riordan now forgotten, the dragon's huge talons dug into Esh's neck and flank. Razor teeth ripped into the old stallion's back severing the spine.

Brónach felt completely immersed in the mystical bond, sensing Esh's adrenaline and rage. Despite their being leagues apart, he felt the fireball's heat, and recognized that a magic attack had just occurred. Having heard rumors about the Dagon being led by an

Anak, riding a tanniyn, he understood that his grandson and the old charger were in a desperate situation. While finding it hard to believe some fool sent a boy into combat against such a deadly opponent, he frantically questioned what he could do to somehow keep them both alive.

All of the Capall knew of the legendary bond the cavalry knew with their horses back in the First Age. Not really understanding how, Brónach knew the legends were moving into his experience. He felt Esh's movements, and . . something else. Their bond gave him strength . . . and increasing power to Esh as well. The red stallion ran like never before, not even when they were both young.

Drawing from combined experience, together they quickly formulated a battle plan. He hoped to evade the tanniyn's front, while remaining close to its flanks, so close the Anak couldn't attack again with magic.

It seemed a good strategy, and if Esh were ridden by an experienced rider, it might have prevailed. Riordan's lack of experience became quickly evident and Brónach through the bond, felt Esh's dismay when the ra`ah flew off his back. He both discerned and encouraged the horses fierce determination to still defend his ward. Suddenly the legs of Brónach went limp and he collapsed. Through mystical bond, he shared the horses frenzied attempts to rise. He felt excruciating pain as claws and four inch fangs crushed and ripped out his old friend's spine. A moment later he lay completely paralyzed all feeling lost below his shoulders. Flat on his back, he offered up silent prayers as he stared at the ceiling of his cottage.

~

At Korah's command the cavalry leaped into motion. They started out at a gentle cantor until they were within twenty yards of the trenches. The captain hand-signaled his troops and two hundred horse broke into a thunderous charge down the slope and over the outer trenches.

Moments later, the captain heard the detonation of a fireball and assumed the worst. He deeply regretted the loss of the boy's life–sensing a real quality in the young man. However, he didn't have time to think about that, his most present and pressing concern was that the combat had ended so quickly. Would it serve as a sufficient diversion? He started second guessing his choices even as his own horse cleared the trenches. Why didn't he pursue Riordan further? Why didn't he face the Anak himself?

He already knew the answers to his own questions. He hadn't told any of his lieutenants his plans or how to proceed without him. For their protection, he gave as little information to them as possible, just in case the king caught wind of the conspiracy. Knowing the reasoning behind the decisions didn't make them any easier however, the cost seemed much too high. Forced to share some details this morning before setting out, several of his officers volunteered for the task of facing the Anak, but he'd already decided against that weeks ago. He would not send another man to die in his place, and there wasn't time to argue. And yet here he somehow . . found himself allowing a mere boy . . . he couldn't finish the thought.

Korah pulled up and swung to the left looking for Riordan and the Anak, he had to know . . As his men swept by, the captain noticed two things; first, the boy miraculously, was still alive–momentarily–for the Dagon forces were still focused on the combat. Quickly sizing up the situation Korah realized that while Riordan didn't know at all what he was doing, the horse did.

Next he noted the Anak intently focused on his young challenger and that no attempt to cut the cavalry off appeared to be forthcoming. A slight chill moved down his spine, what if the sorcerer wasn't distracted at all? What if he just didn't care? Perhaps the Capall Cavalry presented no more threat to the Anak than a young boy on an ancient broken down charger. After all, what possible threat could a few hundred horse hope to bring against an army numbered in the tens of thousands?

Korah started to ride after his men when he heard a roar of celebration from the Dagon camp, a decisive blow must have been struck! Moving to a small rise to see a little more clearly, he watched as the valiant red horse screamed its defiance. Esh's courage moved him to tears, but the captain flinched and had to turn away his eyes as the tanniyn used teeth and talons to sever the old warrior's spine.

He couldn't see the boy Riordan. Surely he must be dead. Yet even now the movement of the Capall wasn't challenged. The diversion, while short proved to be more than enough. More than anything he wanted to go back and face the demon who slaughtered his sons. He also knew it to be more important that he stay alive and lead his men. He could do nothing for the lad now, but perhaps he would have opportunity, on another day. His best revenge would be the defeat of the Anak's army. Then perhaps, Korah would have the opportunity to confront the Dagon shaman himself.

~

After release by his father's guards, Mereah knew from the departure of the sons of Capall that he missed his meeting with Korah. Taking up his weapons, he headed to the observation point to see if the captain chose to lead the cavalry out of the Keys without a diversion, or if he decided to provide it himself (which the Rapha' Prince thought far more likely). Lithos saw Mereah sprinting up the path to the lookout, and ran after him, yelling, "Where have you been, I've spent most the night looking for ya!"

"No time to stop my friend, we must talk while I run. I was held captive . . . no time to explain."

"Or need to either," Lithos muttered as he pursued at a dead run.

Mereah reached the high place just in time to see a rider on a red horse, move forward to meet the Anak. Under constant watch himself to ensure that he did not go out to meet the Anak's challenge, his heart felt a certain thrill that at last someone demonstrated the courage to defy the king and answer the Dagon Shaman's defiance. The Dun Commander, huffing and puffing caught up with Mereah, and didn't receive any greeting other than a strange question, "My friend, do you have an Irial glass with you?"

Puzzled, Lithos declared, "Yes, but not for an eye as big as yours."

"Well then quickly focus on that lone rider–tell me what do you see?"

After a tense moment trying to focus, precious seconds that seemed like an eternity to the young giant, at last the Dun warrior gave a low whistle. Speaking extremely slow, in short incomplete phrases, Lithos drove his enormous, anxious friend almost insane.

"Ah, that will . . . never do, ... what was . . . Korah . . . thinking."

"What? What do you see?"

"Looks like a . . . boy, on a . . . broken down horse."

"A boy? Why would Korah send a boy?!"

"I don't know!" Lithos shouted as he lowered the glass, "Perhaps you should ask Korah, and for that matter, why is anyone challenging the Anak in defiance of your father's orders? And maybe you can tell me what the cavalry is doing, even now they are clearing the trenches and appear to be attempting to break past the Dagon lines somewhere to the East?"

"Ah my friend, I'm sorry I didn't include you . . . In a little conspiracy. I didn't want you to get in further trouble after joining me in my last fool's errand. I have no time to explain right now. I must get down onto the plains. Korah may still need me to provide a diversion."

Lithos yelled after the Rapha Prince's retreating back as he charged down the path, "What diversion?"

Mereah shouted back over his shoulder as he kept running, "I am supposed to be the one to give battle to the Anak!"

Lithos rolled his eyes, gave a deep sigh, and ran once again after his prince.

Twenty-two

Some reckon their age by years,
Some measure their life by art;
But some tell their days by the flow of their tears
And their lives by the moans of their hearts.
~Abram Joseph Ryan

The tanniyn gave a roar of triumph as Esh's limp body collapsed into the desert sand. So intent were they on Esh's prostrate form that neither the serpent nor the Anak saw the ra`ah climb to his feet just a few steps away. A fraction of a second too late the Anak saw out of the corner of his eye the deadly blue arc of the Riail dlí slicing through the dragon's armor scaled neck as easily as it sliced the air. The blade's judgment true, the second edge withheld healing, leaving the serpents long neck and head as well as its lifeless body to writhe and flail about. Foul black blood sprayed everywhere, the gore filling Riordan with revulsion.

Rising from the wreck of his tanniyn the Anak once again held aloft his jeweled scepter. Air molecules condensed above the glowing orb until they formed a dark catapult projectile that flew at Riordan striking him straight in the chest. His ribs and sternum cracked. The

270

blow launched him backwards several feet and dropped him unceremoniously into a heap. Body and spirit broken, the air forced from his lungs once again, he watched helplessly as the sorcerer stooped over and picked up the Riail dlí out of the dirt.

"Any number of attacks I could have used to destroy you boy . . all were dismissed as being too quick—much too painless. Ah, but it strikes me that slow dismemberment by your own blade, now *that* would have such delicious irony . . . even a soul long dead such as mine can still enjoy a good laugh.

My name is Anbhás. I intend to kill you slowly, painfully—violently. Perhaps your screams will prove useful to lure more vermin out of their holes so they may be exterminated."

The Anak's pre-death "I'm about to kill you now" monolog was interrupted by the sounds of thunderous hoof beats as the Capall charged through Jeshurun's Key. "Ah, the cavalry is coming. Too late to save you! However, I must thank you for helping me lure the fools to their deaths."

Riordan struggled to rise to his hands and knees, his cracked ribs screaming in protest. All the while Anbhás continued to gloat. Lifting the blade to allow closer examination, the Anak continued his monolog in an attempt to increase the boys fear and despair, "This is the finest blade I have ever seen. I can't imagine what fool would entrust it to such a helpless whelp as yourself. Or did you steal it? Perhaps I shouldn't kill you after all. I am quite sure the true owner of this blade would flay you alive for taking it, only to lose it to me. Observe how little effort is required to remove your limbs." With a simple flick the Riail dlí passed through Riordan's arm. To the Anak's bewilderment, the boy looked as though he hadn't been touched.

The Shaman muttered a single word to express his dismay, "Impossible." The sword flicked out once again in a deadly arc but this time not to maim or torture, but to kill. Riordan closed his eyes, braced against certain death as he felt the blade pass through his neck. Yet, death didn't come. Once again the blade cut. Once again it healed. How could that be? The boy who'd been called Mamzer for most of his life felt anything *but* innocent. His astonishment almost matched that of his foe.

The Anak stepped back, and lifted the blade again to examine its length for flaws, for anything that might explain what he'd just witnessed, "Apparently I underestimated you young scum. All the better. The blade's magical properties I will learn to exploit, after your death of course, which will . ."

Anbhás focus left the nomos blade just long enough to see Riordan's sling stone on a collision course with his forehead. The only thing and the last thing he felt . . . his own surprise just before the stones impact.

~

The Dagon army watched the Anak fall, as did the armies of Jeshurun. Both sides were struck dumb with disbelief. After a full minute of stunned silence, one of the sons of Dun leapt out of the trenches, and roared his approval. A few more joined in . . . and then almost all of the sons of Capall who manned the defenses added their voice; and so the cheering spread up the canyon and through the camps. The Anak is fallen.

"What?" Some doubters cried, "Impossible! Who killed him?"

"Nobody knows!" Came the reply, "Somebody said just a boy, one of the sons of Capall."

"Impossible!" The doubters scoffed, "Someone's had a bit too much to drink. But why are they cheering down there?"

"I told you already, somebody killed the Anak!"
"Who did?"
"Are you deaf? . . . A BOY! A mere boy, and he

272

killed him with just a rock."

"Impossible!" The doubters cried again.

And so word spread through the camp, but not belief. Completely understandable, not even the people who saw the Anak fall with their own eyes believed it.

Believers were made from among the enemy ranks however, much faster and easier. With the spiritual bondage of the Anak's imposed will removed, one by one the Dagon started to leave the battle lines. Walking slowly at first, after a couple hurried glances back, the early responders started to run. The first few runners infected thousands of others with panic, and it spread like a virus. In mere seconds the entire Dagon army transformed from savage invaders to frightened cattle stampeding across the Cnámh.

The last of the Capall riders raced past Korah and he assumed the position of rear guard for the cavalry's desperate attempt to break past the Dagon flank. When he heard the sudden explosion of cheers, he felt sure it could only mean one thing, the Anak had dispatched the young ra'ah. Any moment now the Dagon would realize what the cavalry were attempting. His first thought, encourage his men to ride like they'd never rode before! His orders died in his throat as he realized, wait a minute, the Dagon weren't cheering, it was Jeshurun. Pulling up hard and straining to see what happened, he couldn't see a sign of the boy or the Anak. He did see the body of the tanniyn however. The dragon was down, lying still in a pool of dark blood. He also saw the Dagon raising a gigantic dust cloud in their frenzied flight across the bone dry plain.

Urging his mount back into a full gallop, he yelled at his men, "Hold, Hold, we have to turn, the Dagon flee! Turn around!" Turning around two hundred hard-charging men however, required Korah to ride a lot faster while yelling a lot louder, especially from well to the rear of the formation. He urged his black mare into her second race of the day in an attempt to overtake the front of the formation.

Mereah arrived at the trenches just as the Riail dlí sliced through the dragon's armor scaled neck. Then he watched as the Anak rose from the tanniyn's wreck to blast his opponent. Best he could tell from that distance, it did appear to be a boy, or a very young man. Perhaps if he acted quickly he could still save the lad's life. With a roar he leaped over the trenches and started down the slope. Lithos arrived huffing and puffing, just as the giant vaulted over the trench. Determined to stay with his prince and friend, the Dun Commander did his best to hurdle the span. The combination of jumping too soon while carrying a ton of equipment, plus possessing much shorter legs yielded a most unfortunate result. Only half of the heavily armored dwarf actually cleared the ditch. With a loud ooooff, Lithos bounced off the trench wall, and fell backwards. His dignity, along with most of his pride plunged down with him as he ended up as a stunned heap in the bottom of the ditch.

Slinging that stone alerted Riordan to the fact that he likely had some broken or cracked ribs. The Anak appeared to be down for the count, and for the moment, the least of the boys worries. He didn't think he could stand, so Riordan crawled to Esh's side. The damage to his friend's hind legs, and spinal area was horrific. He managed to lift the red horse's head to cradle it in his lap. To his wonder he saw the light of life still remained in the dark eyes looking back at him. Esh managed a little nicker to say goodbye, then gently the light faded and was gone. One more loss to trigger the well-springs of pain and grief in his soul. His cries and tears of dismay were lost amidst the roars of celebration erupting from the Jeshurun lines, and camp.

Leagues away, Brónach lay paralyzed on the floor of his home. There wasn't any sensation his legs, or from the waist down and he could feel his own life draining away. Since yielding the right of the First Born to his son Brannan, he lived in his small cottage alone. Yet, he wasn't alone. He could feel Riordan's anguish and tears through the continued mystical bond with Esh.

"It's alright Lad, Esh is a warrior. He chose a noble end . . and now, so must I. I can feel your presence lad, . . . I just can't see you . . . . I hope you know, how proud . . ."

Together, despite leagues of separation, Brónach and Esh said their goodbyes, closed their eyes and released their spirits.

~

Korah finally got the cavalry turned around, and in pursuit of the bolting Dagon. When an opponent turns his back and flees, they can offer very little resistance. The cavalry quickly turned the Cnámh plain into a killing field–still more bones to be added to the dry bones valley.

About the same time, the Jeshurun army abandoned the defenses to also join in the hunt. Perhaps, the biggest surprise for the Jeshurun camp came when the king emerged from his tent. The madness cleared from his eyes, Ruarc appeared wearing his armor, and brandishing his axe. Several of the Rapha` around the encampment looked at the king like they'd never seen him before. Truth is they hadn't, not like this, not for some time. "What are you looking at you idiots, the enemy is fleeing, to arms!"

Frustrated that his soldiers continued to just stare at

him he bellowed impatiently, "Did any of you hear what I just said, this is your KING. TO ARMS! The enemy is fleeing the battlefield!"

Not willing to wait for his warriors to overcome their shock, the king with his guards stormed out through camp to the desert plain below. The remaining surprised and bewildered Rapha` were left to scramble and grab their weapons in a frenzied attempt to not be left behind.

Riordan sat for the longest time, cradling Esh's head in his lap, weeping. He barely heard the quiet dismount of Capall's captain, or his soft footfalls. Korah, quickly took in the details of the scene before him. The Anak lay flat on his back a few yards away, a bloody sling stone lay in the sand nearby. In some ways, Korah almost felt cheated. The sorcerer was responsible for the death of all his sons; his death came much too quick, and not from his own hand.

A few feet away, the ra`ah supported the red horse's head, overcome with grief. That night at the farm by Joktan, when Brannan denied being the lad's father, Korah knew even then, sensed it somehow, the young man would be destined for great things. And here he sat, victor over one of the Anakim riding a tanniyn. His victory obtained through use of a simple sling, the weapon of a ra`ah, a shepherd.

The boy's tears threatened to open up his own floodgates of pain. Grief–mourning, these were a luxury he couldn't afford of late. Now at last, his time had come. The Anak was defeated. The Dagon were routed and fled across the Cnámh plains. So the good captain placed his hand gently on Riordan's shoulder and sat down beside him. That is how Mereah found them both, cleansing their souls through the shared sacrifice of broken spirits.

Twenty-three

"I'll come back to the dew of dear Tara
To restore the strong magick of old.
To make right the sad wrong
And to sing a new song
Of honor and courage, so bold."
~Susan Isabella Sheehan
On The Hill Of Tara

Out of respect for Korah and Riordan's grief, Mereah didn't announce his presence, choosing instead to keep his distance. Walking over to where the Anak lay, he noticed a bloody rock and a magnificent sword that lay close to the fallen shaman's hand. The young Rapha` Prince didn't remember ever seeing the Anak with a blade. Nor did he think it belonged to him, something about the sword made Mereah doubt it would be a weapon of the Shaman's choosing.

The sling-stone he picked up, knowing it needed to be preserved as a valuable artifact. The story of what happened here today would be told again . . . and again. It would be remembered for as long as Jeshurun endured as a people.

Finding a lance abandoned by the fleeing Dagon soldiers, Mereah thrust the blunt end deep into the sand,

277

next to the body of the tanniyn. He then took up the Anak, and impaled his body on the spear so the pale white face, outstretched arms and hands, all faced up to be exposed to the sun and light.

Grimly he murmured to the prostrate form, "No burial or fire for you. Too many of my people, most of them family . . . and friends . . have you fed to the birds, or your lizards. Now we shall see if the birds will touch even you."

Lastly, he looked at the Anak's scepter, laying in the sand. Magnificently crafted from several precious metals, the ruby capstone, as large as a child's fist reflected the sunlight like fiery wisps in a complicated and sacred dance. Clearly an object of great value, the Anak had used it as an instrument of tremendous evil. He reasoned it would be extremely destructive in the wrong hands–in any hands for that matter–so he didn't dare to touch the thing himself. Instead he wrapped it in his cloak, and put it away murmuring, "Perhaps, I'll see Jireh again, he'll know what to do with this."

Mereah then approached Riordan and Korah, sitting in the dust beside Esh. "Well met captain. It seems to be El's will that neither you or I need die this day. But who is this young man? I do not recognize him as being one of your riders.   Our friend Lithos observed your deployment of this young warrior and I believe his opinion to be that you had taken leave of your senses."

Korah looked up at the Rapha` Prince with a slight grin, "So a Dun Captain who joins his prince to meet the enemy with a battle strategy that includes singing to them, thinks *I'm* crazy? Did I hear you right? I don't know where our horizontally enhanced friend is, but if he were here, I would say to be called crazy by *him* is a bit much."

"Well in his defense, I may have employed a bit of creative enhancement of what he may have *actually* said. However, the question still remains who is our young friend here, and did you send him for this combat

278

in my stead? I am sorry I did not appear as promised, I was . . . prevented."

"Well, to answer your questions, no, I did not send the lad. ˈI would have prevented him, but his charger proved to be much like his rider, there's much more there than meets the eye. As to who he is, when we first met, he was a simple ra`ah tending his uncle's sheep. When next we meet he's wearing the crest and tunic of a great captain of our people, and riding that captain's old horse. I can only guess at the many events that must have taken place between those two meetings . . . so I think I will let the boy speak for himself, and tell us his name."

Ashamed of his tears the boy tried to hide them by not showing his face. His voice however betrayed powerful emotions as tears mournfully colored his words thick with grief, "I am orphan."

Not yet fully comprehending the full extent of the young man's grief, once again Korah guessed he had yet to hear the full story, so he prodded him to speak further, "Why would one named Orphan wear the crest of a great captain of our people?"

Brónach, my Grandfather . . my . . he's my Goel, my kinsman redeemer, he is now lost. When Esh's life passed from him, so did my Grandfather's, I . . . heard his voice. My uncle–father . . Brannan, he will never accept me as son, or honor my Grandfather's mercy. I believe he will take away my name. I will be worse than orphan. Once the name Mamzer spoke to my shame. He shall name me Mamzer again."

Mereah scratched his head and tried to make sense out of what the boy just said. He felt like someone who just walked into the middle of a complex conversation. Clearly there existed a great story yet to be told.

Likewise Korah could only guess at the meaning of much that the ra`ah said. However, one thing jumped out as a likely clue to a troubling question that had been on his mind for the last few minutes. He looked with renewed wonder at Esh. If it was true, that Brónach shared the death of his old charger, this spoke of a life bond–a bond not known by their people since the destruction that ended the first age. This bond was a treasure, a gift from Elohim, lost to the people of Capall for thousands of years.

"If Esh had been empowered by this bond," Korah thought, "That might explain how the old charger left me so far behind and eating his dust this morning."

Suddenly, the full extent of Riordan's grief struck home. The lad also said that Brónach, his great captain had perished along with Esh. Korah realized just how much he shared with the boy, they both had lost everything.

Korah gently placed his hand on Riordan's shoulder. "Lad, look at me. I served as your grandfather's armor bearer. I remember him as the greatest man I have ever known. If we find it is true, . . if your grandfather is dead, by my honor, I will not leave you orphaned. I will redeem you myself, if your uncle lacks the good sense."

Mereah's booming voice chimed in, "And lad, I for one refuse to repeat the slur ignorance slandered you with in the past. When your grandfather acted as your redeemer, he must have given you a new name?"

"My mother, she who abandoned me to Brannan's care, called me Riordan. That name my grandfather gave back to me."

Mereah looked intently at the boy, as though he could somehow read his heart, "Names can be powerful things, your mother may have been an unwitting prophetess. Her choice of identity for you as her son is given as a noble calling. Riordan you shall remain, no one will dare challenge a hero of the Capall or Jeshurun the right to bear such a name. Although after your dispatching of an Anak with a sling, you may find that there is a renewed respect for a ra`ah from this day forth.

Now, tell me about this blade Riordan, is it yours, or

did it belong to the Shaman?"

"It is mine."

"Where did you get it? I have never seen its like."

Korah noted a touch of fear in Riordan's face at this question so he quickly added, "It's alright lad, you can tell him, you've nothing to fear."

Riordan looked up at Korah and then at the Rapha` Prince, searching their faces to be sure they spoke true. Finally he answered, "The sword is the Riail dlí, given to me by Jireh, the Shophetim of Jeshurun."

Mereah gave a low whistle and looked at Korah as if to confirm his thoughts on the matter. "Jireh . . he does not give such prizes lightly. This knowledge, while safe with me, may not be so with my father. Hundreds in the army saw this blade wielded by the Anak. I think it would be safer for you if the blade were to be regarded as a trophy of war. My father especially must not know where the sword came from, and most certainly *never* know Jireh as the giver."

Riordan looked at the Rapha` Prince with a puzzled expression on his face. It was Korah who articulated what Mereah felt uncomfortable expressing.

"Lad, this blade is meant to be wielded only by one who was, . . or is, . . anointed as ruler, judge or king of Jeshurun. If Ruarc knew the nature of this blade, or the giver, the king would try to kill you."

Riordan looked up at Mereah incredulously, "But you are the king's son."

Mereah stared off into space, as though his reply battled with memories and thoughts, "Yes, . . . yes I am. I am the king's son, and heir to the throne of our people. I am also my father's son, and I have watched the wearing of the crown nearly destroy him. When my father became king, I became a prince. I would rather be a nobody, . . if it meant I could only have my father back. If Jireh has discerned you are called to one day be the King of Jeshurun, no one will cheer more loudly than I at your coronation.

"Tonight, you will need to stand before my father. I advise leaving this blade hidden, or in another's care. I think it best you appear as a simple shepherd. Let him think the defeat of the Anak to be no more than a extraordinarily lucky shot. I warn you, my father in all likelihood will be angry. Earlier, he forbade anyone to answer the Anak's challenge. But for now, what can a Prince of Jeshurun do for the hero shepherd of his people?"

After a few moments thought Riordan replied, "Can you help me to care for Esh? I can't bear to think of him . . . being touched by vultures, or worms. Also I need to return home, to make sure that my grandfather . . . that he indeed is . . ." Riordan couldn't finish his thoughts but didn't really need to as both men understood.

Mereah spoke first. "Esh, if I understand the old tongue aright, means fire or flame, I would think a funeral pyre fit for a warrior hero could certainly be managed by a giant. This is however, a meager request and the very least I can do. Since you will not ask, I will have to find additional ways to honor our people's newest, and perhaps youngest hero."

Korah then stood up, offered his hand and pulled Riordan to his feet. "You will also need transport to get you home, perhaps tonight after you meet with the king, I can be of service."

Mereah spoke again, and Riordan found it hard to fathom how any being so big could also be so . . well, gentle. His memory went back to his conversation with Brónach on their journey to the mountains, and what it meant to be gentle or meek. Both the prince and Korah by their lives, proved the statement gentleness is weakness to be a lie.

"Lad, the enemy is in full flight. The captain and I must ensure as few of the Dagon as possible make it back to their homes safely. We want them to think long and hard about ever returning. That they will is inevitable, but we prefer that it be later rather than sooner."

Riordan reached to retrieve the Riail dlí, with the intent of following, "No lad. If you never do another thing of note for the rest of your life, for this one deed you will be remembered. Stay here. Honor your friend by remaining as his guard. We shall return before long and then we shall give you both due honor."

That night, as promised, they gave Esh a funeral pyre fit for a hero of his people. As it turned out, Mereah discovered Esh to be the only Jeshurun casualty of the day. An enemy showing his back is seldom in position to offer any real resistance, and without the Anak to control the Dagon forces for an orderly withdrawal, the day's battle proved a total rout.

Mereah prepared the pyre as his father Ruarc spouted mild objections about so much fuss being made "Over a horse."

The young prince responded with a gentle reminder to the monarch about his responsibilities, "You are Jeshurun's King, and by now should know better than anyone that to the sons of Capall a horse is never just a horse. They have an attachment to their mounts that is almost as great as . . . well, that of a centaur."

This comment only received a chuckle from Ruarc as the king left the tent to preside over the wake. Following his father through the flaps, Mereah felt waves of elation and relief. His most fervent prayers appeared to be answered. He seemed to have his father back, after a long journey in the dark.

More than the enemies defeat, he believed the change in Ruarc to be in some way connected to the death of the Dagon Shaman. The madness, the fits and moments of rage, didn't begin until shortly after the enemies first assault. Although the serpent-rider did not reveal himself at first, it seemed certain he'd been leading the Dagon army from the start. Mereah felt certain that the Anak somehow possessed a window through which to conduct war against his father, a window Mereah felt powerless to shut. He knew it couldn't be coincidence that once the Shaman was dead, the attacks stopped. Now he must somehow discover how the enemy gained such a foothold. By what dark sorcery did they manage to attack the king even while inside his inner chambers? If, or when the enemy returned, would they have the same capability to renew the assault?

Lithos waited alongside Korah to provide Riordan, the King and Mereah escort. Standing between the two captains, the boy didn't look that much taller than a dwarf, and much more slight than Korah. Taking a moment to give the kid the once over, the Dun commander remarked, "No offense lad, are you sure the Anak didn't die from laughing to hard? I doubt ya weigh a hundred and twenty pounds soaking wet."

"No wonder the Anak dismissed his opponent so easily," Mereah laughed, "the lad has barely reached puberty. The shaman thought he was being threatened by a puppy still needing its mother's milk. But my friend I would caution you, there is more to this lad than meets the eye. I can assure you, the Anak is indeed dead, and this *boy* killed him. I know of no other warrior in our entire kingdom who could have accomplished this deed, so take care."

Lithos merely snorted in response.

As they drew near to where the ceremony would take place the Dun Captain was stunned, the entire army had showed up! Leaning over to whisper to Mereah so that Riordan, or Korah didn't hear, the stout warrior realized he was speaking to the young giant's knee. Frustrated by the attempt he finally just spat his words out, regardless of who heard. "I have to admit I agreed with your father. Sure did seem like a lot of fuss over a horse. That the sons of Capall would be here in force is a given, and I expected the Irijah. Wasn't too sure about the Rapha` or

Irial, but all of my people are here as well! The Dun don't generally get too sentimental about animals, we're not a people likely to get mushy about most things. That old red horse now, he displayed extraordinary amounts of bravery and courage, two traits my folk admire greatly. Most of the Dun were in the trenches watching when that old horse placed itself between the boy laying helpless, and that dragon."

Mereah stooped over to reply so that his voice could be heard over the crowd noise without shouting, "Aye, as great an act of devotion and sacrifice as I've ever seen."

Unable to push through the throng, Lithos barked "Way, make way. . . make way for the king!"

The cavalry sergeant who stood the night watch when Riordan first arrived at the Jeshurun camp, snapped to attention, saluted and then presented a torch to the young ra`ah. "Half dead bag of bones I said. Shows how well I know horse-flesh eh boy? I've ridden with the cavalry for over fifteen years, . . never seen a braver 'orse. Sorry lad . . the things I said, just the words of an old fool."

Riordan accepted the torch and nodded in acknowledgment. All eyes were fixed on him, as they waited for him to walk forward and ignite the pyre. Esh lay not just on carefully stacked sticks and small logs, but also on a gallery of spears, lances, bows, and axes–war trophies taken from the Dagon dead.

With the time to actually proceed with the ceremony upon him, Riordan froze in his tracks. This was the final goodbye. He felt unaware of anything except for the huge lump stuck in his throat.

Korah gently placed his hand on Riordan's shoulder, offering silent support. After another moments pause and a deep sigh, he started forward. Not wanting to be seen shedding tears in front of the Jeshurun army, he bit his lip and fought his churning emotions with every step. What he couldn't see however, is that in the eyes of more than a few of the sons of Capall, a fine mist clouded their eyes as well. Even several of the hardest veterans were thankful for the darkness of the evening.

Reaching the pyre, Riordan realized someone had taken time to wash and brush Esh. Also the red mane had been combed, braided and neatly arranged. Reaching up, he stroked the long jaw and soft muzzle. Whispering softly, he murmured "Good bye old friend."

It suddenly dawned on him that if indeed Brónach had died the same moment as Esh, the wake must suffice as farewell for both. Hugging the chargers neck he spoke gently into his ear, "Thanks Esh. You were the best. I don't know how I'll go on without you. And thank you Grandfather. Thank you for the gift of Esh, he saved my life. I hope you and him are reunited now. I thank you for being my redeemer, and giving back to me my name, and my honor. I am no longer Mamzer, but Riordan, son of Brónach, warrior son of Capall."

He touched the bottom of the stacked wood with his torch and stepped back a few yards. Suddenly the flames engulfed the pyre and the boy realized Mereah must have placed something underneath the wood to accelerate the flames. Three times the sons of Capall clashed sword or spear against shields in salute, ending with a loud shout.

Watching the rising flames, Riordan gave one final tribute as he sang in a high clear voice.

Yahweh is my light, and my salvation,
Of whom should I ever be afraid.
I have walked in the midst of His great halls,
That He has adorned in splendor and majesty.
The deeply laid cornerstones of His house,
are laid of stone that resists sheol's flame,
The foundations are deep in the bowels of the earth.
But the beams of His temple, glitter from sky's ice
His treasures of light are renewed every morning.

Yahweh rides the clouds as a chariot
He walks upon the wings of the wind.
You alone are the Lord, you are the One,

You who make the four winds your messengers,
receive now Zaquen Esh, the Aged Flame
In your halls of light, wind and storm,
may his spirit be now returned to flame
May he find a place in your house
A minister of flame in the midst of chariots of fire.

Many who were there that night told the story, a tale
often to be repeated, of how the flesh of the red charger
did indeed transform into consecrated fire. Witnesses
swore they saw horse-shaped flames leap from the pyre
and up into sky, to be carried away as though riding on
the wings of a sacred wind.

Transfixed by the sacred event, the army stood silent
a few minutes longer, until the booming voice of the
king brought everyone back to earth. "Now, I have one
last small piece of business that regrettably must be
dealt with. Riordan, come before me."

Slowly Riordan took his place a few paces before
the king, his head hung low. Realizing defiance of the
king's orders would most certainly be punished, fear
crept into his heart, pushing aside sorrow. He heard the
soft footfalls of Korah, Mereah, and Lithos as they
stepped in close behind offering their support.

In a voice commanding respect Ruarc asked, "How
is it lad, that you defied the orders of your king and so
rode against the Anak, the Shaman of Dagon?"

Korah stepped forward, "My king if I . . ."

"Peace captain! I did not ask you to speak. I just
heard the boy lift his voice in song, so I know he has a
tongue, let him answer. Did you know I had forbidden
anyone from this army to engage the Anak?"

"Yes."

"Did you know the penalty of such actions were
death?"

Lifting his head for the first time, Riordan looked
Ruarc in the eye, and said simply, "Yes."

Korah once again hastily stepped forward, "My

king, as his captain, the actions of this young man are my responsibility, . I request . . ."

"Captain, I have yet to ask for you to speak. This is between the boy and I. Riordan, you are new to this camp. You could have told me you were unaware of this ban, perhaps I would have then possessed some reason to spare your life. As it is, I don't know as though I have much choice. Before your sentence is carried out, as your last words, please explain why you chose not to lie."

" Because of my name sir."

"Your name?"

"Once my people called me Mamzer–illegitimate, not a son. But now I am adopted, redeemed, given a new name by Brónach, my grandfather and Goel. I would not dishonor his name, by taking to myself a different name, the name of liar."

At this response Mereah started to say "Father . ." but a sharp glance and an upraised palm silenced the Rapha` Prince.

"Son, I cannot allow those who break my commands to go unpunished. All the people understand this. Riordan you will indeed die." At these words the whole army started to express their dismay. The king silenced them all with a glance and an upraised palm. "You shall die to your past life, you shall die to the life you once knew. You will no longer be your own man. You are a dead man, but I as your king, can *also* choose to redeem you, and so I shall. What say you dead man, will you live again but in the service of your king?"

Riordan stood as tall as he could, and lifted his chin proudly, "I will."

"So be it. Your death and new life will begin immediately. Your first duty in my service is to grow up and be trained as a warrior son of the people of Capall. Korah, my captain, before you is a servant of your king, and all Jeshurun. He must be trained as a warrior son of his people. Will you accept the task of training and instructing

Riordan, son of Brónach as your page and armor bearer?"

Korah stepped forward and answered firmly "It would be an honor my King." At his response, a roar of approval came from the sons of Capall.

Addressing the whole army the king raised his voice further to go over the excited voices of the soldiers of Jeshurun.

"Tomorrow, we shall break camp, and most of you will return to your homes. Let us all say a prayer that upon our return, our stay there will be a long one. The task of watching Jeshurun's Key will fall once again to the sons of Dun. Regular watch must be established to watch over the Cnámh plain should our enemies ever return.

"Your king thanks you all for your service. Let us remember and honor the many who gave their lives for their people. Long may they be remembered, and may Yahweh Elohim be pleased with their sacrifice."

As the army began to disperse, many soldiers from all the races represented stopped to congratulate and encourage Riordan as they passed by. After awhile the numb feeling in his hand and arm convinced him both were going to be shaken off. He also wondered if he would ever recover from all the slaps on his back (a friendly pat on the back from a centaur or giant can crack bones). Every friendly swat sent shooting pain through his side, reminding him of the Anak's attack that most likely cracked a few ribs. Eventually only Riordan, Korah, Lithos and Mereah remained to watch the orange glow from the few remaining embers and dying flames from Esh's pyre.

Lithos spoke first to break the reflective silence. "I know you feel honored by the king taking you into his service boy, and ya should. But, be careful. His intent may have been to simply make a way to conveniently keep his eye on ya lad."

Mereah quickly interjected, "Whatever my father's motives, I for one will gladly accept the wisdom of this unexpected mercy. Riordan, I am not of the Capall, so I can not train you in the ways of mounted warfare or cavalry tactics. But right now, with these companions as witnesses, I pledge my friendship—you will always have an advocate in the king's court."

"Aye, but promise me you won't try to give the boy singing lessons," Lithos growled, "I don't think the lad needs your help in that department."

Always embarrassed by the strength of his emotions the Weapons Master usually prefaced any expression that might be construed as "mushy" with wise-cracks. But no one, least of all Riordan doubted his sincerity when he also pledged his friendship and support. "Now, I don't ride, but I can learn ya a lot about fightin' on yer feet lad, and I also plan to keep both eyes on ya. Always remember, you're never alone."

With that the Rapha` and Dun Commander strode through camp carrying on some absurd argument. Korah watched them go, with a slight smile on his face, and after a moment turned to Riordan. "Son, as my armor bearer you will stay with me now, and I have something to give you that might be of service in your new duties. We can return to camp as soon as you're ready."

Riordan approached the fire one last time. Retrieving a water skin, he sprinkled the dying embers until they were cool enough to touch. He then scooped some of the ashes into a small leather bag. Standing up, he said one more soft goodbye, turned back to where Korah stood watching and said, "I'm ready."

Passing through the camps, they eventually passed the tents of the Capall. Riordan saw Torin standing at the door flap of the family pavilion, watching him intently.

"Captain, may I have just a few moments, I need to speak to my . . . brother."

"You go ahead lad, I'll wait for you here."

Riordan approached Torin. Even in the dark of night it seemed clear he radiated anger, but his words were measured and softly spoken. "Congratulations Mamzer," the old name seemed spat out as way of letting him know he would never be considered a legitimate son, or called by his new name, "Is the great hero of his people ready to return and watch my father's sheep?"

Looking off into the stars, as though for support, Riordan gently responded, "You know as well as I, I can never return. My redemption by our grandfather will never be accepted by Brannan, or you. I refuse to be named Mamzer again. I am Riordan, son of Brónach, but without him there to enforce his will . . ."

"Wait! Hold on, what do you mean, without our grandfather there . ."

"I can't tell you how I know, but when Esh fell on the Cnámh plain, so did Brónach, our grandfather. Without his presence in the house of Brannan, I can never return."

"I'll name you more than Mamzer. I name you Amadán–Fool, Crazy! Brónach is in perfect health."

"And when you return I pray you find him so. But I will not be returning with you. I am pressed into service."

"Yes, isn't that convenient. You steal my father's goods as an excuse to come see the battles, kill our grandfather's beloved horse, and then get rewarded for it. Again, congratulations, but if there is any justice in this world you will prove displeasing to the king. You will receive just payment for your lies and deeds. *Then* the world will know you for who you really are: *Mamzer!* Have you not heard, that a spotted cat never wears stripes?"

"I know to change is very hard, and few things change harder than hate and resentment. Goodbye Torin. Brannan your father, and the family will be glad to be rid of me at last. This is goodbye. I don't know if

I will ever return to the place I was never allowed to call home."

Riordan turned quickly away from the heat of Torin's glare, that burned into his back. As he walked away, he didn't see his half-brother's emotional conflict. A struggle within his conscience and emotions was taking place that fought to surface in his facial expressions. Torin lifted his hand and started to say something, but the words got stuck in his throat. After a moment his hand dropped back to his side as he sadly turned his back and returned to his tent.

Korah smiled sympathetically as he approached. No words were spoken as they continued on until they stopped at a temporary corral. Leaning on the top rail, the captain gave a low whistle. A large black with a white face and two white front socks trotted up to the rail followed by a slightly smaller pure white stallion. In the dim starlight the white horse seemed almost blue.

Korah pulled bits of carrot for the horses. His mare accepted the treat with the comfortable ease of long familiarity. The stallion however, acted much more nervous and shy, dancing away after taking the treat.

The mare's head in contrast, came over the rail and searched the captain's tunic for pockets containing more delicacies. Laughing and scratching its ears Korah made formal introductions, "This is Aella, she has been with me now for twenty years. She is named for the desert wind and she is well named, for so she runs. Though, today I discovered that Esh . . . is the flame that runs before even the wind."

Scratching Aella's chin, Korah looked right into her eyes and talked to her directly. "Don't let it bother you girl. The old man ran today with divine purpose. No horse in all of Capall could have caught Esh in his final race."

Still fussing over his mare, Korah explained to Riordan, the depth of their friendship. "She's given me three foals, gifts for my three sons. All three were bonded to my sons when they came of age, . . they were the finest chargers in all Capall." Strong emotion became evident in Korah's voice, "When my sons were lost, so were hers. She is as bereft as I . . .

"The white stallion is named Sorcha. He is a different breed from what most riders of Capall choose. He's smaller for one thing, not as long of stride. My Aella would beat him in a race for two–three, even five miles. But Sorcha's strength lies in his endurance. He will keep running when most other horses will quit, or die. I purchased him to be a gift for my eldest son . . . now I give him to you."

Riordan started to protest but Korah cut him off. "Before you object hear me out. To keep you out of his hair, the king gave you to me to act as my armor bearer and page. His intent being that I keep an eye on you, and keep you out of trouble. I am a cavalry officer, it's a simple fact that in order to be my page, you'll need a horse. You look pretty spry but I doubt you could keep up with Aella on those scrawny legs.

"It is the will of El that we be brought together lad, not the edict of the king. I'm alone in the world, you took the life of the slayer of my sons . . and I am beginning to understand, that you are also alone in the world. Somehow, I believe your pain may surpass even my own. An orphan can at least imagine that his parents wanted . . . and loved him. However, the pain of a parent, especially a father's rejection, almost never heals.

"I have . . . memories of a loving wife, and my sons, I'm so proud . . ." the depths of his emotions wouldn't allow Korah to finish his thoughts. Riordan waited respectfully while the great man regained his composure.

"You have far too few memories of shared love . . . to apply healing balm to your heart's wounds and loss.

"But, you were given the love of your grandfather Brónach, a great man. The ability to conceive does not make a person a man or father. Brónach chose to be your kinsman redeemer, let him also be the father of your heart. Also as your adoptive father, he gave you a horse, as any father should.

"Years ago a great captain, your grandfather took me on, trained me. As promised, I will take you on as my page; but by law, only a son of Capall may ride, so I will also be your Goel. As your redeemer it is my responsibility to give you a horse, and so confirm my covenant of adoption. Starting tomorrow I will begin your training as a warrior son of Capall."

A soft but deep voice spoke from behind about a dozen feet away, "I approve this choice captain." Both Riordan and Korah turned to watch Jireh step out of the shadows and come closer so they could see him better.

"The boy will need someone to teach him if nothing else, how to ride. He will also need to learn what it means to be in the service of the king. Because of the recent severing of friendship between Ruarc and I, there will be many times I will not be able to be the boy's instructor. I can not think of any one better suited to take my place, or Brónach's place as this lads teacher."

"Jireh," Riordan could barely speak because of the strength of his emotions, "Brónach I believe has died, or did you some how already know?"

"Aye, I knew. I watched your combat from the top of the plateau–that was foolish by the way lad, you were not in any way prepared for that battle. But yes I knew about Brónach, and this is going to sound a bit strange, I knew because of Esh. Esh ran, not as he did when young; but with a strength he never knew before, even in his prime. The strength of bond known by your ancestors is the only explanation I could come up with."

"But all the great horses of Capall are bonded, why would that make a difference?"

It was Korah who responded to Riordan's question, "Aye lad, but long ago, the bond was different, or so the stories passed down from our fathers tell us. When we

294

speak of a bond now, it is not much more than an expression of closeness and affection we feel for our horses. But the chronicles of our people say the bond long ago proved to be much more. More than a connection of thought and spirit, something within the bond powerfully strengthened both horse and rider. I also thought I saw the evidence of a bond watching Esh run today, but Jireh, I have not heard of any rider having this bond for thousands of years."

"You haven't heard of this for thousands of years because it hasn't happened for at least a thousand years. Not since the days of Jephthah, the first Shophetim. The horse and the bond is counted among Elohim's greatest gifts to man. After the Rebellion the bond became eroded and eventually lost. But when Jephthah led the people of Jeshurun from bondage, some of the people began to experience a restoration of their creation gifts, including the bond. I suspect it has something to do with the blade that you now carry lad."

"The Riail dlí?"

"Aye the Riail dlí. The Rule of Law is the very fabric of our universe. When I first gave you the blade, I wondered if you would start experiencing a rebirth of the bond of your people through Esh. But while I saw evidence of an unusually strong love, shared between the two of you, I did not see evidence of the spiritual bond as experienced in days of old. Then I saw Esh in combat and I recognized the bond beyond all doubt– just not with you. Not only uncommonly swift, Esh also seemed guided by a wisdom and experience much greater than a wet-behind-the-ears young pup like you would possess."

Riordan looked up to the Shophetim and asked, "Is that how you knew it was Brónach who bonded with Esh."

"Aye, and perhaps the captain can guess the other reason."

Korah gave a knowing look to Jireh and said softly, "When Esh died, the boy did not."

"Aye. I knew Esh to be guided and strengthened by the Bond. But in days of old, the Bond often proved to be so strong, that when one died, be it the man or horse, so did the other. Because you possessed the Riail dlí, the Bond indeed became restored, but with your grandfather lad, which would make sense. The two of them have been together for many years."

Even in the dark Jireh could see that something disturbed Korah, "What troubles you captain?"

"Jireh, I swore an oath, to be loyal and support Ruarc as my king. His son Mereah is as great a leader and Prince as I have ever known. By placing the Riail dlí in the lad's hands, you have in effect named him king. How do I keep my sworn oaths to Ruarc, without betraying my new charge? I have no desire to be involved in an uprising against the king."

"And you will never be asked to lead one. I did not choose Riordan. Elohim and in a way, the Riail dlí did. The time, place and circumstances of the boys eventual ascension to the throne, that's entirely up to Elohim to establish. Both of you must serve Ruarc faithfully. Just remember this, even when the how of the establishment of Elohim's purpose and promise seem uncertain—even impossible—to try and help Him out is always a disastrous idea.

"Lad, remember when I told you the Riail dlí was offered to Ruarc but he rejected it? What I told you is true, but there is more to the story; in a way the Blade first rejected him. He did not recognize its value because the sword did not reveal its worth. The Riail dlí is not dead metal, it is living, active . . . discerning. For hundreds of years I have been Jeshurun's Shophetim, I knew of rumors of it's, um empowering. To tell you the truth, when I presented the Blade to Ruarc, I hoped to finally discover what gifts the blade might impart . . . but Ruarc wasn't chosen. No one since Jachin,

Jephthah's apprentice has been selected, not even I. The Shophetim have possessed the sword now for well over a millennia, waiting for the next great leader and deliverer of our people to be revealed. To Ruarc, the blade is just that, a simple blade, and a rather short one at that. He cannot be blamed for not realizing its virtue. It seemed merely an ancient heirloom, better suited for historical display than combat.

"Yahweh Yireh is the God who sees. He revealed to me that before I died, I would find the one who is to be the next great deliverer of our people, and I have. Do not forget however, Ruarc, is Jeshurun's anointed leader. Respect this, never raise your hand against him. Ruarc must remain king until it is your time to be revealed."

"Jireh, . . don't get mad, but there's something I'm confused about. You call Yahweh the God who sees, and I have always assumed Yahweh and Elohim to be different names for the same God, is that right?"

Laughing softly Jireh responded, "Bless me lad, of course you wouldn't know, how could I be angry. How can I explain this, . . how many names have you been called since I have known you lad?"

Riordan grinned, "At least a dozen I think."

"The Power or El of Jeshurun, has many names, but He is one only. His names tell His story, and the story is a long one. El's names reveal His nature, and character . . . and his love for His people. His name is Yahweh Elohim, He is El Shaddai, El Elyon and Adonai. As you learn to know him by name, you will grow in your understanding of His heart and His purpose.

"The names of Elohim may be a mystery, but having many names is not. You are an example of that lad, your mother named you Riordan, a good noble name. You have been given other names, some destructive, . . . but none more destructive than those you gave yourself, whispered quietly in the recesses of yer heart.

"And know this, Yahweh Elohim has given you a name as well. A name only He can reveal to you in His time. There is a spirit in this world, a voice of malice, that tries to confuse, and abuse, in hope that your heart can be broken—conditioned and trained to accept a lesser name. The name Mamzer, and you've been given worse, is a name given by a thief to steal from you your greatest treasure. Your name lad, the name by which you must learn to call yourself, the name which Yahweh Elohim knows and reveals, your true name is not just who you are, but who you are called to be. Your true name reveals your nature, and you've no greater gift.

"And now, I must be going. If Ruarc knew of our relationship he would kill you immediately. But our El has surrounded you with the greatest gift a man can have– friends who are true."

The big centaur bent forward slightly and reached down to shake Korah's hand. "I am in awe of Elohim's provision, I couldn't have chosen a better mentor for Riordan if I combed the entire nation."

"I will do my best to meet your lofty expectations, . . . all the people miss you. I know your ties with the king are severed, but where will you go, . . . will we see you again?"

"I will not be too far, I have to keep both my eyes on this one," Jireh indicated with a roll of his eyes he meant Riordan, "He has a very nasty habit of getting into trouble. Look for me to show up at times when least expected."

Riordan ignored the centaur's outstretched hand, choosing instead to leap as high as he could to hug the Shophetim's thick neck.

"You can't go Jireh, I haven't even begun to learn the things I need to know, I . ."

"I'm only one of your teachers lad, Brónach another. You will learn things from Korah I could never teach you. Also you posses the Riail dlí, forged from Nomos law. Learn from the things revealed by the law, and one day rule as king *by* the law. And when times are darkest, remember the name Elohim means covenant.

298

It's a promise that the work He has begun in your life, He will finish."

With that said, Jireh extracted himself from Riordan's death grip hug and gently put the lad's feet back on earth. Then after rumpling his hair affectionately, the Shophetim turned and trotted off into the darkness.

Epilog

Riordan sat up, and looked around a dimly lit chamber. He could tell by the steady breathing, that Korah remained asleep in a bunk across the room. Judging by the light it seemed to be about the fourth watch, maybe an hour or two before the cock crows.

Careful not to wake up the good captain, he slipped out of their shared quarters to a long antechamber. The ceiling in the hallway, built to accommodate giants gave the simple passage a stately, almost cathedral-like effect.

Walking silently over stone floors he came to the tall, narrow entrance for the palace hall and throne room. Twenty feet high double doors, round at the top, and made from dark, rich oaks and walnut, prevented entry as though they were faithful sentinels on guard. Ornamental relief in many places plated in gold and silver told the story of Rapha`, the giant First Born.

Widely rumored to have been paid for with funds lifted from banned Dagon loot, the Dun architects planned a royal residence well suited for King Ruarc. This meant the door handles were placed at eight feet, well above the heads of the tallest man. Since there is precious little leverage reaching above a person's head, the sheer weight of the doors would prevent anyone but a giant, or perhaps a centaur, from opening them, even a crack. This presented the effect of intimidating most visitors to the king's court, which Riordan suspected to be quite intentional. The intended message, "I am King Ruarc and I am a giant, . . and you, my guests are not."

Since entry also needed to be adapted for the king's captains, designer's included a much smaller door within the door, cleverly hidden by trim. Pushing this inner door open the young armor-bearer stepped into the dark hall.

To escape the morning chill, he wandered over to a massive stone block fireplace built along the north wall. Rectangular in shape, the hall seemed to be oriented to create a long walk from the western doors to the dais on the far eastern end. Soon, the rising sun would bring illumination to the high, round eastern window, and cast a beam of light directly over the throne. Sort of ironic, Riordan thought, all that effort to bring luminance to the throne, when of late, the king seemed to much prefer the dark.

Completed shortly after Ruarc's triumphal return,

and the death of the Anak, the palace served to honor the victories of the king, despite the fact that Ruarc did very little to defeat the Dagon and did nothing to defeat the Anakim Shaman. Fair or not, all victories in battle are a king's to claim, so when Ruarc returned, he received a hero's welcome back to the Rapha` city of Flann.

With his back to the failing embers, he soaked in the radiant heat to ward against the morning chill. Riordan looked over the room, and admired the long row of tall narrow lattice windows along the south wall that soon would fill the hall with light. Long heavy tables placed on either side of the center aisle, were made for the comfort of the five races and tribes during court and for feasting. Five steps led up the dais to the Ruarc's throne. No fancy or plush felts or fabrics for the High King. Instead, a simple bench with curled stone armrests, carved from a single block of polished black marble served as the symbol of the Monarch's office.

Riordan knew that his swan harp rested on the top dais step, at the foot of the throne. Although officially Korah's armor bearer and page, of late he spent a great deal of time as court musician.

A few days after the king's return to Flann, Mereah came to him to ask a favor, "My father," he explained, "Suffers from attacks and fits of madness, for which the healers can find no answer or cure. I discussed the problem with Lithos, and I suggested we try singing to him."

Riordan remembered laughing, "Sing to him?"

The sheepish grin on such a gigantic face would have been impossible to miss, "I have learned from past experience that sometimes the only victory against madness and darkness is boldly singing of the light. But, Lithos suggested that my father's madness might be better countered by a singer who can actually sing. That's where you come in my friend."

So that night he began his singing career, and his

playing and singing did seem to help. In truth, when the madness came upon the king, his songs seemed to be the only thing that brought the Monarch peace. Korah proved to be a big help in this endeavor, he loved to sing, and taught Riordan many songs preserved by the Jeshurun people through hundreds of years. The young bard also composed songs of his own that were inspired by his own life experiences. He sang about what he knew.

The night before last, when Ruarc suffered from one of his attacks, the young shepherd drew on his experiences watching Brannan's sheep:

> Yahweh is my Ra`ah,
> because He is my Adonai*
> I lack no good thing.
> From the desert of my soul
> He leads me to a place of rest.
> Beside still waters,
> my thirsty spirit is restored.

While singing the song, Riordan felt spiritual conflict, as though an unseen battle were taking place. When he looked up from his playing, the king seemed at rest, slumped over in his chair, and sound asleep. In truth the whole hall became silent when he finished the song. A healing balm was in the lyrics and melody that touched with shalom peace the wounds in many hearts.

His mother named him Riordan, a king's bard or singer. Would she prove to be a prophetess? Did she somehow see across the years and discern who he would one day become? Did she ever think of him? He wondered where she might be now. What would she be doing, . . or even who was she? He found himself asking the most basic question that every son

(*Adonai means Master or Lord)

deep in his heart wants answered; would she be proud of me, of the man I've become?

His thoughts exposed once again his own deepest ache and wound. Not for the last time he went to the shepherd of his own soul, to seek healing, peace, and restoration in those same deep quiet waters. The waters that are only found by gazing deep into the quiet pools that are the eyes of Elohim.

The End

Coming soon, Riordan's adventures continue in:

Riordan

The Wards of Power

The following is an excerpt of Chapter One.

Riordan looked up from a place flat on his back and could see Korah's grinning face framed by a blue mid-afternoon sky. After several hard falls or throws from his horse, the young armor bearer realized he could see stars, swirling around his captains head, giving him a mystical, supernatural appearance.

"You're doing great kid!" Riordan recognized the sarcastic laugh of Lithos, the Dun commander. "Why I think ya managed to stay on for at least five seconds that time. Five second's, don't cha think Mereah?"

Suddenly the sky disappeared as the lad's vision was filled by the hulking frame and big beaming face of Mereah the Rapha` Prince also looking down at him. "Much more than five Lithos, don't sell our young friend short, I'd say at least six seconds, maybe seven."

It took a few more seconds for Riordan to get his wind back after getting it knocked out of him for the tenth time that day. Finally he managed to ask, "Where's Sorcha?"

Korah answered, "Well lad, after you were thrown that last time, he kicked up his heels and lit out, likely half way to the mountains of Irijah by now. Want me to go on Aella and fetch him back?"

"No, I want somebody to draw a bow and arrow and shoot 'im."

Lithos laughed, "Now we know he's alright, he's as surely as ever."

Korah held out his hand and helped Riordan up out of the dirt. "Sorry lad, I'd shoot 'im, but you're the armor bearer of a cavalry captain, and you'll be needing a horse."

"No, I don't I can run real fast."

Korah started dusting Riordan off, and picking bits of bramble off his back, while speaking gently, "Sorcha's not like Esh lad, he's never been gentled for riding before. Trust and motive are the keys to forming the bond between a horse and his rider. Esh trusted you because Brónach trusted you. Sorcha needs to learn he can trust you. Part of that trust is knowing your motive. When I give orders do you think they're only to restrict your freedom?"

"No, I think you don't want me to have any fun, . . ever."

Korah laughed, "That is the way it feels sometimes I'm sure, but we both know all the orders and training are for your benefit, and that I'm doing my best to keep you alive. Sorcha possesses a lot of spirit, and he doesn't yet understand or trust your motive or intent. He needs to understand you seek a partnership of mutual benefit."

Lithos scoffed, "Is the boy needing a horse or a wife?"

Riordan then jumped in, "Well if this is a partnership based on trust and motive, I can tell you I don't trust that horse because he's motivated to kill me!"

Stifling a chuckle, Korah spoke to Lithos, "I think the lad's had enough riding today, but while I fetch Sorcha, do you mind working with him a bit on the use of a

306

sword?"

"Not at all, take yer time." As they all watched Korah ride off, Lithos growled, "alright lad, get that fancy blade of yours, and let's see what you can do."

Mereah hearing this, offered a suggestion of his own, "Um Lithos, wouldn't it be best starting the young man out with wooden practice swords?"

"Well maybe if he fights somebody using a wooden sword, but since that ain't likely I'll use my iron blade. Don't worry, I won't hurt the lad, I've been training recruits for better'n a hundred years."

Mereah held up both hands palm outward as a gesture of submission, "Alright, I meant it only as a suggestion." And then as he backed away muttered, "The *kid* isn't the one I'm worried about."

Riordan walked forward with both hands gripping the Riail dlí. Mereah marveled at the swords beauty, the blade shown like pale blue crystal, nothing else like it existed, he would bet his life on it.

Lithos watched Riordan's tentative approach and smirked "All right lad, let's see what ya got, attack me." Seeing the hesitation the stout warrior sneered, "Never show fear boy, now attack!"

His face glowing red from the rebuke, Riordan swung the Nomos Blade in a high arc that descended towards Lithos' skull. Lifting his iron blade to easily block the attack, the Dun weapons master had already planned his next move to disarm Riordan; except that when their swords clashed the Riail dlí passed through his best iron sword as easily as cutting air. Two thirds of the Dun's blade flipped through the air and landed a couple feet away. Riordan, on the other hand managed to stop the Riail dlí just before parting Lithos' hair. Looking up at the Nomos Blade resting on his forehead right between his eyes, Lithos slowly reached up, grasped the sword flat between his thumb and index finger and lifted it gently away. "On second thought why take chances? I think Mereah might be right, practice swords would be best."

The young giant laughed, "I tried to warn you Lithos, the lad's blade is more than a decorative wall ornament, that sword has serious bite."

In the short time it took Lithos to fetch wooden practice swords, Korah road up on his mare Aella leading an unrepentant Sorcha.

The Irial captain Ragnhildr rode beside him with another warrior who seemed something of a mystery. The facial features made the rider appear very young. And yet the warrior's armor and clothing were that of someone possessing considerable rank. The face almost seemed the image of Ragnhildr, but the features were finer, without a trace of facial hair. To Riordan, this meant a pre–adolescent boy, maybe about two years younger than himself. That such fine brass armor, silk tunic, and beautiful weaponry would be bestowed on an armor bearer or page, he just couldn't understand.

Lithos tossed Riordan a practice blade, with a growl, "That was my best sword ya cut in half boy, so I'm feeling a bit grumpy. And I bet yer thinking as long as I have a sword like that, I don't need to know how to fight 'cause I'll always have the advantage. But what will ya do on the day when another warrior comes along with a blade to match yer own? Or Elohim forbid, you are forced to fight with a different weapon? We'll begin with the basics, sheath your sword and we'll begin."

Riordan looked down and fumbled with fitting the thicker wooden sword into the sheath that an artisan crafted for the Riail dlí. Half way into the process Lithos shouted, "On guard!" and charged. Desperately trying to withdraw the glorified stick, in his panic the sword got tangled in the sheath. After getting smacked several times very hard by the Dun captain he lost his footing and balance falling backwards looking up into the sky once again.

Listening to everyone's laughter hurt almost as much as the several smacks taken from the Dun's attacks, and despite some padding from gambeson armor, he felt every one. Mostly he felt embarrassed for being made to look like a fool. Lithos' face now blotted out the blue sky and he offered his hand, "What did you learn from that encounter boy, can ya tell me what ya did wrong?"

"Yep."

"Well out with it then."

"What I did wrong is trusting you, and doing as you instructed. What I learned is *NOT* to do what you ask or to give up my advantage. You can keep the sticks, I want the Riail dlí back."

The booming laughter he heard now could only be coming from Mereah, and he could hear the softer chuckle from Korah as well. Knowing the comments scored at least a small point it eased some of his pain, so he took the Weapons Master's hand and allowed himself to be pulled to his feet.

Lithos however didn't laugh. He replied as gruff as always, "Don't get smart with me boy, I did that on purpose. When it comes to sword play, the difference between a second and a half–second is enough to get you dead. Never forget, if it looks like it's to be combat, it takes longer to draw your weapon than it does to strike with it. So rule number one–a sheathed weapon will only get ya killed. If there is any possibility of danger, get your weapons where they are ready to be used. Now, do you know the second thing ya did wrong?"

"I didn't duck?"

A sharp whack and the resulting "OOWWW!" taught Riordan the penalty for not taking the lessons seriously enough.

"I didn't survive untold number of battles in my hunert and fifty years by being a clown boy. I'm going to teach ya what you need to survive, even if it kills ya. Second thing ya did wrong is panic. You fumbled getting your sword out because you panicked. Reaction time of a fighter that is tense is tight, clumsy and slow, and just a fraction of a second slow will get you dead. So rule number two–relax. Fear kills as surely as a sword. Know the third thing ya did wrong?"

Knowing a smart answer would only earn another whap, he thought carefully about his response, "I fell because I didn't pay attention to my footing."

Lithos looked hard at the former ra`ah, and told him to bend down, Riordan hesitated but did as instructed. The weapon's master reached up and knocked on his head with his knuckles, "Now that's using yer head for somthin besides providing me a target. Always remember rule number three, a sword fight is first won with the feet. Never let your feet get too close together. Keep em on the ground. Lifting yer heals or rocking back on 'em and you're in danger of losing balance and your strikes will lack power."

Ragnhildr spoke up from the back of his horse, "As entertaining as this has proven to be, and I truly hate to break this up, but a matter of great importance has come to the attention of the king. He is requesting the presence of all his captains and their available officer's. We meet in an hour in the king's council chamber. I recommend you gentlemen take a break from training and get cleaned up. I'll see you in an hour."

A little less than an hour later, Riordan accompanied Korah to the king's council chamber's. He hated the gatherings. Having no experience or wisdom to offer as counsel, he stood around feeling about as useful as a man's teat. Fortunately Ruarc didn't have the personality that had much use for organized meetings. In fact, only two such meetings had taken place since the young armor bearer's arrival in the Rapha` King's palace. A man of action, when something needed to be done, the monarch just wanted to do it. He didn't want to talk about it. He definitely didn't want to form a committee so he could talk about it some more. He hated bureaucracy and red tape, and while he may have lacked organizational skills, as a king he usually managed to get things done.

The captains and some of their lieutenants filed into the room and took their seats around a table. Riordan as a simple armor bearer with no actual rank, didn't have a seat at the table. Instead he took his place standing behind Korah's right shoulder.

Mereah sat immediately to the king's right and represented the Rapha` along with his father. Lithos represented the sons of Dun, along with his second in command Nahor, and they sat next to the Rapha` Prince, across the table from Korah and Riordan. Then Ragnhildr came in with Quillan and the young page that accompanied him earlier. Only now, without armor or brass cap to conceal the feminine features, only a blind man could confuse her with a boy. The young ra`ah felt his neck and face turning red, simply from watching her walk into the room.

The Irial captain greeted the other commanders in attendance, "Gentlemen, forgive me for not making introductions earlier. When I travel with my daughter, I prefer for her safety that her identity and gender remain known only to a few. Permit me to introduce my daughter, Aislin."

With a gesture that can only be described as a cross between a bow and a curtsey, the Irial shield–maiden greeted every one present with dignity and queenly grace. Quillan pulled out the ladies chair and seated her properly next to her father, just to the king's left.

Aislin, with her helmet and chain mail removed could only be described as a vision. Raven black hair cascaded down her back and the silken fabric of her dress did nothing to conceal her soft curves. Riordan hoped no one noticed his staring. However hard he tried, he couldn't take his eyes off of her. Mereah did in fact notice, but hid his smile and said nothing.

Conspicuously absent from the gathering, were any

of the sons of Irijah, especially Jeshurun's Shophetim. In a sense, Jireh transformed from centaur to the elephant *not* in the room, the one whose absence everyone pretended not to notice.

Ruarc stood up to address the small assembly, "My friends, you know me well enough to understand, I don't put much stock in formalities. I also hate to jaw just to hear myself talk. I know its been but a few Months since the defeat of the Dagon and their Anak. But there is a recent development that demands immediate action. I have appointed Ragnhildr as my Chief Military Adviser, and I have asked him to explain this emergency in greater detail."

With only a nod for acknowledgment Ragnhildr stood to speak while the king collapsed wearily into his chair. "As captains of our respective peoples, I believe we all understand how close we came to losing our nation and our freedom. Just a few short months ago, were it not for a miracle shot from the young man present today, I think we all know the eventual outcome would have been the death or enslavement of all our peoples. The Anak may be dead, but I think not the forces that empowered him. Those powers I believe are as we speak preparing for another strike at our hearts. We dare not be idle. We must prepare for what is coming, or perish."

Tired of waiting for the Irial captain to get to the point Lithos interrupted by asking, "Can we get on with it, Ragnhildr, we all know we barely escaped with our lives. What's the big new development?"

Without a word in response, but rather a throwing motion so fast most at the table didn't even see it, a twelve inch dagger flew and stuck in the table right in front of Lithos. "That is the development. You know a bit about metals and weapons, what do you see my friend?"

Frowning at the Irial Captain's audacity, Lithos extracted the dagger from the table. He quickly forgot about his annoyance however, as he looked at the craftsmanship of the blade. Wonderfully made, a ruby gemstone set in a silver circlet on the pommel finished the pearl handle. However, it was the double edged blade that astonished Lithos, "This blade is forged from an ore or alloy I am not familiar with. It feels lighter than the bronze weapons favored by the Capall, and much lighter than iron. Question is, how strong is it?"

Ragnhildr responded, "Stronger and lighter than both bronze or iron. I don't believe it comes from any known metal, but that rather it is an alloy, a blending of iron with another lighter, yet unidentified ore. Now tell me this my friend, would an army equipped with weapons made from this alloy have a technical advantage?"

"You knew the answer to that question before you asked," Lithos scoffed, "But the fact that we came within a hairs breadth of losing the last war with the Dagon didn't have anything to do with our army having inferior weapons. Attacks of sorcery from the Anak is what almost destroyed us, better swords would not have helped!"

Ragnhildr responded, "Granted my friend, and we must find a way to better counter those attacks, and that will be the topic to be dealt with momentarily. However, let me ask the same question another way: what if the Dagon had swords and axes made with this alloy?"

Lithos hesitated for a moment, then grimly pronounced, "They would have swept us aside and passed through the keys with, or without the Anak's help."

The enormity of that admission produced a chilling effect on the whole room leaving everyone to sit in stunned silence. After a moment Korah asked the obvious question, "Where did this blade come from, who forged it, and how do we obtain more?"

Ragnhildr smiled and said, "Those are all key

questions captain, but Bearach, son of Atara, commissioned this dagger along with many other fine blades. As far as how they were forged, no one alive in the world today understands the process or the composition of the ore by which this blade is made. That is knowledge lost to the world for almost four thousand years. Knowledge of this craft, and of many other things were all lost in the world wide devastation that brought the First Age to an end."

Lithos started laughing and slapped the table, "You can't be serious, are you really going to waste time and precious resources chasing after a bunch of old legends and myths? Do you have any idea how many stories of lost cities and treasures there are? But whoever is telling the story has never seen the place himself! They only heard about it from a relative, or worse a drunken sailor. The one piece of evidence that is always offered however, is a map–a map, for sale of course at a very reasonable price."

Ragnhildr responded a little sharply, "I too have heard the stories and wives tales, don't take me for a fool my friend. In this case we have more than a map. The blade you have seen for yourself, it is quite real. I can assure you no forge in Tebel today could have produced this alloy. Also if you will look, in the silver circlet around the gemstone, you will find something inscribed in an ancient Irial text. Working from ancient scrolls preserved in Bethel, the text translates Bearach Adonai, or Bearach is lord."

Still skeptical Lithos asked, "And this is important . . . because why?"

"Perhaps the Dun have forgotten, but the Irial have not, it is the source of our greatest shame. The Irial First Born Atara is also the First Born of all peoples, and races. Not content to be Tebel's chief ruler and steward he led the rebellion against Elohim and so brought death into our world. Bearach is the name of Atara's First Born and heir. The stories preserved by my people say he eventually killed Atara by his own hand and waged war against all other peoples to subjugate them.

"The inscription Bearach Adonai means the son of Atara declared his crown and authority to be above Yahweh Elohim."

At that point King Ruarc finally interrupted by voicing his objections, "I'm afraid I grow as impatient as Lithos Ragnhildr, so I have to ask, is this history lesson going to eventually go any where?"

"Please indulge me just a moment longer your majesty. This is important because Lithos is right, better swords may have helped against the Dagon armies, but would have been of little use against powers such as were used by the Anakim. Those attacks were of a sorcery from another time and age, as were the tanniyn the Anak rode. Our greatest hope for victory against the next attacks will be weapons to counter ancient sorcery.

Legends and some of the earliest scrolls tell us that Bearach foresaw the coming destruction that ended the First Age. In response, he prepared wards to preserve knowledge and technologies for his continued existence, and future reign. He not only intended to survive the holocaust that ended as the Drochshaol, the Age of Sorrow; he planned to reign over the earth for eternity.

"We now know Bearach did not survive the devastation. However, we have reason to believe at least some of his Wards, did. We also have reason to believe this blade came from one of those Wards."

Mereah spoke up for the first time to express a voice of caution, "I know I am not the scholar that you are Ragnhildr, but isn't it our people's understanding that Bearach proved to be more corrupt than even Atara his father? Would not much of his knowledge come from Conri, the fallen Messenger and Watcher? If so, how could we hope to use this knowledge without it becoming a deadly snare for the whole nation?"

"I'm afraid I have to agree with Mereah," Korah interjected, "We cannot embrace the weapons of the enemy, without surrendering to the enemies values and will, how could this capitulation be viewed as victory?"

"I understand your concerns Mereah, and believe me, I share them. But no one is suggesting anything of the kind," Ragnhildr responded. "I hoped you would have a little more faith in me than this my friends. I am not suggesting we learn the secrets of sorcery. We seek power yes, but the right kind. It is my hope that Bearach's Wards will reveal information concerning two types of powers that came from the First Age. These powers are from Elohim, not from Conri. In fact, they were not originally designed to be weapons at all."

"Alright Ragnhildr," Lithos said. "You have our attention, name these weapons."

"Well," he continued, "It is my belief that the attacks used by the Anak were simply counterfeits of the original gifts of dominion placed within all the children of Elohim on the day of creation."

"But," Korah objected, "Those gifts were lost from the day Atara made his choice."

"Yes of course you are right, and perhaps it is a false hope," Ragnhildr agreed. "But if the attacks of the enemy are spells imitating creation gifts, then it seems to me that the best counter to a fake, is a dose of the real thing. I can only hope that somewhere in these Wards, perhaps we can find a clue as to how gifts of dominion may be restored."

The king remained silent through the entire discourse, so it seemed a little jarring when he finally spoke up, however briefly, "Go on Ragnhildr, my tolerance for endless jaw is coming to the end, tell them the rest. I believe that is where we have our greatest hope for success."

The king's adviser acknowledged his impatience with a nod and continued, "The second power I referred to, is a talisman of such great power, that its misuse by

316

Bearach, is what led to the world's decimation and the ending of the First Age. This device, many believed to be a symbol only; but Atara's son after killing his father, began to experiment with what we believe proved to be the Scepter of Adon."

Lithos scoffed, "What kind of a weapon could you make of a scepter? It wouldn't even make a decent club."

Mereah shifted uncomfortably, remembering the Anak channeled his magic attacks through a scepter. He didn't think the present circumstances the best time to point this out so he said nothing.

"First of all, I didn't say weapon, *you* did. I said power." Ragnhildr responded, "And secondly, you should know better than be glib about matters of such importance my friend. What kind of a weapon indeed? What sort of a weapon could a king make of a device that possessed the power to alter and change Natural Law?"

Korah gave a low whistle to express his dismay.

Ragnhildr allowed the implications to sink in. "Designed, constructed and presented by Yahweh Elohim as a gift to the First Born, the scepter's intended purposes were such that when the Children of Elohim were ready, they would be able to use it to channel their gifts and exercise dominion over all of creation."

"But," Korah responded, "The Legends tell us when Bearach attempted to use the scepter as a weapon, he set off a chain of events that almost destroyed the world. Even if we somehow recovered the scepter, who's to say we would know how to use it any more than Bearach? Sounds to be far worse than children playing with fire, any attempts to use the scepter by persons who don't know what they're doing can result in destroying the whole planet! And nobody alive has so much as a clue as to how to use the bloody thing so what we're talking about is setting up a second devastation! Don't the ancient scrolls teach that the

First Born were warned, that the day they claimed the scepter for their own, they would die? If we take up the scepter will we not be merely affirming Atara's choice? Will we not be inviting our own deaths?"

Here the king voiced an ominous proclamation. "Korah, we must be prepared to make use of any potential power to protect our nation and peoples. If the Dagon once again unleash the sorceries of the Anakim, we must be prepared to fight with powers of our own."

After a moment of silence with the king's words hanging heavy in the room, Ragnhildr made an attempt to bring calm by making some assurances. "First of all, we don't have any other choice but go after the scepter. Just like the secret of the ancient alloy, we must recover these technologies if for no other reason than preventing the Dagon from getting them first–and using them against us. The scepter must be recovered before our enemies find it and attempt to unlock its powers. In our possession it may be studied, thoroughly understood, and hopefully never used–and then only in the direst of circumstances. But if the scepter fell into the hands of the Anakim, . . who knows what evil the demon spawn might attempt to achieve with it?"

"There, you see Korah, you worry needlessly." Ruarc's words were meant to be comforting, but glibly spoken and so fell short of their intent. "Regardless, I am asking that you provide pack animals and mounts for Ragnhildr and for however many of the Irial and Capall he deems necessary to recover the contents of Bearach's Ward. Do you have any questions?"

"Only one sire, will we have maps or something to give direction to our search?"

The king replied, "Better. You shall have a guide, the same person who recovered the dagger and brought it to us." The king then bawled out to attendants in the entry way, show in the son of Dun."

One of the entrance doors for the hall swung open and their new guide strode in. Wearing a weather stained cloak over several braces of weapons and chain mail he proceeded to the end of the table to stand beside the king.

Ragnhildr made a simple introduction, "Captains of Jeshurun, I present to you the explorer Gad."

Gad stepped forward just a bit, and threw back his hood. Riordan softly gasped. Memories flashed through his mind of the Dun Adventurer who bound and gaged him in the mountains of Irijah, before taking the feral horses.

Hearing Riordan's sharp intake of breath, the horse thief looked closely at his face, recognized him and flashed a big grin, "Hello boy, you've grown some."

Korah turned and looked at his young armor bearer, "You know this man?"

Shock still registered on Riordan's face and in his voice as he answered, "We've met, earlier this year, he visited my father's camp in the Irijah mountains."

Gad jumped right into the conversation to cut Riordan off from what he came close to saying next, "And the young feller here served up a lonely, hungry traveler some right tasty Coney stew. A right courteous lad he is, and pretty fair cook."

Korah interrupted with a question, "I have been given the task of supplying horses and pack animals for this expedition. What information can you give that will aide in my preparations?"

Gad smiled easily at Korah and replied, "Well I can't exactly tell ya where yer going cap'n, cause then ya won't rightly need me along, . . and well, to be plain, I intend to profit from the trip. What I can tell ya is you'll need horses that can withstand a good three to four weeks of hard riding, much of it through rough mountain terrain, just to get there. And it's getting late in the year, we might see some cold weather where we're going. Also, I'll need a pony. I don't trust horse critters. Why just a short while ago I paid good money for pack horses, up in the mountains of Irijah they were; only got em half way home when this big black stallion crashes my . ."

This time Ragnhildr became impatient and interrupted once more, "It's clear why we need your guidance to find this ward of Bearach's, but it is not clear to me why you would have need of us. Am I right in assuming you have been there once already? Why not go yourself and enjoy a greater profit?"

"Well now, yer sharp as a knife and no mistake, and ya have got right to the heart of the matter cap'n that ya have. Well, . . it's like this ya see, whether left by yer Irial ancestors, or e' just showed up on 'is own, but that there treasure is guarded see?"

Mereah looked the adventurer in the eye in an effort to discern whether or not the man spoke true, "A guardian, what sort of guardian?"

Gad's sun-browned face blanched white, and his fear became palpable, "Can't say, I rightly know. I never really saw clearly, . . and there may be more than one. The lads that were with me, they're all dead, all tough men. I think the guardian is a demon, an 'e feeds on blood. All during the night, my lads and I tried to pack up treasure while realizing we weren't alone. One by one they got picked off. I found one of em, his heart ripped out but not a drop of blood–anywhere. Like it was something to precious to be spilt on the ground, or left in the body. Finally, I told the boys to just drop everything . . we're getting out of there. I'm the only one as made it, that fancy knife the only thing I got out."

"I already knew some of the story," Ragnhildr interjected, "But everyone here needs to know why you would dare to return to such a place."

"Because they were good lads that died back there. Now I don't deny there be more treasure than I could hope to scrounge in a hun-ert life times, . . but all the treasure in the world is worthless if yer not alive to spend it. What I'm proposing is an arrangement of mutual benefit. There is a treasure room sure, more importantly an armory. Most important, I think I found a forge, a forge where we can make weapons and armor of our own. Weapons the Dagon can't match. I need help dealing with whatever is guarding the place, in return you get new weapons, and powers to use against the Dagon, a win–win ya see."

Lithos snorted, "If we survive that is!"

Having reached his endurance limits for committee "jaw" Ruarc stood up, clapped his hands together once loudly and made his pronouncement, "So, it's settled, Ragnhildr, Korah, I expect your expedition to be ready to leave no later than three days from now. Have a list of the warriors selected for the journey, and have them here for a feast in their honor in this very hall tomorrow night. Now, if you will all excuse me, I have other matters to attend to."

As the king rose to leave, Aislin rose and spoke for the first time, Riordan immediately found himself captivated by the melody of her voice, "Father, I want to go!"

Ragnhildr immediately replied with an emphatic, "No."

"But father . ."

"Did you hear a word that Gad just said? We have no idea of what we are going up against. It could be very dangerous. Not another word."

Aislin looked directly at Riordan and fired another challenge, "Well, is this one going?"

"Riordan is Korah's page and armor bearer, his presence on this expedition will be Korah's decision, not mine. You on the other hand are my daughter. The decision is mine alone and I am telling you, *no*."

Refusing to back down Aislin retorted, "I have been named as your shield maiden. Is this a honorary title only? I will be shamed publically if left behind. Besides," here she flashed Riordan an apologetic glance, "I am twice this one's age, and you saw his training this morning; I am far more proficient with blade or bow, and unlike him I can actually control a horse!"

Riordan felt his face turning red and heat suddenly rising from his body. Ragnhildr however, responded before he could make his own defense, "Riordan is young, and he has much to learn it's true, but he has already demonstrated the courage to face one of the Anakim. Whatever creature wards Bearach's armory it is not likely to be as dangerous as the enemy he has already faced. Can you say the same?"

"No, especially not if I am left behind at the whispers of danger likely inspired by too much wine or imagination. Long has our people allowed women to take their place in the Fianna (band of warrior bards)."

Riordan leaned over and whispered in Korah's ear, "How can she be twice my age, she barely looks to be older than thirteen, maybe fourteen?"

Korah whispered back, "the Irial live almost as long as centaurs, at thirty she isn't even considered an adult."

After a long moment's thought, Ragnhildr at last partially yielded, "Women have taken their place among the Fianna it is true, but you are not a woman, yet. This far I will yield, and if you speak another word I vow I will leave you behind bound, gaged, and locked up for your own protection. You may accompany us as far as the gates to Bearach's ward. Once there, you will remain behind with Quillan as your guardian, and Riordan as well if Korah is agreed. You will remain behind at least until we encounter whatever defender this ward claims and so have a better understanding of what we face."

Realizing the extent of her victory and the folly of pressing her cause further, Aislin excitedly lost her composure for just a moment and hugged her father's neck. His dignity thus endangered, she released her embrace swiftly, and bowed elegantly, "Thank you father."

Everyone watched her leave, and then Ragnhildr

turned to address his officers for the last time that morning, "I apologize my friends. I regret my daughters impetuousness should be displayed so publically. But one thing coming from our morning's conversation is that I hope everyone understands this undertaking is one fraught with peril. I don't believe attendance is an option for Korah and I. For anyone else, only volunteers who full understand the dangers faced should be selected. Lithos, I'm not sure you should attend, but I believe one or two Dun engineers would be of use to perhaps discern the use and purpose of some of the war craft technologies. Korah, could ponies be found to accommodate a few of the sons of Dun?"

"Oh no you don't," Lithos growled, "Yer not leaving me behind, I ain't 'fraid of no booger–man in the dark. Besides, no one understands forges or weaponry better than me, I'll be taggin' along. And I suspect, so will the Rapha` Nightingale here. Some body will be needed to look after 'im."

Mereah flashed a big grin, "Well I planned on stayin' home, sounded much too dangerous for me. Now that I know I have Lithos along as babysitter and protector, how could I stay behind?"

Ragnhildr looked everyone over gravely, "Don't speak of the dangers so lightly my friends, I fear the realities will render your glib words foolish. Our destination is a place you have heard of, a legend spoken of only as whispers in the dark. Gad, you didn't tell them its name."

The explorer sat with his chin resting on his chest as he contemplated the impact and weight of his answer. Looking up he spoke softly, "It is called Magor–Missabib, the terror on every side."

About the Author

Will McDonald is the sixth child born into a large Irish Catholic family. The story of Riordan has grown in his heart from a life-time of facing his own personal Demons. Growing up in a violently dysfunctional home, there were plenty of giants to slay just to achieve normalcy. While many in similar circumstances have led lives spiraling downward through alcohol and drug abuse; Will was rescued by an encounter with Yeshua Elohim. This empowered him to work his way through High School and College, eventually earning a Master's in Education and a Post-Graduate Degree (Th.M) in Theology.

While drawing inspiration from David's Saga, and his own life, Will insists Riordan is every man's story, everyman's choice–we either use the past as an excuse or as motivation. His writings are a reflection of his core belief that the purpose of life is transformation.

Married, the father of three sons, Will makes his home in Montana.